CW00377159

NO WEY OF KNOWING

(Book Two of the Weys)

S.J. Blackwell

Copyright © 2020 S.J. Blackwell

All Rights Reserved

This is a work of fiction. Names, characters, organisations, places, events and incidents are either products of the author's imagination or are used fictitiously.

No part of this book may be reproduced, or stored in a retrieval system, or transmitted by any form or by any means, electronic, mechanical, photocopying, recording or others, without express written permission of the author.

If I were Weyfare, I would travel back to Christmas 1973. Stand outside the house, and watch Slade debut that song on Top of the Pops through a misted window. Smile at us all watching The Morecombe and Wise Show, the telly surrounded by family and laughter, with the fake white tree dressed in lurid tinsel and us dressed in our bright acrylic rollneck jumpers. Laugh at how full I am with goose and roast potatoes, but still asking for Wagon Wheels and Snowballs for a treat. See me making my bets with copper coins on games of Newmarket until it was way past my bedtime.

To Mum and Dad, wherever you are. Thank you for believing in me.

FOREWORD

The chapter headings tell a story of their own.

Head over to Spotify, search for *No Wey of Knowing* and immerse yourself in the music while you enjoy the story.

CONTENTS

More Fam

(and a few more olds)

2019

Maisie Wharton - me. Turns out I have a secret.
Jasper Lau - my blud, bestie, BFF. Mildly claustrophobic, severely loyal.
Ani Chowdhury - my other BFF. Probably still has more brains than a *University Challenge* reunion party, but whereabouts currently unknown.

1987

Lizzy Brookes – if you dig deep enough you find an unexpected heart. My mother, in about fifteen years.
Glenda and Henry – my nan and granddad, Lizzy's rents.
Paul – Lizzy' s biker brother, my uncle.

Rob Simmons – still the hottest thing on the wrong side of the year 2000. Plays the drums for Fallen Angel. To begin with, anyway.
Valerie Simmons/Bennett – his mother. Less said about her, the better.

Kim Fox – Living up to her nickname and finally loving life. Lizzy's BFF.
Tracy Rutherford – introduces the concept of barbeque to Lizzy's squad.
Elaine Longhurst – Not aware that it's a waste of time flirting with Jasper. Lizzy's squad.

Claire Cook – Panicked about exams. Lizzy's squad.
Ian Hills – Hooked up with Kim for about thirty minutes. Lizzy's squad.

Brian Walker – Rob's best bro. Ani's equal on the brains scale. Plays guitar for Fallen Angel and air trumpet, at first. Lizzy's squad.
Marion - his mother.

Neil Thorpe – drummer with Divine Morrissey
Ed Mitchell – bassist with Divine Morrissey.
Scott Kelly aka Patchouli - Lizzy's ex-boyfriend. Fit and fake. Don't go there.
Tim Wharton - manages the Hippy Shop in Stoneford. My father, in about fifteen years.

1971

Mick, John, Babs and Trev – all the young dudes.
Ted Simmons – Rob's very young dad.
Frank Bennett – lead singer of Monkey Business, also Rob's uncle.

Chapter One – (You Gotta) Fight For Your Right (To Party) (Beastie Boys, 1987)

Celebrations. Some people have birthday parties with chocolate caterpillar cake and sausage rolls. Other people celebrate in restaurants or pubs by eating too much pizza or going out clubbing and drinking cocktails with crazy names. Here at Lizzy Brookes' 18th birthday party, it looks like they are having a sexfest. The worst thing is not that people are snogging. The worst thing is that they are old.

'I don't think we need to worry about blending in, Maisie,' Jasper says, picking up a soggy serviette with a gold 18 embossed on the corner.

Everywhere I look, it's carnage. Empty crushed cans and bottles litter the corn-yellow grass like confetti from the apocalypse, and two couples are being really obvious on the multi-coloured patio. They must be at least 40. Gag. I can see a big silver bowl on a camping table in the gazebo; there might have been drink in it once, but now it's stuffed with what looks like it might have been someone's jumper, scattered with a load of greying wrinkled tiny sausages like rotting sprinkles. What I hope is beer drips down the white sides of the gazebo, and the fairy lights are dangling limply down over the heads of six more people; two on the floor sleeping and four shouting and laughing so violently that they must be at risk from having a seizure. In front of us, another group of four are sitting cross-legged in a circle, sharing a sizeable spliff. One looks up and vaguely wafts it under my nose, and I realise it's being offered to us.

Jasper steps forward, but I push him back and shake my head. 'What?' he says, all innocence.

'I don't need you stoned on top of everything else,' I mutter, sounding like my mother. Oh, the irony. I can hear laughter from the open windows of the house and some woman singing that she'll survive; the sickly, sweaty mix of booze and ganga is everywhere. We're supposed to be the delinquents, and we aren't even home yet.

Brian lifts his leg and removes some squashed pastry from the sole of his white Converse. 'I don't think anyone's sober enough to notice that we all just appeared from Glenda's shed.' He pushes the door to the shed shut behind us and closes the latch, his bleached blond hair past the collar of his denim jacket and short on top, as is today's trend. Today being 1987.

'Are they smoking grass?' Kim asks, the pupils of her eyes huge in the semi-darkness.

'You know Glenda and Henry have always been a bit hippy,' Rob says, squeezing my hand. 'How else would Lizzy get away with it all?'

'These olds sure know how to party,' Brian agrees. 'Is my mother here? I don't think I want to see that. Way too traumatic.'

Traumatic? Does he think so? In the last two days, I've discovered my family are Weyfarere, Guardians of the Weys and Protectors of the rifts (we call them Weydoors) that allow people to travel through Time. My mother in 2019 sent me back here to 1987 to sort out a mess I probably made, and now I'm here at Lizzy's birthday party, where she was given her precious grounding key. Here again. No one knows that I'm Weyfare as well apart from Jasper, and he's sworn to silence. Because our friend Lizzy Brookes, the wild child who just turned 18 today, is my future mum.

So no, Brian has not one idea of how traumatic this is. I, on the other hand, am one freaking outburst away from enforced sedation — me, Maisie Wharton, on the edge of the abyss that is my new life.

Someone is speaking to me. Rob squeezes my hand again. The fittest drummer this side of the Millennium has green eyes that make me catch my breath when he looks at me. 'What do you think we should do now?'

They're all looking at me like I'm supposed to know. Jasper, my best blud from our time in 2019, our worrier supremo with his floppy hair and cheeky grin; Kim, bubbly blonde permed curls on the outside, dark scars hidden away inside; Brian, looking like an angel from an old oil painting but with the brain of Einstein and Rob, still wanting to be by my side despite all the weirdness, hotter than the sun with his tip-bleached hair all spiky on top and long over his collar, wearing the usual blazer with sleeves all rolled up over muscled drummer's arms, still managing to look FAF. And then there's me. Maybe Jasper is right. Stoned sounds like a good option right now.

'Maybe we should have some of whatever they're smoking?'

'As brill as that sounds, I think you were right before - we need to keep a clear head,' Rob says. 'You say Lizzy told you she thought Scott stole the book as well as the key?'

Scott, Lizzy's thieving mong of a boyfriend went from hero to zero in the second he thought it would be a good idea to steal Lizzy's precious silver key. There's a big chance that he took her Book as well. The *Trewthe of the Weyfarere* or *The Truth* is the family history, and it's the only thing around here that will help us make sense of all this time travelling. Especially since Glenda Brookes, Lizzy's mother and my Nan, will be all kinds of wasted and not able to help us make sense of anything tonight.

Something important is trying to work its way to the front of my brain. 'Lizzy wasn't sure that he stole *The Truth*, but if he did, he would steal it tomorrow, wouldn't he?' I ask. 'After this party?'

'After my Stepmonster turned up with my Dad and threw an eppy,' Kim says. It's been a rough few days for Kim too.

Jasper nods towards the cackles of laughter and disco music coming down from the house. 'Which means it should be in there now.'

'So if we go and get it now -' Rob says.

'Then it won't be there tomorrow for Scott to steal,' Brian finishes, playing the little imaginary tune on the imaginary trumpet that we have all just learned to ignore.

'That's got to make a difference, surely,' Rob asks. 'Because it wasn't what happened before, was it?'

No, it wasn't. I look up at the house: my lovely stone house built at the end of a tunnel to a door through Time. Travellers' Rest Mum had called it. I didn't even know it had a name. How many of my ancestors had lived here? A pang of resentment and disappointment races through my brain, that I can't sit down with Glenda Brookes and ask her for the answers to all the questions screaming in my head. I'd had to leave the only person who could help me in 2019 before I could ask her anything important, in a future she didn't deserve. In a future that wasn't even ours. 'It sounds even busier in the kitchen.'

'Let's hope they're all too written off to notice that we're back early,' Jasper says.

'Let's hope we can get away with the Book before the other versions of us come back from Trinity,' Rob squeezes my hand.

What do you do if you see yourself walking up the path towards yourself? I am not going there. Is it not crazy enough that I am holding hands with a guy who probably already has grandchildren? Currently, there are two versions of us here; me, Rob, Jasper, Brian and Kim are also walking back slowly from Lizzy's other birthday party. We go through the Weydoor with Lizzy tomorrow, and until then, we have to watch out that we don't see our backs, which means getting on with this and getting gone.

I push through the open back door, through the little strips of coloured plastic that are supposed to keep the bugs out of the kitchen, into a blue fog so thick I have to concentrate hard not to start choking. The kitchen isn't just busy. It's rammed with dancing olds.

I'm feeling more minging than ever, but a hand gently nudges into my back and pushes me forward. I can't act weird, or the olds are more likely to notice our weird, but the thing is, the further I move into the room, the clearer I can see that these people are too messy to notice a bunch of teens who should be listening to bands up town. I glance up at the wall clock with the clunking jackhammer tick; usually, we'd hear it but not in this row. My ears feel like they're bleeding.

'What is this music?' Jasper says.

'David Bowie,' Rob says evenly.

Jasper turns on him, nearly falling into a gyrating woman with loose curly hair tumbling down her back, singing happily about a laughing gnome. 'Come on, blud,' he says, frowning. 'We know about Bowie too; he's a legend. He did not write songs about gnomes.'

'Yeah, he did,' Rob says evenly.

'He did a great song about a honky cat as well,' Kim says helpfully.

'That was Elton John, love,' Brian says.

'I thought Elton John did the funky gibbon?'

'That was the Goodies,' he says patiently.

'You are all mad,' Jasper says.

I'm approaching the round pine dining table. Last time I saw it, everyone nearby was slumped over it with mugs of tea, hanging. Today you can't see the lace tablecloth, not only for the ashtrays and beer bottles but also just about every strong spirit known to me and then some. I'm tempted to grab the Bacardi bottle on the way past, but now the mission target is in sight: the pine dresser on the far side of the dining area. Stacked with posh dinner plates and two shelves filled with books, the one we are looking for isn't laying out, and that's a good thing. I hope.

There is a board game on the table. It looks like it ought to be Monopoly, but the people playing it are laughing too much. I don't remember Monopoly being that funny when I was a little kid. It says Pass-Out in the middle. Several people are just standing around laughing at the ones playing and laughing, and they're all drinking, so Rob, Kim and Brian join in the watching, and me and Jasper try to see through the blue smog to the spines of the books on the dresser.

Glenda Brookes is a cook and cleaner at Drake's School when she's not protecting the Weys from people who shouldn't be travelling on them, so I guess I shouldn't be surprised to see *Home Cooking with Fanny Cradock* (really?) alongside *The World As I See It* by Albert Einstein. *The New Freezer Cookbook* by Mary Berry (surely you just bung the carton in the microwave and hit defrost) is next to *Travellers in Space and Time* by someone called Patrick Moore. I'm not a big fan of books. I wasn't a big fan of anything to do with the past until this little life-changer dropped in my lap; the day I saw my teenage mother walk out of the Old Library at the Fundraiser Disco with her big hair and pearly neon pink lippy.

Jasper nudges me. I look at him, and he nods meaning-fully forward at a point on the topmost bookshelf, about a third of the way along. He's right. I can see the purple leather spine trying to blend in with *Blue Peter's Seventeenth Book*. I thank any gods that are listening that no one has taken it.

But I'm about to. I look at it for a few moments. How does it all work? If I take this book down from this shelf and hide it in the denim jacket I borrowed from Lizzy to-morrow morning, will 2019 change again? Will anything ever be how it was before we came through the Weydoor? Something so small, like removing a book from its place on a shelf, could change so many things. The thought is frightening, but I have to do this because I don't know what else I can do.

'You get it down,' Jasper mutters in my ear. 'It's yours, after all.'

I drop my head sideways onto his shoulder. He's such a fusser, my Jasper, but he's loyal and he never lets me down. He followed our best friend Ani into the Old Library because she asked him to go with her, and we ended up in in a riot of parties and music and bad fashion choices - until she disappeared. We have no idea what happened to her. He's here with me now because I told him he had no choices. I wasn't lying, but it doesn't make it any easier. I can't guarantee him that we won't disappear either.

I reach out for the book, and someone behind me screams, 'Glenda! What're these kids doing in your house!'

Chapter Two – Wishing I Was Lucky (Wet Wet Wet, 1987)

'Kids?' Glenda sounds like a squawking bird.

'Well, not little kids. Big kids!'

I turn around to face the red-faced man on the edge of his seat, pointing at Kim, who is nearly as red in the face as he is, for different reasons. I look at Glenda, who is staring at Kim as well.

Then she laughs. 'That's not kids. That's Kim, that is. She's sound. Sound as a bell. You're sound as a bell, aren't you, little Foxy Loxy?'

Jeez.

'I'm good thanks, Glenda,' she says, flicking an amused glance back in my direction.

Glenda suddenly checks us all out. 'You all back so soon from the gig? Where's my birthday girl?' she slurs, sloshing more tequila from a bottle into her mouth, and a little down her chin.

'She's with Scott,' I say because I know that's true, but where they actually went after Trinity, I can't be sure.

'Scott?'

'He works at the hippy shop in town,' I say.

She eyes me speculatively and then bursts out with another totally unnecessary blast of laughter. 'The Hippy Shop,' she says, convulsing like I'm the funniest thing she's seen in weeks. 'That's not a hippy shop! Hippies don't run shops!'

'What kind of a shop is it then?' another woman at the table asks, taking a huge drag from a cigarette and almost disappearing in the haze.

'Well, it sells incense and perfume oils and crystals, and silk scarves and these terrific embroidered tunics from India,' Glenda says.

'Like the one Val's wearing?' the woman in the fog asks.

'That's a hippy shop,' another man says, trying to take a swig from a green bottle of something and discovering it empty.' And those aren't kids. Those is jail bait. And I'm not interested. Are we playing this game or not?'

'It's a pagan outlet. And I'll thank you not to call my son jail bait, Tony,' a woman standing by the sink calls over. The woman sitting beside her is propped up on a stool and she giggles like a pre-schooler.

I feel Rob actually jump beside me. 'Mum?'

Valerie Simmons looks less housewife and more vampire priestess today, with her bobbed dark hair hugging her chin and long black embroidered tunic over black jeans. Her friend is less goth in a tangerine shift dress with massive shoulders and big golden chains hanging down her front. 'Don't look so surprised, son, you're not the only party animal in the family. The General can cope without me for a night, you know. Say hi, Marion.'

'Hi, Marion!' the other woman says brightly, waving, almost falling off her stool. Valerie grabs her arm, and they both giggle. 'I mean Brian!' she adds, waving at him like he's leaving.

I look at Brian, and he's bright red. I realise I've not been breathing and take in a massive slug of not very clean air.

'You want to join in with the game?' Glenda asks, her words slurring so badly it sounds more like wanjoyinagame?

'I think we've had enough fun for tonight,' Jasper says over my shoulder, nudging me in the back with something hard. Something book-shaped. I stand up straight.

'Suddenly well tired,' I agree.

'He's right. Could definitely do with some kip,' Brian says, picking up momentum from Jasper and me.

'Going to motor in a bit,' Rob says, 'though that looks like a great game.'

'Lightweights,' the man with the empty bottle sneers. I wonder vaguely if he's related to me.

Glenda waves an arm around her head as if it's signifying something. 'You go then, and I'll see you on the other side. Yellow take a drink. Oh bugger, that's me,' she says inexplicably, pouring more of her drink down her throat as we take our chances and get out of the blue haze of the kitchen as fast as we can move through the wasted olds watching, past the ones dancing to Michael Jackson, out into the clean air of the night.

'Sod's knacker bag,' Brian leans forward, hands on his thighs, breathing hard. 'Did you see the state of my mother?'

'Did you get it?' I swing around and face Jasper once we are up on the road.

Jasper moves his hands from his chest to reveal that he is clutching the purple leather volume of *The Truth*.

It's a moment in Time, as all five of us look at this book, and I guess it's a different moment for all of us. For Kim, I'm guessing *The Truth* is the start of her mission to find out if she

13

can use the Weys to escape her awful family. For Brian, *The Truth* could have the answers to the question of why his new girlfriend vanished into thin air at Trinity, and whether he will ever see her again. For Jasper, *The Truth* is the start of the road home again, back to the security of 2019, and for Rob, *The Truth* is the beginning of the end, because it means me and Jasper will leave them all again soon.

But for me, it's the beginning of a much bigger journey. For my whole life up until a few days ago, I was just Maisie Wharton. I wasn't that smart, I wasn't that ream, I fought with my mum all the time, and I lived for my squad, Ani and Jasper. Now I'm a gatekeeper of some dimension I never knew existed where you can travel through Time; I have all this family history, and I had no idea about any of it until today. Mum in the future would be so proud; I'm actually keen to read this old stinky book and find out about our past. The history of the Weyfarere.

'We can't stay here,' I say into the silence, as we all stare at the book in Jasper's hands. 'It can't be long until the other us come back from Trinity now.'

'If we go the long way across the back of the Park, we'll avoid them. We could go to my place,' Rob says.

'Too risky,' Brian reaches out and touches the purple book with a single finger as if it's something religious. 'Your house is next door to Claire's, and if she gets a whiff of us being at your place, we'll have to go to Tracy's garden party with her tomorrow and that way will lead to a catastrophic rupture in the fourth dimension.' He stares back at all of us. 'We'll meet ourselves over a hamburger, and that way lies pain and suffering, I'm sure of it.'

'Well, we can't go to my place,' Kim says, almost laughing, 'I haven't even walked out yet, and none of you has enough money to bribe me to go back.'

'We can bunk down in my garage,' Brian says. 'It's not cold out, and there's some blankets and stuff at the back with the old camping gear if it gets that bad.'

They all look at me. 'Since when did I get to be the one in charge?' I ask, hoping they don't hear the wobble in my voice.

'It's obvious, Maisie,' Jasper starts, so I glare hard at him, and fortunately, the hard stare is in the Brookes' genes, and he realises his mistake. 'I mean – well you saw Lizzy, and she told you what to do. She gave you that key,' he finishes meaningfully.

'Lent me. She lent me a key,' I say irritably, instinctively touching where the old silver key fell against my chest under my black T-shirt. The key Lizzy did give me in the future, but if they knew that, they would want to know why she gave the one remaining Weyfarere key to someone who wasn't in the family. It's not the only key right now, though. Right now, Lizzy is still wearing her key, and Glenda, I imagine, is still wearing hers.

'Yes, she lent you a key. You,' he persists, and I know I'm not going to win this one, and I need to keep Jasper on side.

'Why did you never tell us you knew Lizzy in the future, Maisie?' Kim asks.

Finally, someone asks the question I've been expecting ever since I turned up in the Music Room in 2019 with a Weyfarere key. 'I thought it would be too weird for Lizzy. And like I keep saying, it doesn't do you any good to know too much about your future.' I say aloud. Or how much it changes, I think.

'It would've wigged me out, that's for sure,' Brian says, 'if you said you knew me.'

'Fine. Let's go cotch in Brian's garage.' There is silence. 'Chill. Hang out?'

Finally, we move. Living in the past is exhausting.

Late May 1987 is warm. I notice this happens a lot as I've got older; we get blistering hot weather in May while we're studying for exams and when we finish, it pisses down with rain for forty days straight. So the plan to spend the night in Brian's garage isn't as crazy as it sounds; we probably won't even need the old blankets he's pulled out from a trailer at the back, which is just as well because they smell a bit funky.

I feel a bit like a teacher from Reception Class must feel with all the kids at their feet on the carpet. Jasper, Kim and Brian are snuggling under one of the better blankets looking at me expectantly, and Rob is laying with his head in my lap. The purple book is on the concrete floor in front of us. *The Truth.*

'Aren't you going to open it then?' Jasper asks, more than a bit salty.

'It's a big deal,' I say and wish I hadn't.

Kim comes to my rescue. 'It's okay,' she says kindly. 'Glenda won't mind you having her book if it means that you're helping them all somehow.'

'Lizzy trusted you with a key,' Rob says. 'We already know a lot of stuff about her. She'd expect us to read it.'

I reach forward, pick up the book and open it to the title page. It's handwritten, and the original writing is quite faded, but underneath each line, there is a darker hand. 'It's in a foreign language,' I say. *The Trewthe of the Weyfarere.* The Truth of the Weyfarere. Trewthe. Something sets off a bell in my head. 'Glenda said it was Middle English. At school, we read Chaucer and a poem about some warrior called *Beowulf.* I think it's in the same language. It's not easy to see in this light.' The strip lights overhead are full of black stuff that I don't want to overthink.

'You can read Middle English?' Brian gets up and walks towards the back of the garage. 'I'm well impressed.'

'Sadly not, but there's a translation underneath each line.' I carefully turn a few pages to confirm what I think, and it looks like I'm right. 'It's going to take some time to read through this lot.' I turn a few more pages, and the writing changes. A few more, and it changes again.

Brian returns with a black rubber torch. 'See if this helps,' he says, placing it next to me.

'Don't you think you should be wearing gloves or something to protect the pages like they do on those antique programs the olds watch?' Jasper asks.

He has a point, but for all that it must be ancient, it's still relatively sturdy, and although the leather is worn and cracked, and the original writing is fading, the pages themselves are not in bad condition. 'I don't have any, do I?'

'There's probably a pair of Dad's old driving gloves back here if that's any help?' Brian offers, but I shake my head.

'Read a bit of it to us,' Rob asks.

'Bedtime stories,' Kim grins, snuggling a little closer to Jasper.

I pick up the book and turn slowly and carefully to the

first proper page of writing. Rob picks up the torch, presses a button on the side and shines the fierce white light onto the delicate pages. The lines are quite far apart, although they're now filled with translation. There's not much writing on each page, and now and then there is a picture that looks like it's been drawn by a five-year-old with their wrong hand.

' Copied for perpetuity in the year of our Lord 1730 by Mary, firstborn daughter of Alice. Here be preserved forevermore the sacred words of our foremothers who seek to impart the truth of the noble and ancient bloodline of the Weyfarere who guard the Weydoor through Time on the land bequeathed to Drake's Manor on the Stone Ford. Someone's written the Old Library in brackets in different handwriting.'

'Noble and ancient, eh?' Brian says. 'Not the first two words I would come up with to describe Lizzy Brookes.'

Or me, I think silently.

'In the year of our Lord, 627 did our unequalled father Wayland discover the vast and fathomless truth of the Weys that traverse the seven kingdoms of Man and beyond. Wayland,' I repeat. 'I've heard of him. I think he pops up in *Beowulf* as well.'

'Wish I'd listened more in History,' Jasper says.

'Saxon, I think,' Rob swaps the hand that is holding the torch and shakes the other one. 'There were seven kingdoms here before it became one big England.'

'Oh, like *Game of Thrones!*' Jasper cries and then shakes his head. I sigh. 'No, not like that. Forget I said that.'

Kim rubs her arms. It's getting colder.

'When Wayland did marry All-wise the Valkyrie, their firstborn daughter was gifted with the key to travel the Weys - '

'Hold your blinking horses up a sec,' Brian sits up, and

the blanket falls away from all three of them. 'Did you just say Wayland married a Valkyrie?'

I look back at the book. The writing is beginning to dance in front of my eyes as the strip light flickers overhead. 'That's what it says here.'

'Lizzy is descended from the Valkyrie?' Brian says, and for the first time since we started talking about time travel, he sounds unsure.

'I thought the Valkyries were something to do with Norse Mythology,' Rob says.

'Myths aren't true though, are they?' Kim asks.

I slap the book closed and put it back on the concrete as hard as I dare. 'Yeah. Well, Wayland's in an old poem about a monster, and you know what? Until a couple of days ago, I didn't believe I could walk through a bookcase and travel back in Time to save my ... to save someone's ass and have to spend time with a load of tools who dress funny, but hey, here we are!'

There is silence. Rob rolls over and looks up at me, his eyes regretful. 'Sorry, baby,' he says. 'It's just a lot to take in, you know?'

'It is,' Kim pipes up, 'but we went to the future with you. I know we weren't there long, but it was still all kinds of strange. We know you're not making this up.'

'I'm a scientist,' Brian says gruffly. 'I can deal with dimensions and energies and ruptures in time fields, but I'm a bit off my game with mythology.'

'I remember M ... my history teacher telling us once that many myths and legends were based on truth,' I pick the book back up and dust it off. 'Maybe she was right.'

'By the way,' Rob says, sitting up, 'just checking, but "tools who dress funny"? That's not a good thing, is it?' I pull a face, and he grins. 'If I didn't like you so much, I'd be offended.'

'We don't dress funny, anyway,' Kim says. 'You're the ones who showed up in the Common Room with hair that looked like it had been ironed.'

I can't help it, and I start to giggle. '*Straightened*. Not ironed.'

She shrugs, but she's giggling too. 'And you were wearing a jumper with a hood on it. Don't they have coats in your time?'

'Jumpers with names on,' Brian says, joining in the smiles. 'Like little kids that wear name labels around their necks in case they get lost.'

'Do you want to hear any more of this or not?' I snap playfully.

'I'm not being funny, Maisie, but are you reading the translation or the original?' Kim asks. 'I've never pretended to be all that smart, but I don't understand much of it.'

'Thus it was that Wayland's daughter walked the Weys that bind the energies of this land to the length, width, height and time of travel, for her forebears charged her with the safekeeping of the faults therein.'

'I think it's saying that this guy Wayland's daughter was put in charge of the Weys and their doors by his ancestors,' Brian hugs his knees toward him, and Kim pulls the blanket better over him.

'Maybe Lizzy needs to do another more modern translation,' Rob suggests.

I put the book into my lap. Suddenly I pull my hands

over my face, still smiling at how stupid and unbelievable and terrifying this all is. Suddenly I can't remember the last time I got any real sleep.

Rob's read my mind or my body language at least. 'I think we should get some shut-eye,' he says. 'The book's not going anywhere.'

'Trailer's at the back if you want a bit of privacy,' Brian says, moving over to the light switch.

'What, in front of you lot?' I say lightly, curling up on the concrete floor that could have been covered in upturned ten-centimetre nails for all I care. Right now it feels like a feather mattress, and *The Truth* is my pillow. Rob switches off the torch and leaves me in the dark to worry about us.

It feels like only seconds later when a crash wakes me, followed by loud shouting and then laughter. I'm no psychic, but I reckon Brian's mum has just made it home, and by the sounds of the male voice, Brian's dad is with her, so she's either got him up or he must have been at the party too. Through the dirty garage window, the night sky is turning a lighter shade of blue.

Rob nuzzles into my neck behind me, his arm on my hip, but he doesn't wake. I reach under my head for *The Truth*, gently remove Rob's arm from my side, take the torch and make my way to the back of the garage, to more funky-smelling blankets that I can hide under behind the trailer and read more of this strange book in peace, like a kid trying to finish a good story after their rents told them lights out.

By the time the sun is bright in the garage window, I

have discovered from *The Truth* that things might be worse than any of us could've imagined.

Chapter Three – Notorious (Duran Duran, 1987)

I can't remember ever reading for so long, and my eyes are streaming from the strain of struggling to read bad news in tiny handwriting under itchy blankets. I peer over the trailer. Rob is still curled up like a kitten on the cold hard concrete, Kim and Brian are leaning on each other like old-fashioned bookends, and Jasper is sitting up, looking straight at me.

I jump, and recovering myself, point to the garage door. He nods, and we quietly make our way out of the garage, into the bright, sunlight street.

'Have you been crying?' he asks me, a supportive hand on my shoulder. 'Are you upset about something you read? I know everything's crazy but -'

'Not upset, no. it's just eye strain. But I've been reading *The Truth* while you all slept and there's some interesting stuff in it.'

'What kind of interesting stuff?' He pushes his fingers through his bed hair and comes out looking like he spent hours styling it.

'Smugglers interesting stuff.'

He stops mid-ruffle. 'Smugglers?' I nod. 'Like Johnny Depp?'

I punch him lightly. 'No, fool,' I say. 'Like contraband goods.'

'I'll get the others,' he replies.

'No.' I put a hand on his shoulder. 'No, don't. Leave them for a bit. I need to talk to you alone. Brian's rents didn't come back from the party until daybreak.' I wipe something gritty from the corner of my eye. 'I heard someone fall through the front door so I wouldn't expect them up for a while. The others will be safe there for a couple of hours. It can't be later than eight now.'

We walk away. 'I don't know that it's such a good idea that we split up,' Jasper says, sitting on the wall on the corner a few metres down from Brian's house at the entrance to some garages.

'We're not splitting up. I just need to speak to you. About stuff.'

'You want to talk about smugglers.'

'Well, yes, and about this Weyfarere stuff,' I sigh.

'You're a Weyfarere,' he says. 'Like Lizzy. Aren't you?'

'I'm Lizzy's only daughter. And it's Weyfare.'

'Pardon me, oh great and mystical Guardian,' he sneers. I glare at him and he glares back at me. Then we both smile and kind of laugh a bit, and the standoff is gone. I guess, when it comes to the crunch, there isn't much more to say. He's right. I'm Weyfare. I have to deal with it.

'Scott changed everything, Jasper.'

'He's a senior manager at Drake's,' Jasper stares forward at the empty road. 'How is that even possible? Scott never struck me as the educator type.'

'I can't leave her there. Mum, I mean,' I say. 'Not with the future all wrong like that.'

'Well, we'll go back when we get this sorted,' he says.

'We've already saved *The Truth*. All we need to do now is save Lizzy's key, and make sure Glenda doesn't vanish later today. After that, we can go home and you'll be able to see Rob whenever you want.'

I sigh. 'Don't say that.'

'It's true. Why wouldn't you want to? You're Weyfare, and you have a grounding key. So you can travel back to see him as often as you like. You're going to have to tell them you're Weyfare though,' he adds. 'That could be tricksey.'

'No, I'm really not going to tell them. The fewer people who know about this the better.'

'But that key is yours. Lizzy gave it to you, didn't she? You're her daughter. So you can travel through Time. Surely you want to tell Rob about that bit?'

That's the trouble. I'm not sure I do.'

'There you are.' I turn to see Brian walking up the road towards us. 'Were you planning on going somewhere and abandoning us doppelgangers to a fate worse than death when my mother goes to the freezer in the garage to get the breakfast sausages and discovers she's got two sons?'

'Explain that like I'm five?' I say.

'Why are you sneaking off out here?'

'We just didn't want to wake you.' Jasper leans forward and pats my knee. 'Maisie's been reading.'

'Is that an event?' Brian asks innocently.

'To be honest, yes. I don't normally do books,' I say.

'School must be a drag,' he comments, 'if you don't like books.'

'School is a drag,' I echo, 'but we don't use a lot of ... Look. I just finished reading the first chapter of *The Truth*.'

'What are you all doing out here?' I turn and see Rob and Kim emerging from the garage.

'Getting some sun,' Jasper says.

'I just go pink and peel,' Kim says, sitting beside him.

Rob sits on the wall beside me. Even his bed hair is cute. 'You look upset,' he says, wiping a gentle finger under my eyes. What is it with guys who can sleep all night and still wake up looking buff?

'Not upset, no. But I've been reading *The Truth* while you all slept and it's thrown a few balls in the air.'

'Balls?'

'We need to get somewhere quiet so I can tell you what I think I found out. Lizzy will need to know as soon as she comes back. Where can we go?' I ask, putting the book into my pocket.

'Better not go back into the garage in case one of my olds wakes up,' Brian says. 'I'm back in the house now, remember.'

'We could go down town.' Jasper stretches long arms above his head. 'Remind me not to sleep on concrete again any time soon.'

'You may not be getting a choice,' I remind him. 'Town's not a bad idea. And it's well away from where the other versions of us are right now.' How did my life get so complicated? 'But I'm not talking about this until we find somewhere we can't be overheard.'

'Mum's the word,' Brian says. 'Mission accepted.'

'Show us the sights,' Jasper says. 'I could murder a Nandos.'

'I think you'll be lucky to get a Maccy D,' I say.

With every footstep in danger of waking the houses and bringing some kind of time-clash catastrophe down on our heads, we disappear into the quiet roads of the Saints' Estate. Brian, Rob, and Claire, another friend from 1987, live here. Unlike Jasper's Poets' estate, which hasn't even been built yet and is currently just hundreds of rows of apple trees, the Saints' Estate has been around a lot longer, and all the roads are named after birds. No, I jest. Brian lives on St John's Road; it's the main road through the estate, and it comes out halfway down the Top Road that leads into Stoneford.

It's a Sunday and Rob is right: it's like everyone left the place. There are hardly any cars about. There are even fewer people on the pavements. There are a couple of shops on the Top Road: one that has loads of washing machines in the window; the chippy that the kids from FCAB and Drake's all use at lunchtimes; a butcher with sausages hanging in the window and what looks like half a pig mounted on a skewer. None of them is open. Down Town Hill, past Neil Thorpe's flat, over the railway line. If we keep going, we go back up the hill to Tracy Rutherford's house, where her family are hosting their very first barbeque with other friends of Lizzy's that we met when we were here before. We can't go, because we're already going to be there, so we take a right at the Station and wander up the High Street. The centre of town is no more lively.

'I haven't heard of most of these shops,' Jasper says, as we walk past a Foster's shop window with loads of boy mannequins wearing thin cotton blazers like Rob's. The High Street is wholly deserted; even the doorways have no occupants.

Our version of town is mainly full of shops that sell

things for a pound, but there are loads of restaurants, bars and clubs that liven the place up after dark. We'd never come here to buy anything. If people want to actually go out and buy something, they head to the shopping centres on the outskirts of town. The kids who go to school in town might hang out down here, but we don't. I can't remember when I came here last in the daylight.

I don't recognise half the stores either. We walk past a Chelsea Girl window full of big-haired mannequins in cropped denim jackets, a Tandy window stacked high with massive black boxes with VHS printed on the front, and a bright red Our Price sign above somewhere that looks like a place where you go to actually buy music, with vinyl record sleeves in the window. I guess without the Internet, people here have to leave home to go shopping; there's no choice about it. As long as they don't want to go shopping on a Sunday. Crazy.

We wander down as far as St Peter's Hill and my feet are beginning to burn. Kim sits down heavily on a slatted bench at the edge of the road.

'We can't just keep wandering around here for the next few hours,' Brian says. 'There's nowhere we can sit and talk privately down here. Why don't we go back to the Railway Gardens? Find a quiet bush and talk about time travel?'

'Why didn't you suggest that in the first place?' I moan.

Back up the High Street and past a huge building called C&A here that's a bar and nightclub in our time, we finally arrive at the Railway Gardens. Jasper and me wouldn't come here in our day if you paid us because it's full of joeys and junkies and, if you come down here, they assume you're into that scene. It looks different now, though. More wholesome, somehow. There are flowers in the beds, and there's even an old couple sitting on the bench by the bandstand holding hands. We pass a public toilet block that I don't recognise from 2019, and we head for the row of bushes at the back.

There are more signs of life here. Groups of kids our age are sitting around, smoking and drinking. I can smell the ganga, but it's not the crack den of 2019. We find a quiet bush or three and sink down onto the dried-out grass.

After a while, Rob looks across at me. 'So come on then. No one can hear us. Spill the beans. What exactly did you find out when we were all napping?'

'It wasn't easy to read,' I say. 'Even the translations are out-dated. I managed to read the first chapter, though. It was more about Wayland.'

Brian crosses his legs and puts his hands in his lap like a little schoolboy. 'Hit us with your best shot, lady,' he says. 'I'm ready for more of your weirdness.'

'Good. Because there's massive crazy in this book.' I pull off my jacket; the sun is climbing higher in the cloudless sky; it's going to be another hot one. Rob puts an arm around my shoulder. Kim lays flat on her front at my feet. 'So, Wayland had two brothers. They all married Valkyrie women, and the women were in charge of where people's souls went after they died, especially if they didn't die in battle. When they found out about the Weydoors, they used them to dump the dead that didn't make it to Valhalla.'

'Nice. Very respectful,' Brian nods, picking at a solitary wild dandelion.

'I've heard of Valhalla,' Jasper says.

'It's been in a couple of films we watched.' I say. 'Anyway, Wayland's daughter got fed up with the wives abusing the Weydoors, and they all disappeared one night, including her mother. I couldn't read the bit that explained why. Wayland's brothers were so pissed off that they went off after the Valkyries and he never saw any of them again.'

'A Saxon Eastenders then.' Jasper lays down and stretches his hands under his cheek for a pillow. 'Family feuds and murder. Nothing ever changes.'

'Wayland worked the silver from the rings the Valkyrie left behind into seven keys -'

'Sod's knacker bag! Are you saying that's a Saxon relic Lizzy lent you?' Brian exclaims.

I pull out the silver key from under my now pretty rumpled and skanky T-shirt. I'd wondered the same myself, but I wasn't going to torture myself with the thought of running around in my mother's timeline holding a priceless artefact, on top of everything else. There were worse things to deal with. 'No. They must have made copies.'

'But it could be priceless, couldn't it?' Kim says, looking a bit stagestruck as the key glints in the sunlight.

'So Wayland's daughter passed a key onto her first-born daughter, to link her to her heritage,' I say, trying to ignore the sudden interest in my chest. 'The Weyfarere are descended from those girls. Glenda was right. The Weydoors glow in the presence of Weyfarere, and over the centuries, the Weyfarere girls were sent to any place where there was word of "mysterious happenings", and if they found a Weydoor, they had to stay there, protect it, and start a family so they could produce a daughter to carry on the work.'

'Well, that sucks,' Kim comments.

'Any boy children were sent off to be hunters and warriors, and the eldest girls always had to stay home to protect the Weydoors with the older females of the family. But that's not the most important thing I read,' I say, leaning forward instinctively, although what I expect to happen if we're overheard is your guess – we'd probably be referred to a mental health team if such a thing exists here. 'The brothers left Wayland, but they found their wives and had kids too. Their ancestors made a living by using tokens to travel on the Weys to steal goods from different timelines and smuggle it through the Weydoors.'

'Like pirates?' Kim asks, looking up from the dandelion head she's shredding.

'More like gangsters,' Jasper says, echoing the single word I gave him back on the wall outside Brian's garage.

'Gangsters?' Kim asks, the dandelion head forgotten.

'A family, with traditions, passed down like the Mafia in the Godfather,' Brian says, his fingers wriggling manically. 'The Mob.'

'The book calls them Weyleighers,' I say, picking up the book. 'Weyleighers didn't have any keys, but they knew about using tokens so they could travel out to different times, take valuable things to sell, and go back. *The Truth* said most of them came to a bad end, either because the tokens failed or the got caught. It said most Weyfarere girls abandoned the Weydoor during the Industrial Revolution when people left their home villages and went to find work in the towns and cities. There are hardly any Weyfarere or Weyleighers left. Glenda wrote a footnote in 1972 that Lizzy was the next in line of the only Weyfarere family left in the south.' I'm virtually extinct already. FML.

'Just as well the tokens aren't reliable without the keys to boost them,' Jasper says. 'If they had keys, they could travel through the Weydoors and make all kinds of trouble. Not to mention a fortune. Well, it's been a *fascinating* History lesson.' I can now hear the impatience in his voice, 'and forgive me for not being more excited about it all, but I thought that book was going to give us a bit more information than telling us that there are good guardians and bad ones.'

'I haven't finished,' I say quietly.

'Let joy be unconfined,' he says snarkily.

'Weyleighers used to settle near the Weydoors to carry out their work. If they discovered the identity of the Wey-farere family, they tried to steal the keys. It said the keys were a great prize for the Weyleighers.'

'Well, they would have been a great prize,' Rob says, 'since the keys would allow them to travel more safely on the Weys.'

'So Weyleighers stole the keys,' Jasper repeats. 'They were thieves. And?'

'Scott stole Lizzy's key,' Kim says, her eyes big and bright in the sunlight.

Someone from one of the other groups of kids dotted around the Gardens lets out a scream of laughter, and we all jump.

'Sod's knacker bag. Are you saying you think Scott Kelly is a Weyleigher?' Brian is leaning forward like a dog waiting for a treat.

Everyone laughs nervously.

'But he did steal Lizzy's key, and he wanted to take the

one she lent to Maisie!' Kim says, slightly subdued.

'And he stole *The Truth*,' Jasper says quietly, all the impatience gone from his voice. 'The first time around, I mean.'

'The shop would be a good cover for a smuggler,' Rob rubs the beginnings of the stubble on his chin. 'To be fair, he's never short of money for a bloke who works the counter in a trinkets shop. Look at how he was flashing the cash at Trinity.'

'The keys are real silver, they're worth nicking just for their value,' I say.

'But a Weyleigher could do some real damage with a key,' Rob says.

'They could really mess up the time-space continuum. It is a thing,' Brian adds with a sigh as Kim goes to ask something. ' It's not just *Back to the Future*.' He breathes through the word like it tastes bad. 'A Weyleigher though? Scott Kelly? You said the families had all died out.'

'The book said that.'

The thing is, back in 2019, I remember Mum said something about a trust fund Scott inherited when he was 25. I'd have laughed at the thought of him being connected to the Weys yesterday, but that was before he attacked Lizzy on the path to the Main Hall at Drake's in 1987, and before I'd seen the look in his eyes when he tried to bribe me to hand over the key Lizzy had given to me only minutes before, after telling me that Glenda vanished later today. Was it greed or something else that I saw in those piercing sky-blue eyes? Either way, it had chilled my bones.

'It sounds ridiculous,' I say aloud. 'Except that Lizzy suspected he was the reason behind Glenda's disappearance. We have to be there at the Weydoor waiting when Scott and

Lizzy come back through. We have to take the key back from Scott. I don't think he's a Weyleigher,' I tell them. 'but I'm pretty sure he changed Lizzy's future when he stole her key.'

'Did she say he was a Weyleigher?' Rob asks.

I shake the thoughts out of my head, no. 'She didn't say anything about them.'

Jasper looks at me. 'Glenda is supposed to disappear later today. What if Scott got rid of her through the Weydoor?'

'She would've just come back again, surely,' Brian says. 'The key would bring her straight back to 1987.'

'Unless Scott took her key as well,' Kim says grimly.

'Or she wasn't able to get back through the Weydoor,' Rob adds. 'They smuggled stuff through the Weydoor, so no one looking for it would ever find the evidence. What if they smuggled bodies too,' Rob says, his cheeks flushed under the bright sun.

'Just think if they wanted to kill someone. If the body was found in another Time, it'd be untraceable. Anything, like dental records or DNA, that could be used to identify the body would be all out of synch with the records of that time.' Brian says. 'That would be brilliant.' He pulls a face as he catches Kim's shocked look. 'I mean, technically brilliant. Terrible though, of course.'

There's a rustle in the bushes behind us, and we all stop talking. It turns out to be nothing more than an enthusiastic blackbird.

'Stop it,' Kim says, and I can see she's nearly in tears, and I put an arm around her shaking shoulders.

'Yeah, shut up already,' I tell them. 'You're not helping. This is Lizzy's Mum we're talking about.' And my Nan.

They all look at me. 'Anyway, if Scott got rid of Glenda, why didn't he do the same to Lizzy?' Brian asks after a few moments of silence.

Rob says, 'Maybe someone paid Scott to get rid of Glenda, but not Lizzy.'

'Who would pay anyone to hurt Glenda Brookes?' Kim asks, her voice a bit wobbly. 'Everyone loves Glenda. She's the nicest oldie any of us know.'

'I think we need to read a bit more of that Truth book,' Jasper says. 'I get the feeling we're working with half a story here.'

'Not even as much as a quarter; I only read a couple of chapters,' I say, 'and that was like wading through syrup in wellies. There was no mention of any killing. We're all a bit extra here. I think we should go to the Hippy Shop.'

'This is a good time for retail therapy,' Jasper says.

'They do lovely perfume oils,' Kim says absently. 'The Jasmine is lovely, but it's a bit sickly.'

'It's Sunday,' Rob says. 'It won't be open.'

'I don't want to buy anything.' I stand up and brush the dead grass from my clothes. 'Scott won't have the book now, but pretty soon he should have the same knowledge from the conversation the Other Us will be having with Glenda. The chances are he will still crawl back to the shop once we start fighting with Kim's rents. I want to talk to him. Maybe stop him from taking the key in the first place.'

'I'm not sure I want to go to the shop,' Kim says, getting to her feet. 'I don't want to be involved with people who hurt other people for a living, even if it's Scott.'

'The book said nothing about anybody killing anyone,' I

say, giving her a reassuring squeeze.

'He may have stuff in the shop about Weyleighers,' Rob says. 'It's a hippy shop. There could be all sorts of useful stuff in there.'

'Maybe even a Middle English dictionary,' Brian adds.

'I'm sure he's not a Weyleigher,' I repeat, a little more firmly.

'But he runs a shop full of folklore books and pagan stuff, so I say it's still worth a rummage around,' Brian says, a bit more insistently.

'Wouldn't anything that secret be hidden away?' Kim asks.

'Glenda left *The Truth* lying about in her dining room,' Brian says, standing.

Jasper staggers to his feet and brushes the dust from his hands. 'I'm getting a numb bum sitting here. And I'm hungry, and I need a wash.'

'Apart from that, you're great. Have any of you got any money?' I tuck the key back under my T-Shirt, and bat at Kim's hands as she reaches into her pocket. 'No, put it away, Kim, that's all you've got.'

'I've got a few notes,' Rob says. 'Enough to shout us a Wimpy if we share. Burger,' he adds for my benefit, and Jasper's. 'Could splash a bit of water around in the loos while we're there.'

'You take me to all the best places,' I say with a smile, but from the expression on his face, I think my comment is lost on him. 'I know it's a risk, but I want to see what Scott says to me, now he doesn't have *The Truth*.'

I want more than that. We can't go over to Lizzy's house

too early or we will bump into ourselves as we hear the news of the Weyfarere the first time around, watching Lizzy's future crumbling in front of her hungover eyes.

So I want to see if I can stop Scott from destroying the future I thought I have. Whether or not he's a Weyleigher, I need to get to the Old Library and stop him from stealing Mum's key. It's possible that he just steals the key to flog for a few quid at the 1987 version of Cash Converter, or he may use it to jump through the Weys whenever he likes just for the craic, knowing he'll get home again. But if he is descended from the Weyleighers, who steal valuables from backwater timelines and flog them to get rich, I want to know whether he would hurt Glenda, and why.

Because I also want to know why he didn't then hurt Lizzy, and why he didn't hurt me last night. Because, when Scott looked into my eyes outside the Old Library, he must've known who I was. I even stupidly told him my name at Lizzy's party at Trinity. If I was Lizzy's daughter, there was a strong possibility I was Weyfarere, and he'd known whether I was her eldest daughter by the time I got back to 2019.

There's another thing I want to do if I go to the Hippy Shop, of course. That would be to meet my teenage Dad.

Chapter Four – We Care A Lot (Faith No More, 1987)

Then someone puts a heavy hand on my shoulder.

'So what brings you lot down to the dark side of the Gardens on a Sunday?' Cigarette smoke puffs into the air past my ear. 'Thought you lot would be in bed with major league hangovers.'

'It's been a long night,' Rob says. 'Gig was good though, Thorpe.'

At my side in a blue paisley shirt, narrow cotton trousers and a long black cotton trenchcoat, the drummer of Divine Morrisey nods his agreement. 'Yeah, considering it wasn't our usual crowd, we went down okay. You do know your gear's still all up at Trinity?'

'What?' Brian exclaims. 'Will was supposed to bring it all back last night!'

'Will shouldn't have been allowed anywhere near a steering wheel, but it never stops him,' Neil grins. 'Yeah, we've just been back up there to finalise a gig for next month. There's an SG, a Fender bass, a couple of mike stands, a Marshall and a Peavey up on the stage.'

They could be talking Mandarin for all the sense it makes to me, but Rob and Brian have gone from zero to ballistic in five seconds.

'I'll bloody kill Will,' Brian seethes. 'If that lot gets nicked, I'll have him.'

'Don't talk about killing people,' Kim says.

Neil smirks and steps in front of me. 'So what did you think of Divine Morrissey, baby? Fancy coming to another gig next Friday as my special guest?'

'Back off, she's with me,' Rob says, with just a touch of ice.

I'm half amused by the guys pacing around me like panthers, and half irritated at being made to feel like a piece of meat. 'Back off both of you,' I say lightly, 'I'm not anyone's property.' I turn to look at Rob. 'I can fight my own battles,' I say, reaching out and squeezing his arm, and turning back to Neil, 'and I don't expect I'll be around in a week, but thanks for the invite.'

'Fiery. Good luck with that,' Neil says and turns to leave. 'By the way, my mate Kevin has a good deal on acid at the mo if you're up for a proper adventure.' He swaggers off like he thinks he's Batman. See you at Tracy's do.'

Rob looks a bit put out, but honestly, I can do without the protection racket. As lovely as he is, we still haven't talked properly about the elephant that follows us everywhere like a menacing shadow; the fact that at the end of my natural timeline, I am currently a few days off 18 and Rob is a few years off his retirement. Looking at him gives me butterflies and shivers at the same time. At some point, we're going to have to have A Proper Conversation. I know it would be easier if I just told him I was Weyfare, and that yes, I probably could come back and see him all the time if Kim lent us her necklace, but where would it end up? In piles of tissues, empty multi-packs of Jaffa Cakes and too many share size bars of Galaxy? At some point, I'd still have to say goodbye or risk living in a world with the me that's born in 2001. It'd be even harder by then. And if I tell him I'm Weyfare, he'd work out that I must be related to Lizzy and I really don't think I can face that on top of everything else.

'Don't look like that,' I kiss him on the cheek. 'I'm a big girl, I don't need a protector against tools like Neil Thorpe.'

He shrugs. 'Maisie, we need to go up to Trinity to get our gear. Can the Hippy Shop wait?'

I nod. Dad can wait, he's going nowhere. 'As long as we are there for Lizzy and Scott when they come back through the Weydoor this afternoon.'

'Where are you going to put everything, though?' Jasper asks. 'We can't go back to Brian's, the other us is going there to talk to him about Weydoors, and Will is going to take us to Tracy's barbeque.'

'He has a point, and also, I don't know about you, mate, but I don't fancy carting my Marshall through the middle of town on my back,' Brian adds.

'Thorpe!' Rob calls out. 'Have you got a minute?'

Neil has started talking to another group on the grass, but he says something to them, and they laugh, and then he makes his way back to us. 'What's up?'

'Have you got any transport that we can borrow for a few hours?'

'I might have. Where's your bro?' Neil looks at Brian.

'Unavailable,' Brian says.

Neil grins. 'Yeah, I saw the unavailability he left with last night. Ed's got wheels, but he's had a fair few tins. Any of you got a licence?'

'Only a provisional,' Jasper says.

'That'll do. Ed!'

'I've only had a couple of lessons with my dad!' Jasper squeaks.

'It'll be fine, Mary, it's like riding a bike.' Neil's grin grows even wider as Ed saunters over and slings a very unsteady arm around Kim's neck. She nearly falls forward with the weight of him. 'Ed can sit in the passenger seat and tell you what to do if you forget. All right, Ed? They need the shagmobile for a couple of hours. They're cool. They helped us out yesterday. They play with Fallen Angel.'

'Ah, Fallen Angel. Great tits,' Ed slurs, and reaches around for Kim's. She smacks him in the face, and he laughs.

Honestly, I don't think Ed can remember his name right now, let alone how to drive a bloody car. I look at Rob, who shrugs, and Jasper, who mouths "help me".

'Don't any of you have a provisional?' I ask the others.

'No insurance,' Rob says.

'Oh, and you think we have some?' I reply, frowning,

'They can't trace you guys, can they?' Brian points out.

I glance at Ed, but he's too wasted to question the comment. 'And that's going to help at the police station when they pull us over?' I can hear my voice getting higher.

'Oh FFS, I'll do it,' Jasper says. 'How hard can it be?'

Ed's shagmobile is in the Station Car Park. Ed's shagmobile is gold with a lumpy bonnet and a grill at the front that looks like it was made for another car. It is the ugliest car I have ever seen in either of my lives.

'It's an All Aggro,' Brian says, his upper lip curling beneath the faint blond stubble.

'I'll thank you not to insult the babe magnet,' Ed slurs, stroking the car's roof lovingly. 'This is an Allegro Vanden Plas Estate, and if you want her to take you to Trinity, you have to be fucking nice to her.'

I look at Jasper, but he seems resigned to his fate, and I wonder idly whether we needn't actually worry any more about whether Scott Kelly is descended from a family of violent smugglers because Jasper is about to end us all by driving into a lamppost. 'You don't have to do this,' I say to him, quietly.

'It's fine,' he replies in a very high voice. 'Trinity is only a few roads away.'

'We still haven't decided where we are putting the gear,' Brian says, his disgust at the car still plastered to his face.

'Caravan,' Kim says. We all look at her. 'By the time we've loaded everything up at Trinity, everyone will be at Tracy's, won't they?'

'Possibly not everyone, but I can't think of anywhere better than Lizzy's caravan right now,' Rob says. 'What's the time, Ed?'

Ed peers down at the wrong wrist. Kim grabs the right wrist and peers at it. 'Just after twelve,' she says.

'I'm sure we're all at Tracy's barbeque by two,' I say. 'I'm sure I remember hearing a clock chime the hours there. If we can kill a couple of hours at Trinity, we should be okay.'

'Don't say kill,' Kim says.

'You know what I mean,' I pat her on the shoulder, and she gives me a grateful smile.

'Sounds like a plan, Batman,' Brian says, and he plays his imaginary trumpet, so we all know he's feeling okay.

At least one of us is.

So Ed slides into the driver's seat, and it takes Rob, Brian and Jasper to get him back out again, round the front of the car and into the passenger seat. Then we have to get him out again because it's a three-door car and the driver's seat doesn't go far enough forward to let us get in the back. It's just as well it's an estate car; even if it looks like something my dad wouldn't drive there is no room in the back for anything other than us, but there is lots of room in the boot, which is already home to a blanket and a couple of cushions. I try not to let my mind go there. Jasper just about manages to keep Ed upright as we pile in, and Brian is looking lit with Kim propped on his lap.

'When does the seatbelt law come into force?' Jasper asks, pulling his over his shoulder and looking at the four of us crammed in like sardines.

'You have to wear one, and so does Ed,' Kim says. 'We don't.'

After another five minutes of trying to fight with Ed, who is wrongly convinced that he can put his own seat belt on, Jasper starts the car.

'Mirror signal manoeuvre,' Ed says, and his head slumps against the passenger door.

The car jumps out into the road like a frog. I am so grateful that this is Stoneford on a Sunday in 1987, as there is hardly any traffic for Jasper to avoid. Trinity is only four streets away from the Railway Gardens, and they are long straight roads, but by the time we pull up outside, I'm convinced I have whiplash. We are all about to vom because Ed farted so much in his unconsciousness; it stank like rotten cabbage, but none of the windows are electric. They all have these silly winder things, and none of them work so we've been sealed in the Car of Eternal Stench. Jasper is paper white and shaking as he steps out on to the pavement and pulls Ed out of his seat so that we can escape. Ed laughs like he's on meds and curls up into a little ball on the ground. I give Jasper a huge hug, which I don't do all that often, and I'm surprised how tightly his arms wrap around me. Rob and Brian heave Ed onto his feet and drag him inside.

Trinity looks more like the church it used to be in daylight; there is even a wooden cross at the top of the roof peak. The front doors are wide open, and inside, at the back of the hall where there was a packed bar last night, there is a woman pouring water from a silver urn onto instant coffee and teabags in worn blue and green plastic beakers, handing plates of Rich Tea biscuits to old people sitting on metal camping chairs. They slump Ed onto one of the chairs. At the front of the hall, as Neil told us, there is some musical equipment. I look at the old people. They are probably the same age as Glenda would have been in 2019.

Rob's hand is in mine. 'Are you okay?' he asks.

I shake my head. 'That stink gave me a bad head. Mind if I get some air? I can carry something if it helps -'

He shakes his head, no. 'It's fine, there's not much to carry, and we need to hang around for a bit anyway. You go. I'll come and find you.'

I watch him walk down the hall, the floor covered with marks in the dust from the hundreds of boots and shoes that danced here last night, and turn to see Brian, standing in the light from the high plain windows that remind me of the sun streaming down into the Old Library. Yesterday he had a new girlfriend; my bestie Ani. Yesterday she vanished here in front of his eyes, and we still don't know why. It was a mystery I hoped *The Truth* would help us to solve, but things are moving so fast that I can't keep on top of all of it. Today is May 24th – again. Even if you take into consideration the days I've done twice, I can't believe how much has happened in such a short time. I leave Brian to his thoughts, and make my way out to the bench by the lychgate.

The cemetery here is not cared for. Most of the stones are crooked and covered in so much moss that you couldn't read the inscriptions if you wanted to, and some have fallen over completely. You couldn't put your arms around the tree trunks, they are so old. I wonder to myself if my family has always lived here, forever having to stay in town to protect the Weydoor. Would any of us be buried here? I would 't know where to start looking. I don't know the names of my family, apart from Brookes; I don't even know what Glenda's name was before she married Henry. I don't even know when Glenda and Henry married; I know they were pretty young.

I was never bothered about the past. It bored me. It bored me up until I became a part of it. I suddenly wish I could speak to Mum, not Lizzy the 18-year-old wild child but my Mum, Elizabeth, and tell her that I get it, I get the past now. I want her to tell me everything. I want her to tell me the names of my great-great-grandparents, and what town was like when they lived here. It's all-important now, as I may end up visiting them all.

I'm not aware I'm crying until gentle fingers brush the tears away from my cheeks, just like he did when he found me crying at the Fundraiser Disco.

'You must be so fed up with me crying all the time,' I say, snuggling into his shoulder as he sits down beside me and puts an arm around me.

'Not fed up. Just concerned.' I feel him take a deep breath. 'The last time we sat here, it was pretty intense.'

He's not kidding; the last time we sat here, we were a couple of layers of clothing away from full sex. The thought of it makes me blush. 'I know.'

'Do you want to talk about it?'

'*What*?' Okay, I'm really scarlet now.

'No!' He laughs to cover his embarrassment. 'No, not that. Whatever it is that's making you sad.'

Hell yes, I do want to talk about it, but hell no, I can't. 'I'm fine.'

'Maisie, it's obvious you're not fine.'

'I've just got a lot on my mind.'

'We all have. All this time travel and Lizzy being who she is, and Scott turning mean on a dime.' He pauses. 'But it's not just that, is it?'

Jeeez. 'Isn't that enough to be going on with then?' I ask, poking him playfully in the chest, but he's not taking the bait.

He leans forward so that I can see his face, outlined with the sun shining down behind him, making him glow like an angel. 'You're not telling me everything, are you?'

I try not to let my fear show on my face. 'Why do you say that?'

'Honestly? I'm not sure. Instinct? I think there is more to all this than you've let on. You've been different since we came back through the Weydoor. '

'Time travel takes it out of a girl.'

'You know what I'm saying. Did the older Lizzy tell you stuff you haven't told us? '

Yes, but I can't tell you the truth. I'm not ready, and I won't tell you that I'm Lizzy's daughter. You're not ready. I'm not ready. I don't even know who I am any more. It's all too soon. 'I don't know what else there is to tell you,' I say brightly, maybe too brightly. 'It's all too much. You know I'm from 2019. You know I can't stay here forever -'

'I know!' he exclaims unexpectedly. 'You don't have to keep telling me! I know! I get it! Can't we just enjoy being together while we can? Does it have to be so uptight and serious all the time while you're still here?'

'You just want to have a laugh, you mean.'

'No! Well, yes!' Suddenly his arm is not around me, and he's leaning forward with his head in his hands. 'Everything else has got so heavy. I just want to enjoy being with you for as long as I can. Is that so wrong?'

'I guess not,' I say.

'Do you feel the same way about being with me?'

I tickle a stray bleached end of his hair between my fingertips. 'You know I do.'

He turns and looks up at me. 'And I want you to know that you can talk to me about anything.'

All aboard the Nope train then. 'Okay.'

Neither of us says another word for a minute or two. If he's waiting for me to reveal my big secret, he's going to have to wait a long time, and in the end, he realises, and it's like someone has planted a glass wall between us.

'Okay. Well, as long as you know.'

'I know.'

He gets to his feet, leans down and runs a finger down the cheek where the tears have stopped. 'I'm going in for a coffee. You coming?'

'Give me a minute or two?'

He nods, pauses as if he's going to say something, and then walks off, and I feel like we've just broken something extraordinary and it was all my fault, but I had no choice, and now the tears are falling again.

Chapter Five – To Be With You Again (Level 42, 1987)

The coffee from the urn looks like watery mud, and it doesn't taste any better than I'd expect, but we manage to pass some time talking about everything and nothing, slowly sobering Ed up with the extra Rich Tea biscuits that the woman behind the serving hatch gives us for free. I'm hoping we can eventually get him dry enough to drive us to Lizzy's house. I don't think Jasper's nerves will manage that journey; it's a lot further than back to the Railway Gardens.

Ed being around also means we can't talk about Weyfarere or Weyleighers, and it's actually good to just sit at the metal table and have a laugh. Maybe Rob is right about me enjoying the time I have here. I wish I could make my mind up what I want.

Ed is the bass player with Divine Morrissey; he keeps telling Kim "birds love that", and it looks like he expects Kim to love it as well. She is obviously flattered but keeps smacking him, as his hands wander too much for anyone's liking. In truth, he's a bit of a sleaze; it seems to be the standard way here for a lot of the older guys I've met so far in 1987. I don't know how the girls here put up with it.

So we talk about cars, and music, whether Fender guitars are superior to Gibson ones (they can't agree) and why in the name of Sod (Brian's words) Ed is driving an All-Aggro (Brian's words again).

'It was cheap, man.' Ed's not slurring now, and he lights a cigarette the first attempt. No one seems to object. Even the woman behind the serving hatch is smoking. 'You wait till you have to get some wheels. Bloody insurance alone is a few hundred notes. I wanted an estate so I could lug the band's gear around, and I couldn't afford a Sierra.'

By the time we all get back in the car, to Jasper's relief, Ed looks and sounds like he can drive, even if his blood count says different. The watch on his wrist says it's nearly two, so we make the journey over to Lizzy's house, and the caravan at the bottom of her garden.

Time is not on our side, though. As we pull up, Henry and Glenda are walking down the garden path towards the garage, and, by the time I engage my brain to shout 'Dive!' above the din of The Smiths tape cassette playing full blast in the car, Glenda has already seen us, and no one in the car seemed to know what I expected to happen by saying 'Dive' anyway.

'Bugger, she's seen us.' Rob smiles and waves falsely as Glenda peers in through the window. She doesn't smile back.

'Hi, Glenda,' Ed slides out of the car and leans on the roof. 'I gather this lot belong to you?'

'Not exactly,' she says, and she's staring at Kim, and a prickle of anxiety itches in the pit of my stomach.

'Is Paul about?'

Does everyone know my bloody uncle?

'He's gone off to some cookout in Lizzy's friend's garden,' Henry says. 'How did the gig go?'

'Sweet.' Ed reaches in and pulls a clip beneath the dashboard. The rear of the car clunks. 'Listen, I got to shoot off. I spent way too long with these losers. Nobody paid me any

NO WEY OF KNOWING

babysitting rates.' He grins at Kim. 'Wasn't all a nightmare though.'

Kim and me help the boys pull the guitars, microphones, stands and amplifiers out of the boot of the little gold Allegro, and then with a wave and a blown kiss at Kim, Ed's gone back up the dirt-track in a clatter of grit and dust.

'What's going on?' Glenda asks.

'We were going to have a jam in the caravan,' Brian smiles encouragingly at her.

'No, Brian Walker, you were going to a garden party at Tracy Rutherford's,' Glenda says, crossing her arms. 'At least, that's where Paul and Lizzy have gone. And you three left to go to Brian's ages ago, Rob.' She's still staring at Kim. 'This is a loop,' she says before any of us can come up with an excuse.

'A loop?' Jasper asks, his voice unnaturally high.

'A time loop,' Glenda says. 'Kim, you were dragged out of my house about two hours ago, pretty much by the hair. Are you telling me your delightful stepmother and father happily let you leave the house to hang out with your friends after that debacle?'

FML. Of course they didn't. Kim walked out. The original her is probably on the bus right now heading back into town to bump into the original us coming back from Tracy's barbeque. I look across at her, and I can see she's thinking the same.

'You're right,' Rob says. I open my mouth to shout him down, but what's the point in lying to Glenda? 'We time travelled, and we got back here earlier than we left. Is that a loop?'

'Where are you all at the moment?' Glenda asks quietly.

'I take it we're not going to the Foxes now,' Henry says,

leaning against the garage wall and lighting a cigarette.

'I'm not sure we need to,' Glenda says, giving me a look that I don't like too much.   'Where are the originals now?'

'Coming up to the Park from town,' Brian says. 'We meet Kim at the Bus stop opposite Edward Betts Comp.'

'And you ended up there how?' Glenda asks her. This is beginning to feel like an interrogation.

'I left,' Kim says simply, and takes a cigarette offered by Henry.

'Understandable,' he says, lighting it for her.

I'm too tired to take any of them out for smoking any more. 'We came to hide out down here until everyone goes through the Weydoor and completes the loop,' I say, using her terms.

'You went through the Weydoor?' Glenda asks. 'Lizzy took you through?'

I let out a puff of air. 'She took us back to our timeline.'

'Then why did she bring you back again?' Her eyes are narrow now, she almost looks mean, which for Glenda Brookes is quite an achievement, she couldn't scare a puppy ordinarily. 'Where is she now?'

'Lizzy told us to come back,' I tell her, avoiding the question. 'The older version of Lizzy, from our timeline told us to. But don't ask me why, because you know as well as me you're not supposed to learn too much about your future.'

One single eyebrow lifts. I never knew she could do that, but then, I never knew her on my natural timeline, she passed away when I was tiny, and Henry faded away a little bit more every year until he finally joined her.

'You know Lizzy then. In your future,' she asks.

I nod once. We are on dodgy ground. Everyone seems to be holding their breath, especially Jasper.

'Well?'

The word detonates like a bomb. 'Well enough for her to ask me to come back here to fix a few things.'

'So you didn't come back because you wanted to have a happy-ever-after with Rob.'

'No, she didn't,' he says quickly before I can answer. Maybe he's still salty about the conversation up at Trinity. 'We've been back here since last night. We're waiting for the loop to close so we can get on with sorting out the mess Lizzy told Maisie about.'

'You've been back? Just how many of you did she take through the Weydoor?' Glenda puts out an impatient hand. Henry lights another cigarette and passes it to her. I'm guessing she's mad about that; Weyfarere aren't supposed to travel on the Weys for the craic, and there's nothing in *The Truth* about free passes for your squad.

'Kim, Rob, Scott and me,' Brian says. 'And obviously Maisie and Jasper because she was taking them back. Forwards. We were only going to have a quick look at the future, but then it all went arse over tit.'

'Arse over tit how exactly?' Glenda snaps.

'Brian,' I warn him. He looks at me and seems to catch on.

'Can't say,' he says sheepishly.

'So where is Lizzy now?' Henry asks.

'She'll go through the Weydoor with us, and then come back with Scott Kelly not long after that,' Kim says, taking a deep drag on the cigarette.

'She didn't bring you back with her?' Glenda sits on the Peavey amplifier and puts her forehead in her free hand. 'She left you there? With no means of getting home?'

This is all getting too tight for comfort. I realise I'm going to have to come clean about all of it. Well, almost all of it. Maybe most.

'Not exactly. The older version of her helped us, remember? We used Kim's necklace to guide us back as well. Claire gave it to her last night, so that's when we got back, and we were at the party here with you guys. We've been trying to avoid bumping into our other selves since then. We've even managed to do one of the things Lizzy asked us to do.' I pull *The Truth* out of my jacket pocket. I don't want to give it to her. I want to find out more about the Weys and the Weyleighers. I want to know how much danger my family is really in. But it isn't my book, not yet, and since it wasn't on the dresser for Scott to steal earlier on, I guess it needs to be returned to its owner.

Glenda snatches it from me as if I'm the common thief. 'What are you doing with that?' she hisses angrily. 'Where did you get this? Did you steal it from me? Why would you do that? Who are you?' As she snaps out the final sentence, the expression on her face changes and she doesn't look annoyed with me any more, she seems wary. Scared even.

'We've got it because Lizzy asked Maisie to get it,' Rob says. 'And now we're giving it back.' He looks at me. 'Maybe you should give her the -'

'Truth about the future?' I cry out, because I know he's going to say the key. He thinks that's not mine either, but it is mine, Lizzy gave it to me, because I'm Weyfare. I can see the silver of Glenda's key glinting through a gap in her blouse. There is one more truth that we're going to have to tell her, but it has to wait until Lizzy and Scott come back through the Weydoor. Once Lizzy's key has been stolen, and Scott has revealed himself to be the slimy git he is, we can tell Glenda everything. Apart from the bit about me. I'm hoping that she will agree with me that I have to give the key I'm wearing back to the Lizzy of 2019, but Rob doesn't know that. 'We can't tell her everything, Rob. We're not allowed to.' He stares at me, not understanding. I look back at her. 'I can't tell you why we took *The Truth* yet, but Lizzy asked us to make sure it was safe this morning. So we did.'

'So Lizzy charged your token with her key?'

'She helped us,' Jasper says, not completely untruthfully.

'All right.' Glenda sighs and stands up straight. 'There's no point in you hiding down here now. You may as well come up to the house for a cuppa and wait for the loop to complete. I can watch from the dining room window, but you must stay back from the glass.'

'But we have to go to the Old Library!' I exclaim. 'We need to be there when Lizzy comes back through the Weydoor!'

After all, this is the moment Scott and Lizzy burst back into 1987, fighting each other for possession of the key. If we can grab him when he's least expecting to see us (he did just abandon us in 2019), maybe we can get the key off him before he goes on to do any damage with it. Perhaps it will even change what happens to Glenda.

Glenda frowns at me. We really are beginning to piss her

off. 'You can't,' she says sharply. 'In real time, the moments that pass between a Weyfare going onto the Weys and back again are barely measurable. If you go after them through the tunnel now, the chances are Lizzy will be back before you even get to the Old Library. Wait for her here.' She gives me a narrow look. 'Or is there something else you're not telling me?'

FML. 'No,' I say. We've already spilled too much.

It's probably the most awkward half-hour of my life, as the assembly where headteacher Elizabeth Wharton told everyone I was her daughter only lasted about twenty minutes. Henry escapes to the front room and the TV, to the closing music from *Eastenders* and then something that sounds black and white and war-like. I can't look Rob in the face. I know he knows that I blocked him from telling Glenda I have a key, and he doesn't know why. Does he think I mean to steal it? I keep catching Brian and Kim giving me odd looks as well. Maybe they think I'm a Weyleigher. Perhaps they think I'm working with Scott? Surely they wouldn't believe that, would they? I can't look Glenda in the face either. Glenda hasn't put *The Truth* back on the dresser, she's clutching it to her like a kid holding onto its favourite doll. I feel like a total tard, and I wish for the millionth time that I could just come out and tell them all who I really am. And now, on top of everything else, we've lost the best opportunity we had to grab Scott when he was least expecting it and get Lizzy's key back.

Glenda is topping the teapot up for the third time when she turns away from the sideboard towards us and puts a simple finger over her lips. I can hear it too. The faint voices of many people chattering as they walk down the side of the house from the front. They aren't expecting anyone to be in. Fortunately, Glenda thought ahead, and she's already closed the back door.

'Move down to the floor,' she says so quietly I can hardly hear her. 'Do not look on yourselves. It may still cause nausea, even if they don't see you. I'll tell you when they've left.'

We slide off the pine dining room chairs onto the green and white carpet tiles, watching Glenda as she watches us go down the steps and into the Old Shed. Inside, there is a trap-door that leads to a tunnel connecting this house to the Old Library. Glenda's expression is unreadable. She looks cross, sad and wistful all at once. After about five minutes, I'm getting a crick in my neck looking up at her, but finally, she looks down at us and gives an 'up' signal with her hands.

'The time between the transition shouldn't be more than a few seconds,' Glenda says, pouring more tea into our mugs as if nothing unusual just happened. 'I reckon you've got about twenty minutes, depending on how quickly you can get through the tunnel.' She pauses, and wipes her hands on a yellow picture tea towel that says "Greetings from Torcombe". 'What is it like in there now, the tunnel?'

'Dark. Dirty. The floor's a bit uneven,' I say. 'When was the last time you went through it?'

She gives me another of those looks that tell me she doesn't trust me, and I wish the ground would open a Weydoor right beneath me and transport me straight back to 2019. Do Not Pass Go, do not collect a mystical key, do not make your new squad start wondering if you're the one who's descended from an ancient clan of smugglers.

'I think I'm going to wait outside for them.' I finish the last of my tea and my insides gurgle.

'You think she needs a welcoming committee?' Glenda asks.

'We think she might,' Brian says.

'Is there anything else you want to tell me?' Glenda asks. I close my eyes, but there is silence all around me. Rob may not trust me very much any more, but he's no grass, and that's good to know. 'Just go then. But bring them straight back here,' she adds quickly, 'and don't you dare go gallivanting off on the Weys again. I want a word with my daughter about responsibility.'

I wish I could tell her just how responsible her daughter turns out to be.

The sun is still quite high in the sky and hot like mid-summer. I take off my jacket, feeling less protective about it than I did when it hid an ancient textbook, and I sit on the red-bricked step in the shade of the vast rhododendron bush, next to the multi-coloured patio that Henry built.

'Well, that's screwed everything up big time,' Brian says. 'Scott's not going to come back through the tunnel with the key, is he? Now, what do we do? How are we going to find him?'

'I don't know,' I say, 'but what choice did we have? Glenda wasn't going to let us go through the Tunnel after our-selves -'

'We could've just left,' Brian interrupts. 'She didn't lock us in or anything.'

'It would've looked shady if we'd made a fuss -' I try to

explain.

'Why didn't you give your key back to Glenda?' Rob interrupts. He doesn't sit down beside me, or put a hand on my arm, or any of the things I've already got used to, and realise I already miss.

'It's not my key,' I say, impatiently. 'She would've taken it from me, and I think I should give it back to the Lizzy that gave ... lent it to me. Back in 2019. When we go back. You know.'

Yes, there's a part of me that wants to sting him a bit for not backing me up, but he doesn't seem fazed. 'You didn't want me to tell Glenda about it, though. Why not?'

'That's true, Maisie. You were happy enough to give her *The Truth*,' Kim says.

'That's because *The Truth* belongs to her.'

'Doesn't the key belong to her then?' Brian chips in, and I feel myself losing it in the face of all this lost loyalty. I've come to think of all of these people as my squad.

'No! It belongs to Lizzy!'

'Get off her back, she's doing her best here,' Jasper says evenly, taking a step toward me.

'What is this?' I stare up at the audience of faces looking down at me. Fifty shades of accusation. 'Why are you attacking me? You're acting like you think *I'm* a Weyleigher! What, am I going to run off with Scott, nick all the keys and take up bank robbery in the 1960s?'

'Stop it. No, don't be daft,' Kim says immediately and drops to her hands and knees to bend forward and give me a hug. It's a few seconds before I relent and hug her back. I feel sick. This is all going wrong.

'No, of course not,' Rob says, but maybe I'm getting paranoid, but he doesn't sound as convincing as Kim.

'I just don't get it,' Brian says. 'I don't get why Lizzy would have lent you something so important. I remember Glenda giving a key to Lizzy and saying it was the single most precious thing she would ever own, and yet Lizzy just handed a Weyfare key over to you, not knowing when she'd ever get it back again? Just how well did your Mum know Lizzy, that she trusted you with something like this?'

'I can't tell you that,' I reply, staring at the concrete under his feet.

'Why can't you tell us?'

'For fuck's sake, I just left you lot in the future!'

We all turn as Lizzy steps out of the Old Shed and our disagreement is forgotten, as we scramble to our feet, ready to do anything and everything possible to make sure that Scott doesn't get far with Lizzy's key.

'It's a time loop,' I exclaim, and my words come out all breathless like I've been running. 'We'll explain later. We're here to help you get your key back from Scott. We would've come to the Old Library, but – well, it's a long story – '

'Your mum grounded us in the kitchen,' Brian says.

'Not that long a story,' Jasper says.

'Where is he, Lizzy?' Rob asks.

'Last time we saw you, you were fighting and he had the key in his hands -' I carry on, but Lizzy holds up her hand and opens it.

A large silver key falls about twenty centimetres below her palm and dangles on its chain.

We all gape stupidly at her.

'How? When?' Jasper asks.

'Have you got any beer?' Lizzy asks.

'Didn't you have enough last night?' Kim asks and steps forward to give her friend a hug. Lizzy Brookes, newly 18, a new guardian of the Weys, a little bit wild, a little bit my future mother, a little bit This Girl Can.

'I don't want a drink. You lot are going to need one though.' Lizzy steps back and opens the Old Shed door a little wider. 'Come on out,' she calls. 'There are people here who will think they know you.'

Out of the door of the Old Shed steps my best friend Ani.

Chapter Six – Love Removal Machine (The Cult, 1987)

I know something's wrong the second I see her step out of the Old Shed. There is something indescribably different about her that I couldn't explain to anyone, except maybe Jasper. I can feel him tense beside me. Something's wrong, even without the strange way Lizzy introduces my other best friend, my missing best friend, even before I can register Brian rushing forward and flinging his arms around her. She looks like my best friend: Ani whose fault it was we ended up travelling the Weys in the first place; Ani whose left-field genius attracted Brian like a magnet; Ani who mysteriously vanished into the air in front of Brian's face at Lizzy's party at Trinity last night.

Brian only realises there's something wrong when she doesn't hug him back, so he steps away looking like she's slapped him, and we all look on her totally unimpressed face. 'Do you mind?' she asks, primly.

'I didn't think you would,' he says, frowning.

She sounds like my best friend. 'Ani?' I say eventually, my voice feeling as if my throat is lined with sandpaper.

She turns to me, looks me up and down like a dress she's not too keen on, and puts a hand on her hips. 'You're Maisie Wharton. 13ES. What are you doing here? That girl told me this is 1987.' She points at Lizzy, who has crossed her arms and is watching us like we're a particularly good episode of *Stranger Things*. It's Ani, but not as we know her. This isn't my best friend. There is no spark of insanity, no quirkiness, no lovely giggly face. She is stone-cold snarky to the bone.

'Lizzy?' Brian asks, his little face full of more hurt than it did the day she disappeared. 'What's going on?'

'I did warn you,' Lizzy says unhelpfully. 'She doesn't know us.'

'I've been investigating a portal in the Old Library for weeks,' the imposter says. 'Is that a perm? Very big, ha!' she asks Kim, pointing at her hair. Kim pats her curls as if she's been insulted. 'Great jackets. Have I really travelled through Time? How on Earth did *you* manage to get here before *me*?'

I hold her patronising look, feeling totally unfamiliar feelings of dislike for the girl who looks like my bestie.

'Who are you, and what have you done with Ani Chowdhury?' Jasper says, his voice sounding as dry as my throat feels.

'Jasper Lau? You're here as well?' Ani steps a little further out onto the pathway that leads down the garden to the garage and the caravan. 'I suppose I shouldn't be surprised since Maisie is here. I guess I'm actually cross that you both got here before me.' She sniggers. I use that word on purpose because it's an old fashioned word, and that noise she makes is an old fashioned laugh, not a nice one. Not how she used to giggle. 'I mean imagine, *the two of you*. Working it out before *me*. No matter. I'm here now. Then she stares up at the stone bricks of Travellers' Rest. 'Hang on a second … This is Orla's house!'

My brain feels like a microwave popcorn bag, slowly inflating, yet to go bang.

'Lizzy help now please?' Jasper says, and his voice has gone all high again.

Lizzy holds her hands up in a perfect double talk-to-the-hand without knowing that's what she's doing. 'Not a frigging clue,' she says. 'I need a fag.'

'What you need is to come inside for a chat,' Glenda says. None of us has noticed her waiting at the top of the steps; we've been too shocked by the apparent transformation of my quirky, funny bestie into an insensitive robot. 'All of you. Please?'

Now it's Lizzy's turn to look like someone just slapped her in the face. 'Yeah, I thought that might be on the cards,' she mutters, and she climbs up the steps away from the Old Shed towards the house, and we all follow her like we're in a bad remake of a Pied Piper film, Ani included.

Glenda sits at the pine dining table, leans forward and puts her hands together like a steeple against her chin. Even Henry has dragged himself away from the war film on the TV in the front room to join us, leaning against the pine dresser, twisting the silver bracelet round and round his wrist the way he always did when he was unsure. He puts a gold packet of cigarettes in the middle of the table.

'Explain yourself,' Glenda says eventually.

'All of it?' Lizzy repeats, looking down at her mother, and then at us standing next to her in a disturbing mirror image of the headteacher's office. Glenda nods slowly, once. 'Where do you want me to start?'

'The beginning. You were supposed to be taking these bystanders back to their timelines, and apparently, you took a few friends along for the ride! And where's Scott Kelly?'

'Mr Kelly? Is Mr Kelly here?' Ani asks.

'Why are you calling him *Mr* Kelly?' Lizzy sneers.

Ani looks away. 'Oh, he wouldn't be Mr Kelly yet, would he? Silly me.'

'And you told me Maisie's friend here was extinguished!' Glenda snaps.

'In all fairness, you were the one who told us she was extinguished,' Brian says, but the look on Glenda's face makes any additional contributions evaporate in his mouth.

'Extinguished?' Ani says. 'That sounds a bit final.'

'Stop. Lizzy, you were supposed to take them back to their timeline, and they're all here again,' Glenda says, with irritation. 'Explain, please.'

'I didn't bring them back, Mum,' Lizzy says, truthfully. 'I didn't bring any of them back.'

Glenda sighs and takes a cigarette from the packet on the table. Ani coughs politely.

I shake my head at her. 'There's no point coughing. They all smoke here. It's not like our time.'

'How disgusting,' she says, her little nose wrinkling. 'Don't they know how bad it is for their health yet? Not to mention the stink.'

Glenda stares at her for a few moments, then she turns back to Lizzy, who is reaching slowly for the packet on the table but stops when she catches her mother's eye. 'Lizzy, just tell me what happened when you went through the Weydoor. We can talk about why you took these others with you afterwards.'

'Okay. Can I have a fag first?' Glenda shrugs, and Lizzy doesn't need to be told twice. 'So I know you told me not to, but I was pissed off and I took them through the Weydoor, and it worked like a dream,' she says, after lighting up and drawing on the rancid little stick like it's oxygen. 'The Weydoor was all pretty and purple, and I put my hand on the key over Maisie's calculator thingy like you said as that was the token; we boosted it up, and we all held hands, and out we popped onto their timeline. It was well weird, but then Scott went from being the nicest bloke I've met in ages to being a complete bastard! He tried to steal my key, Mum! But it's okay, don't freak. He nearly got his hands on it, but I wasn't having any of that; he tried to run back through the Weydoor and I grabbed him as he went through, and we came back to now.' She holds out her other hand, which is still clasping the silver key on its chain, snapped from being pulled violently from her neck. Something about her words jars on my thinking, but I can't pin it down. 'And then, when we got back, Frank the caretaker was in the Old Library, staring at the Weydoor! He looked totally shocked to see Scott and me there, so I took advantage and managed to grab the key back from Scott, and I kicked him hard in the leg.'

'I'd have chosen somewhere softer,' Glenda comments.

Henry, Jasper, Rob and Brian wince as one.

'Frank tried to grab hold of us, but Scott smacked him one, and he fell down.' I think it's the first time I've ever seen Lizzy look ashamed. 'Scott ran through the main door out into Drake's – I tried to follow, but he was too fast, and I lost him, and when I went back into the Old Library,' she turns to look at the elephant in the dining room, 'this was standing at the back by the Weydoor, and I realised the others weren't with me.'

'Go up to Drake's and check that Frank is okay,' Glenda

says to Henry. 'Don't use the tunnel.' She turns to Ani, as Henry disappears out through the back door. 'So I'm guessing that you don't have any idea who we are, do you?'

'That's not true,' Ani says pompously. 'I know Maisie and Jasper vaguely from school. They aren't in *my* circle of friends, but I know of them. Everyone does.' She stifles another one of those ratchet laughs. 'Lizzy here is the girl who opened the Portal. You're her mother.' She turns and looks at the others like they are covered in rat poo. 'I don't know about these others, but I know Scott Kelly, and you've got this all wrong. Mr Kelly would never steal anything from anyone, it would be more than his job was worth -'

'Stop!' I shout, probably loud enough to be heard up at Tracy's barbeque. 'Don't! Don't tell them any more things from your timeline! Our timeline!'

Glenda blinks, and her head drops slightly to one side. 'That is good advice, Maisie, but you didn't need to rupture my eardrums to share it.'

Ani shrugs, shakes her head, folds her arms and stares at the grill above the cooker. 'Fair enough,' she says, tight-lipped. 'Don't have a benny on me.'

'So Lizzy left you all behind. And you told me you came back because you spoke to the Lizzy that exists on your timeline?' Glenda asks me.

'I spoke to Lizzy's future self,' I say carefully. This was going to take some handling.

'You know me in your timeline?' Lizzy asks, her eyes big with surprise.

'My mother knows you. Her.' Not a lie, is it? Not really. 'I knew she was Weyfare, so I thought she was probably the only person who could help us.'

'That was smart of you,' Lizzy says. 'What am I like as an oldie?'

'Things on my timeline had changed,' I tell them all, refusing to answer Lizzy's question. 'Lizzy didn't know that, though. She just asked me to come back and stop Scott from stealing her things.'

'Like my key?' Lizzy asks.

'And our book, at a guess?' Glenda pushes her fingers into her eye sockets and rubs.

'How did you get back here?' Lizzy asks.

'Kim has the necklace that Claire gave her last night.'

Lizzy nods her approval. 'Smart. I'd never have thought of that.'

'You did. It was you who told us to use it.' I breathe in deeply. Now for the first big lie. 'You also lent me a key to get back here.'

Glenda's jaw drops so far I'm concerned she's dislocated something vital. 'You did what?' she exclaims, glaring at Lizzy.

'Don't you have a go at me for something I don't do until I'm fifty-odd!' Lizzy snaps back.

'Where is the key now?' Glenda asks. I point to where it lays hidden under my T-shirt. 'Well, you don't need it any more. Lizzy has her own key, and she can get you three back to where you belong again using your token, and the sooner, the better. Give the key to me.' She holds out her hand like a determined toddler, waiting for a sweet.

I look Glenda squarely in the eye. 'I'm sorry, Glenda, I can't give you this key,' I say, with a sideways look at Rob.

I'm expecting Glenda to erupt all over me like a human volcano, but her eyes just widen a little. 'Why not?'

'Because it belongs to the Lizzy of the future, and I think I should give it back to her. When I see her again,' I say, and hold my breath.

Glenda looks up at the ceiling, sighs a couple of times, and then looks me in the eye. Her expression softens a little. Maybe she's just fed up of arguing. 'You're right. We don't want to disrupt the Weys more than they have already been disrupted by all this travel. If that key belongs in the future, it had better stay there. I'll make us all a cup of tea, and then Lizzy can put you back to your timeline.'

'I can't drink any more tea,' I say. 'And I can't go back either. I haven't done everything that Lizzy asked me to do.'

'This is doing my head in,' Lizzy says, sitting down at the table. As if she's broken an invisible barrier, Rob, Kim and Brian sit down as well. Jasper stays standing beside me, though. He may worry for England, my blud, but he's loyal. Ani leans up against the wall under the clock with the ticks like a jackhammer. It's like she's observing us. All we need is for her to put on a lab coat, and for us to run around in little plastic wheels.

'And what else did Lizzy ask you to do?' Glenda says, refilling the kettle from the tap anyway.

'She said I had to protect you.' I take a deep breath. 'When we took *The Truth* last night, we took it because we thought Scott stole it from you this morning. Before the loop.' I pause. 'And the Older Lizzy thought he stole it too.'

'I don't think Mr Kelly would stoop to common theft,' Ani says. 'Sorry, did you just say *The Truth*?'

'Ani, please! No more!' I cry out. She gives me another look that could wither a spider plant.

'And that's why you took *The Truth*. To make sure Scott didn't steal it this morning,' Glenda remarks.

'We didn't steal it, Glenda,' Rob says, finding his voice, playing with the edge of the lace tablecloth. 'We were just looking after it.'

'Protecting it,' Kim adds.

'So it didn't get stolen by Scott,' Brian adds. 'And it didn't. This time.'

Glenda turns back to face us. 'Well, that much is evident. If you're not making all this up.'

'They aren't,' Lizzy says. 'I was there too. There was a fight between Kim's stepmonster, her dad and us, and then Paul said the book was missing.'

'That fight still happened. Scott disappeared when things got ugly, and Kim left with her family. Paul didn't say anything about *The Truth* being missing,' Glenda says, switching the kettle off at the mains as it boils for what my bladder reckons must be the thousandth time.

'We think Scott might originally have taken *The Truth* for an important reason,' I say, 'I had a read of it.' I speak the last sentence quickly, hoping that she can't interrupt me with squawks of outrage that I have dared to look at the frigging sacred book. I'm not wrong. Her face becomes a pretty shade of fuchsia. 'I have to tell you something else about the future!' I yell out before she starts the inevitable shouting.

That worked. Sort of ish. 'Abso-bloody-lutely not!' she yells back at me.

'Lizzy told me we had to protect you from Scott as

well!'

In the silence that follows, the faithful clock jackhammers a ton of the next minute into the room.

'We are from a timeline where Scott Kelly stole *The Truth*, and then he stole Lizzy's key,' I go on quietly. 'and then - she thinks he hurt you. Some of us - well, we think he may be a Weyleigher. The Lizzy in the future wanted me to come back here and help you. So I'm here. To fix it.'

'I have no idea why you have such a bad attitude toward Mr Kelly, but I wish I had a notebook so I could record all this,' Ani says primly. 'Clearly, I can't use any modern technology, so it would have to be old school, but I don't even have a biro on me. You keep talking about *The Truth*. Can I just ask -'

'I think you were doing just fine when you were sticking with the shutting the hell up,' Jasper snaps at her. I've never heard him speak to Ani in that way, but then the old Ani would have probably burst into tears if he had, and this one doesn't.

'Just as much of a mong as ever,' she snarls. 'How someone like you got to investigate a potentially world-changing phenomenon like this is totally beyond me.' They glare at each other. How did she turn into such a tard?

'You read *The Truth*,' Glenda breathes the words slow and low.

'Only the first chapter,' I say, breathing hard. 'It gave me a headache; it's all faded and some of it isn't that easy to read.'

'You had no right to read from our book,' she mutters with menace, but now I'm beginning to get just a teensy bit pissed at being told I have no rights.

'I had every right,' I snap out loud. 'Lizzy gave me the right when she ga ... lent me the key. She trusted me with it.

She trusted me with trying to help you. Why can't you trust me?' After all, I have all the rights, but I just can't bloody tell anybody about it.

'She has a fair point,' Lizzy says. 'Mum, can I bum another smoke off you?'

Glenda throws the packet at her like a pitcher without taking her eyes off my face. 'You say you think this Scott is a Weyleigher. There are no Weyleighers left.'

'Can I please ask something without someone sniping at me?' Ani says, sounding bored off her face.

'That all depends whether we find it offensive or not,' Kim says. Sheesh. Even Kim's pissed at her.

'This book you keep talking about. *The Truth*. Is it a small purple volume written in Middle English?'

No one seems able to reply until Glenda finds her loud voice. 'Is there anyone here who hasn't seen *The* fucking *Truth*?' she cries out.

'Language,' Lizzy mutters. Oh, the irony.

'Plenty, I'd say,' Jasper turns to look on his former BFF. 'It's just they aren't in the room. Where did you see *The Truth* then?'

'If it's the same book, Mr Kelly had it in his library.'

I turn toward Ani. 'Look, things are nasty right now, but you need to understand – the world you've come from? You can't tell these guys the details about it. It's crucial.'

She considers me like she's choosing a new top to buy. 'Since when did you get to be in charge?'

'That's a good question, but we don't have time for that one right now.'

'Scott's future's probably all changed again anyway,'

Brian tells her casually.

It hits me like a brick that he's got a point. Is Ani's Mr Kelly the same, if we already changed his fortune back here in 1987? I don't know why Ani's the way she is yet, but maybe if we ever do get back to 2019, she will be as confused as we were. Are. FML.

Glenda sighs, and her shoulders slump. She goes over to the dresser and pulls out the little purple book that she took from us earlier, the book that started all our troubles, way back when on some timeline that may not exist any more. She puts it on the table, and Ani gasps. 'That's it!'

'Did you read this book as well, Ani?' Glenda asks as if she's inviting her to have tea and scones at a posh spa hotel.

'Not all of it. My friend Orla and I only managed to read a few chapters last night. Why have you got it?'

'Because this family are Weyfarere,' Glenda says, not without a hint or seven of pride. 'It's our book. It's our history.'

Ani reaches out to touch it, but Glenda reacts, picks up the book and clutches it to her. 'You're actual guardians?' Ani breathes, her pretty brown eyes wide as she stares down at Glenda in what can only be described as awe.

'We are the last remaining known Wayfarere family in England,' Glenda says, her voice little more than a whisper. 'We are the gatekeepers, the descendants of Wayland the Smith's daughter. The guardians of the Weys.'

'So you're the time travellers,' Ani says, looking totally awe-struck and nicer for it.

'It doesn't do for anyone to travel the Weys. It creates anomalies.' When we all look at her blankly, Glenda adds, 'Total fuck-ups like this.' Well, she's not wrong there. 'We just protect the secret.'

'And Mr Kelly really stole *The Truth* from you?' Ani says, her words barely audible.

'Apparently so,' Glenda says.

'If you saw it in his future, it looks like he did steal it, on that timeline at least. But now Glenda has it back, so things will have changed. He tried to steal Lizzy's key as well, but now she has that back too.' I sit down at the pine table.

'There are no records of Weyleighers in these parts for over a century,' Glenda says. 'Whoever your Mr Kelly is, he's no Weyleigher.'

I take a deep breath. 'Whatever. I guess his life will be very different now.' And maybe mine, too.

The thought seems to subdue our new Ani a little. 'It's turning out to be a quite extraordinary day,' she says. ' If I may say one more thing though. Some of the translations of the original text aren't very accurate.'

'Is she for real?' Lizzy asks and slumps forward onto her folded arms.

'I have to say I preferred the Mark One model,' Brian replies sadly.

'Do any of you read Middle English in the vernacular?' Ani takes a step forward. 'Do any of you know what the vernacular means? No, don't answer that,' she goes on, ignoring Brian's raised hand. 'The vernacular is the dialect of the area where a language is spoken or recorded. Where was your book originally written?'

As Elizabeth Wharton was always telling me before I fell through the Weydoor, every day is a school day. We all look at Glenda, whose cheeks have gone a greyish-pink.

'I'm not entirely sure,' she says unexpectedly. 'I've not translated any pages myself. They were passed on to me like that. Do you read Middle English?'

'Extensively,' Ani replies, and she couldn't sound any more up her own backside if she stuck a hose in it and blew. 'But to be completely accurate, I need to know where the book was originally written.'

'You need to know who wrote the original version of *The Truth*?' Brian asks.

'Someone who knew Wayland's daughter maybe?' Rob asks. "Maybe Wayland himself?'

'Maybe someone who lived in the same village?' Kim asks. Ani nods.

'So where did Wayland live?' Jasper asks.

Lizzy stands up suddenly, and the chair scrapes noisily. Glenda spills the tea she was pouring into mugs from the teapot; Kim, Brian and Rob all jump like she's hit them and Jasper makes a little squeaky noise. Lizzy puts the palms of her hands flat on the table and leans forward; her eyes closed. Then they blink open.

'I was 18 yesterday,' Lizzy says quietly. 'It was supposed to be the biggest day of my life. All I got was the hangover from Hell after being given a key that locks me into slavery for the rest of my life, and my boyfriend assaulted me and tried to steal it. I'm sitting here listening to you wankers talking about it all like it's some kind of stupid fantasy story. It isn't.' Her voice is getting louder and higher as she continues to speak. 'It isn't a story. It's my bloody life, and right now, every sodding one of you seems to know more about it than I do. So why don't you all just shut up wittering for a second and explain it all to me properly, so I can get this crap straight in my head?' She closes her eyes again and toys with the silver key. 'Why couldn't you have given me a watch for my 18th, like normal mothers?'

'The key is our heritage,' Glenda says sadly.

We all turn away from her distress, respectfully. All but one of us.

'See, that's exactly the problem,' Ani says. 'Everyone keeps on about keys, and depending on the vernacular, they've completely got the wrong end of the stick.'

Chapter Seven – Never Take Me Alive (Spear Of Destiny, 1987)

'It's still yapping,' Lizzy says, her eyes still closed. If I were Ani, I'd be taking cover under the pine table by now, but I'm not Ani, and she isn't. 'Doesn't it come with an on/off switch?'

'Do. You. Want. Me. To. Help. You?' Ani says as if Lizzy is five.

'No. I. Want. You. To. Sod. Off,' Lizzy says in the same tone.

'Charming!' Ani is all fluffed up indignance, with her hands on her hips.

'Ani, just leave it,' Brian says wearily. 'Now is not the time to shine, Einstein.'

The faintest of smiles crosses Ani's lips. 'Fine,' she says quietly. 'I won't say another word about any of this unless I'm asked.'

'Praise be,' Jasper remarks.

'Sit down and have a cup of tea,' Kim says, more kindly.

I move forward tentatively. 'Lizzy. We read the first part of your book. Weyleighers are smugglers, and they steal keys if they discover a Weyfarere family, so we put two and two together and thought it might mean that Scott is a Weyleigher. The Older You told me your mum's in danger and that the danger may come from Scott. That's about it, really.'

'Missing out much?' Jasper remarks, but I silence him with the look I learned from the other Lizzy, and Brian gives him a supportive nudge, and he backs down. 'Okay, I get it.'

'That's what's important right now.' I look at Glenda. 'You have your book, and Lizzy has her key back, but Scott knows you're Weyfarere now, and he may still try to steal your keys. Or worse.'

'Right. Stop there. You said smugglers.' Lizzy replies slowly, opening her eyes. 'Mum? There are smugglers in the family, and you take me out for hiding the Garibaldi in my room?'

Glenda takes a sip of her tea calmly. 'Wayland the Smith had two brothers, and all three all married Norse Valkyrie women, ordained by Odin to choose the dead worthy of Valhalla. That's the resting place for dead warriors. But Wayland and All-wise had a daughter, Mildred, and she was gifted with seven keys to the Weys.'

Brian coughs politely. 'I thought they were just stories in a book,' he says quietly. 'I don't mean to be rude, Glenda, but we read those Norse myths in school when I was a little kid.'

'All history comes from stories and books. Who are we, who live in these times, to say which of the old stories are truth and which ones aren't? We weren't there when they were written,' Glenda says sternly. 'Even photos can be manipulated. Don't judge what you haven't witnessed yourself.'

A shiver goes down my spine as Glenda speaks. Maybe the spirits of my Norwegian ancestors are here listening to us dispute the fact that they existed.

Brian nods slowly. 'No, actually, that's a very fair point,' he says. 'Is there any more tea?'

Glenda gets up and goes over to the silver kettle. '*The Truth* tells us that when the Valkyrie discovered the Weys, they used them to discard the bodies of those who were not seen to be fit for Valhalla or Folkvangr, the two heavenly realms, rather than sending them to Hel.'

'I thought Hel was a Christian place,' Rob says.

'Not a place, a person. Hel the ruler of Helheim, land of the dishonoured dead. The Valkyrie fled when Hel realised that they were depriving her of bodies, and therefore their souls, and Wayland's brothers fled with them. Their descendants are known as Weyleighers.'

I must've been struggling by the time I read that bit.

'So they were good people then? The Valkyrie? If they were saving people from being sent to this Hel woman?' Kim asks.

'Hardly. Sending someone through a Weydoor back in Time to die, with no knowledge of where they are going, isn't far from the Hell you recognise, Kim.' Glenda opens a flowery metal tin, takes three teabags and puts them in the brown teapot. 'It was said that the souls were lost, with no sense of where they should be. In limbo.'

I wonder then if there is some truth in the school legends of the ghosts that were rumoured to haunt the Old Library.

'So do the Weys lead to these places?' Brian asks.

'Only the dead can go to the realms of the dead,' Glenda replies. 'so I would say no. The Weydoors are ruptures in Time, like wormholes in Space. The Weydoor in the Old Library maps the existence of the Old Library through Time, so you can travel through Time, but you will still be in the same place.' She sighs. 'In all honesty, my mother just told me about my duties. Find the Bystanders, send them back on their Wey.

I never needed to understand the mechanics.' She smiles at us, trying to lighten the load. 'There was never a written test.'

'But the Valkyries were trying to piss the HellWoman off?' Rob asks.

'*The Truth* suggests they were doing it for Odin. He wanted to reduce the number of souls led by Hel at Ragnorok.'

'Good film,' Jasper says. I poke him harder than I needed to.

'So how did the Weyleighers go from helping lost souls to making money?' Lizzy asks.

The already warm water in the kettle boils quickly, and the kettle whistles. '*The Truth* says that descendants of those families eventually became smugglers. At first, they would work for the lords, using the local Weydoor to go out and gather monies for the manor. Later, they moved valuable property through the Weys to line the pockets of those who paid them. They were particularly sought after as spies and agents during the Reformation. Some of the most famous spies in History were rumoured to be Weyleighers.' She pours the water into the teapot. 'And like I said, there haven't been any active Weyleighers in this area for at least a century, and we are the only Weyfarere family that I know of.'

'Christ on a bike,' Lizzy says, lighting yet another cigarette.

'Maybe there weren't any Weyleighers for a long time,' I say, 'but maybe they haven't been back long. How would you know? It's all supposed to be a big secret, isn't it?'

Glenda sighs and says nothing, but she reaches for the chain around her neck and pulls out the key.

'Did you get your key on your birthday as well?' Lizzy

asks.

Glenda nods, looking down at it. 'On my 21st birthday. December 30th, 1971.'

I knew Nan had had her kids quite young, but I hadn't realised just how young until now. If my GCSE Maths still works, she was only 17 when she had my Uncle Paul, and 19 when she had my Mum.

'21st?' Lizzy asks. 'Not your 18th?'

'When I was 18, people didn't get their majority until they were 21,' Glenda says. 'Become an adult, I mean. So when they changed the law, Mum made me wait until I was 21 anyway.' Taking a large gulp of tea, she puts the mug on the sideboard and looks at us. 'I don't believe that Scott's family are Weyleighers.'

'Would you know, though?' Brian asks.

Glenda shakes her head firmly now, but there's a guarded expression on her face. 'I'm sure of it.'

'But in the future, I'm convinced that something bad is going to happen to you, and I'm convinced it's to do with Scott,' Lizzy says. Then she turns to face me. 'You know what happens, don't you, Maisie? I bet I told you. I asked you to come back here to help us protect Mum from him. What did I ask you to do?'

'Nothing. We didn't get that far into the conversation.' Suddenly I feel exhausted. 'We got interrupted.'

'Can I make a suggestion?' Jasper asks, putting his hand up, looking at it, and then thinking better of it. Lizzy waves at him dismissively. 'Only, if the key and the book are safe, surely Scott won't try anything else. Whether he's a Weyleigher or not, he knows we know he's a liar and a thief, and we're on to him.'

There is a polite cough from under the clock, but no one is taking any notice of Ani now. I feel bad, but she's behaved like a mong, and no one likes an asscloth.

'Oh, we're onto him all right.' Lizzy rubs her face as if she's trying to wake herself up. 'Okay, I've decided. First things first. I'm going up to the Hippy Shop to tell him he's dumped, and to tell him to keep his skanky hands off my family and my belongings in the future or I'm going to the Old Bill.'

There is a loud mess of noise that suggests that we don't all think that's a great plan.

'Shouldn't we be making sure nothing happens to Glenda?' I eventually make myself heard through the fog of disagreement. 'Older Lizzy told me she was in danger today. The day after the party.'

'I said this before, I don't think we should be going any-where near Scott,' Kim says. 'I've already had enough dealings with sociopaths to last me for a lifetime.'

'Attack is the best form of defence,' Brian says firmly.

'Yeah, but running fast in the other direction has also al-ways worked well for me,' Jasper says.

'Maybe we should just back up to Tracy's garden party and take you with us, Glenda,' Rob suggests.

Lizzy, who seems to be looking to me for some kind of clarification, snorts and shrugs. I've wanted to go to the Hippy Shop for a few hours now, but if Scott is responsible for Glenda's disappearance, then the last thing we should be doing is dangling her under his nose. I look at Ani in desperation, out of habit I guess. 'Do you have an opinion on this?'

'Oh, now you're asking?' she sneers. 'I'm sorry. The Helpful Person has left the building. Please try again tomorrow.' She stares past me.

Sheesh, she really has become a mega douche.

'I really don't think it's going to help anyone with me tagging along,' Glenda says, her eyes fixed on her daughter's grim face.

Lizzy turns to Rob and Brian. 'Well, I'm going to find Scott. Can you two stay here with Mum?'

'We can do that,' Brian says. 'But what if he tries something?'

'We really ought to be making sure everyone's safe,' Rob says.

'We can look after ourselves, you know,' I tell him gently.

'So you keep telling me,' he says a bit sharply. 'Okay, fine. We'll stay with you, Glenda.'

'Lock the doors and don't let anyone in unless they can prove they're Paul or Dad. Or us.' Lizzy pulls a face at Glenda. 'Sorry, but the idea of you bearing witness to me chucking my boyfriend brings me out in hives. I need you here safe.'

I consider all the things my mother has recently borne witness to in my life, but I keep my mouth tightly shut on that matter, as always.

'I'll stay too,' Kim says. 'I have no desire to go anywhere near someone who might get paid to hurt people – or their shop.'

'You three come with me,' Lizzy says. 'Since you seem to be the only ones who really know what's going on around here lately, I'd better keep you close.'

The Hippy Shop, or new age shop, or pagan outlet as Rob's Mum Valerie called it at the party, is off the High Street, up a narrow road with houses whose doors open straight onto the street. The road is ordinary, apart from a couple of pubs with smoke billowing out into the air you breathe as you pass, and a massive white-domed church that looks like a gurdwara. Trinity isn't far from here, but that party is long over. Ani is captivated by all the differences we pass in the shop fronts. Listening to her, I realise how much me and Jasper have already got used to 1987.

The Hippy Shop has a real name: Serendipity. The white paint on the door is cracked and is peeling away from the wood in places. Windows either side of the door are showing a range of stuff through the grubby glass; one side has a couple of bald mannequins wearing Asian embroidered trousers with elastic at each ankle, and sandals made from leather thongs and beads, like festival veterans. Their ponchos are mustard yellow and also heavily embroidered.

The other side of the window is a bit less Woodstock, a bit more goth. Here there are animal skulls and sharp knives and tiny grey cauldrons surrounded by crystals of every shape and size; not the pretty ones you see in jewellery but the ones that look like they've been mined straight from a cave in an unspoiled part of Africa.

'Kim buys her stuff from here?' I ask Lizzy. I'm not being funny, but she doesn't seem like the sort of girl to buy her perfume from a place with skulls in the window display. At least, she didn't until she left home.

Lizzy nods. 'You can't get proper scented oils from any-

NO WEY OF KNOWING

where else. Although there is a place just opened in town called The Body Shop that looks like it might do them.'

'Tell her to try the White Musk,' Ani suggests. 'My mother still has a bottle of Ananya.'

Sometimes you have to choose your battles. I ignore Ani and try the front door. 'It's locked.'

'It's Sunday. Nothing opens on Sundays apart from garden centres and garages,' Lizzy says. 'And the corner shop near Rob's.'

Jasper steps away from the door and stares up at the three levels of drawn curtains above the shop. 'Is that flats upstairs?' He looks across at Lizzy, pointing to a door next to the shop, covered in the same cracked paint design, but this time it's the pale blue of the duck eggs Mum liked to boil for her breakfast in 2019. Next to the door is a plastic box, with six black button doorbells inside. The names next to the buttons are faded, but one definitely says '2b – Kelly'.

Jasper pushes against this door, and it gives a little, catching on the doormat, which is covered in what looks like piles of junk mail.

We all stare at the open door.

'We can't just go up and knock on his door. What do we say? "Hi, Scott. Making any more plans to pinch your girlfriend's sacred necklace?" ' Jasper asks.

'I don't think anyone's in,' Lizzy says. 'The curtains are open, and he always shuts them when he's home.' She gives me a small smile. 'And I'm not his girlfriend any more. He's dumped, remember?'

Suddenly there is a clattering beside us that makes me jump; Jasper grabs me and I cry out. Only Ani and Lizzy remain sensible. The next thing I know, the shop door with the peeling paint is opening outwards, someone steps through it and I am looking into the face of my teenage dad. Or thereabouts.

If Lizzy's 18 now, Tim Wharton must be 21, a year older than her brother Paul. Tim's hair is thick, wavy, dark and hangs past his shoulders, and his blue eyes twinkle behind rimless glasses. He's still tall and slim like he is nowadays, although nowadays he has less hair and what he has got left is grey over his ears. I always wished I inherited more of his genes. I got his hair, but I got Lizzy's green eyes and big arse, although the curves look good on her at 18. Having spent so much time with my teenage mum and my nan over the last days, you'd think I'd be used to seeing my family popping up in the past, but it doesn't get any easier. It's all I can do to keep the tears from my eyes.

'You okay there?' Tim asks.

'Dust in my eye,' I say. Pathetic, I know, but it was the best I could come up with at short notice.

'You waiting for someone?'

'Where is the deceitful bastard?' Lizzy says, stepping forward.

'So sorry, our special offer on deceitful bastards finished last Friday,' Tim grins at her. 'We sold right out.'

'Don't you bloody cover for him, you jerk.' She pushes him against the shop window, and he pushes her off, playfully, but firmly.

'I didn't catch your name,' he grins even wider, and then he catches sight of Ani, and all of a sudden he holds out his hand like an old-fashioned gentleman. 'But this is -?'

'I'm Ani.' She grins back at him. 'Who are you?'

'I'm the wingman.' When we all look at him blankly, he laughs. His laugh hasn't changed in 32 years, he's still all laid-back surfer dude. 'Tim. Scott's not here.'

'Where is he, Tim?' Lizzy seethes. 'I'm serious. He's pushed it too far this time.'

'That's what happens when schoolgirls like you play with the big boys, babe.' He reaches into his pocket and pulls out a silver tin. Well, this is just lit. My mum and dad have already met, and there's no love lost between them. My existence starts to fray a little.

'Have you seen him since the delivery this morning?' I blurt out, my voice is so much higher than usual that everyone turns and looks at me.

'I haven't seen him since he went out to Carrots' party last night.' Tim pulls a thin white stick out, puts the silver tin in the back pocket of his faded blue jeans, lifts the stick to his lips. Why the hell does everyone smoke in the '80s? 'He never shows for deliveries during the week, let alone on a Sunday. Why do you think he hires a schmuck like me?' As he's lighting it, he scowls at me. 'How did you know we had a delivery this morning?'

'Are you open?' Jasper tries to peer through the gap in the door.

'Course not, mate. It's Sunday.'

'I don't suppose you'd mind us having a look around since we're here and waiting?' Ani asks, giving him a huge toothy grin.

Tim is definitely giving her the green light as he winks, shrugs and looks up and down the street. It's uncomfortable, but since I've been watching Lizzy play tonsil tennis with

Scott for a couple of days, I'm becoming more immune to the dutty. It doesn't look like Lizzy and Tim are going to be getting together any time soon, but I can't add another thing to the long list of worries I'm currently fielding about extinction. 'Don't expect it's going to hurt anyone if you just come in for a quick shufti,' he says and pushes the door open behind us. 'He's not up there, Carrots,' he adds, clearly for Lizzy's benefit. 'Your guess is as good as mine when he'll show up again.'

A little bell tinkles, like in the olden days - more olden than these ones – and we're inside.

You know that one cupboard at your house that everyone just chucks stuff into when there's nowhere else to put it? Mum calls ours the Stuff Cupboard because it's rammed full of stuff, and you have to have two of you to open the door; one to open it, and one to catch all the crap as it tumbles out onto the floor. This shop is like a massive version of a Stuff Cupboard. There are shelves everywhere full of stuff. Someone at some time tried to organise it by putting little paper labels over the edges of the shelves to tell hopeful shoppers what they might expect to find there. I only know because the ends of the bits of paper are still stuck to the paint under the sellotape. I guess it is a new age shop, there are a lot of jossticks, crystals, little black sculptures of dragons, silk scarves and Tarot cards, but it's a weird mixture of tat and what looks like serious witchcraft. I wouldn't want to tangle with some of those daggers. It smells like neither Tim nor Scott know how to work a vacuum cleaner.

Ani is fingering the silk scarves with their swirls of bright colour, her eyes sparkling like they used to, as if she might have to take one home. They are pretty, in the '80s wild hairstyle sort of way. 'Mr Kelly *owns* this shop?' she says as if she can't believe it.

'Manages it, we think.' Jasper is at the back of the shop, looking at a tall bookcase that puts Glenda's dresser in the shade.

'Found anything interesting?' I ask, sidling up closer to them while trying not to knock over an African tribal statue holding a pretty blue paper parasol that looks Chinese.

'Lots of books about how to read tarot cards. A few books about witches. Nothing about Weyleighers,' Jasper says.

Instinctively, I shove him. 'Don't say that here!'

He manages to stop himself from falling by grabbing hold of a large stone bird table. 'What was that for?'

'I don't think we should be saying those words here,' I say.

'Awww. Have the skulls and tribal masks freaked poor Maisie out?' Ani teases, but she's right in a sense. I am not only weirded out by everything that I've learned, but also by the thought that Scott Kelly might be dangerous, and we're in his shop. I am so out of my depth. I decide to forget the sight of Ani's sparkling eyes because it's beaten into submission by her smug smile.

'Over here,' Lizzy calls, and we follow the sound of her voice to the other side of the shop. In the darkest of corners, she's looking at more shelves where the books look less exciting than the brightly coloured paperbacks describing how to predict the future. I'll tell you how to predict the future; you don't need a book. Go through a Weydoor, and show your future mother an *iPhone Ten R*. I predict a riot.

'It stinks something terrible here.' Ani's nose is wrinkled like a cute pug.

'Oldness. Rot. I'm not sure. Look at the titles on some of the spines.' Lizzy pulls a book away from the others. It's called *The New Leyhunter's Guide'* by a guy named Paul Deveraux. 'Didn't Mum mention ley lines when she was telling me about being a – Ow! What was that for?' She looks down at where I've grabbed her arm.

'Don't say the W-word, Maisie gets lairy,' Ani says. 'The book does mention ley lines, but one or two books by some guy in a junk shop isn't going to cut it as evidence.'

'I thought you said you weren't going to say anything else about it,' Jasper says tetchily. She scowls and turns back to the bookcase.

'Maybe we should buy them anyway,' Lizzy says. 'Got any cash?'

The bell rings again over the shop door, and then it rings again. Tim has come back into the shop, and he's not alone.

'Scott's not here,' Tim is saying. 'Maybe I can help?'

Someone puts something down heavily on the floor. 'I doubt it.' A female voice. Familiar. Some instinct in me makes me freeze. I can feel Lizzy's decision to lurch forward as she makes it, and I grab hold of her hand and hang on for dear life.

'No. Stay here,' I hiss at her.

'Why?' she hisses back at me, but at least we're only hissing. I don't think we've been heard. It's dark in this corner where there is no artificial light, and there's an enormous wooden spike eight feet tall full of more hanging silk scarves and ponchos in front of us, so I don't think we've been seen, either. And somehow, that feels important. My spider-sense is now telling me that we need to stay hidden.

'We'll hear more if they don't know we're listening. Just hold on,' I hiss again. The others appear to be staying quiet too. Even Ani.

'He left a message on my answerphone concerning some other work he was doing for me,' the female continues, and something jangles like she's leaning against a cabinet full of crystal. 'It sounded urgent, or I wouldn't have bothered coming all the way into town on a Sunday. Looks like you're open though. Have I caught you illegally trading?' She laughs.

'Nope. Just airing the place,' Tim says. 'Scott told me he thought he'd found a book you were looking for. I don't know how long he'll be.'

Found a book? I close my eyes and try not to breathe and hope the others don't react.

'Did he tell you the name of the book he found?'

'Some old artefact. It's none of my business, anyway. You're welcome to wait for him. He's popular today.'

Don't you let us down, Dad. Don't you dare give us away.

'Meaning?'

'Nothing. I meant nothing by it. I'll tell him you came by.'

There is another noise now. It's unexpected. It sounds like a yelp.

'Yes. Yes, you will. Or I will remove this in a heartbeat.'

I am torn between the urge to see the woman that Scott Kelly is working for, and an equally sudden fear of doing so. Despite the heat in the airless shop, I shiver.

Eventually, the bell rings again, but there is a silence afterwards that feels like a death.

It's a few seconds before we leave our hiding place and

go to the front of the shop, but Tim's vanished. The shop door is wide open, on a Sunday, and he is nowhere to be seen. In front of the desk with the old brown cash register on it, there is a large, brown cardboard box.

'So Scott's working for someone who's looking for a book,' I say quietly. 'And he told Tim he found one.'

'Her voice sounded familiar,' Jasper says, 'like we've met her before.'

'If I didn't know that she was up to her eyeballs in study at Clare, then I would have sworn that was Yvonne,' Lizzy says.

'Who's Yvonne?' I ask.

'Brian's sister,' she replies.

We all look at each other, and run to the front door and look out onto the street. A few people are hanging about, especially down by one of the pubs, but there's no way of knowing if one of the women just left the massive box in the shop. The box hasn't been opened.

'Why would Scott be working for Brian's sister, though?' Jasper says as we walk back in.

'She's not even due home from Uni for a few more weeks,' Lizzy says, and she looks at me, and she looks a bit uncomfortable, and I have no idea why.

'This must be what she said she would remove if Tim didn't tell Scott she'd been here,' Jasper pushes the box tentatively with his foot. 'Whoever she was, she sounded a bit hardcore.'

'I guess Scott likes his girlfriends hench,' Ani says.

Lizzy scowls at her, grabs one of the decorative knives from a nearby glass shelf and plunges it into the cardboard.

'Lizzy, no!' I exclaim.

'Why not?' Lizzy replies, still sawing through the top of the box as if she's imagining it's Scott's arm.

'What if Tim comes back?' Jasper asks.

'If he were that bothered about it, he wouldn't have abandoned it here in the first place with the shop door left wide open,' Lizzy says.

Ani kneels down and starts pulling at the severed pieces of board. They smile at each other, partners in their crime, and my stomach lurches. They get the top layer off, but whatever is inside is protected by another layer of white plastic.

'Please tell me it isn't hard drugs,' Jasper says.

'It isn't hard drugs,' Ani says. 'She wouldn't have just left it on the floor, and she wouldn't have left it with the wing-man.'

Jasper is helping Ani and Lizzy to pull at the packaging now, and suddenly with a dramatic ripping noise, the top of the layer tears away to expose what's inside.

We all look into the box.

After a moment or two, Ani says, 'I think it's fair to say none of us was expecting that.'

Chapter Eight – The Right Thing (Simply Red, 1987)

I look up at Lizzy. 'That's a lot of cigarettes.'

'I reckon about a thousand packs,' Ani says.

'So Scott is a smuggler then,' Jasper says, pulling a packet out of the box.

'It can't have been Yvonne, then,' Lizzy says.'She's reading Medicine at Clare. She's a complete anti-. Smoking, I mean.'

'Clare?' Jasper asks.

'Clare College, Cambridge,' Lizzy says.

It's odd; these cigarettes aren't wrapped up in plastic sheeting or anything to protect them from the damp or damage. There's just a single cotton sheet across the top. I don't smoke, never have, but I'd expect them to have better waterproofing. Ironically, it was Mum put me off smoking by showing me a video when I was twelve of a dead smoker's lung dripping with black tar. I know cigarette boxes used to be in pretty colours like Glenda's golden boxes, whereas now they are hidden away in plain sight, but these look different to the ones that Glenda and Lizzy smoke.

'So here's the evidence that he's a smuggler,' Ani says, 'but not evidence that he's a Weyleigher.'

As I watch, Lizzy reaches across and takes the blue and white striped packet from his hand. She turns it over two or three times, and when she looks up, she is the colour of the ash those dirty things produce. 'There's no government warning on these Players,' she says quietly.

Jasper picks up another packet, red and white this time and still recognisable. 'Nor on these Marlys!' he exclaims.

'Do foreign cigarettes have warnings on them yet?' I ask.

'These aren't foreign, they're British.' Lizzy shows me the back; I assume she's pointing out the English writing. 'They are old.' She tears the little cellophane strip around the lip of the pack, opens it, pulls off a piece of silver foil and sniffs. 'But they are fresh. These are new tabs from back when they didn't have to print a health warning. They look like the tabs Mum used to smoke when I was little. They haven't been smuggled overseas.' She looks at me. 'They've been smuggled through Time.'

'So Scott's smuggling goods through the Weydoor?' Jasper asks after Lizzy's bombshell has sunk in a bit. 'There's the evidence then! Scott is a Weyleigher!'

'Permission to speak?' Ani says.

'Don't be a moron your whole life,' Lizzy snaps, 'take the day off.'

'I'll accept that as a yes. Surely if Mr Kelly ... Scott was this time traveller smuggler you're all accusing him of being, he could travel back to nineteen-before-health-warnings and buy his own cut-price cancer sticks. He wouldn't need anyone else to do it.'

Much as I hate to admit it, she has a point. 'He isn't the Weyleigher then,' I say. 'The woman who left him that box is.'

No one says anything for a few moments.

'She wouldn't have a key. How could she be sure of coming back? She couldn't smuggle stuff through the Weydoor without a key any more than Scott could,' Lizzy says.

'Well, that's another story completely, but none of you was interested when I tried to explain it before.' Ani stares around at us all, her on fleek eyebrows way high on her brow. 'Do you know how many words the Saxons had for a key?'

'Maybe we should hear Ani out, but find somewhere else to talk about this.' It makes me uncomfortable talking so freely about the Weys in the middle of this shop. Anyone could overhear us, including the mysterious woman who has apparently just deposited contraband cigarettes from a different decade in my dad's shop.

'Good idea.' I look up, and Tim is standing in the doorway. With the sunlight outlining his thin frame, he looks a bit like an angel. He's got a grey handkerchief with a blue 'T' embroidered in the one corner, and he's holding it to his neck as if he's hot. The laidback surfer from earlier has vanished. 'I need to lock up the shop.' He removes the cloth from his neck to point at Lizzy and snap, 'Scott's not here, so you can bloody well take your mitts off those right now!'

Lizzy and Ani immediately drop the packets back into the box. He catches me staring at his throat, and he puts the hanky straight back in place, but as we all troop past him I glance up and see him looking down at me, and we both know that I saw in those few seconds what he didn't want any of us to see; the small cut in the front of his neck, still seeping tiny droplets of blood.

'Tell him he's dumped,' Lizzy snarls at him, as we step out into the sunlight.

'A couple of nights in the sack doesn't make a relationship, Carrots,' he sneers back.

After a walk where the only conversation was deliberately unimportant, we arrive back at Travellers' Rest. Glenda puts the kettle on again, and I swear I have drunk more tea in these past few days than I have in my entire life. Lizzy and Glenda start arguing about tradition and heritage and timelines. Kim, Brian and Rob just kept muttering under their breaths to each other.

When Glenda puts another green mug of tea in front of me at the pine dining table, I accept it, because it's comforting, and it's consistent. The pine table is like the Round Table. No, I never liked History, but I loved that *Merlin* show on the TV when I was a kid. We are all sitting here like the knights: Glenda, Lizzy, Jasper, me, Rob, Brian, Kim and Ani.

'I'm telling you now,' I hugged my mug to my chest. 'You may not have seen it, but I did. He had a cut on his neck that he didn't want us to see, and he didn't have it before Cigarette Woman arrived.'

Ani says, 'You keep bleating on about your fine traditions and your ancestral rights, but the fact is, your translation is flawed. Now we can speak freely, I can tell you that if I'm right, Scott wouldn't have needed anyone's pretty necklace to travel the Weys safely if he's a Weyleigher, and the woman wouldn't need a key to get his contraband for him.'

So now we are all looking at Ani because she's just said something that has changed the game. Glenda has put *The Truth* in the middle of the table again in a weird echo of the drinking game all the olds were playing last night.

'We told you. The keys are the tokens that ground the Weyfarere to the ends of their natural timelines,' Glenda says, her words coming out in a sigh. She touches *The Truth*. 'You can travel out using grounded tokens, but the key will always bring you back to where you left. It's all in here. These facts have been known to our family for generations -'

'I'm not disputing the facts,' Ani says calmly. 'I'm disputing your definition of the word 'key'.'

'How many ways can you define an object that unlocks a door?' Jasper says sceptically.

'Oh, I can think of several,' Ani says. 'A key opens and closes a lock. If something is key, it's vitally important. It can be a code used to unlock a puzzle or read a map, or a support in a building. It can be a series of notes on an instrument. It can be a way of sorting out groups.'

'I'm in love all over again,' Brian says, leaning on a hand and gazing at Ani, whose upper lip curls in disgust.

'And this is important because -' Lizzy asks, bleeding boredom from every millimetre of her face.

'This is important because keys are not just metal forks,' Ani says. 'They aren't all literal, and I don't believe your ancestors translated the word properly!'

For the second time since she's been back with us, I see the faint echoes of my bestie in her excited words. My Ani isn't here. But there is definitely a little something of her in this new, colder version.

'Explain,' Glenda says, lighting a cigarette from the gold box and throwing the box into the middle of the table. I can tell the stress levels have increased as Lizzy, Kim and Rob all help themselves.

'Middle English originated not long after the Battle of Hastings, but Wayland was alive about 300 years before that.'

Ani leans forward, blinking at us like a barn owl through the swirling blue smoke. 'Since the origins of your ancestry seems to be Norse, it is likely to have been translated from Old Norse. A translation must have passed down in the old tongue, Old English, through word of mouth, until your book was written down in Middle English. I suggest that leaves a lot of opportunities for error.

'Middle English also had a dialect. There were slight differences between say, Devon and Yorkshire. So the ancestor who first translated the Old Saxon English into new Middle English did it according to the vernacular of where they were living.'

'Well, that's me lost,' Jasper says, slumping down hard on the table.

'No, Jasper. Stop acting like a tool. It's not that hard to grasp,' Ani says. 'The translation is flawed, that's all. A key allows access; it isn't necessarily a metal device. That's just our modern understanding. They translated it wrong.' She folds her arms. 'I think the Weyfarere are the keys.'

'Run that one by us again?' Glenda says, tapping ash into the glass bowl.

'You. You're Weyfarere. Wayland made the silver keys after the Valkyrie wives left, simply to commemorate the family's heritage for his daughter, Mildred. Those keys wouldn't have anything to do with the Weydoors, or they would have been there from the start. So the Weyfarere themselves must be the keys to travelling the Weys.'

'Still not seeing this,' Lizzy says.

'The Middle English word for a key can translate as house. House can translate as ancestry, and ancestry can translate as blood.' Ani spreads her hands out as if she's revealed a deck of cards.

'Blood,' Glenda repeats into the void.

I look at Ani, and she looks at me. She is my best friend, and yet she isn't, and yet she's speaking words that have been teasing in the darkest pits of my thoughts for days, and she's bringing them to life. Without looking away from her, I say, 'Lizzy, when were you given your key?'

Lizzy snorts at my side. 'You should know; you were there. The afternoon before the Fundraiser disco. In my room upstairs.'

'So the key should have brought you back through the Weydoor to that afternoon, like Kim's necklace brought us back to the party last night. But it didn't. Your key brought you back to the moment you left,' I say. 'Today.'

Ani claps her hands slowly. 'Because the key didn't bring her back here. Her blood did. It brought her back to where she left her natural timeline.'

Which is why when Lizzy opened the Weydoor using the phone that she gave me as my mother, we didn't travel back to the morning that she gave it to me. We went back to the moment I left my timeline in 2019. Because my blood overrules any token, and it anchors me into my natural timeline. Wherever I travel to, when I return, I always return home.

Fuck. She's right.

'Sod's bollocks,' Brian mutters over my thoughts. 'Why didn't I spot that?'

'Now you're all on board with this,' Ani says, 'we can discuss the issue of Scott Kelly.'

'Is she right, Mum?' Lizzy asks.

I look at Glenda. After all, she's known all this Weyfarere stuff for years unlike us, and here's Ani from the future come to tell her her puppy's died. Well, something catastrophic, anyway. 'Are you from a Weyfarere family?' she asks Ani eventually, her voice doubtful. 'I thought we were the only ones.'

Ani laughs. It sounds harsh and tinny compared to the lovely giggle I remember. 'I wish. No, I'm just a nerdy history student who got obsessed with a school legend.'
Suddenly her face softens. 'I'm sorry,' she says unexpectedly. 'I can be like a bull in a china shop when I get carried away. This is your history, and I'm stomping all over it.'

'Not stomping,' Glenda says. 'Poking it with an enormous hot stick, maybe.'

'So let's look at this logically,' Brian says, crossing his arms. 'Scott steals the book and reads it, and so he learns that the keys anchor him to his timeline as it says, and when he finds out Lizzy is Weyfare, he tries to steal her key. So he must be a Weyleigher.'

'Or he just could be on the make; a bloke who's heard Glenda talking about the Weydoor and knows he can make a quid or two selling goods on from different times?' Rob asks. 'I've seen that antique show on Sunday evening. Mum watches it. You can make a small fortune buying old stuff.'

Brian nods. 'Fair comment. Either way, he hasn't got the key any more, but someone else has shown up with fresh goods from the end of the 1960s. So if there is a Weyleigher in town, is it Scott, or is it the mystery cigarette woman? Or is she just someone like Ani who has worked out how to use token objects to travel on the Weys?'

'It's far too risky to travel on the Weys,' Glenda says.

'Even though we thought our keys would always get us home, we couldn't guarantee where a token would take us. Even if it's owned, we were told there was no guarantee that it would control the direction or distance travelled.'

'I've read parts of *The Truth*,' Ani points out. 'And I can read Middle English. Most people wouldn't see the mistake.'

'But if Scott was a Weyleigher, who would be travelling the Weys for him?' Rob asks.

'She sounded like Yvonne,' Lizzy says.

Brian lets out a noise like a strangled duck. 'My sister Yvonne? She wouldn't trade smokes!' he chokes. 'She'd be more likely to burn the lot. You think my family are connected with this? You think my sister is a smuggler? Anyway, if she was back, I'd know, and I bet Rob -' His high-pitched voice is silenced, as everyone looks at Rob.

He is the colour of cold porridge. 'We know it's not her,' he says, shortly. 'We know your family aren't involved.'

'And how is this woman travelling backwards and forwards in Time?' Kim asks.

'And is the book Tim mentioned to her the same as that one?' I ask, pointing to *The Truth* on the table.

'Too many questions,' Lizzy moans. 'You were supposed to be helping me to understand, and it's just getting more messed up. I need a drink. No, not more tea, Mum. A proper drink.'

'Just because you're 18 now, it doesn't mean you have to have a drink every five minutes,' Glenda says. 'We're not made of money. Besides, there's too much at stake here.' She strokes the cover of *The Truth* absently as if it's a sleeping kitten.

'There are too many questions, and no way of knowing

the answers to most of them,' Ani says. 'I think we can assume one thing, though. If Scott hasn't stolen your book, then he still believes your keys are the source of your ability to time travel safely because that's what you've told him.'

'But he knows we're Weyfarere,' Lizzy says. 'So he might still try to pinch the keys.'

'Then you need to hide them somewhere he won't find them,' Ani says.

'Weyfarere are never parted from their keys,' Glenda says.

'That's because you thought they were the source of your control. They aren't, though.' Ani looks at the three of us: Glenda, Lizzy and me. 'You're all wearing nothing more than expensive jewellery. The kind that should be locked away.'

'In a safe,' I say, thinking about how Older Lizzy told me where she'd hidden the key she gave to me. Glenda looks at me sharply.

'Perhaps someone should lock us up as well then if it's our blood that's so important,' Lizzy mutters.

'Assuming she's right,' Jasper says shortly. We all look at him. 'Well, I mean we only have her word to go on that you guys are the real keys to time travel.'

'He has a point,' Kim says, glaring at Ani again.

'He does, except for the fact that I didn't travel back to the time I was given my key.' Lizzy stubs another cigarette out into the rapidly filling ashtray. 'I came back to where I left off. That suggests she's right. Maisie, listen – I get all the stuff about not knowing my own future, but did I tell you what happened to Mum?'

'Spoiler alert,' Jasper says.

'You did.' I'm feeling like Lizzy's request for a stronger drink was a good idea.

'So, what happened to her? I told you to protect her from Scott because - ?'

I think about this. Keep it simple. 'Because you told me she disappeared.'

Pretty much everyone except Ani exclaims loud shock and disbelief.

'I was extinguished?' Glenda says, her voice shaky.

'Lizzy didn't know whether you had been or not. She just told me – that you went out later today and you never returned.' I feel like a tard telling her this.

Everyone seems to be thinking over the implications of my comment in the privacy of their own head.

Glenda goes on, her voice no stronger. 'Well, it's obvious then. On that timeline, Scott stole *The Truth*. He read it. Maybe he came to the same conclusions about what constitutes a Weyfare's key. Maybe he stole Lizzy's and he kidnapped me and I don't even want to follow that thought through.' She looks around at us all. 'I'm actually beginning to be rather grateful that you all came back.'

'Then we've sorted it out,' Rob looks a little less grey. 'Scott hasn't got the book now. He hasn't read it, so he doesn't know any of this new info. And he doesn't have a key.'

'But he still knows about the book's existence,' Jasper says. 'He told Tim about it.'

'We don't know Tim was talking about *The Truth*,' Lizzy says.

'We don't know he wasn't,' I point out.

'He could've spotted it on the shelf when he came over

for … tea one day. Afternoon. When you were at work.' Lizzy's eyes widen as Glenda turns to eye her. 'I had a P.S. All afternoon. Study leave. One of the teachers was sick, so we were sent home. Get off my back.'

'Put the shovel down and step away from the hole you're digging,' I say gently.

'And he knows someone else who's interested in the book.' Brian stretches his arms above his head. 'I'd say it's not just the keys you need to be locking away. To be on the safe side.'

'We need to protect *The Truth*,' Glenda says.

'Well, to be honest Mum, it was a bit bloody daft just having the thing lying around on the shelf like any old copy of *Lace*,' Lizzy says.

'Says the girl who brought a bloke to the house when she should have been studying,' Glenda replies smoothly.

'A guy who could still turn out to be a Weyleigher.' Ani says.

Lizzy pulls a face at her, but her cheeks redden.

'Unproven to be fair,' Kim says. 'The Weyleigher bit, I mean. Sorry, Liz.'

'Unproven my arse,' Brian replies. 'Scott's got a shed load of dodgy fags from the '70s locked up in his shop and an even dodgier female contact. I'd say that's reason enough to track him.' He plays his little imaginary trumpet. Ani looks at him as if he has just blown his nose on the tablecloth.

'Or lose the things he's looking for.' Lizzy stands up. She places the silver key on its broken chain on top of *The Truth*. 'Time we tested Ani's theory.'

Chapter Nine – (Something Inside) So Strong (Labi Siffre, 1987)

'Testing it how?' Glenda asks, reaching for another cigarette, but they have smoked them all, and the little box is empty. She crumples it in her hands, leaves the table, goes over to the dresser, opens a drawer and pulls out another cellophane-covered golden box. Henry must have a good job.

'We need to travel on the Weys back to a time before Scott ever sees *The Truth*,' Lizzy says determinedly.

Glenda stops mid flaring match and stares at her as she lights the little white stick. 'Absolutely not.'

'Why not? I've done it. I'm not disintegrating or vaporising or extinguishing, am I?' Lizzy sweeps her arms in front of herself as if bowing to an audience.

'No, but you have no idea what damage you are doing to yourself! Or your timeline!' Glenda leans back hard against her chair.

'To be honest, I think that's a lost cause now,' Jasper says unexpectedly. 'I have little hope of things ever being the same by the time we get home for good.'

I reach to touch his arm as I can hear the regret in his voice. Sorrow for life changed, change that we never intended. He looks up at me, attempts a smile but fails miserably.

'All we need is a token to get us back in Time to before Scott is on the scene,' Lizzy says. 'I can hide *The Truth*. When I come back through the Weydoor, I'll get us all home automatically. Well, if Mrs Einstein here is right.'

'I don't like your tone,' Ani snaps. 'Bullying is unacceptable.'

'Whoa,' I say, 'bullying?'

'You are constantly mocking me for being intelligent,' Ani says primly, the shutters coming back down on her personality, 'and it may be acceptable in this decade, but I won't put up with it.'

'Who's bullying you?' Rob asks, his face open and genuinely confused.

'They aren't mocking your intelligence, they're mocking the fact that you're behaving like a tool,' I snap at her.

'No one mocks intelligence on my shift,' Brian says gently, and interestingly, the ice in her eyes thaws a little again.

'We don't mock anyone,' Kim says. 'We accept everyone. We always have. No one here is a bully. You're just rubbing people up wrong.'

I remember having a similar conversation with her not long after we had tumbled through the Weydoor the first time.

'Okay, stop.' Lizzy puts her palms flat on the table. 'All I meant was that if Ani is correct, I can use tokens to travel the Weys out to other times, but I will always come back to the end of my own timeline. Have I got that right?'

Ani pauses, and then she nods. 'I'm pretty sure that's what your book said, yes,' she replies.

'So I need a token that can take us out to say … January this year? I can hide the book somewhere that Scott will never see it, so he will never know we have it.'

Kim reaches out and smacks her on the shoulder. 'You so haven't been seeing Scott for that long!' she cries out.

Lizzy looks up at Rob. 'On and off. Sorry,' she says sheepishly.

'I knew your heart wasn't in it,' he says evenly. 'All worked out, though, didn't it?' He sounds more like he just missed out on a lottery win though, and he won't meet my eyes. I wish I could put this right. I wish it could be the way it was when we first got together. I wish it hadn't got so serious so quickly.

'Mum,' Lizzy goes on, after giving him a confused look, 'talk to me about tokens. Can I just use anything that was given to me say, last Christmas?'

'It's not that straight forward,' Glenda says. ' Tokens are not just owned by words. They are owned by emotions. They are owned by physicality. Touch. They have a spiritual connection. Don't put your hand up like you're in school, Maisie,' she says, and I lower my hand, feeling stupid.

'Sorry. It's just, well, we used Kim's necklace to get back here without Lizzy. It's only a plastic bead necklace. It's not valuable or spiritual. Sorry, Kim,' I add, and she shrugs acceptance.

'How did you feel about being given the necklace, Kim?' Glenda asks.

'It meant everything to me,' Kim replies. 'I know it isn't expensive, but I don't care about that. I don't get a lot of presents, except from you lot, so all of them mean the world.'

Glenda opens her palms in front of us. 'There you go. The emotion of her gift made it spiritual.'

Lizzy looks a bit downcast. 'The best thing I got given

for Christmas was money for driving lessons from you and Dad,' she says. 'I can't use that, can I?'

'No.' Glenda leans forward. 'Okay. I have taken on board everything Ani here has said, but I am too old and cranky for change now, and I can't get my head around all these modern ideas about blood tokens. I was raised with the belief that our keys bind us to specific places on the Weys. I don't want you to travel on the Weys, Lizzy, but I can see you're not going to listen to me any more now than you ever have so -' She reaches into her blouse and pulls out the silver key on its chain, lifts it over her head through her dark coppery hair, and places it next to Lizzy's on *The Truth*. 'I was given my key on my 21st birthday. December 30th, 1971. You were given your key on your 18th birthday. If you must travel on the Weys, I lend you my key to use. If Ani is right, it won't matter. But if Ani is wrong and the keys are what grounds us, you will still come back to me. My key will take you out to 1971. Yours will bring you back you to 1987.'

We all stare at Glenda. It's very likely the first time she has ever taken off her key. This is a momentous deal.

'Mum, you can't lend me your key. You never take it off,' Lizzy says quietly. 'Put it back on. And you can't stay here. Maisie says we need to protect you.'

'Travelling the Weys takes but a second to the people you leave behind,' Glenda says without smiling. 'Even if you spent a whole week in 1971, you'd be back here again moments later. When you come back, Scott should have no idea about the existence of *The Truth*, and he should be hiding out with his tail between his legs, having failed to steal Lizzy's key.'

'Doesn't sound very smuggler-y,' Brian remarks.

'I don't believe he's a Weyleigher, as I've already pointed out,' Glenda sighs, 'but he's clearly involved in some kind of trafficking, and the future Lizzy believed he was a danger to me for some reason, so you need to hide *The Truth* someplace where we can find it again later. Somewhere Scott will never find. Don't stay there too long.' She opens *The Truth* and takes a biro from the top of the dresser. 'At the back of *The Truth* are the names of all those that have ever protected our Weydoor. Write your name in it now you are Weyfare. It will help if we have to identify it from others,' she says, holding the pen and the book out for Lizzy, who takes them. It feels religious all of a sudden. As Lizzy finishes writing her name, Glenda adds, 'Try not to interact with anything while you are there.'

'That's pretty much impossible, surely,' Ani says. 'Simply by being there, she changes things.'

'She? You mean us. I'm not travelling the Weys on my own,' Lizzy exclaims.

'Bystanders aren't supposed to travel the Weys,' Glenda says.

'Neither are Weyfarere, but you've accepted that I'm going to do it. Everyone will be safe if they're with me, and I'm not going back in Time alone to a place where I can't even talk to my family. Shit!' Lizzy's eyes widen. 'I'm already there!'

'You will be two and a half,' Glenda says slowly, rubbing the heel of her hand into her eyes, 'and if you meet yourself, your body will go into a state of paradoxical confusion. At best, you'll be sick for a couple of hours.' She takes a deep breath. 'At worst, if you should touch, the chances are your internal organs will shut down. You must not meet your baby self under any circumstance, as she is more vulnerable.'

I'm glad I didn't watch us all go into the Old Shed earlier.

'Okay. So, I don't get to read myself a bedtime story. Check,' Lizzy says, her pale face betraying that she's not feeling as brave as she wants us to think. 'Still taking you people with me. Even more so now. I need you to watch my back.'

'You asked me to sort this out, and I'm not going back to 2019 until I know everyone's safe,' I say, and if anyone questions why I'm so loyal to the adult version of her, nobody says out loud.

'If Maisie's going, so am I,' Jasper says, giving me a look. 'Maisie's phone is our token back. I'm not leaving her side.' Of course, he knows that it's not really the phone that takes us back; it's me, and it's me he's not leaving.

'If Maisie has a token for 2019, I'm staying with her,' Ani says, jumping on Jasper's bandwagon.

'You can't all go!' Glenda says, exasperatedly.

'We all went before,' Brian says shortly. 'All for one, and one for all, it was.' But he doesn't play his imaginary tune. 'All the same, this time, I'll give it a miss. Not being born with the super-blood, one time-travel trip in a day is enough for this nerd.'

'We could all spend a year in 1971 and still come back today to take the new kids home. Couldn't we?' Lizzy looks hopefully at Glenda.

'In theory, but please don't test it out,' Glenda says.

'Definitely still not coming,' Brian glances at Ani. She's looking at her fingernails. After all, why would she be bothered whether he's decided to come with us or not? She hardly knows him, and he knows that, and it's hurting him to the point where any distance will be a relief, no matter how short in real terms.

I look across to Rob, who I realise is staring at me with those deep green eyes, and I'm stunned in my stomach to see that there is a little hurt here too. 'I'll stay here with Bry,' he says, his eyes not leaving mine. 'Just in case. You need to get to the bottom of what's been going on here. We'll be here when you get back.' I give him a small smile and this time he does return it; I know he's not just talking about the situation with Scott. Or the situation with Brian and Ani. Too many situations.

'So much has already happened to me today, why stop now?' Kim says. She squeezes Lizzy's hand. 'You don't think I'd leave my bestest friend in the lurch?'

'Lurching into oblivion together,' Lizzy replies, squeezing her hand back.

Glenda sighs. 'If you're really going, you need a plan. You can't just travel through the Weydoor and come up to the house through the tunnel in 1971. It may be my birthday, but things were different then. If your Nan sees you, she will just send you straight back through the Weydoor again, party or no party.'

'Can't I just tell you who I am?' Lizzy asks.

It feels like the blood has drained from my head to the bottom of my feet, and I instinctively steady myself on the table. Jasper pats my shoulder once. Out of the corner of my eye, I'm sure I notice Rob giving us both a questioning look.

'Not a good idea,' Glenda says. 'We shouldn't know too much about our future.'

'So if I'm not coming here to the house to hide *The Truth*, where am I going?'

'I didn't say don't come here at all, I said don't come through the tunnel, or we will think you are bystanders,' Glenda says impatiently.

'How did you return people to their timeline without a token?' Ani asks.

'Everyone tends to carry something we can use. A piece of jewellery or a watch. We just used that,' Glenda touches the key on the book. 'I used items of clothing a few times.'

'But if people weren't given their tokens on the day they found the Weydoor, they wouldn't get back to the end of their timelines,' Jasper says.

'And surely most of them wouldn't be able to find the entrance to the Tunnel,' I say. 'I only just worked it out. Most people would just go straight back through the Weydoor.'

Glenda frowns. 'Before it was a school, the Weyfare had to keep watch at the Weydoor itself. It was much harder once it became part of a school. They dug the Tunnel and it was the Weyfare's duty to unlock it every day. I was told it wasn't our job to worry about where the bystanders ended up, we just had to make sure they didn't affect their timeline - so if we found them, we sent them back on their Wey.'

'So they could have ended up years from the end of their timeline,' Brian leans back in his chair. 'There could be millions of displaced people over the centuries. Seems a bit brutal, Glenda. I thought you were the good guys.'

'Brutal? Of course it's brutal! You think all this has a happy ever after?' Glenda shakes her head in irritation, her eyes wide. 'Generations of girls like me, left with no choice but to stay here and guard the Weydoor? Bystanders appearing from nowhere and ending up back into anywhere? Apart from the keys, tokens are unreliable. The Weydoors are dangerous! They are passages to nowhere, and anywhere. You can leave, but you may never come back, and Weyfarere just have to try and do the best for bystanders that stumble through. Like I told you, no one's come through since 1982, and I don't even unlock the Tunnel now. And this girl,' she splutters the word as if it's an insult, 'this girl from the future just turns up and says we are the key as if it makes it all better! It makes it worse! There is nothing fun about this, Brian! Have you not realised that?'

'No, but I'm beginning to get it,' he says quietly, with a glance at Ani, who has gone as pale as I feel.

'I didn't mean to cause any trouble,' Ani mumbles, looking genuinely upset.

'No one ever does,' Glenda mutters.

'So where am I putting *The Truth*?' Lizzy says, not smiling.

'In the safe,' me and Glenda say at the same time.

Now everyone is looking at me. FML. 'Don't tell me,' Glenda says, her voice even more heavy with irony, ' my adult daughter told you we had a safe.'

'She did,' I say, my hand going instinctively to the key around my neck. It had been kept hidden in the same safe years before, on another timeline before it was given to me. 'How else would I know?'

'We have a safe?' Lizzy asks.

'It's in the back of the fitted wardrobe in my bedroom,' Glenda says.

'We have a safe?' Lizzy repeats.

'There was never any need for you to know about it,' Glenda replies sharply. 'You know now.'

'So how the hell am I going to get into your bedroom in 1971 and open a safe?'

'Not my bedroom. It'll be your Nan's bedroom.' Glenda stood up. 'And it should be reasonably easy. The code is your birthday, and the door unlocks with a Weyfare key. You're going back to December 30th. It's the night of my 21st birthday party. As long as you don't come through the Tunnel, people will just think you are friends of mine. We'll be close-ish in age. If I remember, everyone was trashed that night. Not that I remember all that much, apart from someone babysat for you and Paul, so I could let my hair down.' She walks out of the kitchen towards the foot of the staircase. 'Much the same as last night, really. I'll get you the keys to the Old Library. I don't remember them changing the lock, so hopefully, it'll still work. I'll get you a new chain for your key as well. You can't travel the Weys with a key loose in your pocket.'

Great. So we're going to another bloody drunken riot of a family birthday party, this time with a younger Glenda and Henry and my Great-Grandma and Great Grandad. It's a good job none of them is expecting me, because I don't have the funds to buy them all a week in rehab until the beginning of the 21st century.

'Does it look like this all the time?' Ani says, clearly awe-struck as we stand in front of the now-familiar purple glow of the Weydoor in the Old Library at Drake's School.

'Only in the presence of a Weyfare.' Lizzy unexpectedly squeezes her arm. 'Don't worry about Mum. She gets on her high horse about stuff, but she's usually pretty laid-back. Everything's arse-over-tit at the moment.' She turns to face me. 'And don't worry about Rob either. He can be a fickle sod. I expect it's the mention of Yvonne Walker earlier made him all moody.'

'Brian's sister? Why?' Jasper asks. I don't comment as I think I already know.

'We all thought they were the real thing until she dumped him out of the blue two weeks before she was due to go up to Cambridge last year.' Lizzy shrugs. 'Rob was broken. She was the love of his life. Well, until he met Maisie, of course,' she says, with a little laugh that sounds hollow to my ears as I process what I knew subconsciously back in the Hippy Shop. 'You being from the future is a bummer, but just give him a bit of time to come round. Rob's all right. He won't mess you around.'

There are too many variables here.

Lizzy takes hold of Kim's hand, who then holds me, then Jasper and Ani in a crocodile line the teachers used to get us to make to lead into Assembly when we were little kids. She holds her other hand out; the one that is holding onto Glenda's key. 'Ready?'

The arm holding Glenda's key just seems to slip through the bookcase as if it is a kind of projection, and the next thing I know we're falling against the bookshelves, and there's white heat, purple light, black – nothing.

Chapter Ten – Imagine
(John Lennon, 1971;
Ariana Grande, 2019)

When I open my eyes, I know something is not quite right. I see moonlight coming through the high windows that line the tops of the old stone walls of the Old Library at Drake's School. Jasper is behind me, his arm draped over my waist. Ani is crumpled under the nearest table. Moonlight. There is moonlight, and the heavy oak door at the other end of the Old Library is ajar. Through it, I can hear slow music and loud cheers. Slow, modern music. And Lizzy isn't here. Kim isn't here. For a second, I think I can see movement in the shadows, but maybe I'm just spooked.

I turn and shake Jasper awake. He's slow to stir, but as soon as he does, he's sitting upright. He instantly looks to the open door, and turns back to me, because we both recognise the song that is filtering through. Not her best, by chart standards.

'It's 2019, isn't it,' he says.

'They aren't here.' I stagger to my feet; I'm still not coping with re-entry all that well.

'Ani?' he asks. I point at the crumpled heap under the big oak table in the centre of the long room. 'Where are they then?'

'1971 at a guess,' Ani says, rolling over and crawling out

from under the table as if she's been doing it her entire life, clearly not passed out as I thought. 'But we're not with Lizzy, and this isn't 1971. That's Ariana Grande playing in the Main Hall.' She nods towards the front of the Old Library. 'That door is open.' She stands up and brushes the dust off her jeans. 'At another guess, it's pretty much the moment I followed you guys through from the Fundraiser in 2019. Lizzy travelled out from her timeline, but we've clearly travelled back to the end of one of yours.' She puts her hands on her hips. 'So which one of you is Weyfarere?'

Jasper splutters unconvincingly. 'You are such an asscloth. Lizzy is the Weyfare; something obviously went wrong with the token, you heard what Glenda said about them being unreliable.'

Ani regards him as if he is an irritating little brother. Then she looks back at me, and she raises an eyebrow. 'Please tell me it isn't him, or we are all doomed,' she says patiently.

Not much point in lying when she's almost at the finish line. 'It's not him,' I say quietly.

'Explain it like I'm five,' she replies.

'I'm Weyfare,' I say shortly. Jasper mouths like a goldfish but no words come out.

Ani nods. 'Well, quite. A little more information would help.'

This is crazy. I'm staring into the eyes of one of my closest friends, but this person isn't my closest friend, and I don't know if I can trust her. 'You don't need any more information. I'm Weyfare.' I pause as something sinks in. 'And it looks like you were right about the keys.'

Jasper gives a slow handclap.

Ani ignores the heavy sarcasm. 'Lizzy travelled out using Glenda's key.' Ani perches on the edge of the oak table. 'But you were returning, so you've come back to your time-line. Your blood's obviously stronger than any token.'

'We followed you through, Maisie,' Jasper says, finally finding his voice. 'You were between Lizzy and us.'

'Well, this is a bit of a fuck-up,' I say. A roar of applause comes through the open door. 'Okay. What's the last thing you remember happening?'

Ani cocks her head to one side. 'A mob dragged Mr Kelly down to the Main Hall to dance with one of the cleaners.' She stares at me for a minute. 'Mr Kelly being Scott. Hang on. If you're Weyfare too, are you related to Lizzy?'

'Perhaps we need to go see if Scott is still the Head of Drake's,' Jasper says quickly, 'before we decide what to do next.'

As we walk out, I hear an electronic voice, and a man dressed in dark combats with the words *Security* written in small white letters across his chest and what looks like a pro-tective vest speaks into a two-way radio, and waves us on. 'Back to the Hall now, Miss Wharton,' he says.

I'm too shocked to reply, and I just do as I'm told for once.

'Since when did Drake's need security guards?' Jasper hisses at me as we walk down the path. 'Did they have them at the Drake's you know, Ani?'

She shakes her head. Neither mentions the fact that the guard knew my name.

The Main Hall is jammed with people pointing their

screens at whatever's going on, so it's almost impossible to get in through the fire door to see who is the subject of the viral *Instagram* footage. It's hot, and it's dark, and the base in the music makes my bones shake, like at Trinity, a day ago, when I stood wrapped in Rob's arms and watched the live bands with him. I shake the image away. There is no point in wishing he was here. Or even that I was back there. Jasper and Ani mingle in the crowd nearby.

'What's going down then?' I ask a girl standing next to me with her phone held high to catch a shot.

'Palmer's dancing with one of the cleaners,' she says. 'He said he'd donate a hundred to the Fundraiser if she agreed.'

'Palmer?' I ask.

'Head of Drake's,' the girl says, looking me up and down like I'm all kinds of chode and moving away to get a better view for her footage.

I think I need to sit down. Maybe lie down. With chocolate. And several scented candles. To hope all this goes away. Which it won't. I make my way back out of the Main Hall, walk back up towards the relative quiet of the Old Library and take a few deep breaths of air. Eventually, Jasper and Ani join me.

'They told me it's a Mrs Palmer who's in charge here now,' Jasper says. 'The cleaner's less well-known, but someone told Ani it was a wrinkly called Mr Harrington. He has a crush on Mrs Palmer, apparently.' Ani is looking a bit green; I imagine it's because the people in her memory of today have suddenly changed, rather than the fact that the cleaner has a thing about his boss. 'So Scott's gone.'

'Gone where, though?' Ani asks. 'Where exactly has Scott gone? Why has it changed? Why are there security guards hanging around? And the place is a state.' She points up at the windows of the Main Block. Everywhere I look, it's all peeling paint and faded. Even the grass beside the path is overgrown. 'Did we make this happen?'

'It's only your first time-travel,' Jasper sneers at her. 'Think of us poor bloody tards having to cope with yet another version of our future.'

'I don't understand,' she says.

'Well, of course you don't,' and this time, Jasper sounds really angry at her, 'because you aren't even the right Ani!'

'What do you see in him?' she snarls at me.

Whoa. 'See in him? He's my blud is all.'

'Yeah, and the rest.'

'No, there is no rest. Nothing else,' I say firmly.

'He's a complete tool.'

'Standing right here while you piss me off!' he shouts at her.

I step forward between the two of them, noting Ani's hands are balling into fists. 'This isn't helping,' I say, in the headteacher voice that I seem to have inherited from a mother who isn't a headteacher any more. Not at this school, anyway.

'It is helping,' Jasper says thickly. 'It's helping me a lot.'

'I just wanted to know what you meant by versions of the future, and you launched all over me with the salty attitude!' Ani yells. 'What exactly did you mean by 'I'm not the right Ani'? What, am I a different version of your future as well?'

I fix my eyes on a particularly fascinating piece of broken black plastic guttering that is pouring the rainwater from the roof of the Performing Arts Block down into a growing puddle on the path in front of the entrance. Rainwater? It hadn't rained for days last time I was here. Is everything different, even the weather?

Jasper says nothing.

'Oh. My. God,' she says, shocked. 'I am, aren't I? I'm different from the Ani you knew. Oh, my god.'

I glare at Jasper, and for the first time in the last few minutes, he is actually looking a bit shame-faced. 'You shouldn't have found out like that,' I tell her quietly, 'but it's true. We knew a different Ani. In our original 2019, we were all friends. Besties. It was actually your idea to come looking for a portal in the Old Library, and we all went back to 1987 together and met Lizzy, and all her friends. Then -' I stop talking and my voice breaks. I don't know how to tell her the next bit.

'Then we were at Lizzy's party, and you felt ill, and you vanished. You just disappeared. Right under Brian's nose,' Jasper finishes for me. 'We thought we'd lost you forever,' he goes on, swallowing hard. 'One of the reasons they all came back before, was to see if you were still here. Brian ... you know?'

'No, I don't know,' Ani replies, but she's stopped shouting, and her fists aren't clenched.

'You were with Brian,' I say.

'With? As in going out? I can't have known him more than a couple of days!'

'The other you was a lot more ... impulsive,' I think about my own experience. 'Things just happened really quickly.'

'Impulsive?' she says, looking at the weed-strewn gravel path. 'You're the impulsive ones. That's why we weren't even friends.' Suddenly the whole area is flooded with light as the Main Hall signals the end of the Fundraiser Disco. Then she looks at me, and the anger leaves her face. 'I'm sorry. You thought your friend had come back. It must have been hard for you.'

'I'm getting used to things being hard,' I say, not without an element of bitterness. 'We need to chill out and plan our next step.' I turn to Jasper, whose face is still shadowed with unexpressed contempt. 'It's not her fault, Jasper.'

'Well, I have to have someone to blame for this fucking mess!' He sinks down onto the grass beside the path, and I can see his shoulders shaking.

I can't bear the thought of another stint trending on everyone's *Instagram*, so I crouch down beside him and whisper in his ear, 'Let's go up to the Big Willow and regroup.'

Eventually, he wipes his face roughly with his sleeve, and he stands back up after a few more moments.

We leave the school site through huge wrought-iron gates carrying a faded school logo I don't recognise. The Top Gates must be at least six metres high now, and on either side, they are connected to chain link fencing that stretches away as far as the eye can see. On top, there is what looks like razor wire. I'm guessing Mrs Palmer takes security a bit more seriously than my Mum ever did.

It's a warm night; the top road is full with rents waiting in their cars for the younger ones, while security guards look on, their arms folded, from the edge of the school grounds. At first, everywhere is swarming with teenagers, but no one is walking home; everyone seems to have a lift or a cab. After a while, the crowds move on, and we sit in the semi-darkness at the edge of the Park, our faces barely lit by the streetlamps, looking at each other.

The willow is now a Big Tree again. 'My mum and dad met at University,' Ani says after we finish telling her a little more of our version of her life, where my Mum is her head-teacher, and she is our mad genius BFF with a crazy laugh. 'We only moved to Stoneford a couple of years ago, and I only knew you and Jasper at school by reputation.'

'What reputation?' I ask lightly.

'Well, your mum was one of the cleaners,' Ani says apologetically as if that explained it. 'My best friend was Orla Kelly.'

'Orla *Kelly*?' Jasper vocalises my inner scream. 'Her surname is Kelly?'

'Yes. She's Mr Kelly's daughter. They lived in Lizzy's house. It was there that we found *The Truth*. He had a library full of books up in an attic room. They were very wealthy. Mr Kelly ... Scott managed the family antique business for years, and then the Mayor asked him to act as School Business Manager at Drake's because of his business acumen. It was in all the papers.'

Family antique business. Doesn't sound like one little local Hippy Shop. Looks like Scott might have used Lizzy's key to launder some money back to his rents at some point. 'It doesn't matter now,' I say aloud. 'That timeline has gone. We have to find out where Scott and Lizzy are on this version of the timeline.'

'As I said earlier, Lizzy's in 1971,' Ani says.

'Not that Lizzy,' Jasper says, a little calmer now. 'The

older one.'

'Oh, of course,' Ani says. 'Do you know her then?'

Jasper looks at me. 'Get out of that one, David Blaine,' he says.

I have no choice. I don't know this girl. I certainly don't trust her; she opens her mouth, and all kinds of crap come out of it. 'Yes. I know Lizzy. Last time we were here, she was a cleaner.'

'Oh, so she must know your Mum. Fucking Hell!' she exclaims suddenly, more like our Ani in that one phrase than at any other time since we met her. 'Fuck! You said you were Weyfare! She's ...' She stops talking and slowly puts her hand over her mouth.

'My mother,' I say. 'Lizzy Brookes is my mother.'

'Does she know?' she whispers after a short while.

'Of course she doesn't bloody know,' Jasper says, but the malice has gone from his voice. 'How would you like it if your 17-year-old daughter from the future walked up to you right now and said 'Hey Mum, look what you made. Let's party!'' Instinctively we all look across to the path, but it's deserted.

'In your timeline, Scott was the school business manager and Mum - Lizzy – was a cleaner. That's not how it was when we started out on this madness,' I say, 'and I don't expect that's what's happening now. We need to find Lizzy and find out what's going on.'

'You mean find out why there are heavies with tazers all over Drake's,' Jasper says dully.

'Okay. But after we've checked on them; what about if they are safe?' Ani asks.

'Explain it like I'm five,' I say.

'Well, if your Mum is okay and well, and Scott is okay and well – doesn't that mean we can all just carry on here as if nothing has happened? As long as Jasper's rents are okay? And mine? I mean, that original timeline? The one where you said we started when your Mum was the Head? We can't get that back, can we? We can't get my timeline back either. We've travelled on the Weys. You've done it twice. Too much has changed.' She glances across at Jasper. 'The best scenario is that everyone's okay, and we can pick our lives up again from here.'

'You mean to stay here then,' Jasper says.

She nods. 'We're not Weyfarere. Maisie here can hop on and off the Weys whenever she feels like it, but you and me, we're just ordinary.'

'Bystanders,' he says, with a sideways look at me. 'But I'm a Bystander with a bestie with amazing talent.'

I smile despite wanting to thump him. 'You've changed your tune,' I say to her. 'What was all that stuff before about being obsessed with finding out about the Weydoor?'

She shrugs. 'Well, I know about it now, don't I?'

'Don't you want to do a bit of serious time travelling with Maisie?' Jasper asks sarcastically. 'See the world in twenty-one different centuries?'

'Not if it means I could end up wiping myself off another timeline,' she says quietly, and I realise with a rush what's caused her change of heart. 'Glenda said the Weys are dangerous, and I think she's right. So if everyone's safe, I'm staying here. I'm never going to be your Ani,' she adds, getting to her feet, 'but I don't want to ... what did Glenda call it? Extinguish. I don't want to extinguish anyone either. Can't we just see what kind of 2019 we've come back to and if it's a reasonable fit, can't we just stay here?' She sighs. 'Maybe this time around we could even be friends.'

'I think we have to go to Travellers' Rest and see if any of my family are there this time.' It felt weird saying 'my family' out loud.

'It was your house then?' Ani asks. I nod.

Jasper looks at me. 'Glenda said we couldn't use the tunnel in 1971,' he says. 'She didn't say anything about not using it in 2019.'

'We can't get back onto the school site now,' I point out. 'It'll be wired, and with all those guards about we'll have to go the long way round.'

I wonder idly to myself as we mooch back to the path across the Park; what am I going to find this time I visit Travellers' Rest. Party? Conference? More to the point, will it still be my home?

Chapter Eleven – Someone You Loved (Lewis Capaldi, 2019)

It must be getting on for eleven at night by the time we cross the Park and approach my home, Travellers' Rest. It's an old grey stone house with chimneys like the turrets high up on the Old Library; a three-storey home utterly different to any of the modern estate houses that surround it, because it has been here since the Old Library was built to mask the Weydoor from the world, and I never even noticed the resemblance until very recently. Beyond the house, I can see the lights from the Poets' Estate rising up towards the sprawling modern buildings of Stoneford General Hospital; only this morning when we parked up with Ed and his golden shagmobile, there were orchards. I look at Jasper, but if he's thinking about going back to his home, it doesn't show on his face.

The lights are blazing as if there's a party going on.

'Please God not another bloody wrinklies' party,' Jasper says, echoing my thoughts.

'It's no one's birthday I can think of,' I say.

'It doesn't have to be. It still might not be your house,' Jasper says. 'You have to be prepared for that.'

'Last time I was here, it was Orla's,' Ani points out.

'Yes, thank you both for the reassurances,' I snap.

'No need to go all extra on us,' Ani says. 'Just saying how it is.'

Jasper squeezes my hand.

We open the wooden front gate, and it still creaks; the sound is familiar like the opening bars of a well-known song. We walk down the path past the rose bushes and the single apple tree that looks unchanged. My heart is beginning to beat normally, then a large man with a goatee beard in full biker leathers launches himself from the inside of the house pretty much onto my feet. We all stop walking.

'State your business,' the man says, pulling a radio, suspiciously similar to the one used by the guard at Drake's, from the belt of his jeans. 'Three juveniles approaching base.'

'Dave?' I say, peering into his face, my voice letting me down and squeaking like a small child.

The man peers at me through the darkness of the garden. 'Maisie? For fuck's sake. Aren't you supposed to be at the school disco?'

'It's finished,' I say, and I'm feeling some hope because, despite him acting like an extra from CSI, this man is my Uncle Paul's biker friend Dave from when they were kids. 'Is Paul … Uncle Paul about?'

'Inside,' Dave says as if I should have known. 'Abort,' he says into the radio. 'It's Maisie plus two. Disco's over. No, I don't know what happened to three-six. Give him a chance to call in. Where the fuck are the Guard? Over.' He walks back to the shadows at the side of the house.

Looking at Dave here, still in his leathers and talking into a radio, I'm wondering what version of Paul I'm about to meet now.

'Is he your fam?' Ani asks as if I've asked her to clear the dog mess from the grass in the Park.

'Dave is my uncle's friend,' I say. 'I'm not sure who lives here yet. Or why they would have security here.'

'You still want to go in and find out?' Jasper asks gently.

He sounds like he thinks I need his support. Strangely, I feel quite strong at the moment. 'No other choices available,' I say, with a thin smile. 'Unless you want to try your place?' He pulls a face and shakes his head.

More people in bike leather fill the rooms. The wallpaper is familiar, although it's not what was on the wall when I left to go to the Fundraiser 300 years ago. The hallway looks sleek and well, classy to be honest. It doesn't look like 1987, but it doesn't look like 2019, either. Stormzy is playing quietly in the front room, and a few people are sitting around chatting with beer cans in one hand and their phones in another, watching the biggest screen I have ever seen that was not in my house the first time I left it. The sofas are all plush leather with big cushions. People look up as we walk in, nod, and go back to their screens. They must all be a similar age to my Mum now.

I walk into the kitchen diner, where I'm pleased to see there is an island and a breakfast bar instead of the round pine dining table and dresser, but everything looks like something from a makeover show. The worktops gleam like black marble, and the screen at the end of the room where the dresser used to be isn't much smaller than the one in the lounge. Flashy pendulum lights hang down over the people sitting at the island, tapping onto their screens. A woman is taking a beer from a large double walk-in fridge, and where the larder used to be there is an extension, full with a dishwasher, washing machine and what looks like a tumble dryer. Several people are sitting at the breakfast bar talking into radios while they watch their phones, and one of them is my Uncle Paul.

The Uncle Paul I know, two years older than Mum, is a lawyer in the City taking significant divorce cases for rich people, sometimes even famous ones. He's got a bit of weight on him, and his hair is cropped short to hide the bald patch. He only wears designer labels on his clothes, and he has his suits made for him in the City. He's nothing like the Paul we met in 1987.

This Paul is completely bald apart from a goatee, dressed entirely in black leathers and puffing on a big black vaporiser. Much fitter than I remember, he's definitely not wearing anything with a designer label, unless you call the Harley Davidson T-shirt a label. He's actually still not bad looking, for an old guy.

'Hey Maisie,' he says, looking up from his phone, 'we didn't expect you back so early. Fundraiser okay?'

Everyone stops talking and looks at me. Oh, this is lit. Not so much. 'It was not what I expected.'

'Isn't life always,' he says tonelessly. 'Mum's upstairs. I expect you want her, not me.'

My heart misses a beat. 'Lizzy?'

Paul's eyes narrow. 'Glenda,' he says, and my heart misses a couple of beats and dives straight into my throat. A couple of people put their radios to their mouths.

'Glenda?' I repeat, my voice unexpectedly high. She's dead, isn't she? 'Where's Lizzy?' I ask out loud. 'My Mum?'

He slips off the breakfast bar stool and rubs his hands over his face. 'She was right then,' he says without explanation. 'Code Green, we'll have to move them tonight,' he says inexplicably to the others at the breakfast bar, who are all muttering into their radios and walking out of the back door. 'Go on up, Maisie. Your Nan's upstairs. It's fine,' he adds, giving me a smile that doesn't reach anywhere near his eyes. 'Just another situation. You know. Well, maybe you don't know. I'm not the one who needs to explain things to you. Talk to Mum. The women in this family are the ones who matter, so I've been told all my bloody life.' He takes a huge draw on his vaporiser and is engulfed in blackberry-scented clouds. 'I'm so not ready for this,' he mutters, as we leave the kitchen.

'Glenda is alive?' Jasper hisses in my ear, as we walk along the narrow corridor to the bottom of the staircase.

I shrug. Glenda had died before I was old enough to properly know her the first time around, and Jasper is the only one left who remembers that. I don't know what was wrong with her, but I'd always had this memory of a little wizened woman in my head, and I'd thought it was her. It's going to be strange meeting Glenda here.

'She will remember us from 1987, won't she?' Ani says.

'I guess,' I reply, starting to climb the stairs. 'But it's been over 30 years for them. I mean, she'll know us, the us that went to the Fundraiser tonight, but whether she'll remember meeting us in 1987, I'm not sure. Do you remember everyone you meet in your life? On that timeline, we were only there for a few hours. Glenda must have known loads of bystanders.'

'Only one of them was her granddaughter,' Jasper says.

On the first floor landing, the door to my room is closed, and a part of me is desperate to take a look inside, throw myself on my bed and spend a few hours on my laptop catching up with my social media, ignoring all this total bonkers, but I know deep down I can't do that. Whatever else Jasper and Ani decide to do, I think I have to go after Lizzy in 1971. She's my mum; she's my friend now. Plus, I think we need to stick together, and all these changing timelines are bothering me. For the first time, I don't feel comfortable in my own home.

The room at the end of the landing that used to be Paul's in 1987 is what looks like a study, with built-in bookshelves up to the ceiling and a big old-fashioned brown writing desk with a large red leather sofa covered in buttons. I remember this just as a box room and a place for the stuff that didn't fit in the stuff cupboard.

'This is nothing like when Mr ... when Orla lived here,' Ani says. 'They didn't have any of this old crap.'

As there is no sign of Glenda on this floor, I go up the second staircase. There are more tasteful, expensive-looking paintings on the walls. I'm sure I recognise a print of Damien Hirst's diamond skull as I reach the top step. In fact, everything all over the house is just that little bit more expensive than I remember. Mum and Dad could never have afforded all this glamour.

There are four bedrooms and another bathroom up here. My mum, Older Lizzy, had always used the biggest of the four with Dad until he moved out, and then she started sleeping in the spare room next to mine. I wonder if Dad's still around, but I don't let my thoughts dwell on that for too long.

A woman is sitting on the edge of a massive four-poster bed that I don't remember either. Two of the bike crowd are sitting up here with her, pointing out places on what looks like a large map on the floor. The woman has white hair cropped in a flattering pixie cut; she's dressed in black with a leather biker-style jacket, long slim legs in black jeans and a black T-shirt similar to the ones that Kim likes to wear. Liked to wear, I mean. I have to say, Mum is looking a lot better than she looked in both the last 2019s.

'Is that Glenda?' Jasper asks, and my spirits soar at the same time as my stomach sinks, and I crumple into an embarrassing heap against the door frame.

The woman in black stands up, and I can see, through eyes misting over with tears, that Jasper is right; this isn't Lizzy, this is Glenda, and she couldn't look more different from the wrinkly I was expecting to see. Hell, I half expected to find her hiding up here in bed with a cup of cocoa and a thick book about sexy highlanders. But, now I think about it, of course Glenda wouldn't be ancient or wizened. She can only be in her sixties. And jeez, is she looking good.

'Maisie?' she says, and I'm stupidly relieved, but of course she knows who I am; I only went to a disco for a couple of hours.

'Hi, Glenda,' Jasper says, stepping into the room next to me.

Glenda looks at me, and then at Jasper and Ani, and she cups her hands over her nose and mouth. One of the women on the bed is standing up as well; she is vaguely familiar, but I can't put my finger on her name. 'Maisie? Are you all right? Have you -?' but she doesn't get to finish the sentence because I don't care about how thirsty I look, I'm hugging my nan like I haven't seen her in 32 years because she is here now in 2019. How can I leave here, now I have my Nan back? This is so much better than I expected.

'Is Granddad here?' I ask, letting her loose just enough to look into her lovely face, which crumples into what I realise is an ever-deepening frown. "Where's Mum? Is Dad here? You guys must have been expecting us.'

'Fundraiser Disco, 2019,' one of the men poring over the map says. 'She was right, after all.'

'You came through the Weydoor tonight,' Glenda says out of the blue, in front of everyone in the room, none of whom strangely seem to find this an odd thing to say.

'Do you remember me? Us? From 1987?' I ask, still holding her. But she gently prises my hands away and keeps them between us instead. Her eyes are dry. She looks more serious than I expected.

'It was 32 years ago,' she says quietly. 'But yes, once we realised who you were, we knew you would come through, but we didn't know when. Your mother said it would be tonight, and the maps have confirmed it. And here you are.'

'So where is she?' I ask, confused about the lack of contact that Glenda is accepting.

'Come and sit down, Maisie,' Glenda says, drawing me over the bed.

'You're freaking me out, Nan,' I say because suddenly she is; the expression on her face isn't the one I expected to see. But then, she only saw me this evening before I went out, and I only saw her a few hours ago in 1987, so maybe my excessive hugging reaction is a little highkey.

'Sit down, all of you,' Glenda says, her face grim. 'There is no easy way to say this.'

I don't really hear the words. I feel them, like someone slowly pushing a thin blade into my back.

Like swallowing bleach. Slow, feral pain that I didn't expect.

Didn't see coming.

Didn't want.

Don't want.

No. You're lying.

Don't lie to me.

'I'm afraid your mother's dead.'

The sob I hear is mine. 'Don't be stupid. Lizzy can't be dead. Maisie's not extinguished,' Jasper says, his voice high and anxious.

'No, indeed. Lizzy only died about three years ago,' Glenda says. 'Not long after Maisie's 15th birthday.'

That's not possible, I say, but I think it's only in my head, as all I can hear is the sound of my grief pouring out like a river roaring as it breaks through a dam wall.

'She was too young to ... what happened?' Jasper says, and suddenly I can feel his arms around me as he drops to the carpet beside where I have landed.

'She died of old age,' Glenda says quietly.

'Old age!' I spit out at them suddenly, tears pouring down my face. 'Don't be fucking ridiculous! She was only 50 yesterday!'

'In true years, yes,' Glenda says. 'She would have been 50. But in Wey years, the medics think internally she was well over 100 when she collapsed. She was dead four days later.'

'I'm sorry, did you just say Wey years?' Ani asks, from the door where she's still standing stiffly.

'Did you say over 100?' Jasper says, his voice now all low and breathy.

Glenda nods. 'You all need a drink. Something strong. I have tequila in the Office. Get onto the Witan and let them know that Maisie Wharton has completed her Maiden Return,' she says abruptly to the other woman. The man on the bed with the map stands up. 'Put that back in the safe,' she tells him.

Two straight tequilas later, and I am sitting on one of the blue leather sofas in the study, my head starting to spin. There is another in a cut-glass tumbler on the dark wood side table waiting for me to drink it.

'I can't believe she's gone,' I sob.

Ani's hand touched my arm, and I accept the sympathy, cold as it is. 'She's not gone,' she says. 'She's just not here. As long as we can get out of this house and go find her, we can put all this straight. I'm sure of it.'

I smile at her weakly. She's right, of course. I have hope.

'How are we going to find her though?' Jasper says mournfully, sitting at the writing desk, playing absent-mindedly with an old fountain pen, scratching away at the leather inlay with the narrow nib as he sips his own tequila. 'She's got Glenda's key. We don't have a token to get to her.'

I frown at him. He's right, of course. My hope evaporates.

'Jasper, please try to be a bit more positive,' Ani says, sounding for all my ears like my mum.

My eyes are sore, but I just about manage to pull myself together enough to stop crying. For now. There will never be enough tears.

'We'll work something out,' Jasper mutters.

Glenda has left us here, surrounded by books and more expensive-looking items that I don't recognise. Even the sofa feels old and valuable. I can hear people talking downstairs, but it doesn't feel like a party. The more I think about it, it never did. I take another mouthful of tequila and wince.

Jasper gouges another vein of leather from the inlay on the writing desk. The sound is deafening me. Sympathy over, Ani moves to the other end of the sofa, peering up at the bookcase. Suddenly, she squeals, just like she used to.

'Found a first edition of Fangirl?' Jasper asks without looking up.

'Far better than that.' She sits up on the arm of the sofa, reaches up to the highest shelf and pulls down a purple leather book, covered in runes. I don't believe it. 'Recognise this?'

'Is it the same book?' I ask.

'Does it matter?' Ani says. 'Having a version of *The Truth* at least means we have our hands on the source of the knowledge again.'

'If it is the same one, Lizzy's name will be at the back, where she wrote it,' I say.

Ani carefully turns the pages, and there, like yesterday, printed in clear blue biro, is Lizzy's name at the end of the list of my ancestors, all the Weyfarere that have ever protected the Weydoor in the Old Library.

'I wonder if she made it back to 1971,' Jasper says.

'She didn't make it to 2019,' I say, and another sob bursts out of me. I take a big swig of tequila, and the burning sensation in my throat strangely helps. 'How could she have died of old age when she was only 47?' I say once I've got my voice back under control. 'Where is my father? My brothers?'

'What kind of man would stay home waiting for a wife who spent all her days on other timelines?' Glenda says, coming back into the study and closing the heavy door behind her. 'She was a stranger to your family. Tim left her years ago and took your brothers with him. I have no idea where they are now, and I'm not sure your mother even noticed they'd gone. You were the only one that mattered.'

'Start by telling us what "travelling the Weys too much" means,' Jasper says.

Glenda takes another tumbler from a polished wood drinks cabinet in the corner and pours herself three fingers of tequila. 'Your mother spent more time away from her timeline than she should have. For every day that she was here, she was away for at least two or three days. They all added up.' She looks down into the amber liquid and takes a large mouthful. 'I think she knew what was happening to her, but she wouldn't stop travelling the Weys, once she realised that we were the tokens and not the keys we used to wear.' She glances at my chest then, and suddenly I don't want my Nan to know I have a key. Does she remember that I have one?

'And no one thought to tell her what might happen to her if she travelled too much?' Ani asks, pushing something into the depths of her jacket while Glenda is staring at me.

"We had no idea what the effects of constant time travelling would be.' Glenda replies, and okay, now there is definitely an unexpected sharpness in her voice. 'No one even knew about the blood tokens until you appeared in 1987.'

'Me?' Ani says, suddenly frozen as she reaches out for the glass of tequila beside her.

'You instigated the revised translation of *The Truth*,'

Glenda sips at her drink. 'Up until then, it was believed that travel on the Weys was controlled by the keys and token objects. We owe a lot of our new knowledge to you, Ani Chowdhury. Much of the damage was done before the translation was complete of course, but now you know too much for your own good. Both of you.'

'Excuse me?' Jasper turns away from his destruction of the leather on the writing desk to face her.

Glenda just laughs, but it doesn't sound sincere. 'Just my joke.'

'So what's with the protection racket up at Drake's, and why has everyone at your party got a two-way radio on them? This is 2019. We do have smartphones, you know.' Jasper's trying to sound all edgy, but it's not coming across.

Glenda sits down between Ani and me. 'This isn't a party. It's a Moot. And smartphones are not secure forms of communication.' She pats my knee. 'I'm going to give you a lot of information very quickly, and I want you to trust me. Can you do that?'

Chapter Twelve – Old Town Road (Lil Nas X (Feat. Billy Ray Cyrus, 2019)

Why would my Nan be asking me to trust her?

'I imagine this is nothing like the 2019 that you left,' Glenda sips daintily from her tequila. 'There is security at the Old Library because the Witan requested it of the Police, and the Police advised the school to accept it. The Witan is the Council for the Weys,' she adds, as Jasper opens his mouth to speak. He closes it again.

'There is a Council now?' I ask.

'I asked you to trust me and listen,' Glenda says, a little more sharply. Jasper pulls a face. 'When Ani revealed what she knew about the false translation back in 1987, I decided to contact an old friend of mine, who used to work in the British Library. To cut a long story short, she confirmed that much of *The Truth* was badly translated from the original, and most of my beliefs were based on flawed information. She also revealed that she knew about at least twelve other books that contained similar folklore.'

'Twelve other books?' I repeat.

'So there were other Weyfarere families,' Ani says.

'That was just in this country. Eventually, we came together to meet, and a council was formed to share advice and support each other. We called it the Witan. Then the Weyleighers appeared.' I glance across at Jasper.

'Scott Kelly?" Ani asks.

Glenda looks at her blankly. 'I don't know that name,' she replies.

We were wrong all along then; looks like he *was* just a petty thief and scumbag. 'How did you find them?' I ask.

'*They* found *us*.' Glenda sips more tequila. 'A copy of the newly translated *The Truth* went missing around 1994, and then other things were reported to the Witan. Reports of burglaries tripling. Local families becoming rich and powerful overnight. People going missing. Then Weyfarere started vanishing. Time and again there were reports of violence at the Weydoors. The police had to be involved.'

'Our Weydoor?' Jasper says.

'They use all the Weydoors for various of their purposes.'

'All the Weydoors?' he repeats.

'The Weydoors are fractures in the fourth dimension, located on what bystanders call the ley lines.' Glenda frowned. 'Does he always talk like a parrot? I thought you knew all this.'

'We did. We also thought we'd found out who the Weyleighers were, and we planned to put a stop to it,' I say. 'Who are all those people downstairs?'

'Everyone in this house tonight works for the Witan, one way or another. Most of the people here are connected with the Weys by family. The ones here tonight are here to protect us.' Glenda finishes the tequila. 'After the troubles, the Witan's role changed overnight from a cosy club to an organization overseeing the safety of the Weys and their Guardians.

There has been a decrease in the bodies delivered through the Weydoor over the years. Here in Stoneford, Drake's School is relocating to new premises on the Railway Gardens. There may still be hope for restoring its reputation and its numbers. People don't want their children attending schools where people are regularly found hurt and mentally ill. In the meantime, The Witan is currently in talks with the local council concerning the future of Drake's site and the Weydoor. It is all very unsatisfactory.' She pauses and gives me a pointed look.

'That explains the heavies,' Jasper says. 'They're here to stop the Weyleighers having a go at you.'

This version of 2019 is awful. I want to go back to 2019. I want to see my Mum still alive and reckless.

'Us. Many of the people you see downstairs live here; either as our personal guards or as security guards at the school.' Glenda puts the empty tumbler on the writing desk.

'If Maisie has a bodyguard, how did she manage to get through the Weydoor without any of you knowing?' Ani asks sceptically.

'This is a good question,' Glenda replies. 'We think she stole the Head's keys, but the Guard on her watch will be punished for her negligence. Reprimanded,' she corrects herself, glancing at me. 'Your mother was always convinced that it was you, her daughter, who travelled back through the Weydoor to meet us all sometime around your 18th birthday, but we couldn't be certain which Fundraiser it was, or whether there would be a timeline cataclysm. I don't have time to explain that part right now,' she adds, looking at Ani. 'What you need to know now is that you are all in danger, and you need to be removed to a safe place.'

'Removed?' Jasper squeaks.

Okay. This is worse than awful.

'I know this is probably quite different to what you were expecting your life to be like when you returned,' Glenda runs her thumb along the tips of her blood-red index fingernail. 'but nowadays, we send all novice Weyfarere to The Bergh.'

'Novice?'

'You travelled on the Weys for the first time tonight, didn't you?'

'What's the Bergh?'

'It's a place of safety for young Weyfarere. You'll have a great time. Everyone does.'

'I'm not everyone,' I say. 'I want to finish my exams and _'

'You overthink your position,' she snaps, 'you were barely around for five minutes back then, relatively speaking. You think Time has stood still since you showed up in 1987? It was something of a shock to Lizzy when she realised who her daughter was, although I must say I always suspected there was more to you than met the eye, even back then. You were clearly no bystander. You and your friends here started a chain of events none of us expected.' She shakes her head as if pushing the memory away. My skin is beginning to crawl. How can this cold fish of a woman be Glenda Brookes, the one who holds house parties where everyone gets drunk and falls down? 'The Bergh was opened about twenty years ago to protect the future of the Weyfarere girls. I was one of the founders.'

'Get you,' Jasper says, but his eyes are far from impressed.

She doesn't smile.

'And what about us?' Ani asks, and I look over in surprise as her voice has suddenly turned fearful. 'Jasper and me? We don't exactly have the family skillset, do we?'

'Exceptions have been made over the past decades. Those who discover the Weys are now expected to help protect them. You will be sent away to train as Witan Security.'

I can't stop myself; I laugh out loud. 'This is bloody ridiculous. Witan security? You can't send them away. They're 18. You can't send any of us away like little kids! I'm 18 in a few days – I can do what I want and go where I like.'

Glenda stands up abruptly. 'No, I'm afraid not,' she says. 'You may have rights in the 2019 you left, but you only have duties in the 2019 you have returned to. All of you. As your legal guardian, I have the right to place you under protection.' Her face is a hideous mixture of guilt and triumph. 'The Witan are sending transport as we speak. I'll gather you some clothes and toiletries to tide you over the first few days.'

'I can get my own stuff from my room -' I don't finish my sentence as Jasper is on his feet before I realise what he's already spotted, and he's too late to stop happening; the key in her hand that closes and locks the door behind her.

'Let us out!' he shouts, hammering on the door, but Travellers' Rest is an old stone house with thick wooden doors; the study door is opening for no one if it's been locked.

'Since when has Glenda been such a biatch?' Ani asks as he shouts.

'That's not my Nan. My Nan is dead, and my Mum is alive,' I say, all the anger and dismay and hurt and disbelief beginning to bubble in my stomach as I struggle not to vomit tequila all over the thick carpets. I stand up, and I start banging my fists on the wooden door beside Jasper, but for different reasons – I figure if I can hit them hard enough to hurt, I'll wake myself up from the nightmare version of 2019 that we've ended up in. 'My mum is alive and we need to go find her!'

'Someone? Help us!' Jasper continues to shout.

It's a few minutes before we give up, and turn back to Ani.

She stares up at us from the sofa. 'Now you've both finished trying to break your hands, we need to work out how to get out of this room and back to the Weydoor,' she says.

'How can you be so bloody calm about this?' Jasper shouts at her. 'Our Ani would have been freaked beyond belief at being locked in a room by someone she thought she could trust!'

'And what help would that have been?' she yells back at him. 'Your Ani is gone! I'm the only Ani here now. You think I'm happy about all of this? Haven't you ever heard of putting on a brave face? Maisie's lost her mum, and you're determined to bust up your hands; one of us has to stay sane and think straight!'

She has a point. From his lack of response, I guess he knows it.

We look at her, me with the tears still leaking down my face, and Jasper scowling.

'So come on then, Miss Sanity,' I say, after a moment, 'let's have the plan.'

'The only way is out through the window,' she says.

'We're on the first floor,' I say.

'No one here needs a diet. One of us can lower the two others as near to the ground as we can reach, and we fall the rest of the way. Those two help the last one out. It can't be more than a couple of metres drop.'

'Still far enough to break an ankle,' Jasper remarks. 'And the guard at the front of the house would see us.'

'Well, unless Maisie knows of any other secret passages that happen to lead from this room, I don't have another plan.'

'I didn't know about the tunnel in the Shed,' I said. 'You think I'd know if there were any other secret passages?'

As one, we turn and look at the bank of bookcases that line the wall from floor to ceiling. As one, we walk over and start tapping at book spines, pulling them out from their positions to see if they reveal any hidden doors like the one in the Old Library that leads to the tunnel to the house. Some of them are old, like *The Truth*. I look for something similar again, but I can't find anything.

We are still pushing and prodding when the door opens, and I turn to see Glenda is standing there, looking amused. 'The only thing hidden behind those books is years of dust and neglectful cleaning,' she says. 'Anyone would think you were trying to find a hidden door.'

'Why on Earth would we want to escape? It's a teenage dream to be sent away to an institution against your will,' Ani says, pushing something behind her back.

Glenda frowns. 'I don't expect you to understand. I do expect you to do as I ask.' She smiles, but it doesn't inspire any trust. 'It's a matter of family.'

There is a gunmetal grey transporter van ticking over

on the road past the front of the house. I look for Dave as we are walked out of the front door, but he's gone. In his place are several blank-faced men and women dressed in black combats, lining the path towards the van. Their message is clear: Don't even think about running.

Even Paul has gone, but my heavy heart knows he would have been on this plan as soon as we came back from the Fundraiser.

The van's windows are blacked out, so we can't see inside. I start shouting again when two of the guys take Ani and Jasper around the back, and Glenda opens the passenger door. They look at me in horror; Ani's arms are wrapped firmly around her sides.

'I want to go in the back with them,' I protest.

'You are Weyfarere. *You* don't travel in the backs of vans,' Glenda says in a disdainful voice that I've never heard her use until now. 'Get in. It's a long way to the Bergh. Your friends aren't going there. They will be safe with Tony.'

'What? No! Where are they going?'

'I told you. They are to train with the Witan.' Glenda puts a hand on my shoulder, and I pull away violently. This woman is not my grandmother. I've decided this is all a bad dream, and I am going to wake eventually - I don't care which year, I don't even care which century right now - just not here. Not without Lizzy. Not without my Mum. 'Maisie, please don't make this any harder than it already is,' she says, her voice a little less cold, but not enough.

I have no choice right now. I get into the passenger seat and glance at the driver. Dressed in a dark hoodie and black trousers or jeans, it's impossible to tell who is sitting behind the wheel. It doesn't look at me, it just stares ahead at the road. Defeated, I put on my seat belt.

'You received full instructions, Mark?' Glenda says to the driver. Mark nods, but he doesn't speak. Some journey to Hell this is going to be. 'We will be in touch, Maisie,' she says. I decide Mark has the right idea, and I stare forward onto the road without replying until I feel the door shut beside me, and the van pulls away from the kerb.

We're only seconds down the top road towards town when the driver finally speaks. 'We don't have long,' he says.

I recognise the voice, but I can't place it. I turn and try to see his face more clearly, but he doesn't turn towards me. Out of sight of Travellers' Rest and the black shadow wall of Glenda's guards, the van approaches the junction with the Bottom Road, but instead of turning left to go on into the town centre, it turns right.

Back towards the school.

'Look at me.' I lean as far forward as the seat belt will allow, but all I can make out is dark hair and a goatee beard. 'Where are we going? Who are you? Dave? Is that you?' He still won't look at me, and now I'm feeling really anxious. 'Where are we going?' I ask again, feeling the breath leaving my lungs and not being able to properly refill them.

'Drake's,' he says. 'We need to get you to the Old Library. I have a one minute window. When it comes, please listen to me.'

I don't know whether to be scared, hysterical or excited. Something in his voice excites me, but I'm in a van with a strange guy, and only a tard wouldn't see the potential danger in that. Suddenly the whole van vibrates. Someone in the back is knocking quickly on the roof. Hard.

As if it's a cue, the driver swerves the van into the side of the road, in front of the chippy. I hear shouts in the back and then silence. The driver kills the engine and turns to face me for the first time. When he pulls the hood from his head, I cry out and then cover my mouth.

It's Rob.

He's still slim under the hoodie and jeans, and I can just see the green of his eyes reflecting the neon sign from the chippy. His hair is still thick but floppy on top, there's no bleach and it's shaved shorter at the sides. The goatee suits him, even shot through with silver. Crap, a faceful of spots would suit him. If he has wrinkles, I can't see them. He must be 50, but somehow, he's still lovely.

We stare at each other. It feels like hours, but it can only have been a couple of seconds. 'Mark and Tony are unconscious under the Big Willow in the Park,' he says. 'Paul and me reckon we have five minutes to get you away. I told him I needed one of those minutes. It's good to see you again.'

My heart is hammering like the base at the Fundraiser. 'You too,' I manage to get out. 'Rob – Lizzy can't be dead. She's –' My sentence ends with a sob.

He reaches out but doesn't quite touch me. 'Your mother.' Into my shocked silence, he adds, 'Maisie, I know you're Weyfarere. I know you're Lizzy's daughter. Things have changed. Whatever we did – all of us, I mean –' he stumbles, 'back in 1987, it's led to this world where Weyfarere guard the Weys, and The Witan guard the Weyfarere from the Weyleighers. They will lock you away where no one will ever find you. They'll say it's for your protection, but The Bergh is more like a prison. You can't stay here. And they blame Ani. There's so much more I should tell you, but I just don't have time.'

Mob royalty? 'They blame Ani?' I want to ask so much, but her name is the only thing I say.

'She was the first to discover that Weyfarere blood is what controls travel through the Weys. They think she sold the information, even though the Difficulties date back about 50 years. They aren't sending her and Jasper to become Witan, Maisie. They are getting rid of them.'

'Stop,' I say quietly. 'Difficulties? Getting rid of? I don't get any of this. I don't believe this. And Ani would never sell us out.'

Wouldn't she? A nasty little voice in my head whispers. The Ani you loved as your BFF wouldn't have done it, but what about this snarky version?

'There's no time to explain, you just have to trust us. Paul is in the back, not Tony,' Rob goes on, over my thoughts. 'Lizzy told us you would return today. We always believed her. She kept travelling on the Weys trying to fix all this, but she didn't have the tokens for the right times, and she didn't know where to go to make it right. In the end, it killed her. I promised her before she died that I would help you get away. Paul called me as soon as you came to Travellers' Rest tonight. He's been waiting for you to arrive for years. ' He looks down. 'I've been waiting for years, too.'

I thought his age would matter. I thought that looking into his eyes and seeing an older man there would gross me out. It bothered me so much starting a relationship with a guy old enough to be my father, but here he is, and in the end, he's just Rob. He's in a different package, but he's just Rob. And he's been waiting for me. For years. 'Waiting for me?' I say aloud.

He looks back at the road. 'Dave has replaced the security at the Weydoor. We need to get you out of 2019.'

As if on cue, there is another loud thump on the ceiling. Rob starts the engine, and the van roars back onto the road.

My mind is a mess. I can't take it all in. 'And they want to lock Jasper and Ani up?'

'And throw away the key,' Rob says, eyes on the road. 'If they're lucky. Jasper may get to serve the Witan. If he's lucky.'

'And I have to go to prison?'

'It's not prison, but it might as well be.' He glances across at me. 'They don't want the Weyfarere to travel the Weys any more, and they don't want the Weyleighers to bleed you.'

'Bleed me?' I squeak.

'They sell Weyfarere blood to the highest bidders. People will pay huge sums of money these days, so that they can travel the Weys safely and change the future. Most people only want to make themselves rich or keep someone alive, which is bad enough, but one day someone's going to do some serious damage to the continuum. Maisie, do you remember the night we spent in the orchards behind Travellers' Rest?' he asks suddenly.

How could I forget it? I'm glad the darkness hides my blushes. 'We spent all night talking. You told me about 1987. I told you some things. I tried not to tell you too much,' I say.

'But from what little you told me about your 2019, I know it was nothing like this one,' he says. 'You need to go back to where all this started, and you need to fix whatever happened. I know it can be different from this. You, me and Jasper – we're the only ones who know it was different before. Somehow you have to make it right again.'

'You remember what I told you in the orchard?' I say. 'You know it was different here.'

'It's our secret,' he says. The van pulls up sharply at the bottom gate. 'It will always be our secret.' I want to reach out to him then, but he opens his door and slips out of the van before I can reply. 'They will never hear it from me.'

Drake's is cocooned in darkness now; the Fundraiser is long over. I unlock my seat belt and open the door. As I slip out of my seat, Jasper and Ani appear in front of me, their eyes full and frantic. Paul steps out from behind them. Looks like they got the same story.

'I thought you were on Glenda's side,' I say to him.

'I had to let you think that. I couldn't risk you giving me away,' he says. 'Dave is up at the Old Library. We need to get going. I have no idea whether Mark and Tony have woken and sounded the alarm yet.'

We climb over the gates and sprint into the school grounds. I can see now how rundown everything is. All it needs are boarded-up windows, and it'll be a proper urban explorers' playground. We run past the Main Block, up onto the three paths that converge and then up to the Old Library, where the door is slightly ajar.

They all keep running towards it, but then Rob stops, and instinctively, I stop a few steps later.

'What's the matter?' I ask, my chest rising and falling hard, my legs aching. 'Why have you stopped?'

'I'm sorry,' he says, and suddenly he looks 18 again, this

man in front of me, thrusting his hands into his hoodie pocket. 'I have to ask you this because it's been killing me for years. Why didn't you tell me you were Weyfare? Or that you were Lizzy's daughter? Didn't you think I would believe you?' He hangs his head. 'Why didn't you trust me?'

Despite everything urgent, time slows. I step forward, and I reach out and touch his hands. The hands of a man who has waited over 30 years to save me from a future he knows isn't mine.

'I was confused,' I say honestly. 'I thought the fewer people that knew, the safer the secret would be. I didn't think Lizzy should be told who I was.'

'And you didn't think I would understand?' he asks. 'You didn't think I would respect that? I knew you were keeping something back from me, and I didn't know what it was. It hurt me.' He looks back at me, and we might as well be back in 1987. 'You hurt me.'

With a pang of horror, I know he's totally right. I should have trusted him. I should have told him about my relationship with Lizzy. Rob never gave me any reason to believe he wouldn't be there for me. I was stupid and stubborn.

'I was wrong,' I look into his eyes. 'I know it was ages ago for you, but I didn't tell you for what I thought were all the right reasons. I should've trusted you. I guess I just didn't believe in us enough.' I swallow hard. 'I was so wrong. Can you forgive me?'

He stares down at my hand touching his.' Forevermore,' he says, and he opens my hands and pushes something into my fingers. It feels like a ring. 'I'm lending this to you,' he says. 'It was given to me on November 22nd, 1994. Come when you need answers that you can't find anywhere else.'

'I can't take this,' I say, looking down at the ring's enamelled surface.

'Yes, you can,' he says firmly, closing my fingers over it. 'I've been waiting for years to give it to you.'

'Maisie, get up here now!' Paul shouts from further up the path, and we both break into a run.

Dave is at the door to the Old Library, and as we step into the musty black, he locks it behind us.

'Dave swapped Weydoor duties tonight,' Paul explains. 'It won't take them long to spot the connection once Mark and Tony make contact again.'

'They will come through the tunnel from Base,' Dave says. 'There's no way of blocking that. You need to go now.'

I look at Rob and realise that we have run into the Old Library hand in hand. He is the one who pulls away. 'Go now,' he says.

'I can't leave you,' I say. 'What will happen when Glenda and the Witan find out you helped us?'

'Don't worry about that. You're going to change everything and put it right,' Rob says.

'Paul?' Jasper asks. 'Dave? Will you guys be okay?'

'We can look after ourselves,' Paul says.

'I don't know where to go,' I say.

'You need a token,' Dave asks.

'I don't have anything!' I exclaim, pushing Rob's ring deep into my pocket.

We all turn our heads then as we hear the same noise; there are voices shouting and feet running.

'They're in the tunnel!' Paul says. 'Haven't you got anything on you?'

'I've got this old pen I found in Glenda's study,' Jasper says, pulling it out of his pocket.

'That will have to do – we've run out of time,' Paul says.

'But it could take us anywhere!' Ani cries.

'Anywhere is better than here,' I say. 'Hold my hand.'

As I take Jasper's pen and push it and my hand against the Weydoor, I hold onto Ani, and she grabs hold of Jasper. She's right – we could end up anywhere, but anywhere is better than here.

The last thing I see is the face of the man who never gave up on me. How could I have been such a tool? Why on Earth didn't I think I could trust Rob? I promise myself there and then that I will get back to 1987, and I will put this right. I won't have him waiting 30 years for answers. Not in my time.

The next thing I know we're falling against the book-shelves, and there's white heat, purple light, black – nothing.

I open my eyes, and Lizzy is staring down at me.

'Mum!' I cry out and then put my hand over my mouth.

She stands up straight and puts her hands on her hips. 'Delirious,' she says to Kim, who is now standing next to her. 'What the hell happened there? Why didn't they come straight through with us?'

'Did you let go of my hand?' Kim asks.

I sit up on the floor. It's not as dusty as usual. In fact, there's a carpet. Thick, soft carpet. 'Not sure. Bit confused. Sorry.' I so want to give Lizzy a hug.

Jasper is shaking his head awake, and Ani is crawling out from under the big wooden table that runs down the centre of the Old Library, holding two small books. I recognise one of them. She's taken *The Truth* from the future.

I try to catch Jasper's eye, but he's too dazed to react.

I'm still holding the pen that for some reason has got us to wherever Lizzy is, but before I can even begin to process how this happened, how we managed to get through the Weydoor to the same timeline as Lizzy and Kim, how I ache about leaving Rob in a nightmare version of my future, there is a flash of heat and purple light behind us, and someone else falls through the Weydoor behind us and collapses onto the floor.

It's Scott.

Chapter Thirteen – Behind Blue Eyes (The Who, 1971)

'Is that how we looked when we came through?' Jasper asks. 'Like someone just flung us through the Weydoor like a bag of rubbish?'

'Pretty much,' Kim says. 'Hang on. Is that -?'

Before she can finish, Lizzy has launched herself at Scott's crumpled figure on the floor and she is kneeling beside him, slapping him hard, shouting all kinds of shit at him, grabbing his clothes and trying to get him to wake up and face her, explain himself to her. It's no more than he deserves, and not one of us moves forward to stop her. When he finally staggers onto his feet he's moaning, and he is clutching his side; his usually disarming blue eyes are narrowed.

'Christ on a bike,' Jasper says. 'It's Scott.'

'You are a fucking asshole!' Lizzy yells. 'What are you doing here? Come to have another go at common assault?'

'Lizzy ... help me,' he says, and he crashes into her, losing his footing.

She pushes him roughly away and then looks at her hands in disgust. 'Get off me, you bastard. You're all wet. What kind of crap are you covered in?'

I step forward and look down at Lizzy's hands as she holds them out in front of her. They are covered in dark fluid. I look down at where Scott has fallen back onto his knees, still holding his side.

'Crap,' I say. 'He's bleeding.'

Ani puts her books on the table, runs forward and kneels down in front of him, pulling his hands away from his stomach. She gingerly lifts the black T-shirt, which is sodden. She looks up at us. 'It's a stab wound.'

'He's been attacked?' Kim asks, her voice wobbling.

'Why has he been attacked?' Jasper cries.

'We need to get him to hospital. He's losing blood, and anyone of a load of important internal organs might be damaged,' Ani says. 'How do people make phone calls in this bloody decade?'

'This bloody decade? Which bloody decade is this?' Jasper asks. We look at Lizzy. She's still staring in disbelief at her bloodied hands.

I shake her arm. 'Lizzy? Are we in 1971?'

'I … I don't know.' She seems to come to herself a little. 'We need to get him out of here. Maisie, you take the side with the blood and I'll take the other. Kim, go with Ani up to the phonebox on the top road. Ring for an ambulance. Jasper, you stay with us in case we need help with him.' She stares at the two girls. 'Run.'

'Shouldn't we just take him back to 1987?' I ask. What were hospitals like in the 1970s? I saw a film once; it was a comedy, but the nurses were all female, and all of them wore weird hats and uniforms that made them look like they were wearing fancy dress, and there was a guy in a hospital bed for weeks, and all he had was a broken leg. Could they cope with someone with a stab wound?

'I don't think he should use the Weys again until he's better. Scott? Scott? Talk to me,' Lizzy says, as she helps him onto his feet again. 'Try to stay awake.'

'Hey baby,' he mumbles.

She hauls Scott up onto her shoulder. 'Kim. Get a grip. The keys should be in my pocket.'

Kim pushes her hand into the pocket of Lizzy's jeans and pulls out a chain with an iron key on it, runs to the heavy oak door at the front of the Old Library with Ani, turns the key in the lock and opens the door onto a chill I haven't felt in a long time. They disappear into the darkness.

'Scott, who did this to you?' I ask as we make slow progress towards the open door.

He shakes his head.

'Were you attacked?' Lizzy asks.

He nods, and gasps when the colder air hits him as we leave the Old Library. Whenever we are, there is no alarm system yet. 'Lizzy, you have to understand,' he wheezes, as she locks the door behind us and pockets the key.

'Understand what? Keep walking,' she adds, as he stumbles between us, and we stagger to stay on our own feet while keeping him upright.

'I was a twat. For trying to steal your key,' he says slowly, every word clearly an effort.

'No disagreement there. You are a twat,' she says, 'but not all twats deserve to get stabbed. Keep moving.'

'Come on. One foot after the other. You can do this,' Jasper says from beside us.

'There's a woman. She came to the shop. Looking for stuff. About Weyfarere.' He coughs, wheezing like an old man and clutching himself. 'She said if ever I heard anything about Weyfarere -' His legs buckle beneath him and it's all we can do to keep him on his feet.

'Come on, Patchouli, you can do this,' I say quietly.

He looks at me then; those beautiful blue eyes blood-shot under the moonlight and creased with pain. 'You have to watch out for her,' he mutters inexplicably, and then his head slumps forward, Lizzy looks at me and we both have to work harder as we drag him up towards the streetlights and the Top Road. I'm relieved that the Gates of Hell have reverted back to the white barn gates and the low brick walls that we left in 1987.

Kim comes up to us, with Ani following. 'We called for an ambulance,' she says.

The glass box by the gates on the top road has turned into a red box with little panes of glass. I've seen these boxes in old photos, along with bowler hats, black cabs and Winston Churchill. I have no idea what you do in one of these boxes, so I'm glad that Kim went. 'We told them his name, but they wanted mine as well,' she adds.

'I told her to say Jane Doe,' Ani says.

'Jane Doe? Who's she?' Lizzy asks, breathing hard with the exertion of keeping Scott upright.

'Wherever we are, it's almost certain we don't exist here,' Ani says. 'Jane Doe is an anonymous person. Untrace-able.'

She's watched too much CSI. 'If it's 1971, Scott will exist here,' I say. 'He'll be what ... eight? Nine? He'll be at primary school, won't he? So his health records won't match.'

Jasper pulls the pen out of his pocket under the street-light, peers closely at it, rolls his eyes and puts it away again.

'We haven't got time to worry about that now,' Lizzy

says, too busy watching Scott to notice Jasper. Scott is looking pale, but his eyes are open again. and he is still on his feet, so I'm hoping that's a good sign. 'We're going to have to leave him here, I think.'

'We can't just dump a stabbed man on the side of the road,' Jasper says. 'No matter what kind of tool he is.'

'I'll stay with him,' Ani says unexpectedly. We all look at her.

'Why would you want to do that?' Jasper asks.

'Someone needs to stay with him,' she says. 'Someone needs to pretend they are his family, so they get some information about whether he's going to survive. Someone needs to be there to tell the doctors that you lot are family when you turn up asking questions. If here is 1971, you need to do what you came here to do,' she says. In the distance, I can hear a siren. 'You need to go now,' she says.

'Ambulance is coming,' Kim says. I can see the blue flashing lights lower down the Top Road towards town, and I realise she is right.

I lean down and lower Scott towards the pavement. 'Lizzy, we need to move.'

Lizzy does the same, and Scott ends up on the pavement, slumped against Ani, eyes closed.

Ani puts an arm around him and looks up at us. We can hear the siren now.

'Go,' she says. 'If they move us from the General, I'll leave a message for you to tell you where we've gone.'

The siren is louder now, and the blue lights are clearer as they approach. Lizzy takes one last look at Scott, and then she runs across the road into the Park, followed by me, Jasper and

Kim.

We watch the ambulance stop from the safety of the Park. I call it the Park, but I'm sure there should be a willow tree where we're standing and there is nothing but scrubland up here. To be honest, the whole Park looks rough; like a big bit of land that no one really cares about. There is no gravel pathway, just a dirt track through overgrown meadow grass that comes up to my waist, and sometimes higher. There are trees dotted about, but nothing that gives me a sense of place. We watch from a safe distance as they put Scott on a stretcher, and carry him into the back of the ambulance, and Ani jumps in and then they are gone, blue lights wailing that they carry someone fighting for their life.

'Doesn't look like much of a Park these days,' Jasper says, looking around us. No one else is around.

'Do you think this is 1971?' Kim asks.

'The pen?' I ask innocently, hoping he's alert.

'21st birthday present from Aunt Gladys, apparently,' he says quickly. 'Engraved.'

'Lucky find,' I say.

Lizzy frowns at us and shakes her head in confusion. 'It should be December 30th, and it should be Mum's 21st birthday. So we need to go home and see if there's a party that we need to gatecrash.' She rubs her hands over her bare arms and leaves traces of red all over them. 'It's cold enough for December.'

I shrug. Gatecrashing parties seems to have become second nature to me lately.

Jasper looks from me to Lizzy and back again. 'No one in

their right mind is going to allow you two to walk into a house party. Even without the masks, you look like adverts for a slasher movie.'

I look at Lizzy. She has a red-stained bandage on her ankle poking out under her tight jeans, and her hands, arms and one side of her face are smeared with Scott's blood. If I look anything like her, I wouldn't let me into my party.

Lizzy looks at me and her nose wrinkles up, so I guess I'm not far off. 'We need to find a place to clean up, wherever we are.'

'What about the public toilets at the Railway Gardens?' Kim asks. 'I'm sure that building's been there for a good few years.'

'Well, no one's going to let us into the restrooms at Nando's,' Jasper says.

'Whatever that is,' Kim replies.

Jasper shakes his head mournfully.

Everyone is subdued by the time we make it to the Railway Gardens. It's a good job it's dark, or one of the little police cars speeding past with their little blue lights on the roof would have pulled us over on suspicion of someone's murder.

Me and Jasper, we're used to seeing familiar things all changed, and the walk is weird for us because we can see it on three different levels now: 2019, 1987 and here. When we realise that the estate where Rob and Brian live is just a building site, it feels uncomfortable, but not so upsetting anymore. Lizzy and Kim are in bits though.

When we walk down past all the little shops into town, the apartment blocks are non-existent, just overgrown brambles and a wire fence with a hole in it leading down to the railway line. I smile to myself as I remember the kiss I shared with Rob on the basement level outside Neil Thorpe's flat. I recognise even fewer of the names on the High Street: Woolworths with an enormous rack of sweets in one window by a huge silver Christmas tree; Fine Fare, a supermarket; so many shoe shops with names that sound like comedy acts - Freeman Hardy and Willis, Lilley and Skinner. The shops all have awnings out the front, like the kind on the side of our motorhome back in my 2019, and the shop windows are covered in tinsel and white spray-on snow. We pass a particularly ratchet butcher's window with dead pigs wearing Santa hats labelled Dewhurst's.

Kim has fallen silent, just gazing at everything that she took for granted every day, now changed. Lizzy just says the occasional random thing in shock, like 'Timothy White?'

There are none of the bars, clubs and restaurants that I remember but there are a couple of pubs with exposed wooden beams and hanging signs. At the "Mitre" there is a poster on the open door for a New Year's Eve party 'this Friday'. At least we know where we are now. On one of the shoe shop windows, we are encouraged to "Step into 1972 in style!" The shoes all have chunky platform wedged soles. Even I would look snatched in a pair of those.

The Railway Gardens is deserted. No users, no gangs, no joeys, not even a couple sneaking a grope in the bushes on the way back to the station. There are no flowers, but it looks well-kept. It looks a lot better than the Park. There is a building here and, as we hoped, it is a public toilet.

'Won't it be locked?' Jasper asks. 'To stop people getting

in?'

'I doubt it,' Kim says. 'Why would you want to stop people going into a public convenience?'

Half of the homeless people in town would thank her, I think to myself sadly.

It's open, and inside it's clean and bright and there's not a trace of graffiti to be seen. There's an empty wooden bowl on a stool by the door with a cardboard sign saying "Please Pay for Your Convenience."

We would if we had any funds.

The water is cold, but we clean ourselves as best we can using hard blue industrial tissue paper and soap that smells of nothing. Both mine and Lizzy's jackets are unwearable but not ruined, and there is an old paper Pricerite bag abandoned on a bench by the wall, so we put them inside it. Lizzy drops the bloodied bandage from her ankle into a tall dustbin. *The Truth*, fortunately, isn't damaged. She hands it to Jasper, who puts it in his unbloodied jacket pocket. I'm cold, but there's no point in complaining. It would be a lot worse; it could be snowing out there.

'So it's almost definitely Mum's birthday, so it looks like her key has worked.' Lizzy pats her chest, where the two silver keys hang hidden. 'All we need now is to get home, find the safe, and hide *The Truth*.'

'When you say it like that, it sounds so easy,' I say.

'You mean apart from getting the stab victim from the future, currently up at the General, back home again,' Jasper says, thrusting his hands deep into his own pockets as if he's tucking something away.

'I don't think it's going to be easy at all,' Kim says. 'Did you see the mannequins in the shop window of Chelsea Girl? I know we're in the '70s, but did you see those flares? And the collars on the blouses? They looked like aircraft wings. Don't you think we're all going to stick out like sore thumbs?' We all look down at our skinny, very definitely non-flared jeans, T-shirts and various decades of footwear, definitely not platform.

'Didn't the Beatles wear skinny jeans?' Jasper asks hopefully.

'Drainpipes.' Lizzy nods. 'But we're about five years too late for that look, I think. We just have to brazen it out. Mum said not to interact with people. All we can do is try to do what we came to do.'

Whoever's bright idea it was to walk all the way into town, and all the way back again actually did me a favour. By the time we are standing a little way up the road from Travellers' Rest, I'm as warm as if I was wearing a hoodie. Or a poncho, by the looks of the group walking and laughing ahead of us.

Lizzy doesn't seem able to move her feet. I know how she feels, seeing the home she has grown up in a different time. I've now seen so many different versions of Travellers' Rest that I've forgotten which one was mine. Still, it does seem weird, seeing it stuck out on its own this way, without any of the estate houses to hide it. From here, you can clearly see across to the roofs of Drake's, and the turrets of the Old Library that are linked by tunnel. Right now, the Park just looks like an overgrown garden in between the two buildings.

'Where is everything?' Lizzy is saying.

'Not built yet,' Jasper says. 'You think that's freaky? My own house hasn't even been built in 1987.'

She turns to look at him and then towards me. 'I had no idea what you two were going through,' she says, her eyes downcast. Then she takes a big swallow of air, puts her hands on her hips, and adds, 'Let's go party like it's ...'

'1999?' Jasper suggests, smiling.

'Sounds like a good name for a song,' she says, and she walks off, leaving me, Jasper and Kim to follow in her wake.

The group in front of us look like they walked straight out of a vintage Glastonbury photograph. Long, flowing hair all round, trousers flapping around their ankles like maxi skirts with flowers embroidered on the base, apart from one girl wearing a brown mini skirt with a fringe. One is in a poncho in mustard yellow, and another two are wearing what look like mauve and baby blue cardigans that are way too big for them and come down to the floor. The one in the brown mini skirt is wearing long tight white plastic lace-up boots past her knees with what can't be far off ten-centimetre platform wedged soles, and a huge pistachio green floppy hat. I only realise I'm scoping them out when Jasper closes my mouth.

'Don't stare,' he says. 'We're the weirdoes here, remember? Not them.'

We are never going to get away with this.

Another group appears beside us, and stop. 'Hey there, are you going to Glen's bash?' a tall guy with hair longer than mine and a beard to match asks. He is looking at me like I'm wearing nothing at all.

'Fancy dress,' I squeak, for some inexplicable reason.

FML.

'She means, we thought it was fancy dress,' Jasper says, looking to Lizzy and Kim for support, but they have been struck down by my revelation as the biggest mong this side of the Weydoor.

'We came as the Beatles,' I say in a small voice.

'I'm Paul,' Jasper says, suddenly breathless, and 'and she's John.'

Lizzy's jaw is now hanging open like a dislocation. Kim is buttoning her jacket over her very pink, very not-at-all-like the Beatles, top.

'Right on,' The tall guy says. 'John. Meet the Beatles.' They both grin, but I don't feel like they're laughing at us. Tall's friend John is short and tubby. His flowery shirt hardly covers his stomach, and his collars are nearly as wide as his shoulders, but he has a kind smile, and he looks me up and down. 'Why would you think Glen's party was fancy dress? The invite didn't say anything.'

'We got the wrong end of the stick?' Jasper says it like it's a statement he's hoping they'll believe.

'You'd look better with a pair of round glasses, love,' Tubby John says. 'Mick! Come back here, dude. You need to help the little lady out.'

Little lady?

Mick saunters back, all poncho, collarless shirt and flares flapping around his ankles. With him is a beautiful girl with jet black hair all curled up messily on her head, and another long cardigan over a shorter than short mini dress the colour of wheat and cute little ruffled white ankle boots. It looks like he's cut open the seams and added a red and green coloured zigzag material to make the trousers even wider, and it makes my eyes reel. His top looks like it's made from sacking, but he's wearing a pair of round silver metal-framed glasses. 'Say what?' He looks at me, and to where Kim and Lizzy are standing a little further back. 'Peace, baby.'

'Lady needs your glasses, Mick.' The tubby guy John takes them from his friend's nose.

'No, but won't he -' I stop speaking as he pushes them onto my nose. My vision hasn't changed. The lenses are clear. Mick grins, revealing a gold filling in one of his front teeth, pulls another pair of glasses out of what looks a lot like a tasselly handbag and places them on his nose. 'Always carry a spare, sugar. Those ones are my old man's; he won't miss them. Peace Out.'

'Man, she can't be Lennon. She's got the wrong outfit for Lennon. Only the hair goes with the glasses,' Tall says, perturbed. 'Lennon never wore those glasses until a couple of years ago. He was into the scene by then.'

The girl smiles shyly. 'I think you look groovy,' she says. 'Like the Beatniks.'

Mick grins even wider, flashing the gold again. 'Yeah! Far out! The Beatniks! Jack London!'

The guys walk away. The girl keeps smiling. 'I wish I was brave enough to wear something like that. I think the Beatniks were really groovy.'

'Babs, come on,' John calls. 'We got to book it. This Party Seven isn't going to drink itself!'

She smiles again at us and scuttles after them.

'I have not one clue what any of you were talking about,' Lizzy says, as she and Kim step forward.

'That was the best example of flannel that I have ever witnessed,' Kim says, her eyes wide as she fingers my new glasses.

'What in the name of Sod made you come up with that idea?' Lizzy asks.

'It was Jasper talking about the Beatles wearing drainpipe trousers,' I say.

She gives me a hug, and I swallow my emotion down hard. She has no idea how good it is to see her, listen to her voice, and feel her arms around me. If she notices me overreacting, she says nothing. 'Bloody genius. We have our story, whatever the hell beatniks are. Let's go party with the hippies.'

Chapter Fourteen – Gypsys, Tramps And Thieves (Cher, 1971)

There are groups of people standing all over the front lawn; it doesn't have an apple tree planted in the centre. Everyone is laughing. Everyone has long hair. There is no one else around for miles, apart from maybe the caretaker up at Drake's. Perhaps they don't have one yet; there was no other security.

Despite the cold weather, the windows at the front are open on every one of the three floors. I shudder as I look up to the window where Glenda locked us against our will. I'm still not over that. I haven't had time to process how I feel about my Mum being gone from that version of my future, even though being here with her now makes me feel I can stop that happening somehow. I haven't processed how I feel about Nan being alive and mean in my future. My heart still loves my Nan, and I'm about to meet her as a young woman; I should be excited like I eventually was about Lizzy. Still, she has left a nasty taste in my mouth, like I swallowed too much of her tequila back there.

No one takes any notice of us as we walk down the path; they are all too busy having their good times, so we walk through the open front door into a hallway heaving with even more people. There are more people here tonight than I have ever seen before in my house. This one makes the party here on the night of Lizzy's birthday seem lame.

'It doesn't look anything like my place,' Lizzy hisses

into my ear.

'Of course it doesn't – you don't think your mum might have decorated since she was 21?' I ask.

She shrugs. 'That wallpaper is radical.' With its swirls and enormous bursts of orange and brown, I have to agree with her: the hallway walls are eye-bleedingly loud. 'I'm glad that's gone.'

'Should we go find Glenda and wish her a happy birthday?' Kim asks.

Lizzy shakes her head no. 'We need to try not to interact with anyone, remember?'

'Like the guy who gave Maisie the glasses, you mean?' Jasper asks.

We all look at each other. 'Surely talking to a few randoms on the street isn't going to cause any harm?' Kim asks.

'Bit late to worry about it now,' Lizzy says. 'Mum said the safe where we have to put *The Truth* is in the main bedroom upstairs. There shouldn't be anyone in there.'

'There are people everywhere,' I say, struggling to keep upright as someone pushes past me and giggles out an apology. 'Why would that room be any different?'

'We have to try,' Lizzy says. 'Her bedroom will be on the top floor.'

I glance at Jasper. We know. We met Glenda there a few hours ago in 2019.

It's no more comfortable getting up the stairs. People are sat on them, drinking, smoking and laughing. On the first floor landing, me and Kim manage to drag Lizzy away from the room that is hers in her time, but through the smog and the people, we can just make out brown furniture and a carpet that looks a lot like camouflage for cat sick. The door at the end of the corridor is shut. Lizzy is already walking purposefully towards it when all three of us realise what could be in there.

'Lizzy, no,' I say.

'Surely I'm not in there tonight?' she breathes, but she stops moving. 'I'm only small. Paul's not much older. We'll be with babysitters, won't we? I'm sure Mum said we would be with babysitters.'

'We don't want to take that chance,' Jasper says, jumping in front of her, giving me a frantic look over her shoulder. I know what he's thinking; if Lizzy extinguishes herself at this point, then I'm house dust as well.

'I suppose you're right.' She stares at the door, then she turns and starts to make her way up the second staircase, and it is quieter, although there are still people murmuring and snogging in a couple of the spare rooms, and there's another closed door.

The door to the main bedroom is open, and no one is inside, so we walk in.

I've not been in Glenda's bedroom in 1987, but Lizzy doesn't seem too shocked by what's here, so maybe not all that much has changed. A double bed sits with a quilted beige headboard against one wall, covered in a crocheted blanket. Two fitted wardrobes rise either side, painted in a mushroom colour and a pale pink, and high storage cabinets connect the two across the top. There's a brown wood dressing table in the corner, with a big ornate mirror on the top and lots of little drawers with dark metal fastenings. There's a trunk embroidered in blues, pinks and creams at the side of the bed under the window; it looks faded, although it's not tatty. No TV. The wallpaper is a big swirl of brown, black and orange and the carpet is the same, but with a different pattern – nothing is easy on the eye.

'I'm going to need those glasses before much more of this decor,' Jasper rubs his knuckles into his eyes.

'These won't help, they're clear lenses,' I say. 'Lizzy? What now?'

'Mum said the safe was in one of the wardrobes,' she says, 'so we open them up and have a look.'

She pulls the safe keys out of their safe place in her jeans pocket and pulls open the furthest wardrobe door. Watching her as she gets down on her hands and knees, she pulls out a few boxes containing various colours and styles of men's shoes, and finally, comes out shaking her head. 'Must be the other one.' We put the shoeboxes back in the wardrobe and, by the time we come back to the side nearest the door, she exclaims, 'Bingo,' from under a load of hanging skirt material. I kneel, and I can make out a big grey metal box shoved right at the back. There are more boxes of boots and shoes over the carpet now, and I hear a clunk as Lizzy opens the door to the safe, and a rustle as she pushes *The Truth* from 1987 into its new, old safe place.

As she shuffles back out, red hair all mussed up even wilder than usual and covered in a few cobwebs, she grins up at us, standing behind her. 'Mission accomplished.' Her face pales. 'Oh crap,' she adds. 'The Eagle Has Landed.'

Glenda – and it can only be Glenda, with her shiny conker brown hair waving down her arms, and over her chest, her green eyes sparkling in the light from the streetlights outside

– is leaning on the door frame. Her trousers are flared and embroidered at the bottom with paisley patterns. She's wearing a blouse with an elasticated neckline, and a waistcoat that looks like it's made out of knitted squares. 'Are you nobbling my mother's shoes?' she asks. Before anyone of us can come up with an answer, she bursts into completely unjustified laughter.

'We were looking for the bathroom?' Jasper says, using the same tone that betrays his lack of belief in his answers.

'Why, did you want a bath?' Glenda giggles. It's high-pitched and tinkly. 'Come on; I dig it. Trev's already buried Pop's cardigan in the trifle. He's such a spaz.'

'You're right,' Kim says, glancing nervously at Lizzy, who appears to have turned to stone. 'We were going to apple-pie their bed and put a few shoes in there, but as you say, it's a bit spaz ... zy,' she finishes uncertainly.

'Oh I love a good apple-pie bed,' Glenda claps her hands unevenly, and rushes forward, reaching the bed just in time to catch her fall. 'Come on!'

And for the next five minutes, we are caught in this surrealism, with Lizzy sitting on the floor like she's been struck dumb, watching us and Glenda fold up the blankets and sheets of Glenda's parents' bed - Lizzy's grandparents, my great grandparents - and hiding shoes in the folds so that when they get into bed they won't be able to get their feet in, and they will be lying in a pile of footwear. Glenda is giggling all the time we are doing this, so she doesn't notice that Jasper and me don't know what makes an apple-pie bed; we are just following everyone else's lead. Her sparkly eyes may be more due to the alcohol she's drunk or whatever substances she's taken, but she looks great for a mum with two kids under five, not like so many young mums that I see around town in my time, harassed and sleep-deprived. She's so full of life that it exhausts me to look at her.

When we've finished sabotaging the bed, she sits on the end and rocks a bit. 'I'm sorry,' she says, still giggling, 'but I don't know who you are.'

'John and Babs said it would be okay if we came,' I say quickly.

She claps her hands again. 'Ah, Johnno and Babs. Beautiful couple. He's a dude.' She looks at us again, and her eyes narrow. 'Course it's okay. Interesting threads. Are you Beatniks?'

'They told us it was fancy dress. For a joke,' Jasper says. I hope if she ever asks John and Babs about it that we'll be long gone back through the Weydoor.

'So here's the thing,' Glenda says, and she pulls a roll-up cigarette out from her cleavage that, on second inspection, I realise isn't a cigarette. Something silver catches my eye. 'Got a light?' I shake my head, and Glenda frowns. 'Not even matches?'

'Here.' Lizzy's voice is faint and shaky, but she is holding out her lighter with the flame on full, and Glenda draws on the doobie and breathes out enough smoke to get us all wasted.

'Tonight,' she says, 'I got some heavy news. Did any of you know there's a Time Portal in the Old Library up at Drake's School for Girls?'

Before any of us can mask our reactions, another figure appears in the doorway, but someone has put out the landing light, and I can't make out their features.

'What you hiding up here for, Glen?' a voice asks. Female. Smooth and unstressed. Friendly. Strangely familiar.

'Just talking, Ria.' Glenda staggers to her feet. 'I'm just saying,' she says unsteadily, waggling her finger at us, 'that you never know where people have come from, these days. Now they're talking about us joining the Common Market. They'll be digging a tunnel to France next.' She staggers out to the friend waiting in the shadows, who wraps an arm around her waist, and they disappear.

I look down at Lizzy, who is still frozen, apart from her move with the lighter.

'I think it might be time to see how Scott is,' I say into the silence.

'We need to leave here right now,' she says, and she's on her feet and out of the door before I can blink.

We follow her down the two staircases – she isn't interested in looking into the room that will be hers any more – and the closer we get to the ground floor, the harder it is to move. It feels so cramped that I'm sure even more people have turned up since we were playing weird-ass Victorian parlour games in the bedroom with Glenda. We try to get out the front door, but the flow is in the opposite direction, so we grab onto each other as we are pushed to the kitchen, which seems to be the source of the party.

The kitchen is partly separated now from the dining room by fitted cupboards and cabinets with an open hatch. Someone is cooking toast on an open grill high above the black rings of the cooker hob, and there is a small little unit marked Electrolux next to it. Someone opens that door and takes out a slab of Anchor butter. I can't see a freezer. There is a bulky black box on a rectangular table on the dining side of the unit playing vinyl records, and most people are dancing there if you can call it that since they don't really have room to move -I thought the clubs in town in my time were terrible. I recognise this music. As I've said before, I don't have a thing where music is concerned, but I know this. Mum's played it to me. This is David Bowie's Hunky Dory.

'We need to leave, Maisie,' Jasper says, nodding meaningfully back at Lizzy. She has frozen in time again as she stares at the people dancing to what will become one of her favourite albums. Kim is equally wide-eyed and overwhelmed.

I glance up at the wall. There is still a clock hanging there; I don't know if it's the one with the tick like a jackhammer, and we wouldn't hear it anyway, but it says twenty minutes to eleven. 'Will they let visitors in the hospital at this time of night?' I hiss in his ear as Bowie gets Kooky. 'And where do we go if we can't get in? It's not that cold for December, but I don't want to spend the night out there. Me and Lizzy haven't even got our jackets.'

'You could have mine, but it won't go round you both. Is there a caravan here yet?' he asks. 'Could we camp out down there? '

'Even if it's open, the chances are it's taken,' I say. 'I think our best bet is to stay here, bed down somewhere out of the way and get going as soon as it's light. None of this lot will be awake before midday.'

'Fine,' Kim says. I hadn't even realised she had been listening. 'If we're staying, then I need a bloody good drink. This is all a bit too much. I've had a hell of a day.' And she grabs a bottle labelled Martini Rosso from the open hatch, and slugs it back like lemonade. She's not wrong. We've all had a hell of a day. I've had a hell of five decades.

'Hey chica, save some for the rest of us!' Mick of the spare pair of round glasses appears beside her, and she acknowledges him with the bottle and continues to pour it down her neck. Jeeez.

'Brakes on, honey,' Jasper says, prising the bottle out of her hands and taking a swig himself before passing it across. 'Give the guy a shot.'

'Thanks, dude.' Mick takes a mouthful and shakes his head quickly. 'It's the bright one, it's the right one, it's disgusting. Still, got to get loaded here before we have to pay for the grog. You coming down the Crypt?'

'You're leaving? What about the party?' I ask.

'Be cool, sugar, everyone's going. The gig doesn't start till after hours.' He reaches across towards a big red tin in the hatch labelled Watney's Party Seven.

'Can we come with you?' Kim blurts out. I look over at Lizzy. There's still a glaze in her eyes. Surely it didn't take us as long to adapt to Weirdsville? Guess I'm a better time traveller than my mother. I pick another bottle up from the open hatch without even checking the label, and I thrust it into her hands. 'Drink,' I insist. Getting wasted is the least of our problems.

There's a definite shift in the direction people are moving in after a while. There is suddenly space between me and Mick's tall friend, who turns out to be called Trev, and he's been on something organic. He seems to be hitting on Lizzy who, after downing significant mouthfuls of Carling Black Label and whatever else we could reach from the hatch, is finally beginning to calm down. Kim is pink-cheeked and giggly with a bulbous bottle of Mateus Rosé, and Jasper is brandishing an empty bottle of Blue Nun like it's a baseball bat.

'This stuff tastes like horse piss!' he exclaims.

'How would you know?' Kim pushes him on the arm, and he sniggers.

'Come on, man, we need to shake it,' Trev says. ' Everyone's on the move.' He points at the rapidly emptying kitchen. Bowie has long since stopped singing.

'Won't Glenda be upset if we all leave?' I ask.

Mick laughs and slings a heavy arm around my shoulders. 'It was her idea, sugar. Mater and pater say she has to finish here by midnight, so we're all carrying on down town!'

'What about her kids?' Lizzy asks.

'Jeepers, I don't know. Not coming to the gig with us, anyway.' Trev plants a big kiss on the side of Lizzy's cheek, and she physically jumps. He giggles.

We go out the back door, past an outside toilet with a barn door that a guy forgot to close before he took a pee and before I could unsee it. He just nods and salutes me with his free hand. There's a steady flow of people leaving the house, up onto the road that leads down and joins the Top Road down into town. I've got no idea where we're going, but I've got a feeling we're walking there. I wish my jacket wasn't covered in blood so I could wear it, and then I feel bad for not being more concerned about the welfare of the guy whose blood it is. I'm never going to admit to crushing on such a bastard, but I've always been a sucker for brilliant eyes.

As we walk down the road towards town, I look across the orchard and farmland where Jasper's house will eventually be built. Where there should be a vast complex of lights, there is nothing but darkness.

'What are the visiting hours at the General?' I ask Mick. He's still got his arm around me, but my spider-sense tells me he's harmless; besides he's loaned me his poncho.

'The where?'

'The hospital?' I try.

'Oh, you mean St Pete's. Not sure. Afternoons probably, but tomorrow's New Year's Eve, so not sure they'll allow any visitors.' He gives me a sympathetic smile. 'You know someone in there?' I nod. 'Bummer.' He squeezes me. I feel a pang of guilt about Rob, but Rob's not here, we were pretty much on hold when I left 1987, and I'm not planning on having Netflix n' chills with this likeable hairy monster any time soon.

Don't think about Rob. He's in nappies right now. FML.

Down to the Top Road, down to where it joins the Bottom Road, lit up bright like the Christmas trees I can see through some people's curtains as we walk past, all reds and greens and shiny foil clashing with purple paper bell cut-outs. 'That's well vivid,' I say aloud, thinking of my last Christmas at home with Mum and her fake designer table tree, covered tastefully in minimalistic silver lights and matching tinsel.

'Won't last,' Mick shakes his head, looking more serious than I've seen him all evening. 'The miners are banging their shovels. Wouldn't surprise me if they call a strike in the next couple of months. Man, that'll screw everyone over.' He looks down at me, looking up at him. 'Don't worry, sugar. No one's going to spoil your party tonight.'

Back down into the centre of town, we walk up the High Street and turn up the road that leads up to the hippy shop, Serendipity. This road is now littered with pubs, and they all seem to be vomiting people onto the street. Now I think about it; the middle of Stoneford is as busy now at about half eleven at night as it is at about three in the morning in my time. That poster said New Year's Eve was a Friday, so today is a Thursday, but everyone's out partying. We turn into the road to Trinity, and I'm shocked into statuedom.

Trinity is a church. A real one.

There's stained glass in the big arched window at the front of the building. Instead of a peaked roof with the simple wooden crucifix that reminded us of its history, there is a colossal spire topped by a gleaming golden cross. There's a huge wooden sign next to a streetlight that says, WELCOME TO THE CHURCH OF THE BLESSED HOLY TRINITY, followed by a list of Sunday services.

'Chill out, sugar,' Mick says, 'we're not going to Midnight Mass.'

The line of people in front of us that have snaked their way through town this far is now all walking through the lych gate at the entrance to what is now a pretty little cemetery again.

Kim grabs my other hand, and Jasper stumbles into me. 'Are we going to church?' she hisses at me as if the word is cursed.

'Mick says not,' I hiss back.

Jasper starts giggling. 'I expect I'll spontaneously combust as soon as I cross the threshold with all this booze inside me.'

Lizzy is busy chatting to Trev, but John and Babs catch us up, and realising I'm causing a blockage, I start moving again.

'Are you new to town?' Babs asks, kindly.

'What makes you think that?' Kim asks her.

'You don't know about the Crypt,' she says, stopping abruptly in front of us as we go to walk past a black railing. It's protecting a flight of stone steps leading down apparently into the basement of the church. As we try not to stumble, she points down. Mick smiles at me, and I frown and shrug.

'You found us out,' Kim says. Jasper has stopped and is being shoved a bit as Glenda's ex-party-goers file past us down into the darkness.

'Come on, man, skedaddle,' is about the angriest thing I hear anyone say.

As we follow Lizzy and Trev down the steps and into a darkened doorway, I see a small black plaque nailed to the grey stone, which simply reads, 'The Crypt at Trinity', in a gothic white copperplate.

'You're in for a real treat,' Babs says as we walk down a tunnel-like corridor, lit all red from wall sconces that I think are probably fake flames between the glass, even if they are flickering. I visited caves in Somerset once with Mum, Dad and my brothers in our motorhome, and this reminds me of the walkways. 'Monkey Business are hip. Word is they have a record deal.' She giggles. 'The lead singer looks just like Marc Bolan.'

There is an opening on the right, a ticket booth like the serving hatch at a drive-thru takeaway, but there is no one inside waiting to take our money and stamp our hands. Just as well, we didn't have any cash for 1971, and I couldn't expect these new guys to bail us out. Note to self; if I'm going to make a habit of this time travelling, I need to be better organised. Outfits and money as a minimum.

'Manager here is the lead singer. Ria Bennett's little brother, Frank,' Trev says, turning and walking backwards. 'D'you know them? He's called open house tonight in honour of Glen's birthday. Saved us all the entry price.'

'Just as well, they charge 20 pence a pint here!' John says, from behind me, and I realise he's complaining about it.

'It goes towards helping the tramps,' Babs says. 'Don't complain.'

'What's that in proper coin?' Mick says.

'Four bob,' Trev says.

Mick shrugs at me and shakes his head woefully. 'Four bob a pint. Can't be getting along with this new-fangled money. You?'

I just smile, but I feel better when I look at Lizzy, Kim and Jasper as they look as confused as I feel. I hope he doesn't ask me what I think about the price of his beer; the last one Ani bought me in 2019 cost a fiver so I reckon 20 pence is a bargain.

The floor starts to fall away from underneath us, the ceiling opens out and my eyes adjust and widen as I realise what is in front of us.

Chapter Fifteen – Jeepster
(T-Rex, 1971)

We must be in the basement of the church above us. The space is as big as the hall above where Lizzy sang with Fallen Angel on her birthday, but here the ceilings are much lower, and the red lighting on the walls is so dim that it's hardly worth it being there at all. There is a brighter, whiter light at one end of the room where a few people are serving drinks from a large hatch. There are posters on the walls advertising various bands as we walk down a few shallow steps. I don't recognise any names, but why would I? This is 1971; for all I know, Monkey Business, The Mark Jameson Trio and Jethro Tull are famous now. Underfoot when I walk, the floor is sticky like walking on syrup, and my Converse seem to squelch with every step I take. The air is thick with smoke from various types of cigarette that hangs under the lights like a red veil. Mick asks me if I want a drink, but I shake my head no. I need to sober up; right now it's like I'm standing in the mouth of Hell. He shrugs and disappears into the growing crowd waiting for service at the back with Trev, John and Babs.

Lizzy is at my side suddenly. 'Trinity is a church?' she asks as if we hadn't all seen it with our own eyes.

'A church with a bar in the basement,' I say. A girl skips past us in a floppy cream hat covered in blue and orange plastic flowers, a bright orange and brown zigzagged mini dress that barely covers anything and a pair of white plastic platform boots that finish centimetres above her knees. 'I'm going to need sunnies if I spend much longer in this time,' I say, glancing at Lizzy.

'Bizarre place,' Kim says, appearing on my other side, 'but I like the fashions, actually. Some of those dresses are to die for. I might start wearing hats when we get home.' She looks over at Lizzy. 'Are you okay? With meeting your mum and seeing your house and everything?'

'It was a massive deal,' Lizzy says, 'It's left me a bit shell-shocked, but I'll be okay. She didn't know who I was, after all. The only thing that worried me was -' She stops talking and looks at me. 'I remembered you when you went back to 2019, didn't I?'

A lump forms in my throat. 'Yes, you did,' I manage to say aloud. In the first return, I say just to myself in my head. You didn't make it to the second.

'And things were different?'

'Both times, yes,' Jasper says, saving me from having to answer that one.

Lizzy looks away from us across the room now heaving with bodies and still more flooding down the steps from the tunnel. 'Can't do much about it now,' she says, almost to herself. 'They're coming back. Mick's got the hots for you,' she adds.

'I'm with Rob,' I say shortly. The idea of yet another complicated relationship, this time with a man old enough to be my grandfather is really a step too far. Besides, Mick isn't buff. Not like Rob. Oh, God. I reach into my pocket. The ring is still there. I haven't even had a chance to look at it properly. Let me be able to sort this mess out when we get back to 1987.

'I got you a Tab,' Trev says, holding out a pink can with a red and white stripey straw towards Lizzy.

'That was sweet of you,' Lizzy takes a big suck from the little straw. 'So tell us again who's playing tonight?'

'Monkey Business,' Mick says, appearing and wiping beer foam from his moustache. 'They're local lads. They play covers mainly: T-Rex, Jethro Tull, The Doors, Slade, Small Faces, but Babs heard they got a record deal. The bassist works with her on the record counter at Woollies. Lead singer is great on the pipes. Glen used to go out with him before she got hitched.'

'Yeah man, and we all know that if she hadn't got up the duff with Harry Brookes, she'd be back with him,' Trev says.

As I was letting that one sink in a little, Lizzy asks in a higher pitch than usual, 'With who?'

'Frank Bennett. Ria's little brother. He manages the bar here, and the Rev. lets him use the place for Monkey Business to rehearse and gig.' Mick says. 'He's far out. Coolest dude we know.'

Frank Bennett? Where have I heard that name before 1971?

'Sounds like the Rev. is pretty cool too,' Jasper remarks.

'Well he would be; he's their old man.' Trev doesn't seem to notice that my jaw scrapes the icky on the floor. 'Keep it in the family, like. I'm going down the front,' he adds. 'You coming?'

Mick nods and tries to push me forward, but I swing out of his grip. 'You not digging this?'

I shake my head. 'Happy at the back. You go. Maybe we'll catch up later.'

He nods and begins to slope off; there is nothing extra about Mick. 'Laters, sugar,' he says with a wave. Trev blows Lizzy a kiss, and she smiles and waves him off. Then she turns back to us all with a face like a slapped kitten. 'Frank Bennett?' she repeats. 'Who the hell is Frank Bennett?'

'The bloke who was seeing your mum before she got married,' Kim says. 'She would have had boyfriends before she met your dad. You know this. Don't have a pink fit.'

'I'm sure I've heard that name before,' I say.

'She was only 17 when she fell for Paul,' Lizzy replies. 'Mum told me she was terrified that my gran was going to kick her out to a mother and baby home, being unmarried, and my gran being a bit straight-laced. But my gran let her stay, on the condition that my dad married her.'

'They called him Harry, but his name's Henry,' I say. 'Like Prince Harry is really a Henry, I guess.'

'What if she didn't want to marry him?' Lizzy says, and her eyes are suddenly brighter than they were, reflecting the warm glow of the red lighting. 'What if she wanted to marry Frank?'

'She was having Harry's baby,' Jasper says, 'so she married him.'

'Something doesn't smell right at all,' Lizzy says, but before she can carry on, a blast of sound ripples across the room and reduces us all to silence. Nothing can be heard above the guitar screeches that are coming from the front of the big room.

I have heard of Marc Bolan, but I can't remember what he looks like so I don't know if Frank Bennett looks like him or not. He's wearing nothing over his chest except a flowery blazer, along with a pair of flared purple trousers. His red hair is curly and past his shoulders. He looks vaguely familiar, but I can't place him, so maybe I have seen photos of Marc Bolan after all.

Red hair.

I look again. Surely with all the red lighting in the room, it must be an effect, but the tower stage lights at each side of the stage are a chill white, and there's no mistaking that colour. I glance across to Jasper and Kim, trying to work out if they have noticed the latest elephant in the crypt, but they are too busy listening to the music. It's a bit heavy for me, but I've heard worse. I risk a look at Lizzy, but her face is a mask. Is she thinking the same as me, that if Harry Brookes and Frank Bennett both had red hair -?

Suddenly I have a terrible headache, and I need to sit down. There are some simple wooden benches at the side of the room that look like they might have been in the church before they ended up down here. I stagger over and drape myself over one, my head in my hands. It isn't long before I can feel someone sitting beside me.

'Is this what they call Glam Rock?' Jasper says into my ear. I shrug. 'The singer looks very glam. That's Frank, isn't it? The red-headed guy? Do we know him?'

I sit up and look at him. 'Leave me here to drown in the sewage that is my family's history,' I mouth at him.

He shakes his head no and leans closer again. 'What's the point in having a benny now?' he says. 'Four days ago, we were sitting in P.S., moaning that nothing ever happened. All we had to look forward to this summer was revision and zero-hours contracts at Maccy-Ds.' I can't help but smile. I remember that convo. It feels like it was last year, but in terms of days, it probably is no more than three or four.

'Then Ani got all high-key about what Orla told her, and we ended up here.'

'During which time you have faced far worse than a couple of guys having red hair,' he adds. 'So your granddad and that Frank guy have red hair. I have brown hair, does it mean I'm Son of Rob?' He shakes his head.

'It's just too much to deal with,' I say, leaning into him; Jasper, my blud, my rock. 'You think this is easy? Travelling through time with my teenage mum, meeting dead rellies and falling for -' I stumble on an appropriate adjective.

'Old guys?' Jasper says, helpfully.

'Yes, thanks very much.' I punch him lightly.

'Of course I don't think it's easy. We need to leave.'

'Be serious, Jas. Last time we went home, it wasn't home. Mum wasn't there. Nan was a Nazi. It was like something out of The Hunger Games. I can't go back there. We can't go back there.'

He took a few moments before he replied this time. 'Maybe as long as we don't extinguish, maybe we just have to end up wherever we feel we belong.'

I look over at him, and his eyes are glistening red in the reflected lights in the ceiling above us. 'You've changed your story.'

'You know I used to want to go home, back to 2019, but that 2019 died as soon as we went through the Weydoor, and you're right – the last time we went back was a dystopian Hell. There's no point in losing my shit over it. It's just the way it is. Anyway, because of you being Weyfare, we can return any time we like to the moment we left, but maybe what we have to do is find a way to rebuild our timeline. How we do that, I have not one idea.'

'If I travel for too long on the Weys, I'll end up like my mum,' I say bleakly.

'Your mum travelled for the best part of 30 years on the Weys before she got sick,' Jasper says firmly. 'We've been travelling for four days. Don't expect to be seeing any crows' feet on those eyes any time soon.'

Love my Jasper. He always makes me laugh. 'Since when did you get all philosophical? You're supposed to be the worrier.' I nudge him in the ribs.

'I figured there was little point in worrying when Scott turned up all stabbed,' he says. 'You can't feel sorry for yourself when you're not the stabbed guy. Thing is, Maisie, I thought he was the bogeyman, but in all the stories I ever read, the bogeyman doesn't get stabbed.'

I rub my hands over my face. 'I can't process all of this,' I say. 'Scott, Mum, Rob, Glenda – 1970s hippyville; my brain is going to explode.'

'Scott isn't our problem. He's in the best place to get help – well, he's in the best place in 1971.'

'But he is my problem,' I say, and the words that tumble out of my mouth into his ear are only leaving my brain nanoseconds before. I do not have time to process what I'm saying. 'I am Weyfare. Scott doesn't belong here. Neither does Ani. Neither do you. None of us has a life here. You talk about pitching up somewhere we feel safe, but I'm not sure I feel safe here.'

'Can't we just find somewhere we feel we do belong?' he asks.

'I don't know,' I say. 'I don't know where to go anymore. I'm not sure we belong anywhere. We may not have extinguished, but do we actually have a timeline any more? I am Weyfare too,' I say, a chill on my skin that I hadn't noticed before. 'I can't just ignore it. Getting people home is my life now. Mine and Lizzy's. We can't leave Scott here.'

'But the longer we stay here, the more we change.' He takes hold of my hand, and I know it's important; he doesn't do this very often. 'Lizzy put *The Truth* in the safe, that was what we came here to do. Why are we sitting in the bowels of Trinity listening to Frank Bennett warble out some song about Jeeps? Maybe by putting *The Truth* in the safe, we have made everything right.'

'Or worse.'

Whatever he was about to say, Jasper was stopped dead by the sudden darkness that dropped over us like a suffocating blanket. The music died out, the lights faded to nothing and people started talking loudly. I couldn't make anything out except black shapes moving around me.

'What's happening?' I hear Jasper ask someone nearby.

'It'll be the bloody strikes again,' came the reply.

Someone starts shouting at us from somewhere to all leave the building. I am overwhelmed with an urge to run away screaming, but Jasper takes my hand and stops me freaking out. I realise that everyone else is reacting calmly; there are no hard words, no anger, no shouting, no problem.

We file out of the crypt as if we are taking a walk in the Park, not that it's much of a Park now. If anyone had panicked, it would have been a disaster. Still, no one did, everyone talks and laughs as if it is just another part of the evening they expected. We move out onto the side of the road beside the big church, two or three hundred people just standing around in the darkness – even the streetlights are out.

There's a hand on my shoulder, and I turn to see Kim, with Lizzy, Mick and Babs.

'There you are!' Kim exclaims and throws her arms around my neck. 'What a nightmare!'

'Be cool,' Babs says. 'It's all groovy, it's just another power cut. Happens all the time around here. Where do you normally hang out?' she asks. 'Don't you get this a lot?'

'Not so much,' I say.

'Hey dude, chill. We're all cool. We're all here. What you doing for digs tonight?'

'Digs?' Lizzy asks.

She frowns. 'Do you have a place to sleep? You're welcome to bunk down at ours. You won't get a train out of Stoneford if the power's gone down.'

I can't even. I know Jasper is looking at me, reminding me of what he told me, the things he said to me that I already know. We need to leave 1971, we weren't supposed to stay this long, and we have no idea what more damage we're doing by hanging around. I know I would tell him again that I won't leave Ani here, or Scott for that matter, so there is no point in looking at him or any of them. I choose to back off and let someone else make the decisions.

'We could do with somewhere to kip,' Lizzy says, into the silence.

'Groovy,' Babs says. 'Stay here, and I'll go find Johnno and Trev.'

Mick approaches me as Babs walks away, and I look way

up into his Labrador eyes. 'Hey sugar,' he says, 'am I right in feeling that you aren't digging a connection between us?

How do you answer that? What does it even mean? 'I'm with someone,' I say.

Mick raises his hands and blows on each palm. 'Then it was a gas. Peace out, sister.' He walks away, and I'm not sure what he's said, but I think we parted on good terms.

'Is this really a good idea?' Jasper asks.

'What do you suggest – sleeping under the non-existent Willow?' I reply.

'It's too cold to crash in the Park,' Kim says. 'Not that it's much of a Park.'

'Only other option is going back to my place,' Lizzy suggests.

'Lizzy, it isn't your place, is it?' Kim says, surprising all of us. 'and sooner or later, you're going to show up there as a toddler, so surely it won't hurt to sleep on Babs' floor?'

'We can go and see Scott and Ani first thing in the morning,' I say.

'If they let us in,' Jasper remarks.

Babs doesn't just live with John. She lives with John, Trev, Mick and a couple of other girls on the top floor of one of the big townhouses on Tracy Rutherford's road, up the hill from the train station. Unlike Tracy's massive house with a swimming pool in 1987 (home of the barbeque we never got to eat), this place has been divided up into apartments. It's a bit of a climb, and it's pitch black.

It's hard to tell in the dark, but once they've lit a few thin white candles and balanced them on a few white plates, I can see it must have been an attic floor once because there are no walls, apart from the bathroom at one end. The kitchen is like the camping stove we had in our motorhome, and there are low beds scattered around the sloping walls. Old-fashioned green fabric hospital screens give the illusion of privacy.

'It's not much, but it's home, and the rent's cheap,' Bab says cheerily, going across to a cupboard unit and pulling out a couple of bottles labelled Black Tower. 'Best thing is no olds to order you about. Life's good.' She screws the top off the black bottle, takes a big swig and offers it to us. Jasper is the only one who accepts, and, by the look of his face when he swallows, the rest of us made the right decision.

There are a few brightly patterned rugs on the floor in the middle of the room, and everyone seems to be settling there, so I sit down crosslegged as Trev grabs a candle and puts it down in the middle. John puts some music on, and it sounds like everything I'd ever thought the '70s were like.

'Gotta love me a bit of the Jethro Tull,' he says happily, but as he goes to wrap an arm around Babs, there is a sound in the doorway, and it looks like a few more people have joined us.

'Frank!' Mick is on his feet. 'Dude! What a gas!'

'Far out, man.' Frank steps forward into the candlelight, still wearing his flowery blazer jacket under a long grey coat with woolly edges. 'Room for a few more? We bought some gear.' He dangles a small paper bag at the room, and his friends come into the dim light.

Babs claps her hands. The light may be dim, but it's clear enough to see. I'm not bothered by the arrival of the crow; I'm more concerned about the arrival of Glenda and the sleeping toddler in her arms.

Chapter Sixteen – Baby Jump
(Mungo Jerry, 1971)

'You bought the sprog?' John asks.

'Babysitter was only paid up until eleven.' Glenda steps further into the room.

Kim is a few steps ahead of me, as we struggle to our feet and try to shield Lizzy from the toddler. Not that the toddler can see anything with its face turned away into Glenda's chest, but Lizzy can. I don't know how we can explain it if she starts hurling chunks over the sheepskin rugs. Glenda is tickling it under the chin like an expert.

'Your little girl is so adorable,' Kim says. 'What's her name?'

'His name is Robbie,' one of the other girls says pointedly, and suddenly the situation has got better and worse all at the same time. She takes the little boy from Glenda's arms, and ruffles his dark mop of hair.

'Mine are with Mum and Pop,' Glenda says. 'Special treat because it's my birthday. Ria here had to go and pick Robbie up.' Kim's mouth falls open. I stare into a pair of green eyes that I last saw at Lizzy's 18th birthday party. It can't be. I can't even.

'I've dunked his dummy in the gin at least six times to try and get him to go down, but he won't sleep,' Ria frowns. 'Do I know you?'

'Abso-fucking-lutely not,' Jasper says, backing away

fast from the bundle in her arms as if it's radioactive. 'We've never met.'

She looks a bit confused at his reaction, which I guess is extreme, but she holds out her free hand to me. 'Ria.'

I step forward, take it and shake it limply, feeling as if I've been sucker-punched. I look down again at the bundle in her arms, and her toddler is staring at me, green eyes wide and innocent. Kim's eyes are not moving from the top of little Robbie's head. Why did we fear this sweet dark-haired baby was red-haired Lizzy Brookes? As if Glenda would turn up with only one of her children anyway. Now it seems the toddler is actually little Rob Simmons, and it isn't any better. Aged about two, I guess, he's sucking on a pacifier laced with alcohol while his mother hits another party. Surely he'll not remember us, being so young, but it is freaking me royally that I have now met my boyfriend both as a middle-aged man and a toddler.

'Ria!' Babs repeats into the silence where I should be telling Ria my name. 'Awww, look at your little fella all conked out.'

'Can I put him down somewhere? He weighs a fucking ton,' Ria says, and, finding an old quilted leather sofa against one of the walls, rolls Rob onto it, and he curls up, eyes rolling back in his head, the gin finally starting to take effect. 'Chuck us up a blanket.' One of the guys throws her something that looks more like a rug made out of knotted ropes. She slings it over the top of her little boy, joining the two guys she came in with on the mats in the middle of the room, almost instantly lighting a cigarette. It's a wonder any of these kids survived to have us.

Frank is passing the substances around; I decline because one of us needs to keep a clear head, but Jasper, Kim and Lizzy are all over it.

'I'm Ria – and you are?' Ria asks Lizzy.

'Beth,' she says firmly. At least someone is thinking ahead. That's good to know. 'Kim – Jasper – Maisie.' She points to us each in turn.

'Oh, my youngest is called Elizabeth, but we call her Lizzy,' Glenda says. 'Sweet little thing. Though her dad says she's got a temper like a banshee already.'

Lizzy smiles and looks just a little bit smug.

'What time does Harry knock off work?' Babs asks Glenda.

She shrugs. 'Six. Just in time to look after the kids when I go to bed with a colossal hangover.'

'He's at work on your birthday?'

'He's on nights,' she explains. 'Up at St Pete's.'

'This is Ted. He's my worse half,' Ria says. Ted salutes us like we're soldiers, and almost instantly looks away as if he's forgotten us. 'And that's Frank, my little brother.' She takes the joint being passed to her and takes a slow, deep drag.

'Are you having a groovy birthday, Glen?' Frank asks, his hair pretty much covering his face.

'Fab,' she says. 'I got a necklace from the olds. It's … really old.' She giggles. 'A ring. Oh, and I got this watch too, look.'

She thrusts a slender arm under Franks nose revealing a sweet little gold watch, and Frank brushes the hair back from his eyes. As I finally get to look at him close up, it's like someone has punched me hard in the guts for the second time. He has long curly red hair past his shoulders, and yet he's still a fit guy with cheekbones like a supermodel. Unlike so many guys we've met tonight, his face isn't covered in a beard or moustache. Now I know that Rob Simmons is passed out on the sofa under a rug, I've finally worked out who this guy is. Last time I saw him, he was bald and wearing baggy overalls. Rob's Uncle Frank, the caretaker at Drake's School.

Suddenly there are too many repeats on this channel. I stand up so quickly, I nearly stagger into the lit candle.

'Whoa, be cool, princess. Who yanked your chain?' John laughs.

'I need some fresh air,' I say. 'Lizzy? Can we bounce?'

Luckily she catches on to my meaningful look. 'Definitely time for a bounce,' she agrees. 'Kim?'

Kim coughs pathetically. Jasper grabs hold of her hand. 'We'll be right back,' he says importantly, but these people are so laid back they're horizontal. They hardly seem to register that we're leaving the room, let alone think it's weird AF.

Leaving the main door to all the flats on the latch, we step out into what is now a very icy night. The pavements are sparkling in the moonlight as if a child has thrown sheets of silver glitter across them. The streetlights are still out. One car passes us on the road out of town.

'What's going on?' Lizzy asks. 'What's with the major dramatic exit?'

'We're being seen by too many people who know us in 1987,' I explain. 'Glenda was never going to be a problem, Lizzy – when we go back, she will just remember she met us tonight, and it'll be fine.'

'Assuming she doesn't get so stoned that she forgets it

ever happened,' Kim comments.

'Whatever,' I say. 'But that baby is Rob. Our Rob. So Ria and Ted are his parents, and Frank is his uncle.'

'Shit!' Jasper exclaims. 'Uncle Frank! I knew I'd seen him somewhere before! He's the caretaker who let us into Drake's to look for *The Truth*!'

'I think you're affected by the fumes,' Lizzy says, frowning. 'Rob's Mum's called Valerie, not Ria. Oh!' She put her hands over her mouth.

'So Ted is Eddie!' Kim says. 'Rob calls his dad Eddie.'

'Henry, Harry. Valerie, Ria,' I say. 'Ted, Eddie. Different decades, different names, same people. It's not okay that they've seen us in 1987, Lizzy. Even if me and Jasper go back to 2019, (even if the very thought of it makes me want to vom on the spot), they will recognise you and Kim when you go back, and they will wonder what the hell is going on.'

There is a weird noise like crackling in the air, and the streetlights flicker on overhead, bathing our pale faces in an orange glow. Lights appear behind closed curtains down the street like stars appearing in the night sky and, upstairs in the attic flat, there is a cheer.

'I can't not see Val and Eddie again,' Lizzy says quietly. 'I've known Rob forever. We were at the same junior school and everything. He's going to think it's bizarre if I never go around to his house again.'

'You can tell him why though,' I say. 'He knows about the Weyfarere now.'

She looks a little less stressy. 'Maybe we can tell Val and Eddie as well then?'

'Why not throw in the whole hand and tell Frank too?'

Jasper asks. 'Why not just post it on *Facebook*? In the Free ads, I mean.' He shakes his head and rolls his eyes.

'That's got to be up to Lizzy and Glenda,' I reply. 'Personally I think there are too many people finding out about our... your business and it can't be good.'

'We should probably leave now,' Kim says, hugging herself. 'Maybe if we leave now, they won't remember us. I'm sure I don't remember every single person I've ever met at a party.' She looks down at the pavement. 'Not that Monster and Dad ever let me go to all that many.'

'That's because they are evil.' Lizzy throws an arm around Kim's shoulder and hugs her tightly, and some of the confidence that seems to have worn a bit thin over the last few hours appears again in her eyes. 'And it's all going to change. Look at how many adventures you've already had since you left home.'

Kim smiles, but it's watery.

'Well, if we're leaving, where do you suggest we sleep? In a shop doorway? We'll all catch hypothermia,' Jasper says, 'and I can't share my jacket between three of us.'

'Church,' Lizzy says. 'Trinity's a church. Aren't they places of sanctuary?' She looks at Kim, whose parents went to services all the time.

'Search me,' Kim says, 'Ours always felt like a prison to me.'

'But they are left open, aren't they? In case people need to pray in the night or confess to something?' Lizzy asks. Kim shrugs. 'Let's go try. We can't go back up there;' she nods at the light on the top floor; 'Maisie's right. And if we can't get into Trinity, looks like we'll be bunking down in the public loos by the station. We go find Scott and Ani in the morning, and then we get the hell out of here. *The Truth* is in the safe at Travellers' Rest. We've done everything we came here to do. Scott won't ever see the book, so he can't tell the mystery woman at the shop about it.'

'By the looks of that wound he had, he may never get the chance to tell anyone anything again,' Kim says. As no one can think of a reply to such a comment, we turn and begin a slow trudge back down towards town and Trinity again.

At least the lights are on now. A clock chimes the single hour. One o'clock in the morning. New Year's Eve. For everyone else in Stoneford apart from us, it's the day before 1972. I haven't got a clue which year we're going to end up in next.

The Church of the Blessed Holy Trinity is open, but it's not much warmer in there than on the bench under the lych gate. We're surprised to find a few coats hanging up at the back, and blankets in a pile by the font. We make our way down the middle aisle and sit down on the pews, quietly so as not to draw attention, in case we're not supposed to be here. When my eyes adjust, I realise why there are coats and blankets at the back of the church. Here and there, single dark shadows are dotted around, sitting huddled on the pews. I'm glad – it's too cold out there to be without shelter.

I don't have any religious beliefs, but there is something about sitting in a vast cavernous church at night, with just the streetlights outside burning through the stained glass, casting fractured colours all over the stone floors in front of you – it focuses the mind. At the front of the church is a single wooden cross on a brass stand, with a single spotlight shining over it.

I've been staring at it for so long that it's mesmerising, and I only come to my senses when Lizzy nudges me.

'It doesn't feel like the same place,' she whispers. 'Where we had my party, I mean.'

'Well, it isn't really. Sometime in the next few years, someone must decide that they don't want it to be a church any more.'

'Deconsecration,' she says.

'Isn't that something that happens in horror movies?'

'The house in *Poltergeist* was built on a deconsecrated cemetery. Except I don't think they've made that film yet,' she says.

'Trinity never felt scary.' I look around. 'It's a place of safety now.'

She lays her head on my shoulder, and it's warm and comforting. The slow, rhythmic breathing on the other side of me suggests that Jasper and Kim have fallen asleep. 'You're pretty cool, you know,' Lizzy says after a while.

'Me? Why?'

'All this time travel crap. I'm supposed to be born into this ancient Weyfarere family, destined to devote my life to helping people get back to their right time, and I'm a complete fuck-up. Look at that pink fit I threw when we met my Mum. Glenda. I couldn't say a word for nearly five minutes. I couldn't even deal with the wallpaper being different. But you just take it in your stride. 1987. 1971. You got back home, and then you even came back again, just to help me out.' She turns her head and looks up at me, and I can just make out her eyes twinkling in the light shards from the window; the irises look red like foxes in the dark, but I guess that's just a trick of the stained glass. 'Just how well do I know you in the future?'

I hope she can't hear my heart hammering from where she rests on my shoulder. 'You know it's not a good idea for me to tell you that, Lizzy.'

'But I am a close friend of your mum's.'

'As close as you can get,' I agree.

I feel her nod. 'Want to compare keys?'

So in the early hours of the morning, under the watchful severe stone eyes of saints and martyrs and plaques commemorating Stoneford's great and useful, we take out the symbols of our own new faith: the keys of the Weyfarere. It's the first time I've looked at mine since Older Lizzy gifted it to me in the first alternate 2019. The top is ornately twisted into three never-ending loops like an optical illusion, embedded with tiny dark grey stones, hanging on a silver chain-like thin rope. Lizzy is now wearing two keys: her own on a chain similar to mine but thicker, given to her by Glenda to replace the one that Scott Kelly broke. The key itself is plainer, though the same dark grey stones are set into the three interlocking circular part that you hold. The key that Glenda lent to her to get us here is even more flashy with the little dark grey stones making petals around tiny pearls to make a flower of the circles on the handle.

We gaze at them for a bit.

'Did I tell you who that one belongs to when I lent it to you?' Lizzy asks.

'No,' I lie.

'And why did I lend it to you again?' she asks.

A shiver of concern tickles my spine. 'So I could go home again,' I say. 'The older you didn't know about the blood thing.'

'But you could had your whatchamacallit,' Lizzy continues. 'Your calculator?'

I try not to fidget. Lizzy is talking about the smartphone we used to get us all to 2019 the day Scott went rogue. 'I think maybe you wanted us to unlock the tunnel door. You expected the doors to be locked when we travelled back. You knew Kim's necklace would bring us back to 1987.'

'Oh. Yeah, I s'pose,' she replies, not sounding all that sure at all, and let's face it, it's a lame reason to lend someone a valuable silver key – close family friend or no.

'What are you going to do about Scott?' I ask her, hoping to take her mind off the key.

Lizzy sighs, and puts the two keys back under her top, wrapping the coat back over her. ' I ought to hate him, you know? But he's so dishy. Those eyes -' Her quiet voice fades, and we both sit there in silence for a few moments considering the hottie that is Scott Kelly. 'I know, I'm shallow.'

'No, I get it. Besides, he's hurt. And we can't leave him here. He doesn't belong.'

'Exactly. He tried to mug me,' she says, 'but I don't wish him dead.' She gives me a cheeky smile. 'You think Rob is a keeper?'

'If he is, I'm not sure I get to keep him,' I say. 'You think I've got this time travel thing down dope, and it's easy for me, but it's not. You have no idea.'

'Well, yeah I do,' she replies.

Duh. Of course, she does. 'Sorry.'

'No matter. What I don't get is what it must be like to get the hots for a bloke who's on a different time scale. Timeline. Thingy. Jeeez!' she exclaims, and then looks up as if she expects lightning bolts to strike her through the head. 'Sorry, God. It's just I need to read more of *The Truth*. I need to understand what's going on.'

You and me both, Mum. 'Perhaps you need to get another translation done,' I say, 'since whoever wrote yours can't tell the difference between the Middle English for blood and keys.'

'Good point,' she says. 'Maisie, listen. I can't just be stuck here in town for the rest of my life pushing people back through the Weydoor. It doesn't seem right! It seems like such a bloody waste. I had plans, you know? InterRail and TEFL training.'

I can't think of anything comforting to say to either of us, and I guess we must both drop off to sleep.

Sometime later, I jolt awake, as if someone has shaken me. I look at Lizzy, and she is staring forward, motionless as if she has just seen a ghost, or something equally terrifying.

'Lizzy?' I ask her, turning and following the track that her eyes are taking, to a small, dark blue prayer book, left out on the back of our pew from the last lot of services. She is staring at the little book as if it is confusing her. 'Is something wrong?'

'Look at the inscription on the prayer book,' she says.

I look again. A small, dark blue book, bound in some kind of thin material, *The Book of Common Prayer* sits on the narrow shelf and at the bottom is an emblem. I'm guessing it's the symbol that the church uses; I vaguely remember seeing it on the board outside the lych gate as we went to the Crypt earlier this evening.

Then I blink and look again at the intricately inter-woven three circles that form the top part of the cross. At the bottom, two clear teeth spread out to the left, and the pieces that are cut out form another cross on its side.

It is a key.

It is the same bloody key that's hanging around our necks.

Chapter Seventeen – Brand New Key (Melanie, 1971)

'What the hell?' I say before I can stop myself. Jasper stirs, turns a little, and continues to sleep.

Lizzy thumps me hard on the arm. 'Maisie! We're in church!' she hisses.

'I don't see any lightning bolts. I'm sorry, but that's just mad,' I whisper back. 'You know it is: you made me notice it! Why is there a Weyfarere key on the symbol for this church?'

'Maybe it just looks like our keys?' Lizzy asks, unsurely.

'You didn't think so, or you wouldn't have woken me up,' I say, and now Jasper reaches over and nudges me roughly with his arm. The message is clear. 'You were staring at it like you'd seen a ghost,' I hiss, more quietly.

'A ghost of a chance. Okay, it is our keys. What are the chances of it being a coincidence that a Weyfarere key is part of the symbol for this church?' she asks.

'Not a lot, when you put it that way.'

She stands up and stretches, and I realise that I have been able to see the little symbol on the book quite clearly because there is a greyish light filtering through the coloured glass. It's morning. We must have been asleep for a while. 'We need to get up to the hospital,' Lizzy says. 'We need to get Scott, and get the hell out of Dodge.'

'Shouldn't we try to find out more about the link between Trinity and the Weyfarere?' I ask.

'If there is a link, Mum will know about it. Proper Mum, not Now Glenda,' she says. A man in a grubby coat the colour of strong tea shuffles past us towards the exit. I look at his feet: he's wearing trainers the same colour as mine. Poor guy looks like he hasn't washed in a week. At least Trinity is open so they can shelter from the cold.

Jasper and Kim take their time to wake up, and even longer to take on board what we're telling them about the symbol. We leave the blankets where we found them, but we borrow a couple of the coats – Lizzy assuring someone's God that we would bring them back again - and step out into the drizzle of the last December morning of 1971. A mist hangs over the spire, obscuring its golden cross. As we pass through the lych gate, I catch sight of the wooden board announcing Trinity's status in town, and my tongue gets stuck in the back of my throat.

'Lizzy,' I manage to growl out loud. 'Stop. Look.'

All three of them look at the writing underneath the welcome. Above the list of Sunday services, there is another line that I missed last night.

'Come hither ye all who have lost their Wey,' Kim reads.

Beneath the words is another Weyfarere key symbol.

'Wey – with a capital letter,' Jasper remarks.' And an e.'

'We haven't got time for this now,' Lizzy mutters. 'We have to find Scott and Ani. That's more important.'

I think Trinity's link to the Weyfarere is probably pretty important too. Still, I can't make a fuss about it because it isn't supposed to be that big a deal to me. We do need to find Scott and Ani, but this latest weirdness needs to be discussed at some point.

'So are we heading over to the General?' Jasper asks.

'Mick had never heard of it when I asked,' I say. 'He talked about somewhere called St Peter's. Have you heard of it?' I ask Lizzy.

She nods. 'I was born there. I think they knocked it down or converted it into flats or something when they built the General. Mum had Paul and me there. I don't know where it is though.'

'Well, there must be a shop open by now so we can ask inside,' I say, wrapping the scratchy old coat tighter around me. 'It's Friday, isn't it?'

'New Year's Eve,' Jasper pushes his hands deeper into his pockets. 'It's not a bank holiday in 1971, is it?'

Lizzy shakes her head no. 'Pretty sure not, but only one way to find out,' she says.

The Railway Gardens and the Station are at the far end of the High Street where it meets the bottom of Town Hill; at the other end of the High Street is St Peter's Hill. The newsagent on the High Street was busy filling racks in front of his shop with the final daily papers of the year when we passed. His shopfront was still covered in blue and red tinsel and flashing green and red fairy lights. He told us where St Peter's Hospital is: at the bottom of St Peter's Hill opposite a bus station. There's a Mall there in 2019, and the Bus Station is underneath it in a long, noisy tunnel usually filled with kids from villages on the outskirts of town that travel in for school, but it's still called St Peter's Hill.

'Bloody obvious really,' Lizzy says, echoing my thoughts as we stand in front of the building.

St Peter's doesn't look like a hospital. It seems more

like a small stately home like a mini *Downton Abbey* squeezed in between a load of terraced brick houses stained with years of soot. There is a car park in front, but there aren't many cars in it, and the ones that are there are all sharp lines and right angles; they look like the pictures of cars that toddlers draw. As we walk past them towards the entrance, I see a few names on the back that read like another language: Zephyr, Corsair, Viva and Maxi.

As we walk into the entrance, the smell of bleach hits me like a fist. Kim starts coughing. In the corner there is a man in a beige overall, sweeping the floor. Someone has thought to put a few straggly lines of shiny foil decorations around the outside of the large room, and a single limp yellow paper star hangs at one end of the strip light. He looks at us, shakes his head, and continues to sweep. Behind a counter like a hotel receptionist, sits a woman in a knitted cardigan that exactly matches the jumper underneath, a necklace of a double row of pearls on top. There is a bright red miniature tinsel tree next to a round silver table bell.

'Can I help you?' she asks, in a tight, prim little voice. I ignore the fact that she has just looked us up and down like a total biatch.

'Yes, I hope so.' Lizzy strides across the shiny tiled floor. 'We were told our friend Scott was bought in last night.'

Kim sniffs loudly. 'Poor *cousin* Scott,' she says pointedly.

Lizzy frowns at her and then catches on. 'Yes, sorry, poor *cousin* Scott. He was... attacked.'

'What's the full name, please?' Pearls asks, flicking through a file of paperwork.

'Scott Kelly. Our cousin is with him. Jane Doe,' Jasper says. 'She told us he was here.'

Pearls continues to flick through her paperwork, glancing up at us every now and then. Look, we slept last night in a church and me and Lizzy are wearing donated coats, I want to tell her. We're from the future. You try looking your best in a time when the guys have longer hair than the girls, when you've recently discovered your mother's dead and your grandmother wants to lock you up like a criminal. Just tell us where he is.

Eventually, Pearls looks up at us. 'Are you related to Jane Doe?'

'Absolutely yes,' Jasper says, way too enthusiastically. 'She's our sister. We are the Doe family. Mum just kept breeding. It's hard to get any privacy in our house.' He stops talking, aware that everyone is staring at him.

'You said Jane was your cousin?' Pearls asks.

'Jane is our sister,' he finishes simply.

Pearls is staring at him as if he needs to be admitted to hospital, but she closes her file sharply and points towards a lift, covered across with a metal shutter like black tessellated diamonds. 'Matron has noted here that you are expected. Fifth Floor from Lift Three. CC Ward.' Suddenly she looks apologetic and her whole approach changes. 'CC Ward? Golly Gee. At least the waiting room up there is nice and warm. I hope your cousin is okay. Happy New Year,' she adds, as we all walk away.

'Should old acquaintance be forgot,' Lizzy says, as we walk over to the rickety-looking lift.

'CC Ward?' Kim whispers in my ear.

I point at a white enamel notice on the wall next to the

lift. The fifth floor is home to the Critical Care Wards. We get into the lift. Lizzy pulls across the metal shutters, and no one says another word until the doors open onto a long corridor, painted the colour of mouldy cheese.

Opening the metal shutters again, we step out into a cold and characterless corridor. Above our heads, a metal sign swings gently in a breeze from somewhere.

'Critical Care. Please report to Matron and wash your hands in the sinks provided,' Jasper reads. 'Matron? Seriously? Like in those *Carry On* films from the sixties with that lady with the huge boobies?'

'Hattie Jacques,' Kim says. 'It's 1971. Those films are new.'

'And completely sexist,' I say. 'I saw that one where Barbara Windsor from *Eastenders* is all dressed up like a sex worker in a nurse's uniform.'

'Barbara Windsor is in *Eastenders*?' Kim asks.

'Those *Carry On* films aren't that bad. It's only a bit of smutty humour. Do they really get offended about a bloke smacking a woman on the arse in your time?' Lizzy asks.

'Too right they bloody do,' Jasper says, 'and men do too!'

Lizzy rolls her eyes at us. 'Remind me not to visit any time soon.'

We approach the desk at the end of the long corridor, but as she reaches out her hand towards a little round silver dome, there is a noise behind us, and Ani appears from what looks like a waiting room at a train station.

'In here!' she whispers urgently.

Once inside the little room with its shabby black plastic seats and a low coffee table covered in magazines such as

Horse and Hound, the *Lady* and *Punch,* Ani closes the door behind us.

The skin under her eyes is dark, and her eyelids are heavy. She looks at us all. 'What the hell are you wearing?' she says, pointing at my coat. 'It looks like you stole that coat from a tramp.'

'We kind of did,' Lizzy says, 'but we're going to give them back. What's going on? What's Critical Care? Where is everyone? It's like everyone already died here.'

The little bit of light left in Ani's eyes seems to go out. I sink down onto one of the chairs. 'Oh, no.'

'No, he is alive,' she says, waving us all into a seat as if we've arrived for a meeting. 'Just.'

'Just?' Lizzy squeaks, sitting down.

'They won't tell me much,' Ani sits down. 'There's a Matron in charge. She won't tell me much, but I think Critical Care is what they had in hospitals before ICU.'

'So he's in Intensive Care,' Jasper asks.

'He's in a coma,' Ani says.

It's the worst news, but it could be even worse, I guess. Kim makes a tiny sound like she's trying not to cry. Jasper scuffs his feet over the tiles on the floor. I look at Lizzy. Every trace of colour has left her face.

'Is it an induced coma?' I ask. 'To help him heal?'

'I don't think they have those here,' Ani says. 'He's on a life support machine in a room all by himself. I looked through the window in the doorway. He's wired up to bags of blood on a drip and a huge box with loads of dials and little screens. They won't let me go in, so I don't think there's much point in you asking if you can. The nurses go in all the time with clipboards, but they won't tell me anything, apart from a doctor is supposed to be doing his rounds later this morning. The Matron told me he'd lost a lot of blood, but they didn't think anything vital was damaged. They are more concerned about infection in the wound, which is why she won't let anyone in with him.'

'Have you been here all night?' Kim asks.

'Matron didn't want me to stay, but I told them I wasn't leaving, so she said I had to stay in here. One of the kinder nurses brought me a blanket and something hot and milky called Ovaltine to drink.' She looks at Lizzy. 'He's not going to get better any time soon.'

'Have they asked you anything awkward?' Lizzy asks.

'Loads of stuff. What's his name, where does he live, who are his next of kin, what's his religion, what size shoes does he wear.' Ani's shoulders slump down. 'Not the last one. If he wasn't so sick, I think they might have pushed me harder. They're concerned about keeping him stable, but they are worried, and they want to know who he is.' She closes her eyes. 'I'm hungry, and I'm tired. There isn't anything we can do for him. He's in the best place. We may as well leave.'

'Are you suggesting that we just abandon him here?' Lizzy exclaims into the silence.

'Have you got a better suggestion?' Ani snaps back. 'You want to unplug all the wires, stick him in a wheelchair and whizz him across town back to the Weydoor?'

'Oh, you're so quick with your smart mouth,' Lizzy sneers.

'If we leave him here, we do have a guarantee of getting back to him,' I say loudly, trying to diffuse the situation.

'Glenda's key is grounded to her birthday.' And of course, so is the pen in Jasper's pocket.

Lizzy and Ani just stare at each other.

'Lovely. So every time we travel back here, we have to go to Glenda's 21st? A guy can have too many parties, you know,' Jasper says. When he catches my eye, he has the grace to look a bit shameful. 'Sorry. Not about me. I get this.'

'We can't go to Glenda's party again anyway,' I say. 'You know the rules. It would be too much of a risk to go again.'

'Will he be safe here?' Kim asks. 'I know he's not a very nice bloke, Lizzy, jumping your bones like that and trying to steal your key, but I don't like the thought of him lying here with no one to look out for him when he's so ill.'

'I don't like the idea of it either,' Lizzy says, glaring at Ani, 'but much as I hate to admit it, Ani's right. We can't get him back to 1987 right now. We will have to come back and get him when he's better.'

If nothing else, you can't accuse Lizzy Brookes of being predictable. Everyone chooses to ignore the unspoken 'if'.

'If the doctors do match his records with his nine-year-old self, they'll call his parents and say 'your boy is in a coma at St Peter's,' Ani says. 'His parents will say their boy is in the front room playing with the truck he got for Christmas.'

'Tonka,' Kim says.

'Bless you. So the doctors just going to think their system's a mess – they're not going to turn off the machine on a potential survivor,' Ani finishes.

'Ani, did he say anything about who attacked him before they took him away?' I ask.

She shakes her head no, her eyes on the floor. 'By the

time they got him into the ambulance, he was unconscious. He never came round. I talked to him all the time, tried to give him a sense of where he was and how he got here, but he never reacted.'

The door opens, and a tall woman in a high white hat and dark blue uniform walks into the room. 'Who are all these people?' she snaps.

'My family. I told you they would come,' Ani says.

She looks at each of us in turn. 'I am the Matron on this Ward,' she says briskly. 'You should have told the sister on duty that you were here.'

'She wasn't there,' Kim says.

'That is why there is a bell.' Matron takes a silver watch on a chain out of her pocket like a gentleman. 'Your cousin is not well enough to receive visitors.'

'Will he survive?' Lizzy asks, a gulp at the end of the question like she's swallowing a sob.

'That remains to be seen,' Matron replies, and then, maybe seeing the lack of colour in Lizzy's cheeks, adds, ' We are doing all we can, but your cousin is very badly hurt.' She takes all in the tatty coats and hair that hasn't seen a brush in five decades. I can't remember the last time I put a decent face on, but now I come to think about it, I can't remember the last time I cared. 'I believe you should all go home and get some rest. There is no point in you sitting around here cluttering up the place. Jane has given us her contact details. We will call if there is any change, but in all honesty,' she clasps her hands together like a prayer; 'I do not see any chance of that this side of Epiphany.'

'You gave her contact details?' I ask Ani as we walk into the lift.

She shrugs. 'Landline from 2019. What's the worst that can happen? Some old dear picks up the phone and says she's never heard of me? More likely it'll be an unrecognised number.'

The light is grey with the cloud cover, but at least it means it isn't as cold as it could be. We spend the walk back through town telling Ani everything that seemed significant to us that happened while she was at the hospital. When we tell her about the Weyfarere key symbol turning up on a prayer book and a notice board at Trinity, she's more interested than in anything else we've told her.

'You know that one of the oldest known symbols of the Trinity is the Triquetra?' she asks.

'You're the geek historian, not me,' I say, maybe a little too unkindly.

'Yes, thank you. Okay, for the uneducated;' she gives me a significant look; 'the Triquetra is used to denote the Trinity in the Christian faith, but it pre-dates Christianity by some centuries. It's most likely Celtic, and there are lots of other similar symbols, not least the valknut, which is Norse.'

Norse. The word jags in my brain, reminding me of laying under blankets in Brian's garage an eternity ago, reading about Wayland and his brothers in *The Truth,* and then later drinking tea at Travellers' Rest while Glenda gave us all a lesson in Norse Mythology.

'Valknut. Is that related to the Valkyrie?' I ask.

She looks at me as if I've just spat on her boot. 'You'd

think it was a possibility, wouldn't you?'

'Glenda talked about them.'

Ani claps her hands slowly. 'The penny drops.'

'Valkyrie. I'm related, according to Mum. So you reckon the symbol that's on our keys and at Trinity; they're all connected in some way,' Lizzy says.

'Most likely,' Ani says. 'Christianity uses the triquetra to represent the Father, the Son and the Holy Ghost. But the triquetra is an infinity symbol. Maybe an earlier meaning could well have been the past, the present and the future.'

'Time Travel on the Weys,' I say.

'It's a symbol that's been adopted by many belief systems,' Ani says. 'Whatever way you look at it, Trinity has to be linked to the Weyfarere and their ability to travel through Time.'

'Do you think that's important?' Jasper asks.

'Well, there has to be a reason for it,' Kim replied, 'and it's probably worth finding out what the reason is.'

Kim's right, and Ani's right as well, much as it makes me crazy to admit it. The more I travel on the Weys, the more confused I become, and the less I feel it's ever likely that I'll find a way back to the 2019 I called home.

Chapter Eighteen – Five Get Over Excited (The Housemartins, 1987)

As we walk back up Town Hill for what feels like the 30th time today, I see the old-fashioned sign directing people along the road to Edward Bett's, the co-ed comp where in my day they wear blazers, smart trousers and kilts. Something occurs to me.

'Lizzy, you do know things might be different when we get back to 1987, don't you?' I say, when I get a word in between her and Jasper arguing about whether Marc Bolan or Jimi Hendrix died in a car crash.

'They weren't different when we went back before,' she says. 'When I had the fight with Scott in your time.'

'Yeah, but you travelled forward, not back,' Jasper says. 'You can't change the past by travelling forward in Time. And you didn't interact with anyone when you were there. None of us did, except Maisie.'

'Whereas we've all just spent the night partying with your Mum and all her besties,' Ani remarks. 'So I'd say that changes things a bit, wouldn't you?'

'And now Scott's being kept alive by machines, on a hospital ward that no longer exists,' Kim says.

We are almost at the junction with the Top and Bottom Roads before Lizzy mutters, 'Crap.'

One or two cars drive past us as we approach the Top

Gate of Drakes, but there's no one around. It's so quiet, and it's the middle of the day. It's New Year's Eve. Maybe everyone's at work. Perhaps everyone's sleeping. Based on last night, maybe everyone's still stoned.

'At least we know we won't be setting any alarms off this side of the Weydoor,' Lizzy says, as we leapfrog the low wall onto the school grounds.

'There's an alarm in 1987 though,' Kim says.

'Yeah, but Frank's hurt, he won't be coming to investigate any alarms after Scott kicked him in the nuts,' Lizzy says.

'Apart from the fact that Scott kicked him in the nads in the 1987 you left behind,' Ani points out,' and not necessarily the one we're going back to.'

As they continue to argue about the likely state of Frank's balls, Jasper reaches out and holds me back. As I open my mouth to ask him what he's doing, he puts his finger on his lips. I watch as Ani, Kim and Lizzy walk off down to join the path to the Old Library.

'Maisie, this is your third return,' he says, once they are out of earshot.

'My third what?'

'You travelled to 1987, and you returned. You travelled back to 1987, and you returned. You travelled to 1971. You're going to return again.'

I stare at him as what he's saying dawns on me. Lizzy will travel back to 1987, but my blood will ground me to the end of my own timeline and back to the nightmare that has become 2019.

'Do you think anything we've done here might have changed things for the better?' I ask. 'Jasper, I don't want to go back to that hell!'

'I know,' he says, pulling an old dirty rag from his pocket and thrusting it into the pocket of my borrowed coat. 'This might help.'

'Ugh, Jasper, that's disgusting!' I exclaim, smacking him on the arm. 'I don't want it!'

Lizzy's voice carries up the path towards us. 'What are you two playing at?'

'Maisie, listen to me, please don't throw it away,' he hisses as I start to pull the disgusting cloth out of my pocket, 'trust me, please? And don't say anything. Just tying my laces,' he calls down lightly, dropping to the floor to tend to his perfectly knotted Vans.

'Get a move on,' Lizzy calls up impatiently.

I wait for him to finish pretending, and we run down the path towards where the others are waiting. His eyes plead with me as he stands up, and I sigh, but something stops me dropping the stinky rag on the floor and I push it back deep into my pocket.

Lizzy takes the iron key from her pocket and opens the main door to the Old Library. We walk into the dusty room; up the aisle towards the Weydoor that lies hidden behind the bookcases at the back, glowing as she approaches. As we reach the back, Ani reaches out and picks up the two books that are on the central table.

'Everyone link hands,' she says, like the Headteacher she ought to become, and suddenly Jasper puts me between himself and Ani. Lizzy reaches out, and her arm just seems to slip through the bookcase as if it is a kind of projection, and the next thing I know we're falling against the bookshelves, and there's white heat, purple light, black – nothing.

I must be getting better at this time travel stuff in one respect because I don't wake up on my ass; in fact, I don't wake up at all, I stagger awake on both feet into the Old Library. There is no light coming through the high windows. There is no sign of Lizzy, Kim or Ani.

'Where is everyone?' I gasp. Okay, I may be on my feet, but time travel is still a fist to the gut.

'I'm going with 1987,' Jasper says, also on his feet, just – panting behind me.

'And we aren't there,' I say. 'So where are we?'

'I'm going with 2019. Jeez, Maisie, don't tell me I'm the only one who gets this?' he exclaims. 'I told you outside. Lizzy the Weyfare, travels out to 1971, travels home. Maisie the Weyfare travels out to 1971, travels home.'

'If this is 2019 when we left it, where are Rob, Paul and Dave?' I ask.

'I have no idea,' he says, sighing. 'We can go and find out, or I have another suggestion.'

'Would it have anything to do with the dirty rag you put in my pocket?' I sneer.

'It's not a dirty rag. It's Lizzy's bandage,' he says. 'It's covered in her blood.'

'Her blood,' I repeat, as a few cogs whirr in my exhausted brain.

'I'm not the brightest bead on the bracelet, Maisie, but Ani said you Weyfare were all anchored by blood, right? So Lizzy chucked this bandage in the bin at the public loos, and I thought, surely if it's her blood, it might come in useful in anchoring us back to her timeline. If we lose her.'

I pull the manky bandage out of the pocket. 'You think it's like ... a blood token?'

Jasper nods. 'She threw it away, but I dug it back out of the bin. I took it, so it wasn't a gift. The bandage might have some effect, but I figure Weyfarere blood overrides any normal grounding token.' He looks at me. 'It's Lizzy's blood token.'

'Won't it connect to the end of her timeline?' I say.

'She's dead,' Jasper says carefully. 'So I thought, and I'm probably being a total mong, but I figured it would connect us to the Lizzy that's living. I don't understand any of this, but it sort of made sense at the time.'

I don't usually do this, but I can't help myself; I throw my arms around my BFF and hold him tight. 'Jasper,' I mutter, 'you fricking genius.'

He goes as rigid as an ironing board at first, and then he relaxes a little and pats me gently on the back. 'Someone had to take over from Uranium-Knickers. Don't jinx it. We haven't tried it out yet.'

'Tried it out?'

'If I'm right, this should anchor you to 1987. It should anchor you to Lizzy's timeline.'

'And if it doesn't?'

He snorts. 'Then toss it in the freaking bin already, and let's go find your psycho grandma and her psycho cronies.'

I look at the bloodied bandage. 'I'm not willing to go back down that road just yet,' I say, holding out my free hand towards him.

He takes it. The hand holding the bandage just seems to

slip through the bookcase as if it is a kind of projection, and the next thing I know we're falling against the bookshelves, and there's white heat, purple light, black – nothing.

This time I definitely land on both feet. It's almost as if I have stepped through a regular door rather than a Weydoor. Jasper is wobbly, but he's upright again as well.

'Why do you keep doing that?' Lizzy asks, her face all twisted in confusion. 'We arrive, and you appear a couple of seconds later?'

'Weird shit this time travel,' I say, pushing the bandage into the pocket of my jeans.

'Maybe she just let go of my hand,' Ani says, but I can see her watching the hand that hides the bandage away.

Then the alarm goes off.

'No hurry. Frank won't come,' Lizzy says.

'We can't be sure of that,' I say. 'We don't know what kind of 1987 we've come back to. We'd better be quick.'

Lizzy takes one of the keys from around her neck and unlocks the door to the Tunnel that leads underground, back to Travellers' Rest. Seems we're coping better with walking through the Tunnel, now we know what to expect. The damp ceiling dips sharply in places, and in others the Tunnel becomes narrow, but we make our way through much more quickly than before. It isn't too long before we are piling out of the Old Shed in what we hope is stil Lizzy's back garden.

'Glenda's at the window,' Kim says. I look up at the face peering out at us.

'She doesn't look all that happy,' Jasper remarks.

I say nothing. I'm looking forward to seeing the real Rob

again: not the fit DILF, or the cute toddler with his gin-soaked pacifier, but my Rob, the 18-year-old I let down badly when I didn't trust him with my secrets. One of the reasons I'm still here is to put that right. Not that I have any desire to walk back into the waking nightmare that is my current future any time soon.

As we push through the familiar blue and green plastic flycatcher in the doorway, I'm relieved to see that the place looks pretty much as we left it, apart from one glaring gap. There is no sign of Rob or Brian.

Lizzy, obviously forgetting that her mother only saw her a few minutes ago, launches herself into Glenda's arms. Glenda looks a bit shocked; Lizzy was never one for the big PDAs before the last couple of days.

'Mum! We're back! We did it!' she exclaims, as Glenda pulls her away, and looks into her face. 'Do you remember us?'

'Of course I do, love,' she says, 'you've only been gone a couple of minutes.' She smiles at us all, but the smile is thin. 'What are you doing back with these bystanders though?'

My heart relocates to the bottom of my Converse, and I reach out blindly for reassurance and find Jasper's hand waiting for me.

'Come again?' Lizzy asks.

'Why have you bought the bystanders back with you?' Glenda shakes her head. 'No matter. We must get the Bystanders back to their Weys quickly, and then we can talk properly. There is so much in the *Book of the Witan* that I need to share with you.'

Witan. I look at Jasper to find he's looking back at me, with equal amounts of horror. I haven't heard that word in

1987 before. I didn't ever want to hear it again.

'What is the *Book of the Witan*?' Lizzy asks. 'We hid *The Truth*. And what are bystanders?'

Glenda nods in our direction. 'They are Bystanders. You can't have forgotten already?' She makes an irritating clicking noise with her tongue like old teachers do. 'I don't know what you mean by *The Truth*.'

There is a big cold void in the air between us. Where at least there was familiarity before between us and Glenda, there is nothing. I glance across to Jasper, and I can see the sinking I'm feeling in his eyes too.

'Where are Rob and Brian?' Ani asks.

'Ian and Brian are up at Tracy's cook-out with Lizzy's brother, which is where she's going to be once you Bystanders have finally been sent on your Wey,' she finishes pointedly.

Sent on our Wey. It sounds like a punishment.

'Mum, you're scaring me,' Lizzy says. 'Rob and Brian were supposed to be here to keep you safe.'

'Rob who?' Glenda asks.

'What do you mean Rob who?' Lizzy exclaims, the words falling out without a break for breathing.

'You don't have a friend called Rob. Not that I know of.'

Oh, no.

Anything but that.

Is this some kind of punishment for smugly warning Lizzy that her life might have changed?

Kim goes over to the pine table and sits down, her chin in her hands, her watery eyes betraying her emotions. Jasper and Ani stand still as statues, just behind me. Their position is clear: you're the Weyfarere, you two sort it out. My position is also clear. My boyfriend has been extinguished.

'Maisie?' Lizzy asks helplessly.

I shrug. A tear drips over my filthy face, and I rub it away as if it were a bug. What's the point in crying? Mum is gone from my future. Now it looks like Rob is gone from my past. Still, I have to carry on. What else is there to do?

'Maisie.' Lizzy comes over to me, and for the first time, she puts her arms around me as if it really matters. It's all I can do not to collapse into a heap of steaming emotion on the carpet tiles. It feels like several minutes before anyone speaks. Kim has covered her face with her hands. Jasper wipes his cheek with the back of a hand. Ani's expression is grim. Rob is gone.

Out of the corner of a blurred eye, I see Glenda giving us what can only be described as a scowl. 'Wayland's First Rule,' she mutters at us like it's an incantation, "Do not befriend the Bystander." Lizzy, don't do this.'

'What is Wayland's First Rule when it's at home?' Lizzy snaps, as if she was just told to clean the toilet bowl.

'From the *Book of the Witan*,' Glenda says, looking back at her daughter. 'Have you forgotten everything I taught you this morning?' Lizzy steps away from me, and the older woman's hands cross her chest. 'Perhaps things will be clearer once we've all had a cuppa,' she says. She glances up at me, Jasper and Ani. 'We are a Weyfarere family. This means we are pledged to help bystanders who fall from their own Weys back to their timelines. We explained this to you before you left. You are permitted to take refreshment with us before we return you to your Wey. *Again.*'

'Oh yeah?' Jasper remarks, dryly. 'Which of Wayland's

rules is that?'

Glenda goes over to the kettle and starts to boil the water.

'Mum!' Lizzy shouts. 'What the hell is going on here? Why are you talking like some religious fanatic? You know Maisie, Jasper and Ani. They know all about the Weyfarere. You were the one who told them about us.'

'I'm not sure this is a good idea, Lizzy,' I say. 'I mean, we aren't supposed to tell people about the future, that's a given. Your mum doesn't know us, does she? Can we tell her about a past she doesn't know?' Older Lizzy didn't want me to tell her about the past, but could I, if she'd wanted me to?

'I told you about what exactly?' Glenda looks as if she's about to lose her footing and stumble, and me and Jasper rush forward to help Lizzy get her into a seat. She looks up at us, and now there is something far worse than the distance that was in her eyes. There is fear.

'You told us about the Weyfarere. You told us to hide *The Truth* in 1971 where no one could see it,' Ani says.

'I don't know what *The Truth* is,' Glenda stutters. 'I told Lizzy to take you bystanders back to the Weydoor and send them on.'

I thump Ani hard on the arm, and she instantly whacks me back. 'We have to tell her!' she goes on. 'Don't you remember meeting us at your 21st birthday party, Glenda?'

The colour is draining from Glenda's face as if she's being exsanguinated. 'My birthday? When?'

'We all went to the Crypt after your party, and there was a power cut,' Kim says. 'So we went up to Bab's flat.'

Glenda's eyes are now huge. 'The Crypt?' she whispers.

'Babs? I haven't seen Babs in years. I didn't tell you to do any of this,' She looks sharply up at me. 'How can you possibly know all this?'

'John and Babs had a friend called Mick who wore round glasses with no lenses because he thought he looked like John Lennon,' I say.

Glenda looks at me as if I have the plague.

'We were there that night,' Jasper says patiently. 'We aren't making it up.'

'You told us all about the Weyfarere. There was a problem with a bloke called Scott Kelly – oh, it doesn't matter what it was now, but you told me to go back to 1971 to put *The Truth* in the safe so it couldn't be stolen or seen,' Lizzy says. 'You gave me the spare key so that I could go into your bedroom – well, Gran's room – and put *The Truth* where someone could never see it.' She takes the safe key out of her pocket and places it on the table. Prickles of unexpected alarm ripple in my stomach.

'Scott Kelly?' Glenda says, her voice barely louder than a whisper. It is as if all my Weyfarere ancestors are dancing on my grave. 'No. Stop now.'

Looking back, I wish we'd listened to her. '*The Truth*. It was on that shelf.' I point over at the pine dresser. 'It got seen by someone who caused a load of trouble. You told us all to get rid of it in 1971.' I look into her eyes. 'We read parts of it.'

'You're telling me things about a life I haven't known and never will know. The Witan will have me extinguished me for this,' she says, and she leaned forward with her elbows on the table and puts her head in her hands as if we've just told her that Henry's died. 'Bystanders aren't supposed to know our secrets.'

'Mum? Will you stop banging on about that word! What are the Witan? ' Lizzy shouts.

'What are the Witan?' Glenda looks up sharply, her face now a mask of shock. 'Where have you come from? What kind of past have you known?'

'One where you were in danger,' Jasper says.

'We took *The Truth* back to the past to protect it and you. You told us where to go and what to do. You lent me your school keys, so I could open the main door of the Old Library.' Lizzy pulls the iron key out from her back pocket. 'You lent me your key so that we could travel out to 1971.' Lastly, she pulls the ornate, silver key with the triquetra at the top from her neck, and she places it on the table next to the iron door key. 'You gave me those keys, Mum. When I left here.'

There is a roaring in my ears but, as I open my mouth to form the words to tell her no, Glenda is already reaching for the key. One hand goes to her chest, and lays flat over what I instinctively know is already hanging from her neck. The other touches the tip of the silver key on the table.

There is no lightning strike, no thunderclap, no booming voice in the sky, but as her fingers contact with the metal, Glenda sits bolt upright, her eyes staring halfway between hurt and horror, and then she slumps sideways off her chair onto the carpet-tiled floor.

Chapter Nineteen – Land Of Confusion (Genesis, 1987)

Everyone is out of their chair in an instant and crouching on the floor beside where Glenda has fallen.

'She's out cold,' Lizzy says, holding her mum's hands and patting them. 'What happened? Call 999!'

We seem to be doing that a lot lately.

'Don't over-react. She might have just fainted,' Jasper says.

'She touched the key, and then she fell off her chair,' Ani says. 'Am I the only one with any functioning brain cells in this room?'

'If you don't shut it, any brain cells you have will be gone by the time I've finished with you,' Lizzy howls. 'My mother has just passed out, and you need to give it a rest with the smug shit!'

'I wasn't being smug,' Ani says into the thickening silence. 'I was trying to point out that Glenda touched the key before she collapsed.' She sighs. 'I just think the key is a paradox.'

Kim pats Glenda's cheeks gently, but there is no response. 'Lizzy, does your Mum keep smelling salts?'

Lizzy gets up, goes over to the cupboards by the sink and starts opening them.

'A paradox?' she adds, looking at Ani.

'Can you check to see if she is wearing anything around

her neck?' Ani asks.

'Carefully, and very respectfully,' Lizzy growls.

'Well, obviously she's wearing her... Oh.' Jasper kneels back on his haunches. 'Maisie. You check.'

Glenda may be family, but I'm still not comfortable patting the front of her blouse. Instantly, my hand falls over a hard shape. I know what it is without looking. 'She's wearing her key.'

As one, we look back at the silver key lying on the table next to the others, so innocent, and apparently with the power to floor an adult just with one touch.

'Exactly. Same key. Different timeline. Paradox,' Ani says.

'Did you read about them in *The Truth*?' Kim asks. Lizzy is still rummaging through drawers muttering to herself, in search of the salts Kim asked her for.

Ani shakes her head no. ' Before me and Orla found *The Truth*, we read a lot about time travel: Richard Gott's *Time Travel in Einstein's Universe*; Joseph Gabriel's *Quantum Physics of Time Travel*; Leon Rodrigues' *Practical Time Travel for Beginners*. The Rodrigues book talked about how if objects from the future are taken back to a past where they exist, and they connect, it creates a paradox.'

'Like people,' I say.

Lizzy finally slams a drawer shut and comes back to Glenda's side with a tiny glass bottle full with tiny multi-coloured stones. 'Found them.'

'Waft them under her nose,' Kim says.

'She's wearing her key, but it's also on the table,' I say. 'The key is in two places at once.'

Lizzy takes the cap off the tiny bottle and waves it randomly under her mother's nose.

'The one she's wearing was given to her in 1971. The timeline changed since she was given the key, which is almost certainly our fault. So the one on the table that she lent to Lizzy is from an alternate 1987,' Ani confirms. 'It's the same key, existing on two timelines.'

'Christ on a bike,' Jasper says.

Glenda isn't responding to the salts. I'm not surprised. They smell like hair bleach. Did they really think it would help? 'We need to call for an ambulance,' Lizzy says.

'We so need to put that key where it can't do anyone else any harm,' Jasper says, eyeing the keys on the table.

'The safe upstairs?' I ask.

'I can think of worse places,' Jasper agrees.

Lizzy stands up, hands on her hips, looking as if she is in charge. 'Right. You put that thing up in the safe,' she glares at the table, 'and I'll call an ambulance.'

'Don't touch it!' Ani yells, as I reach out for the silver key on the table. 'Use something protective. Just in case,' she adds.

'This is ridiculous,' I say, as I climb the stairs to the first floor with Glenda's silver key dangling between a pair of plastic tongs that Ani found in a kitchen drawer. 'I'm not connected with this key.'

'Sure you're not,' Ani says. 'Just as the key you're wearing isn't yours, and you're not Weyfare. Downstairs they don't know who you are, but we do. You think we can explain it to them if you pass out as well?'

'I'm not wearing another version of that key,' I say patiently,' and Lizzy's been wearing them both around her neck, so I can't see how us touching it is going to have the same impact.'

Ani finally has the sense to look beaten. 'Well,' she says lamely, 'it's not worth taking the chance, is it?'

We left Kim and Jasper down in the kitchen diner trying to wake Glenda up. Lizzy is ringing for an ambulance. Ani is the one with the safe key in her hands.

'I'm so tired of all this,' I say suddenly, feeling everything heavy in my bones. 'I just want things back the way they were. I can't cope,' I say feebly, and I stop, my back sliding down the wall at the base of the staircase, managing to avoid the jutting nail in the floorboard that cut Lizzy's ankle before.

'Yes, you can,' Ani says. She squats down in front of me. 'Look, we don't know whether Rob's Gone gone. Glenda just didn't know Lizzy had a friend called Rob.'

'Is this supposed to make me feel better?' I wipe another couple of tears away with the back of my hand. 'The Rob we all knew doesn't exist.'

'I'm not your best friend. But even if I was,' she sighs, 'I wouldn't be doing you any favours by blowing sunshine up your arse, Maisie. Maybe he'll come back.' She stands up and holds out a hand to haul me to my feet. 'I did.'

'And you weren't the same!' I exclaim.

'Still ended up in this nightmare of a dystopia with you, didn't I?' We approach the second floor and the bedroom where the safe is hidden in the wardrobes. 'You have to man up. This is your life now. With or without Rob in it.' She looks down at the silver key from another 1987. 'This is our life now. Nothing any of us took for granted exists ever since you,

Jasper and the former Miss Chowdhury went on a Time Trip. All we can do is make the best of what we have, and hope that at some point it resembles the futures we all thought we were going to get.'

Jeez, how to make a girl feel even worse.

The bedroom is warm as the sun starts to dip in the sky and send beams of heat and light through the glass, and Ani opens the fitted wardrobes on the left of the big bed. I sit down, trying hard not to rub my gritty eyes. When was the last time I had a proper shower? Put on a decent face, or did my hair? My clothes are grubby, and I need a good sleep, but Glenda is downstairs on the floor, and like Ani says, it's probably our fault. Again. Because we messed her up too.

As Ani shuffles forward on all fours, digging out open boxes of shoes and boots, I take the downtime to get things ordered in my head.

The first time I came here to 1987, we extinguished Ani. I haven't even begun to consider why she now exists again, or why she vanished in the first place. The second time I came back to 1987, it was to stop Scott Kelly from ruining my family's future. We stopped him from stealing the key and *The Truth*, and my family's future went from being ruined to being a living nightmare. We thought Scott was descended from the bad side of the family's ancestry, but he turned up with a knife wound to the guts. Now he's stuck in a hospital bed all wired up to 1971, and Glenda's become a scary echo of the grandmother I met in 2019. Could things get any more confusing? Could things get any worse? How am I going to put this all straight? Can I even? FML.

'Maisie?' Ani calls out from the wardrobe.

'What is it? Is the safe not there?'

'No, it's -' Her voice trails off. 'D'you think you could get down here and check something for me?'

I close my eyes and breathe out a sigh. When I open them again, things are no better. 'Hang on.'

Glenda's cupboard smells a bit musty, like many of the clothes in here haven't seen daylight since she bought them. By the look of the enormous collared blouses and flared trousers, she could've been wearing some of these clothes at her 21st birthday party.

'Just what I needed to set off the boho look I'm going for with my hair. Cobwebs!' I splutter, wiping the stringy tickly lines out of my face as I crawl under the clothes. 'It's going to take years to get a brush through this mess!'

'Save the Kardashianing for someone who cares,' Ani says. 'I need a second opinion. Can you reach the safe?'

I shuffle forward a bit more, push one arm out blindly in front of me while supporting myself with the other, and my hand slips into what feels like a metal box. 'Yes. My hand's inside now.'

'Have a feel around for me?'

'Why can't you do it? There's not something mushy in here, is there? Like in those challenges they set on *I'm a Celebrity -*?"

'Nothing mushy,' she replies. 'Please?'

Some tone in her voice makes me quit the questioning, and I have a good feel around the inside of the box. The metal walls are cool to the touch, and it isn't very spacious. I can feel a few papers in there, maybe a couple of envelopes, and a book. Definitely nothing squishy.

'What can you feel?' she asks.

'A few sheets of paper, maybe an envelope or two? A book. Probably *The Truth*. Why?' I can feel her body tensing beside me in the dark. 'What's wrong?'

'Have you still got the key?' she asks.

'It's here. What did you feel?'

'Can you put the key in the safe and take the book out?'

'Why are you acting all extra about it?'

I hear her sigh. 'Why are you being so salty about it? I'll explain once we're out in the bedroom again, but I'm not getting all uptight with you in a wardrobe. I'll lock the safe back up.'

'We're taking *The Truth* back out again?' I exclaim. 'After everything that happened in 1971?'

'Only for a minute or two,' she says. 'Come on, Maisie. Trust me.'

Not needing more encouragement, I drop the silver key in the safe, grab the book, shuffle backwards out of the wardrobe and clamber to my feet. My clothes are now even more filthy if that's possible. I hear a couple of clunks, and then Ani shuffles backwards out of the wardrobe and shuts the door. We both look up at the same time.

'Siren,' she says, as the familiar wail fills the bedroom.

'Ambulance must be here. Come on, we'd better go down -' I begin, but she holds back my arm. 'Now what?'

'Show me the book.'

We both look down, and my stomach lurches as I see the book in my hand.

'*The Truth*,' I whisper.

'In more ways than one,' Ani says. 'Why hasn't Glenda

heard of this book?'

'By the state of the outside of that safe, I'd say she hasn't opened it in years.'

There is a sudden babble of voices rising up from below. Ani looks suspiciously like she's avoiding my question as she runs out of the room and down the stairs.

I look at *The Truth*. No matter how much we need to sit down and read it, right now it's better it stays where we know we can find it. I lock it back in the safe, and go quickly down the stairs.

The kitchen now resembles an amateur episode of *Casualty*. Two paramedics are kneeling beside Glenda, while Lizzy, Kim and Jasper all look on, their faces pale and their mouths tense, but I realise to my relief as Glenda's face comes into view that her eyes are open, and she's sipping some of the water given to her by the female paramedic.

'Mrs Brookes? My name is Tammy. This is Rick. When was the last time you ate a meal?' the female paramedic is asking, while the male paramedic Rick wraps a cuff around the upper part of Glenda's arm.

'Er -' Glenda says, and I think, Have any of us eaten properly in days? Probably not.

'Thought not. It's the most common cause of feeling faint. You're probably suffering from low blood sugar levels,' Rick comments. He squeezes a thick black balloon, and the cuff on Glenda's arm inflates and sends silvery fluid up a test tube that he's balancing against his leg. 'What about alcohol intake?'

'It was my 18th yesterday,' Lizzy says. 'We had a skinful.'

The female paramedic, Tammy, grins. 'I guess you

haven't read the new guidelines for drinking then.'

'Guidelines? For drinking? What is this, bloody Red China?' Lizzy exclaims. 'They'll be telling what food we should be eating next.' She catches Tammy's eye and shrugs. 'Sorry.'

'Blood pressure normal,' Rick comments. 'Pulse a little on the high side but within reasonable limits.'

'How are you feeling now, Mrs Brookes?' Tammy asks.

'A little better,' Glenda says weakly.

'I'm not sure there's a lot more we can do for you, love.' Tammy turns and looks at us all. 'Which one of you is Lizzy?' Lizzy puts her hand up; after all, we're all still in school. 'We'll put her to bed; you boil the kettle for a hot water bottle. Have you got any soup? Or boil an egg and make toast for eggy soldiers. Something simple, nothing too heavy. And bed until the morning at the very earliest. Any problems, call in again.' She passes the bottle of salts up to Lizzy. 'Best get a new bottle, these have lost their potency.'

'Could've fooled me, they nearly blew my freaking socks off,' Jasper remarks.

Kim puts the kettle on, and Lizzy finds a tin of oxtail soup in the larder by the back door and a pan to heat it in. She puts two slices of startlingly white bread under the grill above the cooker hob.

'Did you put the key in the safe okay?' she asks.

'Yes,' Ani says quickly. 'It's in there.'

'So is *The Truth*,' I say.

'Why didn't Mum know about it then?' Lizzy asks, stirring the soup.

'It doesn't look like the safe's been opened in decades,' I

tell them.

'Blimey,' Kim says, from the kettle-side. 'Do you think she even knows she's got a safe?'

'Maybe not,' Ani says.

'But where is *The Truth* now?' Kim asks.

'I put it back,' I say.

'Just as well.' Ani reaches into her jacket and pulls two small books out from the inside pocket. One of them has a purple leather cover. She drops them onto the pine dining table, and everything falls into place. For me, at least.

'How in the name of Sod did you get hold of that?' Lizzy asks. 'You were at St Pete's when we put that in the safe!'

'It's not the same book,' Ani says.

'It's from Glenda's place in the future, isn't it?' Jasper says.

I remember seeing her stuffing something into her jacket. Something that she then left on the table in the Old Library in 1971, and then quickly picked up again before we all travelled back. 'You took it off the shelf in the study,' I say out loud.

'Didn't it occur to you when I asked you to put your hand in the safe upstairs?' Ani asks.

I scrunch up my lips. 'Didn't think about it much.'

'So you didn't think about what you might be touching?'

'I actually have a lot of stuff on my mind right now; forgive me I'm sure if I didn't get your subtle little clues,' I snap. 'I guess you wanted me to put my hand in the safe upstairs first because you were worried there might be another paradox. With two versions of the same book. *The Truth*.'

Ani nods.

Kim leaves the kettle and peers down at the little purple book that has caused us so much trouble. 'So it is back here, after all that?'

'No,' Ani says. 'This is a different version. It's a paradox, like Glenda's key. The other one is upstairs.'

'You said it was from the future,' Lizzy says, turning the toast under the grill, which is beginning to smell past its best. 'You haven't been back to the future since I told you to come back to 1987 and stop Scott from stealing things.' She stares at us. 'Have you?'

'Let's have a look at the other book,' I ask lightly, avoiding her look as I glance down at the table.

'Answer the question,' she repeats.

'Yes we have, but it's too complicated to explain right now,' Ani says. 'The fact is, we have a copy of *The Truth* that we can carry around, and still know that the one Scott originally stole is locked up safe. The other book is one I thought might come in useful. It's called *The New Ley Hunter's Guide,* and it's by a guy named Paul Devereux. *The Truth* said that the Weys and the Leys were effectively the same energy fields. All we need now is to get hold of a *Book of the Witan*, then we can sit down together and really get our teeth into –'

'You're changing the subject,' Lizzy says. 'When and how did you travel back to your own timelines without me?'

Chapter Twenty – Victim
Of Love (Erasure, 1987)

The kettle whistles as it boils away and the soup makes a glopping sound in the pan.

'I had a key, remember?' I say quickly. 'The key that you lent to me in the future, that would always take me back to 2019.' Plus a whole load of Weyfare blood pumping through my veins, but we won't talk about that right now.

'When did you use it though? Why?' Lizzy asks, picking up the two charred pieces of bread, pretty much throwing it on the table and blowing on her fingers.

'It was when we came back from 1971,' Jasper says before I can speak. 'We wanted to see if anything had changed.'

'And had it?' Kim asked.

You. Have. No. Idea. 'Just a bit.'

Lizzy takes the pan and puts it on a placemat. 'Kim, get me down something to put this lot in. Not enough had changed to make you stay there then,' she adds.

'Understatement of the century,' I agree, my voice sounding small. Lizzy looks at me, and I pray to whatever gods are listening that she doesn't ask me if she's okay in that future. Our eyes lock for a few seconds, and then she looks away.

'How did you get back to 1987 again though?' Kim asks, hunting around in a cupboard. 'I mean, we know Lizzy is anchored here, and my necklace is linked, but you didn't have either of those.'

Jasper stole Lizzy's bloody bandage from a bin, and I have it in my back pocket. 'Luck, I guess,' I say aloud, shrugging.

'You could've travelled anywhere in time on the Weys, and you still came back here?' Lizzy asks, putting the blackened toast on a side plate. 'That's one fine coincidence.'

Even Ani is looking curiously at me now.

'Well, we're here, aren't we?' Jasper blurts out. 'Deal with that soup, will you? It smells like bad feet, and it's making me want to vom.'

'Keep your hair on,' Lizzy grumbles.

My granddad Henry stumbles through the back door just then; his eyes wide and his hair all sticking up on end. 'Is everyone all right? Lizzy? My God – someone said they'd seen an ambulance stop outside, and I came back as fast as I could. Your mother, is she -?' He takes a huge gasp, leans forward with his hands on his thighs, face bright red where he's obviously been running, and he's not used to it.

'Relax, Dad, she's fine.' Lizzy pours the mud-brown soup into the bowl that Kim placed on the table. 'She had a bit of a turn, is all. We panicked a bit and called an ambulance. They're putting her to bed upstairs. I made soup!' she finishes brightly as if it's an achievement. 'And toast, but it's a bit burnt.'

'You're a good girl. I'll take it up to her,' Henry says.

'How's Frank?' I ask.

'Frank who?'

'Frank, the school caretaker. Weren't you up the pub with him?' Ani asks, lightning quick.

'Strange question.' He looks at me, and then at Jasper and Ani. 'I wasn't. I was at work. I got a call. And you are?' He isn't quite so red-faced now, and he's breathing more easily. 'Don't bother. Look, chicken, I'm here now. You go enjoy yourself. You said yourself the medics didn't think it was anything serious. I can take care of Mum. It's your special weekend. Wasn't your friend having a cook-out this afternoon? I thought you'd be up there by now.'

Tracy Rutherford, one of Lizzy's closest friends, lives in one of the big townhouses on the same road where John and Babs rent their bedsit in 1971. Lizzy hasn't seen Tracy, or her other friends Elaine, Claire and Ian since the Weyfarere crap hit the fan. Me and Jasper were there at her barbeque briefly, on some long lost timeline, with Rob and Brian.

When Rob and I were still together. Before I blew it all with my lack of trust. Before I expected him to just accept that I was a time traveller from the future, but I couldn't trust him with the fact that Lizzy and I were family. Because if I did, he'd have known we could be together indefinitely, and I wasn't ready to commit to a future living a messed up version of *The Time Traveller's Wife*.

Now Henry is all distant, and even Glenda's acting like we're pretty much strangers, and Rob has gone, maybe into the ether like Ani 1.0 did. Perhaps he's vanished forever. I had my chance, and I blew it on more levels than I could possibly imagine. Jasper wipes another tear from my cheek.

As Henry takes the brown soup and the charred pieces of toast on a metal tray up the stairs, Lizzy slumps down into one of the chairs as if she's just prepared a banquet. 'Should we go and face the music?' she asks.

'Maybe we should go and catch up with everyone,' Kim says. I wonder if she is thinking like me, how much will have changed since we were all last here, until she adds, 'because if the stepmonster and Dad come looking for me here again, I'd rather be someplace else.'

'Maybe we should get our stories straight before we meet anyone else,' Ani says.

'Stories?' Kim asks.

'The party was only last night. Your friends would have gone to bed, got up, popped a couple of pills to kill any hangovers, had a shower and change of clothes and rolled up to your friend Tracy's house.' Ani sits down at the table. 'You, on the other hand, have gone through considerably more.'

'Will they even know who we are?' Jasper asks.

'I think it's unlikely,' I say, ignoring the concrete beginning to set around my heart. 'I think our stay in 1971 has changed too much. We're going to need another cover story.'

'You don't think any of them are going to remember you?' Lizzy says, more like a statement of fact than a question. 'Harsh.'

'Should've realised, to be honest,' Jasper says. 'We came back here, and everything changes in the future. We went back there, and now we've changed this future. Maybe we should just curl up somewhere and not do anything else,' he finishes, more mournfully than he's sounded for a while.

'I don't agree,' Ani says. 'We didn't interact with any of their families, did we? Just your family, Lizzy, and Rob's.'

'Well, if they don't know who you are, you can be my cousins.' Lizzy stands up. 'We'll tell them you've come to stay for my birthday.'

Jasper splutters fakely. I smack him on the back, probably harder than I needed to. Lizzy looks at him, frowns and shakes her head.

'Cousins it is, then. And while we're sitting here all together where we can talk, I'd like to raise the matter of the Witan,' Ani says.

'This isn't a meeting of the WI,' Lizzy sneers. 'We don't have the book.'

'Not the book, the people,' Jasper says, unexpectedly. We all look at him, surprised that he's supporting Ani.

'So? The Witan is probably just something she hasn't got around to telling me about yet.' Lizzy gets up, goes over to the pine dresser, opens a drawer and pulls out a gold packet. 'Thank God – I need a smoke.'

'No. She thought she'd told you about them. And we've heard of the Witan,' Ani says. 'In the future.' She pauses until she's sure everyone is looking at her. 'And they weren't very nice.'

'How not very nice?' Kim asks quietly.

'Lock you in a room against your will not very nice,' I say. 'Send you to some kind of detainment centre not very nice.'

'Sounds like something my stepmonster would enjoy,' Kim says. 'She's probably a fully paid-up member.'

'It suddenly seems more sinister than before.' Lizzy lights a cigarette and blows the smoke across the table. 'You know what? I've had just about enough of Weyfarere and Weyleighers and Witan and Weydoors to last me till September. What I really want is to just go out and forget about all this crap for a while. Be 18, stuff my face with hamburgers and hot dogs and drink a crate of cider.' She looks at us each in turn. 'Is that so wrong of me?'

Even if it is, no one's going to tell her because right now, by the looks of the jaded expressions on our faces, we're all tired of the mess time travelling is making of our lives. 'We can't exactly talk much about it if we're going to the barbeque anyway,' I say, looking particularly at Ani. 'A break from it all would be a good thing.'

She shrugs, nods and gets out of her chair in one graceful, fluid action. 'Fair enough. How many bathrooms has this place got? I can deal with having to have big hair while I'm here, but I am not going another step without a hot shower and a change of clothes.'

'Looks like I'm going to be Paul's clone again,' Jasper says, still mournful.

The jackhammer clock on the wall in the dining room says it's just after six by the time we are all ready for another walk down Town Hill towards Tracy's house. Kim tried to put me in a little denim mini skirt with pink leggings and short white suede boots, but I managed to convince her I was happy in the bleached blue jeans she called acid-wash. I did give in to a cropped top though since all the other girls were wearing them. Ani suits the mini-skirted look, but despite the heat, she insists on an oversized acid-wash denim jacket with deep hidden pockets, because she refuses to leave her books anywhere. Jasper is wearing a plain black T-shirt; it was the only thing in Paul's wardrobe that didn't have a band name splashed across the chest.

After another endless walk into town, we are finally

standing outside Tracy's front door. Again.

'Party's going well, by the sounds of it,' Kim says. 'Funny how I never thought I'd get to come to this one.'

'I hope they still have some of those hamburgers left,' Lizzy says. 'When was the last time we ate properly?'

I shrug, but, to be honest, I don't think I can face anything right now. My heart is filling my mouth and my throat and refusing to go back into my chest, as I think about a party without Rob. A future without him. Or a past.

As if he knows what I'm thinking, Jasper takes my hand and squeezes my fingers. 'Time to get your game face on,' he smiles, encouragingly.

When we were here before, the barbeque had only been going for an hour or so. Now it's nearer to seven. The noise level is louder, the music coming from the record player system is louder, and there are a lot more drunk people around. There are people in the swimming pool. I'm about to comment sarcastically that I regret not having a costume with me, when I'm knocked flying into Ani as a tornado of white jeans, red stilettos and big hair flies past us and almost takes Lizzy off her feet. Tracy is closely followed by Elaine and Claire, both with shiny, giggly faces, clamouring for our attention like puppies that haven't seen their owner in weeks.

'Where the hell have you been?' Tracy shouts. 'Talk about arriving fashionably late, you skank. Good job I like you, and I saved you all some grub.'

'Have a drink!' Claire thrusts a can labelled Harp into my hands. ''Lizzy, where have you been?'

'Long story,' Lizzy replies. 'These are my cousins; Maisie, Jasper and Ani.'

'Nudge nudge wink wink say no more,' Tracy says. 'I just told the olds they were new mates from school.'

There is a beat, and then they all stare at Ani.

'I thought you went home,' Tracy says.

'Without saying goodbye,' Claire points out.

'She came back,' Jasper says flatly.

'You ran away again?' Elaine exclaims.

Ani shrugs. I actually feel sorry for her, but what can I say to help, other than wing it.

Kim is a step ahead of me. "Don't you give her a hard time,' she says. 'You never give me the Spanish Inquisition.'

So they do remember us; the runaways from the day of the Fundraiser. We haven't changed their lives. It gives me hope, and I look around, as Kim tries to get them up to date with her escape from home. I'm trying to catch sight of dark hair with bleached out tips, and a cotton jacket with the sleeves rolled up, but there is no sign of him. I can see Neil Thorpe sitting on the side of the pool. He's with Paul, Dave, Brian's brother Will, Ed with the Shagmobile from the Railway Gardens and a few other faces I recognise from the band at Lizzy's party. Then I see Brian watching us, with Ian beside him.

They amble over towards us, Brian with his crooked smile, his blonde hair all up spiky and mussed like before. Then he looks at Ani; his eyes widen a little, his smile reaches a little further into his cheeks, but he doesn't play his little imaginary trumpet.

He just stands in front of her. 'I feel like we've met before,' he says.

Tracy shakes her shaggy blonde mane. 'At least have

something to drink before you start snogging again.'

I hold my breath, waiting for Ani to come out with some totally incomprehensible comment that we're going to have to spend the next three hours explaining. I really should have learned, shouldn't I?

Ani's eyes are a bit wider than usual. She reaches out and takes Brian's hand, and they stand there, almost formally, like a couple of old people at a reunion. 'It's nice to see you again,' she says solemnly.

Brian smiles at her just long enough to diss the rest of us. 'Can I get you a drink?' She nods, and they walk off together. Didn't see that one coming.

'Love the croptop,' Elaine says, reaching up and fluffing the silk scarf that's tied in a bow in my hair to hold back the backcombing riot. 'Pretty scarf. Is it from Miss Selfridge?' I'm still not over Ani's 180-degree turn, and I just smile and shrug.

'I can't believe how many turned up here today!' Tracy says proudly.

'You invited every bloke you spoke to last night,' Elaine says, reaching for Jasper's hand and holding it as if it's the most natural thing in the world. Jasper looks at their hands as though they have turned into bananas, and I choke.

Lizzy pats me on the back, hard. 'Dry throat? I think we could all do with a drink,' she says. Tracy does a theatrical bow and points towards where a pubload of cans are sitting in a yellow plastic tub of melted ice. Lizzy is gone, taking Kim, Tracy and Ian with her. Elaine pulls Jasper in the direction of a rack of beefburgers that have seen better days.

Claire stays by my side. 'You look like you've just seen a ghost,' she says kindly. 'Are you feeling all right?'

'No, I'm really not,' I say, sitting down where I stand and cracking open the can she gave me. 'I need a drink.' Harp is lager, apparently.

'Are you from very far away?' she asks kindly.

It takes me a few beats, but then I remember that to these guys, we are Maisie, Jasper and Ani – the runaways. 'Somewhere miles from here,' I say, not without an element of truth. I'm sure some writer in English Lit. said the future was a foreign country. Or maybe it was the past. Am I even registered to take my 'A' levels in my future any more? 'I was hoping to go to Uni this Autumn but -' My sentence just trails off as I don't have the words to finish it. But I've been travelling through Time, and I altered the future? But being a Weyfare has changed everything? But I don't know whether my home even exists any more?

Claire clearly misunderstands my hesitation for anxiety. 'Well, we're all hoping for that. Don't worry about it for now. No point worrying, that's what they tell me. I made myself a revision timetable for this week.' She goes on to tell us about her homemade highlighted paper timetable which tells her when to revise, what to review and for how long. She already had this conversation with us, on the day of the Fundraiser, up by the Top Gates of Drake's by the Park.

Except clearly, she didn't. 'D'you know anyone called Rob Simmons?' I say. The words are out before I've even had the chance to consider the possible implications of asking her this.

She gives me a funny look, but then it was a bit random of me to come out with that question on the back of her monologue about crucial points being on yellow Post-It notes. 'Rob Simmons? No.' She cocks her head to one side. 'Do you?'

'I used to,' I say sadly. 'I just wondered if he was still around.'

'Is he at FCAB?' Claire asks. I nod yes. 'Best to ask Brian or Ian then. If your fella is in the Upper Sixth, Brian and Ian will know.' She sits down beside me and gives me a sympathetic look. 'Were you keen on him?'

'You could say that.' I take a huge mouthful of the lager from the can. It doesn't taste any better than the first try.

What did we do in 1971 that extinguished Rob Simmons from 1987? I know we met his mum and dad, and we left a guy in their version of ICU – but Rob already existed in 1971. We saw him, a toddler fast asleep with a pacifier laced with alcohol, under a scratchy old rug on the sofa. When Ani was extinguished, she was a time traveller from the future, and we did something that prevented her from even being born. We couldn't have done that to Rob.

So, he can't be extinguished, can he? He may not be the Rob Simmons we know, but he must still be here. All I have to do is find him. Except when I do see him, he won't have a clue who I am. So should I even bother trying to find out what's happened to him? Should I just concentrate on trying to repair the wreckage of my life, and making a future that I can actually recognise?

'Maisie?' Claire has obviously said my name a couple of times already. 'Did you want to come over to get some food? I can recommend the chicken; it's lovely and juicy even if it is a bit pink.'

Salmonella all round for the Bank Holiday then. 'Maybe

just a corn on the cob,' I say, emptying the last of the lager down my throat, and holding the can out. 'And another few of these.'

She gives me an unexpected, but strangely welcome hug. 'It'll all work itself out. Give it time.' I'm glad she can't see my face. 'Oh,' she says suddenly, as she's still looking over my shoulder, 'One of the Robs from FCAB has just arrived.' She pulls away and gives me a serious look. 'But I don't think you can have been talking about him.'

Chapter Twenty-One – Still Of The Night (Whitesnake, 1987)

It wasn't our Rob, and neither were the other three that came through Tracy's patio doors during the rest of the evening. As the clock in the house chimes midnight, Will and Ed offer us all lifts home in the silver-grey Escort and the Shagmobile. It makes me strangely happy to see Kim choosing to go with Ed. She spent a bit of time talking to Ian earlier at the barbeque, and they've obviously just decided to stay as the friends they always were. Right now, as we weave our way up Town Hill in Will's Escort towards Travellers' Rest, I'd do pretty much anything to get to just be friends again with Rob.

'Maisie wanted to know if you knew a Rob Simmons at school,' Claire says, her head wrapped under Brian's arm in a really uncomfortable-looking angle.

Jasper, in the front seat, turns around so fast that I worry his head is about to do the full circle like those creepy dolls in '90s' horror films. He glares at me, rammed in like sardines on the other side of Ani, who is half next to and half over Brian's knee. I give him my 'what' face.

'Simmons? No.'

'Well, Rob anything really,' I say lamely.

Brian turns to me, his face scrunched up. 'Not fussy? Just fancy going out with a Rob?'

'No! No, I just... knew a Rob. Here in town. Way back when,' I finish, feeling pathetic.

'If he's 18, it could be Rob Dryden. He was at the party,' Brian says, but he's eying me suspiciously, and with good reason, he's no noob.

'The Rob I'm looking for wasn't at the party,' I say.

'Isn't it 30 through here?' Ani asks, peering forward through the gap in the front seats.

'I'm doing 30,' Will calls back. 'Who's driving here?'

'That speedometer says 43.'

'It doesn't work,' Will replies. 'You want to get out and walk? I'm happy to pull in at the bus stop.'

Ani slumps back.

'The only Rob I can think of who wasn't at the party is Rob Bennett,' Brian adds.

Mine and Jasper's eyes meet over a particularly vicious speed hump on the entrance to St James' Road. Bennett. Like his Uncle Frank. 'That could be him,' I say.

'Hope not,' Brian says. 'Rob Bennett's a prize jerk.'

'Why say that?' Jasper asks.

'Complete poser who thinks the sun shines up his jacksie. The family runs a hotel business down opposite the Bus Station. You might have heard of it – it used to be the old hospital before they built the General up at the back of the orchards.'

'St Pete's?' I ask faintly.

'That's the one. St Peter's Hotel and Restaurant. Posh joint. Apparently, he has his breakfast made every morning by a chef, and he never does any chores because they have staff to do it all. The meals there are all tiny, and even the buttered spuds have names.'

'Dauphinoise,' Will says, his voice all plumy and artificial. 'Five quid for fish and chips they charge! They call it fillet of sole with julienne potatoes but even so … Five quid!'

'He thinks he's too good for us. Even brags he's not going to turn up for his exams because he already has a job for life.' Brian sighs and shakes his head as if it's the worst crime he can think of; then again, if Brian is anything like he was before, not pursuing an education would seem pretty heinous.

'You know an awful lot about him for someone who claims to think he's a jerk,' Ani says.

'Well, we would,' Will says, pulling to a halt outside a familiar garage. 'He's going out with our sister. You getting out here, bro?'

Brian takes a look at Ani, and she gives him a small smile back. ''Drop me off at Lizzy's,' he says.

'Are you going home, Claire?'

'I think so. I'm beat,' she chirps, 'and I've got a whole load of revision to work through tomorrow.'

As Will pulls away from the kerb, I remember to breathe again.

Jasper is still twisted up in knots, looking back at me. 'I didn't know you had a sister,' he says to Brian, without looking away from me.

This, of course, is garbage. If he's forgotten how embarrassed they all got when they mentioned Yvonne back up at the hippy shop, I haven't. Yvonne, the love of Rob's life who dumped him and went off to study at Cambridge. Clearly, on this version of the timeline, she didn't get around to the dumping.

'Yvonne. She's at Clare College,' Brian says. 'I'm hoping to get into Trinity.'

As he starts talking about his plans to take over the world (he may not even be joking), I wipe the edge of my hand through the steamed window and stare out into the still of the night.

Lizzy's already back by the time we come back from dropping Claire at home, and so is Kim. Claire used to live next door to Rob. As we drive away, I look back at the little semi-detached house where the Simmons family used to live, re-membering how we'd come back before with Elaine to watch *Grandstand* in his front room, while Ani 1.0 started to fade on the sofa, and Rob took a phone call from Neil Thorpe.

It was only yesterday. All those memories, now left with no foundation in any reality we can access.

'Mum's still not right, and Dad doesn't want her dis-turbed, so I told Dad we'd go down the caravan,' Lizzy says, as we pad down the garden path. The layers of my mind feel like they are beginning to peel apart. At least the caravan hasn't changed.

'Brian, this is really important,' Lizzy says, pulling on a plastic cord by the curtain and lighting a yellowish fluores-cent strip bulb in the ceiling. 'I need you to tell us what you re-member about today.'

We are all sat on the bench seats, three either side: me, Lizzy and Jasper versus Ani, Brian and Kim. Brian puts his hands on his thighs as if he doesn't know what to do with them.

'I got in late after talking to you people down here after the party at Trinity. I went to Tracy's party. Why?'

'A bit different to the original then,' Kim says.

'Is it? How? Brian asks. He gives me a pointed look. 'You

obviously knew a Rob Simmons.'

'We're not supposed to talk to you about lives you haven't known,' I say.

'Lives I haven't known?'

'Your sister's going out with Rob Bennett, for a start,' Lizzy says.

'We're not supposed to tell him,' I say.

'Tell me what?' he asks.

'He seems to have lost all the memories since Scott stole the key,' Jasper says. 'So we're sitting here with Ani who isn't Ani, and Brian who isn't Brian. Someone pass me a cigarette.'

'You don't smoke,' I snap. 'Brian, maybe it would be better if you went home.'

'Who are you? My mother? Brian asks. 'What is all this crap about lives I haven't known? Brian who isn't Brian? Lizzy is a time traveller. We've all been time travelling. We went forward to somewhere. You're from the future.' Brian says evenly. 'I was hardly going to blurt it all out at the garden party, was I?'

'And Ani?' Jasper asks.

Brian takes a few deep breaths. 'Time traveller. Some bird from the future.'

Ani nods.

Lizzy snorts.

'You wouldn't take the piss, would you?' he asks.

'I think you'd know if I was,' Lizzy says. 'You're an intelligent bloke. She was more than "some bird from the future".'

He nods slowly. 'Well, that's a thing we can't sort out easily.'

'Perhaps we could start with you not referring to me as

"bird",' Ani says, but with a smile.

'The more we try to fix this, the more damage we do,' I say out loud. 'The more we travel, the worse it gets. We can't go home. We can't go back. I had thought maybe we could stay here but -' I can't finish the sentence, but I'd started to hope that there was a chance I could somehow share a part of my future with Rob. That dream has extinguished, along with him.

Lizzy reaches forward and takes my hands. 'You can stay here as long as you need to,' she says earnestly. 'All of you. Kim, you know I'll protect you from your monster of a stepmother with my final breath. Maisie, Jasper, Ani - I don't care what my Mum says about you having to go back on your Weys. I don't care about these new Witan rules. Things are going to change.'

It's hard not to cry when she says that. I can't tell her that I can't stay here too long, because I can't watch her grow into the woman and mother I hope I still have, somewhere.

We talk for another hour or so, and then exhaustion takes over, and they all find a place to curl up and sleep. All except me that is; I'm wide awake, and shifting my body centimetre by centimetre off the bench seat until my backside gently meets the thin carpet on the floor. I wait a minute or so to check that I haven't disturbed anybody, and then slowly get to my feet and move over to the door. Millimetre by millimetre, I turn the inside latch that keeps the door shut, looking back all the time to make sure that I haven't woken anyone from their rest.

Because I'm making this journey on my own.

Closing the door behind me, I walk quickly and quietly up the garden path towards the house, past the back door and then up to the gate onto the road. Obviously, no one in 1987 is much concerned about climate change; the bright orange streetlights stretch away in both directions, leaving nowhere in creepy darkness.

I'm not really scared. I mean, I don't usually wander around town in the middle of the night, but I did a Self-Defence unit at Drake's in Year Eleven, and I can make good use of the silver key around my neck to stop an attacker in their tracks. All the same, when I realise there are footsteps behind me, it's almost too late to react, so I just turn and scream and hope it's enough to deter whoever is there.

Jasper puts both hands over his ears and waits for me to register who he is. 'Was that totally necessary?' he snarls. 'Now you've probably woken the whole bloody estate.'

'I thought you were asleep!' I hiss at him.

'It's likely that my bestie's boyfriend now lives in a hotel in the middle of town. It was almost a given that she would go looking for him, and besties don't let each other wander around town on their own in the dark.' He links my arm through his. 'I can't believe you even thought about doing this without me. If we weren't already up shit creek, I'd so be giving you a slap.' A couple of upstairs curtains twitch. 'I tell you something,' he says, more quietly. 'My thigh muscles are going to be like iron from the number of times we've walked Town Hill this weekend.' We walk on a little way in silence. 'That is what we're doing, isn't it? Walking to this hotel that might belong to Rob's family?' I nod, yes. 'Okay. What's the plan then?'

'I don't have a plan. I can't just show up and say "Hey! We knew each other in another life", can I?'

'Not really. So why are we going down there in the middle of the night to see someone who will think we're strangers?'

I sigh. The night sky is littered with stars tonight, so it's colder than it has been. It's the kind of night you want to be sitting out under with someone you care about – as I did here last night, in the orchards with Rob Simmons. 'Because I just need to make sure he's okay,' I say quietly. 'I know he won't know us. I know he's with Brian's sister. I just need to see him. To make sure it's him. To make sure -' My voice breaks, and I cough to cover my emotion.

'To make sure he hasn't been extinguished,' Jasper finishes for me. He pushes his arm tighter against mine. ' Makes sense to me. Wonder how they ended up running a hotel? Was she in hospitality before?'

'Who? Brian's sister?'

'No, his mum.'

'I think she worked at the old Hospital,' I say. 'I think I remember hearing that somewhere. Maybe she was in catering there. I think my granddad worked there as well.'

'That's a massive leap on the pay scale for a hospital cook,' Jasper says. 'Did they buy the whole bloody hospital?'

When we get there, we can see that St Peter's Hotel and Restaurant is not the whole old hospital at all. Houses have been built to the left and right. However, the original entrance building with its Downton Abbeyesque pillars and stone brick walls still remains, and this is the bit that's been converted into a hotel. There is ivy growing up around the windows and a large placard outside. The car park is full, and there are lights on in the entrance hall. We stand looking at it for some time before I realise Jasper has taken my hand.

'Come on, Wharton,' he says, tugging on my fingers. 'If we hang around out here for much longer, they'll think we're checking the place out and be calling in the rozzers.'

'What are we going to say?' I ask, confidence draining from my system as if someone turned on a tap.

'It's a hotel. Maybe we could ask for a room?' he replies, and now he's practically dragging me into the place.

Whoever converted the entrance of St Peter's Hospital into a hotel reception was a master of their trade. The faded green walls are now silver grey with floral patterns, the floor is covered in thick dark grey wool carpet. The reception desk is dark, polished wood with simple carvings around the edge. It looks like somewhere James Bond would stay. The lights are warm, not like the unforgiving fluorescence of 1971. There is a woman in a white blouse with a waistcoat over the top in navy blue, sitting behind a large computer screen. When we approach, she gives us her best welcoming smile. Her shiny gold name badge tells me her name is Amanda.

'Good morning, and welcome to St Peter's,' she says chirpily. 'Do you have a reservation, or can I fetch your key?'

I'm about to speak, and then Jasper squeezes my hand so tightly, I nearly cry out.

'Room 33, please,' he says, all teeth and confidence.

Amanda smiles and turns to face a wall of numbered hooks that I only just noticed, but Jasper has obviously already seen, analysed and plotted, because she reaches out for one of the few hooks that are still holding keys. She turns back and hands the keys over. 'Did you have a good evening, sir?' she asks, completely straight-faced.

I must be doing a worse job of disguising my amusement than I think because my fingers get another dose of Jasper's vice-like grip. 'Fabulous,' he says, in a not-too-shabby impression of Craig Revel-Horwood, and then he turns and pulls me towards a lift to the right of the reception desk.

I can't believe it. Where are the security checks? How does she know who we are?

This lift must be in the same shaft as the shaky old elevator from the hospital in the '70s, but the wire security gates have gone. There is a framed panel on the wall to the right of the sliding doors identifying the different hotel floors. Most of them I recognise: storeys 1,2 and 3, G for Ground Floor and LG for Lower Ground Floor. The very last level, however, does make me cry out and put the hand that Jasper's not holding over my mouth.

'Is everything all right?' Amanda calls anxiously from the front door.

'Peachy, thank you,' Jasper replies with a big smile in her direction that drops the instant he turns to me and hisses, 'Are you trying to draw attention to us?'

'Over there. Look at the last level,' I hiss between my fingers.

There is a triquetra printed on it.

Before Jasper can reply, and before I can work out why the symbol on the end of my Weyfare key and on the prayer books at Trinity is also a level in this hotel, there is a pinging sound. Above the lift, a light behind the number 1 flashes, and before we can react, the G flashes, the lift doors slide open, and suddenly we are face to face with Rob's mother.

Chapter Twenty-Two – Goodbye Stranger (Pepsi And Shirlie, 1987)

'Do excuse me,' Valerie says, her voice light and precise, her crisp, navy-blue jacket and pencil skirt set suggesting she's on the hotel nightshift. She shimmies around us. 'I hope you rest well.'

As we step into the lift, I start breathing again. Jasper nods and smiles, but clearly, even he can't trust himself to speak. Would Valerie remember two people that she met briefly at a random party 17 years ago? As the lift doors shut her away, he hits the number 3 on the buttons and breathes out heavily.

'Third floor? Why?' I ask, feeling like I've just run the 100-metre sprint.

He holds up the key. 'That's where this room is.'

'Jasper, we can't go in there!'

He pulls a face. 'Where else are we supposed to go? You aren't seriously thinking of pressing *that* button.' He nods at the triquetra button at the bottom of the choices as if it might take his whole finger off if he touches it.

'No. Do you think she recognised us?' I ask.

He shrugs. 'If she did, she's not doing anything about it.'

There is a ping, and the lift doors open onto plush blue-grey carpets and a pale blue walled corridor; one-way signposts to rooms 31-35 and the other to rooms 36-38. There is an expensive-looking vase on a black table with colourful inlaid carvings and a print above of something looking vaguely Van Gogh.

We step out, the lift doors close behind us, and I hear the mechanisms pulling it down from our level. The numbers above the door suggest that it's going back down to the ground floor.

I feel uneasy. I've made a bad decision coming here tonight. What was I thinking? Not thinking at all would be right. I was thinking too much about a boy I used to know is closer. I was planning a grand reunion where he suddenly remembered a life he never had. What a total disaster. 'We have to leave,' I say out loud.

'And go where? You said yourself that we can't go into this room.' He dangles the keys at me.

'You were the one who asked for the bloody key! You were the one who suggested we came up here!' I hiss at him.

'What did you have in mind then?' he sneers. 'Were you planning on going up to Amanda and saying "Hi there. I don't suppose we could have a word with the boss's son? Yes, I know it's after midnight. No, he doesn't know who we are." He glares at me, head on one side. 'Or did you have another equally brilliant plan?'

I hush him down; the nearest room door is only a few paces away and it must be after one. 'We need to get away from this lift. Look, there's a sign for a staircase at the end of the corridor. Let's use that.'

We end up on a brightly-lit landing overlooking the empty bus station. 'We shouldn't have come here,' I say, the sinking feeling of realisation taking over. 'It was a shabby idea. You should have stopped me. Let's just go back to

Lizzy's.'

'You wouldn't have listened to me if I'd tried to stop you,' he says firmly. 'Maybe we should just have bitten the bullet and asked for Rob at Reception. That's what you wanted all along. We can still do that.'

'We can hardly do that now,' I say. 'What about the keys to Room 33? What happens when the people in that room come back and find their key is gone?'

Jasper pinches the skin over his tired eyes. 'Let's just go and put the key in the door for them, and then go back down and ask Amanda if Rob is home.'

I'm crawling with discomfort, but I can't come up with a better idea that that. Still, it comes as little surprise to me that, as we are putting the key into the lock of Room 33, there is a squawk of indignation from the lift, and we turn to face Amanda and two very elderly ladies with purple hair.

'Look, they are breaking into our room! Stop them!' one shouts.

'Stop! Thieves!' The other waves her walking stick at us, and Jasper lets go of the key and holds his hands above his head like it's the Old West, she's the sheriff and the stick is a Colt Peacemaker.

Amanda looks shocked and furious all at once. I guess she might lose her job for not checking we were legit guests, and I feel bad for that – she doesn't seem much older than us – but we're not on safe territory. 'Get away from that door! ' she shouts. We do as she says. 'I've called the police, so there's no point in you running off!'

'There was no need to involve the police, Amanda,' a smooth voice says from behind them, and once again I find myself looking into the dark eyes of the hotel's owner. 'It's just a simple case of misidentification, isn't it?'

'Miss Bennett!' All the colour leaves Amanda's cheeks. 'Those young people asked for a key that wasn't theirs!' Concern lines her smooth forehead.

'And you could have checked who they were against the ledger to see that one of them at least wasn't Miss Harrington or Miss Clarke, and you didn't. It's very late and we're all tired. This is only your third shift. There is no real harm done, is there?'

It could just be me in the face of yet another crisis, or does she look on edge? For all she's being nice to Amanda, there's something wrong here. Amanda seems to be shrinking into the carpet.

'They could have stolen our belongings and be locking the room back up to leave!' one of the purple ladies screeches.

'Nothing to see here,' Jasper squeaks, pulling out the insides of all his pockets. 'We weren't stealing anything.'

A door opens further down the corridor, and a man's tousled head appears. 'What's all this racket?'

'Absolutely nothing to worry about. Go to bed, Mr Hutchins, it's a storm in a teacup. Amanda, please take Miss Harrington and Miss Clarke to their room and reassure them, as I'm certain is the case, that no one has been in their room tonight.'

'Yes, Miss Bennett,' Amanda replies dutifully.

The man grunts something that sounded like 'bloody refund' and closes the door.

Valerie holds her arm out in a sweeping action back towards the lift doors. 'Shall we?' she asks, and there is no refusing as Amanda and the purple ladies scuttle past us towards their room, still burbling away. Valerie waits as we enter the lift, and she walks in after us. She stares at me as if she's provoking me to react, but I feel like I've said enough tonight. Everything's unravelling.

'We really weren't stealing anything,' Jasper says, as the doors slide shut.

'Indeed.' She hits her hand smartly against the triquetra button.

I just about manage not to react. 'Where are you taking us?' I ask, my voice dull.

'Somewhere we can talk without interruption,' Valerie says smoothly.

'What does the symbol on that button mean?' Jasper asks.

The edges of Valerie's lips curl upwards, but you couldn't call it a smile. 'I think you know the answer to that already, don't you?' she remarks. The momentum of the lift stopping makes us all stagger forward slightly. 'After all, we have met before.'

The lift door opens onto another corridor. It's painted the same shade of grey as the walls in the reception area. It doesn't feel menacing or ancient. It just looks like another floor of the hotel, except that it has one door at the end and no others. She waves us forward, and we move as she suggests.

The door at the end of the corridor is not opened with a handle or a key; she opens it with a keycard, and before I can get my head around them having this kind of technology in 1987, I'm slapped silent by the room inside.

It is like how I imagine the penthouse suite at the very

best hotel in the City would have been 30 years ago. In front of us is a vast open-plan room with several black leather sofas, what looks like a skinned sheep on the floor, tall lamps with their shades bent over at weird angles, a bar area with glass cabinets full of coloured bottles and a television inside a dark wooden cabinet. Jasper is staring open-mouthed at the television. It's showing a film I vaguely remember as a classic; *The Breakfast Club, Pretty in Pink, St Elmo's Fire* – one of them anyway, but the picture quality is appalling. I nudge Jasper, and he seems to wake up.

Sitting on one of the sofas next to a beautiful blonde girl is Rob. At least, he's almost Rob. His hair is a little longer down the back; he's wearing a white polo shirt instead of the usual black band T-shirt, and a pair of preppy dark blue cotton trousers. The dark, spiky hair still has bleached ends. He's ream, but somehow he just looks too clean-cut to be my Rob. I know he doesn't know me. I also know the blonde girl is Yvonne Walker. Her legs are sprawled proprietarily over his, and my life skews on its axis again.

'You wanted to check lover boy is still around?' Jasper says into my ear. 'He looks pretty still around from where I'm standing. Let's go. Oh no, look - they won't let us go.'

I scowl at him.

Rob glances up at us. His eyes linger on me a little longer than necessary, and it might be my imagination but I'm sure his cheeks blush a little. He takes a quick look at his mother and turns to the girl on the sofa. 'Time to leave, blondie.'

Yvonne crosses her arms like a sulky toddler. 'It's just getting to the good bit!' she exclaims in a startlingly plummy voice, pointing at the television. 'I want to know if Andie goes to the Prom by herself!'

I stare at her. It's probably not fair to hate her so much so instantly. She's not to know that she's with the boy I tried so hard not to fall for. It's not her fault that he has no idea who I am.

'Take the pirate and go watch it in the bedroom then,' he says, looking at me.

'Aren't you coming with me?' she says, falling back against the cushions on the sofa in a total huff.

'Hotel business,' he says, tickling her under the chin as if she's a puppy.

To her credit, she smacks his hand away. 'Don't patronise me,' she snaps and gets to her feet. 'It's after two anyway. I need to be up early tomorrow to catch my train back to Cambridge.'

'Have a good trip,' he says, without looking at her. There's not a lot of love in his eyes. The green is like coloured glass – beautiful but soulless. I remember what Brian said about him at Tracy's party. I can see there is something missing.

Yvonne drops a kiss onto his cheek, hesitates for a moment or two, and then leaves the room through another door further back.

'Where did you get that television?' Jasper asks suddenly.

'Rumblelows,' Rob replies.

'Why is it in a cupboard?' he asks incredulously.

Valerie's eyebrows lift, and then she sighs and frowns at Jasper. 'Is he always that gormless?' she asks, looking at me.

'Rude,' Jasper says, but he stops gawping at the now

blank screen.

'It took me a few minutes, and I came after you as soon as I realised. It explains the clothes,' Valerie says, lighting a cigarette and grabbing a half-full bottle of wine from what looks like a bar at the side of the room.

'What does?' I ask.

'You weren't exactly dressed for the day, as I recall,' she says, pouring a glass of blood-red liquid into a wine glass. 'You should have done more research. You were never going to get away with skin-tight bleached denim in December 1971. How long ago were you there?'

'Yesterday,' I hear myself saying. Not much point in lying to her, is there?

Valerie nods and sips at her drink. 'Can I get you anything? Beer, wine – something stronger?'

'A rum and coke would go down well right now,' Jasper says.

I shake my head no. One of us needs to stay clear-headed.

Valerie goes behind the bar and starts to fix Jasper's drink. 'And have you been riding for long?'

'Riding?' My voice comes out a lot squeakier than I planned.

She sighs and chucks an ice cube into the glass. 'How long have you been riding the Weys?'

I am aware I'm staring at her with my mouth in a fixed 'O' shape but I can't even. Not only does Valerie remember meeting us in 1971, she knows about the Weys. How did we make this happen? Did she overhear a conversation, and decide to do a bit of research for herself? Did Glenda let something slip over one too many glasses of Blue Nun?

'Oh, time travel has a name. That's nice,' Jasper says. She passes him the glass, and he slugs back half of it in one swallow.

'How do you know about the Weys?' I ask.

She presses a button on the wall beside the drinks cabinet and speaks into it. 'Baby, are you still awake?' After a moment, there is an indistinguishable crackly response. 'Can you come through to the lounge?' Followed by a mumble of something. 'Yes, it's important.' She clicks the button again and waves her hands towards the seats. 'Come and sit down.'

As we join her on one of the plush leather sofas, I try not to catch Rob's eye and stare at my Converse.

'So are you the rogue bystanders that ride with her then?' he asks me.

I don't say anything.

'Possibly,' she replies. 'That's why I asked him to join us, but I couldn't say too much over the intercom because I wanted to get a true reaction from all of them.'

'Could she be Weyfarere too?' Rob says.

Jasper drops the remains of his rum and coke all over his jeans.

I mean, I should've guessed with the triquetra button in the lift, but it's still a bit of a blow just how much they know. That word left me with no choice but to look directly at him, and I'm surprised how much it hurts to look into those beautiful green eyes and see not one trace of recognition, but there is an emotion there; I just can't place it.

Valerie takes the glass, goes over to the bar, and pulls a box of tissues out of a drawer.

I have a second or two to save myself before the pause is

too long and obvious. 'I'm not Weyfare,' I say.

'But you ride the Weys along with Lizzy Brookes,' Valerie says. Into the silence, she adds, 'Is there any particular reason she took a bunch of teenagers with her to 1971?' She drops the tissues into Jasper's lap and passes him another rum and coke.

'Where are you grounded?' Rob asks. 'The future or the past?'

'Look, why have you brought us here?' Jasper asks as she leaves, hands firmly holding the new glass now. 'We think it's a hotel, and now it turns out you know all our secrets. Are we in some kind of shit?'

'Know all your secrets? Hardly. Though, that will come I'm sure,' Valerie says. 'You came to the hotel of your own accord. The first question I have is, why would you do that?'

'Long story,' I say, avoiding Rob's eyes.

'Oh? Do elaborate.'

'I know you're Valerie Bennett, and that he's your son,' I say.

'With all respect, most people in town know that much about us,' she replies. 'I recognised you both from a party on the night of Glenda Brookes' birthday in 1971. You recognised the triquetra symbol, yet it doesn't explain why you came here at one o'clock on a Bank Holiday in May 1987.'

'The what symbol?' Jasper takes another big mouthful of rum and coke.

'Triquetra,' I say. 'The swirly symbol on the button in the lift.'

'I didn't know it had a proper name,' he says huffily, 'I thought it was just the Weyfarere symbol. Like the one on your -'

'Triquetra means Trinity, I think.' I interrupt him be-fore he can say 'key' or 'book'. I don't want them knowing I have my Weyfare key, or that we have *The Truth*. Or at least, Ani has *The Truth*. I'm still bothered by the fact that Glenda hadn't heard of it. I'm equally bothered by the fact that I don't have it with me, although to be honest, it might be just as well if they end up searching us. I'm still thinking about how I can protect my key, Rob's ring and Lizzy's blood token if they search us. I hope Jasper still has Glenda's pen from 1971. I wouldn't want to lose that just yet, either.

'It isn't a triquetra, actually,' Valerie says, coming back and perching on the sofa next to her son with a refilled wine glass. 'It's a stylised version of the Valknut. Have you heard of the Valknut?'

'Nope,' we lie in unison.

She exchanges glances with Rob. 'Yet you know about the Triquetra. Have you heard of the *Book of the Witan*?'

'Oh, of course,' I say airily. 'Just never got around to reading it.'

'I should hope not,' she says sternly like I'm five caught with my fingers in a Nutella jar. The goosebumps are starting to pop out on my arms. 'What's your name?'

'That information is on a need to know basis,' I say.

'Why would you be so protective of your name?' Rob asks. 'You know who we are.'

'You don't seem to be telling us a lot more than that,' Jasper says. 'How do you even know about the Weyfarere? Why is there a tricky sign in your lift, and how did you hear about the *Book of the Witan*?'

Rob and Valerie exchange glances again. 'So where is he?' Rob asks.

'I'm here, and I'm not particularly impressed with being dragged out of bed at some god awful time of the night.' The man, dressed in a short black silk dressing gown embroidered with a Chinese dragon, walks through the door that Yvonne left by, and turns to face us.

In an instant, the air leaves the room, and the colour leaves all of our faces. He stumbles in shock and reaches for the doorframe for support. Jasper's empty glass tumbles to the floor again, and I shoot up onto my feet.

'Well, I think that answers several of our questions,' Valerie says smoothly.

He's older, of course. The hair, cut short on top and long at the back, is not unlike Rob's, and it's still a dirty blond, but there are crinkles around his bright blue eyes and at the edges of his mouth that weren't there before someone stuck something sharp deep into his guts. Scott Kelly has arrived back in 1987, and it looks like he took the long way round.

Suddenly, I get a sense of the danger we could be in. Because this is the man we left on life support in a hospital in 1971. This man knew an alternative world like us, and now he's clearly a part of this new one.

'It is them, isn't it?' Rob asks, barely containing his excitement.

Scott nods yes. He can't take his eyes off me. It's unsettling; they are the same blue eyes that looked me up and down at Drake's when their owner was wearing a staff badge. Beautiful, but deadly. I do a quick bit of arithmetic in my head and work out that he's pretty much the same age as Valerie and Glenda now. The colour has gone from his cheeks, and he's breathing hard.

'But what happened to the other Scott?' I say out loud before I can even begin to think about whether it's worth bluffing our way out of this. 'The little boy who was already living in Stoneford?'

'The Kelly family were given a very lucrative reason to move to the City when he was still fairly young, well away from any chance meetings with a second self,' Valerie says. 'There is a saying, isn't there, that everyone has a doppelganger somewhere in the world?'

'You just sent your family away?' Jasper asks, his eyes big and child-like.

'I found I had a bigger role to play than the one they were offering,' Scott says enigmatically and walks across to take the cigarette that Valerie has lit for him. 'I can't believe you're here. I knew you might turn up one day, but to have you turn up at my home was never on the agenda. Maybe there is something important about the Weys at this point in Time. Or this Weydoor.'

I have so many questions to ask, but the first one out of my mouth is less important than some. 'How did you get here?'

Scott shrugs and sits on the sofa next to Rob. 'I lived,' he says simply. 'I lived the first month on a machine in St Peter's Hospital, and then later I was tended by a very kind and frankly curious nurse, who wondered why I never had any visitors.'

Of course. Valerie Simmons now Bennett hadn't been in catering at the hospital: she had been a nurse. Originally at

St Pete's. More likely, when you think about it. I look at her.

She smiles. 'After a bunch of kids my Matron described as 'rough around the edges' left on New Year's Eve 1971, no one ever came to see him again.' She pauses to draw on the cigarette. 'I assume you were part of that group?'

'We had to leave you there,' I say to Scott, suddenly feeling as I needed to apologise. 'We didn't abandon you. We didn't know if you'd recover. We planned to go back for you.'

'When I checked Scott's records, the number you gave us didn't exist,' Valerie says, 'and when I rang the number on his medical records, his mother was firstly distraught and secondly furious, as I'd led her to believe that her eight-year-old son wasn't playing on the swings in their village green with his father after all.'

'When I finally woke up, Val was there. She nursed me back to health. She gave me a place to stay when I was well enough to leave,' Scott says.

'So you are the rogues he talked about?' Rob asks. His voice is almost in awe. Scott nods.

'And when he was well enough to remember what had happened to him,' Valerie says, 'he had quite a story to tell.'

'I bet,' I say, trying to file my memories into the correct versions of the timeline. This is Scott Kelly, who arrived through the Weydoor in 1971 with a stab wound. This is Scott Kelly, who tried to steal Lizzy's Weyfarere key, but this is also the Scott who didn't get away with it. So this is the Scott Kelly who never stole the key, and he never saw *The Truth* either. 'How much did you tell them?'

'Enough to piece together a few missing parts from a jigsaw that is the legacy of my family.' Valerie gets to her feet.

'Scott showed us where the Weydoor was. Told us what he knew about the grounding tokens and the silver keys. Told us that Glenda Brookes was a Weyfare, and obviously her klutz of a daughter too.'

And her granddaughter, I think, praying to any God listening that they don't see the fear on my face or the key under my top.

'The history of your family?' Jasper asks, frowning.

'I told them about the five teenagers who called the ambulance,' Scott says calmly, 'and I told her I'd know them if I ever saw them again.'

'So Lizzy Brookes is definitely Rogue,' Valerie exclaims, her eyes glittering and excited.

'What is this word that you keep throwing about?' Jasper snaps suddenly. 'What does Rogue mean?'

'Rogue is the name we give to Weyfarere who ride the Weys without the correct paperwork or authority,' Valerie says.

'And who are you to give people these names?' Jasper asks.

'We are the Witan,' Valerie says.

Chapter Twenty-Three – If You Let Me Stay (Terence Trent D'arby, 1987)

'Witan?' I eventually find my voice. 'You can't be Witan!'

'What an odd thing to say,' Valerie says. 'Quite rude, too, in the circumstances.'

I'm on the edge of a major benny here but I swallow my bile and say, 'What circumstances?'

'Well, we have just placed you both in 1971, and you say you aren't Weyfare, which means you must have had a Weyfare to take you there,' Valerie says, placing a hand on Scott's exposed knee. I'm hoping they are looking at each other too lovey-dovey to notice me trying not to vom. Valerie Bennett and Scott Kelly? What the hell is Lizzy going to make of this development? 'We suspected Lizzy Brookes was the one who turned rogue as she grew older and more familiar to Scott,' Valerie goes on, 'but although Scott and I recognised one of her friends, three of you were nowhere to be seen. Now suddenly you two turn up today, and we have unmitigated proof for the Moot. Not only is Lizzy rogue, but it also seems she's been taking bystanders on the Weys with her. Naughty girl. I don't fancy her chances.'

'Her chances in what? That sounds like a threat,' I say, anger bubbling in my chest.

'Doesn't it?' Valerie smiles. 'Maybe you will have that

drink after all?' We lock stares. No one backs down.

'Can you tell us about the Witan since we don't have a scooby what it is?' Jasper asks. 'And I'll have another drink.'

'I'll make them,' Rob says. 'What's your poison?'

'Vodka and Coke Zero,' I say and correct my mistake instantly. 'Diet Coke, I mean.'

'You don't need to lose any weight,' he replies, as he walks to the bar.

In any other situation that would have been an NSV. 'Thanks, Rob,' I reply.

Rob stops in his tracks and turns and stares at me as if I've dropped the 'c' word. Valerie and Scott turn slowly and look at me; her eyebrows have disappeared under her hard fringe.

'I don't think anyone told you my name,' Rob says. He's paper white. 'How come you know my name, but I don't know yours?'

'Your mum mentioned it when we came in – she must've done,' I say quickly.

'I don't believe I did,' Valerie says, her voice low and level.

'How else would we know it?' I retort, forcing myself to be bright. 'Come on. So we know your name. Big deal. You were telling us about the Witan.'

There's an uncomfortable pause when all we can hear is the sound of Rob dropping more ice into glasses.

'Since they've ridden the Weys and they've heard of the Weyfarere, there isn't much point in withholding that information from them, baby,' Scott says. 'It won't matter what they know now, will it?'

We stare at each other for a few moments, then she shakes her head slightly and looks away. 'The Witan are the descendants of the brothers gifted with the responsibility of protecting the Weys. The Weys, as I suppose you've worked out for yourselves, are interdimensional energy channels tracking time. The Weydoors allow people to ride across the timelines. The Weyferere are the Guardians of the Weydoors, and the Witan provide the laws and boundaries that keep the Weys safe from abuse.'

'So you're descended from Wayland?' I ask.

'You may claim not to have read the *Book of the Witan*, but someone has spoken to you about its contents,' Scott says. 'Lizzy, no doubt.'

'Weyfarere are descended from Wayland,' Valerie says smoothly. 'Witan are descended from his brothers Egil and Slagfior.' She pauses. 'Is something wrong?' I guess she's referring to the noise Jasper and me made as she finished her sentence. I look across at him quickly and will him to have the common sense not to say what I want to scream out at the top of my lungs; when I read *The Truth* back in Brian's garage that morning which feels like a decade ago, it said the descendants of Wayland's brother are the Weyleighers, not the Witan.

Somewhere back in all our unintended meddling, it looks like the smugglers have become the leaders.

'No, I'm just a bit impressed. That's one hell of a lineage,' I say, trying to keep my voice light.

'One of the oldest traceable lineages in the country,' Rob says, handing me the drink he's been making, and I can't ignore the note in his words; is it smug or resentful? The trouble is, and my mind is racing through all this so fast I can barely track each thought, that whatever Valerie Bennett is calling herself, whether it be Witan or Weyleigher on this timeline, she is still Rob's mother, so he is a descendant too. Has he always been? Have the family always been? When I was here last time, with Rob, kissing as if our lives depended on it under the lych gate at Trinity, was he the son of a Weyleigher? Has Valerie always been a descendant of the brothers? Glenda said we were the last known Weyfarere family still actively protecting a Weydoor. Did Valerie always know about us? Did Rob know when he was Lizzy's friend? Did he know what her family were? Surely not. No, please surely not.

Someone is speaking.

'Who stabbed you, Scott?' Jasper says into the silence. 'How did you end up in the Old Library in 1971?'

'That happened on a timeline that no longer exists,' he says evenly, 'as did any relationship I had with Lizzy, so the answer to both is irrelevant. More important I think is the question of why you were there. How did Lizzy get you back to that time? It must have been Glenda,' he adds thoughtfully. 'She must have helped you back to her 21st birthday. Lizzy couldn't have done that. Not easily.'

'So what were you doing there?' Valerie asks. 'Why did Glenda send you back to that birthday?'

I'm feeling more and more that the reason we were there needs to stay a secret, and I'm becoming more and more uncomfortable, sitting in this showy room at nearly three in the morning. I need to sleep, and I want to go back to Lizzy, Kim and Ani, and warn them of what we know. 'Lizzy wanted to meet her mum when she was younger.'

'And you weren't told of the extreme dangers of meeting yourself in the past?' Valerie. 'Were you alive in 1971?'

'Not even practised for,' Jasper says.

'But Lizzy was. She would've been a toddler. Pretty much the same age as Rob here.'

And Rob here was passed out on a sofa with a dummy soaked in gin.

'So what happened to Eddie?' I ask casually, looking at Scott, who is ageing well again for a middle-aged guy.

'Eddie?' she asks.

'Rob's dad?' I say, and instantly regret it, because the temperature has just plummeted by about ten degrees again and I have this horrible feeling that we are giving too much of ourselves away.

'My dad is called Ted,' Rob says, eyes narrowing. 'Short for Edward. No one ever calls him Eddie.'

'Of course not,' I say cheerfully, 'my mistake. Like you said earlier, it's hard to remember something that happened 16 years ago.'

'Except for you it was only yesterday,' Valerie says.

Oh, touché, Ms Bennett.

'Did you actually tell us where you were from?' she asks, then turns to Scott. 'Do you remember from before?'

'Too long ago,' Scott says, yawning. 'I don't remember them being around before Lizzy's 18th birthday party. That was the day she found out that the Old Library was a Portal.'

'So you've been to Lizzy's 18th, and Glenda's 21st,' Valerie says. 'Quite the party animal, aren't you both?'

I won't even meet her eyes.

'I don't mean to be rude,' Jasper says, clearly meaning to be rude, 'but I'm shafted and I need to get me some shut-eye.

Are you going to let us go back to Glenda's place, or are you giving us a bed for the night?'

If I'd had any legal currency on me, I'd have gambled the lot on the answer.

'Knowing your propensity for riding the Weys, perhaps it would be better if you stayed as our guests,' Valerie says. 'We can talk more in the morning. I am, after all, supposed to be running a hotel here, but at least by leading us to you, that cretin of a receptionist has earned herself another day's trial.'

The room she gave me is all plush purple velvet, black leather sofas and silvery voile drapes like something out of an emo fantasy, but the bed is clean and warm and comfy, and I so want to drop into the best sleep of my lives. Pretend for a few hours that I'm going to wake up on Bank Holiday Monday to the racket of Elizabeth Wharton yelling at me that I'd promised her I was going to start my revision schedule at nine o'clock every day and if I wanted my place at Exeter University, I'd better pull my finger out – whatever that meant. Instead, I'm still laying on top of the bedcovers an hour later, staring wide-eyed at the blackness.

In the end, I give up. I make a cup of coffee using the room facilities, and pocket the pencil and notebook on the desk; who knows what might come in useful as a token? I get up and turn on the white plastic television set that sits on the large wooden desk, but all I can find is white noise and a static picture of a weird girl in a red dress playing noughts and crosses with a freaky clown. I turn it off and lie down again, but I still can't sleep. I have too much to think about.

They've given Jasper another room. We tried to pretend

we were together and that it was totally cool for us to share a bed, but Valerie was having none of it. I can't be sure the rooms aren't wired anyway, but she won't risk us communicating in other less vocal ways that she can't control. Valerie is Witan, and I remember all too well the technology they'd developed in 2019, but this is 1987, and even James Bond was impressed by whistling at key rings to locate them back then.

Concerned that I'm also being watched, I go into the en-suite bathroom. There is a mirror over the sink, so I hook one of the white towels embroidered with 'St Peter's Hotel and Bar/Restaurant' in blue italics, hoping they aren't that keen to watch people take a crap, and I sit on the toilet lid.

I don't need to check the key around my neck. I can feel it's there, even more so every time my heart pulses with anger or fear or confusion. I'll have a hard job explaining to Valerie and her people why I have it if they find it. It was hard enough explaining it to Lizzy and Glenda.

It's the other stuff I really want to check. Jammed into the back pocket of my jeans, I carefully pull them out: the white bandage covered in the blood from Lizzy's injured ankle and the ring the older Rob gave me, the item I'm most inter-ested in for now.

I've not examined it until now. Until now, it didn't seem significant, just thoughtful, and touching. It's a gold sig-net ring, probably big enough for a man's ring finger. The flat part at the top is covered in azure blue enamel, and when I look closely at it in the harsh bathroom lights, I draw a sharp breath.

There is a triquetra engraved on Rob's ring. No, what did Valerie call it? Not a triquetra. A valknut. However you look at it, it answers one of my questions in the lounge. Older Rob knew he was related to the Witan in the future when he gave me that ring. He was Witan all along.

I was only just beginning to work through that hurt when something occurred to me, and I was shocked at myself for not having thought it before; if only girls could be Weyfare, did the same rules apply to the Weyleighers? Or the Witan, or whatever they were known as now. Was it a girls-only club? If that was the case, then Scott could never have actually been a Weyleigher, even before it all got so complicated. Nor could Rob. I needed to find out about their traditions, for different reasons now.

So Scott had stayed in 1971, and now he was obviously Valerie's partner and step-dad to Rob in all but name. Had he been the reason Rob's Dad left? What had made Scott stay? Had he just not been brave enough to ride the Weys back again? Or not able? Or was there just not a good enough reason to go back to the timeline where he'd been stabbed?

Why exactly were they keeping us here? If the Witan were the law-keepers, did they have courts? If so, what could they try us for? Just how serious was a rogue Weyfare? I tried to remember what Glenda had told us about them the last time we were in 2019. They had been planning to send me to some kind of boarding school, although Rob had said it was more like a prison. At the time, he didn't think much of Ani and Jasper's chances of survival, as they were bystanders who knew too much. With a lurch in my stomach, I realise that they think I'm a bystander too, and I fall into that camp now.

What was going to happen tomorrow? Would they take us to Glenda and demand information about what we'd all been up to? Or would we all end up here, in the dungeons of the hotel, being interrogated by the descendants of the brothers, the people we thought were capable of murder for the right price? Will they throw us through the Weydoor, and dispose of us in some random timeline? Will they kill us first?

I have so many questions, and pretty much no answers. As I'm rolling everything around in my mind, my fingers toy with the little golden ring, and through the swamp of my thoughts, I realise that the underside of the ring is rougher to the touch than the top. I hold it up as high as I can towards the striplight, and see that there is a tiny inscription, written in slanting italic script like the One Ring to Rule them All in the films. This isn't a film though, and I don't have a fire to throw the ring in, and even if I did, I think the writing would be too small to read in this light. It's annoying, but I can't do much about it.

The main thing is that I have my Weyfare blood. They can't know about Weyfarere blood, because Ani translated it from a book they've never heard of. They don't know that I have it as well Lizzy and Glenda unless we tell them about it. I trust my BFF with my life, and I hope Ani's still clever enough to keep her mouth shut. As long as I have my blood, and the bandage with Lizzy's blood, I can control my rides on the Weys. As Rob's signet ring must be a token, that's three ways we can escape. I'm not sure how we can ever get back to the Weydoor again to be able to ride, but if we can, there is hope. I have to protect these items, in a place Valerie and her goons won't easily find.

When I turn the light off in the bathroom and go back into the bedroom, there is a faint light behind the curtains. It

can't be long before sunrise. I lay down on the bed, fully expecting to still be wide awake as Monday, May 25th dawns, but
my eyes close, and when they open a few minutes later, the
curtains are full of the bright light of day, and there is a loud
hammering on the door.

'Are you trying to take the door off its hinges?'

'So you are awake?'

'Duh!'

'Finally! Be in the lounge in twenty minutes,' a familiar voice says, 'and don't be late. We invited some more old
friends around for breakfast.'

Chapter Twenty-Four – Living In A Box (Living In A Box, 1987)

It's like a skewed version of the headteacher's office, with the addition of scrambled egg served on china plates on trays by uniformed waiters. We sit in a straight line on the huge leather sofa where Rob and Yvonne sat last night: me, Lizzy, Jasper, Brian, Ani, and Kim. It's been so long since I ate something decent that even I'm forking the fluffy eggs into my mouth, but Lizzy is pushing little piles around her plate, staring at Scott as he leans against the bar talking in a hushed voice to Rob. Kim keeps looking from her, to Scott, to me then to Rob before starting the whole cycle again.

Valerie is standing by the cupboard with the television inside. 'Explain to me again how you made your mother sick with your token,' she repeats.

'I didn't make her sick,' Lizzy repeats. 'I told you, there are two keys or tokens or whatever you call them now; the key from now that she's wearing, and the one from the alternative future that she lent me. When she touched them at the same time, they created the paradox. She threw a bit of an eppy, but the ambulancemen said she would be fine after a good night's sleep.'

'And you don't know yet if that's the case,' Valerie replies.

'Because you and your heavies shoved us in the back

of your Black Mariah before she'd woken up and we'd had a chance to check on her,' Brian snaps.

'You;' Valerie snaps her head around to glare sharply at him; 'are in no position to be commenting on the affairs on the Weys!'

'Sieg Heil,' Brian mutters.

'It's like *Nineteen-Eighty-Four*,' Ani mutters back.

'Isn't it 1987?' Jasper asks.

'The book, not the now,' she sighs, shaking her head.

'I'm losing track,' he says seriously.

'Explain to us why we're here again,' Lizzy says, putting the tray with the uneaten food on the floor at her feet, still staring at Scott.

Valerie steps forward, her hands behind her back. 'You have broken the Witan code; first, by riding unauthorised on the Weys and secondly, by taking bystanders with you. Now it appears you have broken the Code a third time by bringing your mother into contact with a physical paradox. One of these breaks alone would be a serious matter.'

'So are you sending us to Azkaban?' Jasper asks.

'Azkaban? I've never heard of this place,' Valerie says.

'It's a fictional prison,' Ani says. 'He wants to know if you're going to lock us up.'

'That will be a matter for the Moot to decide,' Scott says. I watch as he finally allows himself to meet Lizzy's unwavering stare. 'Was there something you wanted to ask me?'

'Why on earth would I have any questions?' she asks, her voice laden with irony. 'I'm just impressed with how lightly you landed on your traitorous feet, Patchouli. If it wasn't for us, you wouldn't even have made it to that hospital bed, let alone have Florence Nightingale there find out about your special superpowers.'

'I don't have any special superpowers,' he replies smoothly. 'I had information that I gave to Ria; I felt it was a pretty fair trade for the care she gave me.'

'You gave her information that wasn't yours to give,' Lizzy says.

'But it was clearly meant to be since he passed it on to a formerly dormant line of descendants who were able to take back their roles as fully and dutifully as your family do.' Valerie lights a cigarette. 'Your father has agreed to bring your mother to us later this morning, once she has had a little more bedrest. We will need to ascertain the damage caused by the physical paradox, then we will need to ascertain her role in this mess before we submit our findings to the Moot.'

'And what happens to us in the meantime?' Brian asks. 'I've got exams to prepare for.'

'Don't hold your breath,' Kim says, with uncharacteristic disgust.

Lizzy looks up at Valerie, and then pointedly looks away back again to Scott. 'You don't belong here,' she says quietly to him. 'What are you now – 40? You've lived 15 years of a life that wasn't yours. Why didn't you come back?'

He looks at her pityingly. 'How exactly was I supposed to come back? I was wired up in acute care, I had no idea where I was, and once I realised where I was, I had no key to control my ride.'

Jasper is smacking me on the back as I find myself in a fit of coughing. I try not to make it too obvious that I've confirmed something brilliant and terrifying all at the same time by giving them all-too-meaningful looks.

'Is there something wrong with your breakfast, Maisie?' Valerie asks politely.

'Maybe if I could just have a small glass of water?' I ask, putting the tray down beside Lizzy's.

It's Rob who brings it over. I refuse to let myself look into those empty green eyes, so I stare at the hand that passes me the tumbler of water, and I nearly knock it into his lap when I see the blue enamelled signet ring sitting shinily on his ring finger. I manage to grab the glass before I accidentally touch the ring, because I have a feeling I have its paradox twin, wrapped in a blood-stained bandage in the toe of my sock, hidden deep inside my Converse in the bathroom behind the covered mirror this morning after my shower, just in case they searched me. I'd figured as much as it would hurt me to lose the key that older Lizzy gave me on another timeline, I could travel – no, what were we to call it? – ride the Weys without it, but I need Lizzy's blood and my own blood to control it. I've still not worked out the significance of Rob's ring, but I'm not letting that go either, and these guys have no idea about the power of Weyfare blood because the translation Ani corrected was in *The Truth*, not *The Book of the Witan*. And Glenda had never heard of *The Truth*, and I'd bet good money that neither Valerie nor Scott have, either.

'I'm so sorry,' I splutter, 'I'm such a klutz.'

'Don't sweat it,' he says somewhere above my eye line. 'No harm done.'

Where is *The Truth*? Does Ani still have it on her? 'I really need some air,' I blurt out suddenly. 'I've got cabin fever.'

'They have been cooped up for a while, Mum,' Rob says.

'There's no harm in them having a wander around the Quad, is there?'

'I don't want any air,' Lizzy says firmly. 'I'm staying put until Mum gets here.'

I manage to give Jasper and Kim meaningful looks in time for them to decline the invitation, and Ani and Brian simply shake their heads. I wonder what passed between them in the caravan last night.

The Quad is not dissimilar to the Grotty at the centre of Fletcher-Clark School for Boys; there's a small pond, a couple of wooden benches and shrubs and plants that are just beginning to flower. Rob walks me out to one of the benches and sits down. I can't see any other hotel guests, so I can only assume this is still part of their private quarters.

I sit beside him in silence, thinking back to what might have happened before if we'd got some privacy anywhere, trying to get my thoughts in order. He's wearing a signet ring now. Can I remember him ever wearing one before? Awkward much? Ironically, he is twisting the ring around and around on his finger.

'You know me, don't you?' he says after some time, startling me.

'We met last night, so obviously,' I reply shortly.

He leans forward onto his lap and turns to face me. 'You know what I mean.'

I refuse to meet his eyes. Is this a set-up? Did I miss a signal from Valerie? Is he here to get information out of me, rather than supervise my downtime? 'You're wrong. I don't know what you mean.'

'You've been riding the Weys. I'm betting you knew me

before. On a different timeline.'

I still won't look at him, much as I can feel him willing me to do it. 'As Scott said, all other timelines are obsolete.'

'Were we friends?' For the first time, I can hear the faintest echo of what used to be Rob in his voice: a subtle warmth, a hint of care.

So I'm going to regret this, but hey, why break the habit of several timelines? 'Yes, we were friends. Happy now?'

We both stare forward at the grey stone walls in front of us. Although it's outside, the stillness is eerie; I can't hear any birds or even the traffic from the main road on the other side of the building.

'I thought so,' he says eventually. 'You knew my name, and Mum definitely didn't tell you what it was. And you called my dad Eddie like it was natural.'

'To me, it was,' I say simply.

'What's your name?' he asks.

I sigh. 'Maisie.'

'Unusual name. Like the girl in *Dukes of Hazzard*? No, that was Daisy, wasn't it?' This isn't my Rob. My Rob is gone, regardless of the weird echoes I'm feeling right now. I can't risk falling for a fake with my boyfriend's face.

'Do you play the drums?' I ask, against my better instincts.

'Piano,' he replies. 'Had lessons since I was very young. Always loved music. Would've loved to play in a band though.' He leaves a pause. 'Did I play the drums when you knew me?'

'You played drums in a band.' I say. Okay, I know I shouldn't tell him about the life he'll never live, but no one ever said it was a rule. Lizzy and Glenda just said they didn't want to know, and he does, and I'm hoping beyond hope that somehow I might trigger something inside him, but how can I possibly trigger a memory held by a different person?

'Were we any good?'

'You were,' I say, and I give up and look into his eyes, and my fears are correct because the emptiness has filled a little inside them; there is some warmth, some kindness and some care there, and suddenly my eyes are filling with tears and I turn away, annoyed with myself.

'Was 1987 very different the last time you were here?'

'Hell, yeah,' I say.

'Tell me how,' he says pleadingly, and then he reaches forward and wipes away the single tear that has escaped down my cheek, and I remember sitting in his arms at the Fundraiser while he did the same thing. No, he didn't. This isn't my Rob.

It's hard, but I take his hand from my face and put it back on his lap, carefully making sure that I don't touch the Witan ring. 'I don't think your mother would like it if I did.'

'She's the Witan, not me,' he says, and suddenly he is angry. 'The line descends through the daughters. This great and noble ancestry,' he swings his arms around at the buildings surrounding us, his voice all lordly and fake, then his arms slump down to his sides and his voice returns to normal. 'I'm no real part of this. I've got money because of it, and I have a great life. I've been blessed with a lot. But I'm not important to anyone.' He sighs. 'I've met a few bystanders, but I've never met one that's ridden the Weys with a Weyfare.' He rubs his hands together but doesn't put one back on my knee. 'I've never met one who knew me on a different timeline. I wish you would tell me how it was.'

'Why would you want to know?' I snap suddenly, the ache in my heart spreading out like a spark catching in a catherine wheel. 'What does it matter? It's like Scott said. In my 1987, he was 24 and he was with Lizzy. He let her down, but they were together, and what's the point in digging it all over? Now he's an older guy, and he's with your mother. Lizzy's only just turned 18.'

'We're both still 18,' he says. 'You and me.'

'I'm not 18 yet,' I point out. 'Not that it matters.'

'What did matter?' he asks quietly.

I look up at another bright blue cloudless sky and try to dig myself out of this torture. 'In my 1987? Family mattered. Friendship. Love. Parties and discos and barbeques. Working out how to be independent; how to beat the odds. Learning how to make the right decisions.'

'And which part of that was I?' he whispers.

I stand up then, and for some reason, I'm really conscious of the items hidden in my sock. 'What's the name of your girlfriend again?'

'Yvonne,' he says without hesitation, standing beside me. 'You don't like me very much, do you?'

'I don't think you're understanding my position,' I reply. 'Maybe we should just go in now.'

'I am understanding your position,' he says, 'I don't think you get mine.'

'What do you want from me?' I turn and snap into his face.

'I've spent my whole life knowing about the Witan and the Weys. How I'm a member of a privileged family. How the Weyfarere aren't to be trusted. How the Witan have to keep control of the Weys. And I have dreamed of being able to ride the Weys even though it's forbidden,' he says, and his eyes look down into mine like emerald again, deep, flawless and full of passion, 'and you turn up today and you've ridden the Weys, and you know my name, and I want to know where you've been and what you know. I want to know what kind of life we had.' He looks at his hands. 'I want to know whether I was happy there.'

The unspoken statement hangs between us in the silence. *Because I'm not happy here.*

I close my eyes and let the breath gently leave my lungs. 'We were friends,' I say quietly, 'okay, maybe we were more than friends: you and me, Brian and Ani. Jasper, Kim and Lizzy, at first it was a laugh, but it's all spoiled now. It's all wrong – this 1987 wasn't the one we left and now we all have to live with the life that we've made, the life we created by riding the Weys, and unless anyone can tell us how to undo all the knots we've made, we are all stuck here, waiting for your mother to decide what to tell the Moot so that we can all be trotted off to some prison for messing up big time!'

'More than friends,' he repeats. He has to pick up on the one phrase I wish I'd never spoken.

'But it doesn't matter now, doesn't it?' I say.

'It doesn't stop me wanting to know.'

We stare into each others' eyes for several moments. 'Glenda will be here soon to put the final few nails in our coffin,' I say bitterly. 'Once she's finished speaking, your mother is going to have us up in front of her court to explain crimes that we didn't realise we committed before they lock us up.'

'The Moot are not monsters,' he says. 'They'll listen to the facts and they won't pass judgement until they are satisfied everyone's acted honestly.'

'And then they'll send us away to some prison to rot.'

'You said we were more than friends on your timeline,' he says. 'Maybe I owe you. Maybe you came here tonight so I could save you.'

Why had I come here tonight? That's right – it was to save him. Or at least to make sure that he was safe and well and not extinguished. Funny how things turn out.

'It doesn't matter why I came here.'

'Did you come here to find me?'

'Will you stop it?' I cry out and freeze in my tracks. I figure with everything he's been saying in the last few minutes there's no way we're being supervised, but nothing will make Valerie or Scott come running like me screaming. 'Stop asking me questions about a life you never knew you had. I told you. It was more than another timeline – it already feels like another lifetime,' I add, quieter now. 'You aren't the same boy, and after all I've been through lately, I'm probably not the same girl either.'

'Then why was it that as soon as you walked into the room last night, I felt as if I had been smacked in the mouth? That I had known you forevermore?' He reaches out and I pull away. 'You did. You came here for me.'

That word. Echoing down through the decades, last spoken by an older man in desperation as he gave me another means of escape across the Weys, should I ever need one.

'Don't touch me with your ring hand.'

'Whyever not?' He looks confused, with good reason.

'Just trust me, okay?'

He takes my hand with the other, gently. 'Would it be all right if I touched you with this one instead?"

'Rob! Come back in here now, please,' Valerie's shrill voice cuts through the tension that's building between me and her son. 'The Weyfare's family are here.'

I look down at the ringless hand holding mine and based on that one word, I make a decision that could make or break everything.

Chapter Twenty-Five – Surrender
(Swing Out Sister, 1987)

'What took you so bloody long?' Valerie snaps as we walk back into the vast lounge, which is now even busier since Glenda and Henry have turned up, and they've bought Paul with them.

'She wasn't feeling all that great. Some kind of foot injury so she said, but I couldn't see anything,' Rob says, sliding away from me quickly to hide behind the bar and pour himself a cup of tea from a huge silver teapot. 'Most likely faking it.'

'You didn't say anything about having an injury,' Valerie sneers.

'It didn't hurt until I went outside. Thanks,' I add, as Jasper jumps to his feet to let me sit in his place.

'Better let Ria have a look to be on the safe side,' Scott says, 'she did use to be a pretty good nurse.'

I hold my foot out innocently and accept the glass of water passed across to me by Ani. I look into her inquiring eyes. If she'd been my BFF I know she could have understood my next sentence without question, but she's all I have left. 'It's getting hot in here,' I tell her, 'did you leave your jacket somewhere?'

'It's in a safe place,' she says evenly. I nod. Maybe there's more of my BFF left here than I thought.

Valerie is kneeling at my feet, having already pulled

off my Converse and the sock beneath. 'No sign of injury as I thought,' she says, standing up and taking off a pair of opaque plastic white gloves. 'I think you maybe hit your head though; your friend is still wearing her jacket.'

'So she is,' I say quietly to myself, pulling back on my sock and boot and tucking them around the back of my other boot, with its hidden stash inside.

Valerie coughs pointedly, and a few murmurs die down instantly. 'I called you all here for an informal chat today,' she says, 'to give you an opportunity to talk freely before we inform the Moot of the current situation.'

I notice that the reason the room is so busy is not that there are three more people in it. There are now several people standing around the outside of the room with their backs to the wall, and they remind me eerily of the people in the black uniforms at my house in 2019.

'Is there really any need to get the Moot involved in this?' Glenda says. She's standing at the end of the sofa next to Lizzy, and her arm is protectively along the back. 'It's an honest mistake; surely we can deal with it at a local level. Lizzy is a headstrong girl, she was just overwhelmed by the news of her inheritance and I can assure you it won't happen again.' She sounds confident enough, but she keeps glancing at the people standing at the back.

Lizzy scoffs loudly. 'Inheritance? You called it a burden, not a bit of extra cash.'

'Did she now?' Valerie asks politely. 'When was this?'

Lizzy looks as if she wishes she could nail her mouth shut. 'I don't remember,' she mutters, 'but it wasn't on this timeline.'

'Perhaps we'd better hear the facts from this timeline before we go any further,' Valerie says, taking a lit cigarette from Scott. 'Glenda, you speak first. And will one of you please give up your seat to her? She looks like a wrung-out dishcloth. Are there no manners on your timelines?'

'I'm fine,' Glenda insists, although when Brian gets up, we all shuffle down and Paul helps her sit next to Lizzy before going and standing behind her. Henry perches on the arm of the sofa. 'There's little to tell. Lizzy was 18 on Saturday and, according to the rules of the Witan, I told her of her duties and presented her with her key.'

'And how did she end up with the bystanders?' Valerie asks.

'They appeared with her this morning.' Glenda looks at Henry, and he squeezes her shoulder and nods. 'I'm sorry, but Lizzy didn't take the news of her birthright well.'

'What happened?' Valerie asks, her voice cool and smooth like a snake would sound if it had a voice.

'She stormed off,' Glenda says, clasping her hands. 'She said she was going to the Rutherfords' garden party, and she just left. The next thing we know is she's back today at Travellers' Rest with Kimberley Fox, Brian Walker and these three bystanders.'

Lizzy says nothing, but her eyes are like glass.

'How did you know we were bystanders? We might have been new friends,' Jasper asks.

'You came out of the Tunnel to the Old Library with Lizzy. What else would you be?' Paul replies.

'I'm asking the questions, thank you,' Valerie's smooth voice ratchets up a little. She looks at Jasper. 'Your memories are slightly different, I imagine.'

'You betcha,' he says.

'And this boy?'

'I'm Brian Walker,' Brian says. 'I'm a friend. From 1987 like Kim. I've ridden on the Weys. I know all about it.'

Valerie's eyes disappear under her heavy dark fringe. 'We'll come to that in a moment, perhaps. How did you come to be sick, Glenda?'

I never knew you could slice an uncomfortable atmosphere. 'I'm not sure,' Glenda mutters.

'Oh, I think you are sure. You experienced a physical paradox, according to Lizzy,' Valerie replies. I look at Glenda then, and her face has turned even paler. 'You touched a duplicate of the token key you were wearing, a duplicate that was made when your daughter rode the Weys into the past. Can we assume she was acting under your direction? I think so, as she was wearing your key. Can we assume therefore that, in spite of your protestations, you knew she was taking bystanders with her? Given the rest of the evidence, I think so.' She walks forward, one perfectly shaped leg slowly in front of the other. 'Of course, your daughter changed the timeline while she was there, so we have little idea now of why you might have acted like this.'

'I -' Glenda's voice fades away to nothing. I feel sick suddenly. I turn to look at Jasper. He's staring at the floor. Kim is wide-eyed and terrified; Brian and Ani have their heads in their hands. Lizzy looks angry. Again.

'Or maybe a little idea is enough. You know Scott's background, don't you?'

'You've been kind enough to share some of it with me,

yes,' Glenda replies, her voice seeming to recover a little, her eyes still trained on her hands. Christ, the way she's speaking, you'd think Valerie Bennett was some kind of high priestess. Val and Glenda were lifelong friends; how come she was being so sub?

'Some of it, yes, but not all.' Valerie takes another pace or two across the room towards her, and by default, towards Lizzy and the rest of us. 'I told you that I found Scott in hospital some time in early 1972, with no family or medical records at all. I assumed he was a bystander who had lost his Wey, and as he recovered, we fell in love and he decided to stay.'

Hang on. That's not right. She didn't know about the Weys until he told her. I risk a look at Rob, but he's drinking his tea from a small china cup, and he won't connect. Scott, however, is looking straight at me, and it's freaky. My sick feeling is growing into one of imminent Armageddon.

'That's what you told me, yes.' Glenda replies.

'Scott will tell you what actually happened,' Valerie says, arriving in front of us just close enough to be uncomfortable.

'Lizzy and I were lovers on an alternate version of the timeline. It ended badly. I was stabbed and then abandoned in 1971 by your daughter and her gang,' he says, without looking away from me.

His words act like gunpowder on a lit fuse. Lizzy is out of her seat and running at Scott so fast that I think she's going to make it and actually get to rip his eyes out with the claws she's made of her hands, but one of the big guys from the back of the room manhandles her into a human cage. Jasper, Paul, Brian and Kim are on their feet shouting words that seem to overlap, but not at the same time, words like 'filthy' and 'bastard' and 'lies' and 'thankless'. Rob is shouting at Scott, and Scott is ignoring him, but it seems like even Rob hasn't heard this version of Scott's story and that seems weird; not that all this wasn't weird enough because even though I'm still just sitting gob-smacked on the sofa wondering why Ani looks so pale, the other guys in black from around the room come forward. One is in front of me. I realise there are not several of them; there are seven. One for each of us, including Glenda, who is sobbing openly into Henry's chest while Paul is being held down by another.

'Enough of this insolence!' Valerie shouts, and everyone just looks at her. 'I am Witan, Chieftain of the South Moot, and I will have order here!'

'Or what?' Lizzy snarls.

'Lizzy, please! You'll just make it worse,' Glenda cries out, and faced with the blotchy, wet face of her mother, Lizzy's temper drains.

'We will get nowhere further today,' Valerie says, into the silence. 'There is still much to be discovered and learned about the various timelines that Lizzy has travelled, but there is no rush. For now though;' she turns and faces us with her right hand across her chest as if she were feeling her heartbeat; 'I, Valerie Bennett of the Witan detain you, Elizabeth Brookes, on the charge of riding the Weys without authorization and the additional charge of suspicion of attempted unauthorised extinction. Glenda Brookes, I detain you on suspicion of aiding and abetting your daughter's crimes. The bystanders must remain here for their own safety. Henry, Paul – you are of course free to leave. This is Witan business and as men, it does not concern you.'

'You're keeping my wife and daughter here against their will. I'm going nowhere,' Henry hisses, stroking Glenda's hair.

'Likewise mother and sister,' Paul snarls, still trying to free himself from the guy in black.

'Then we will have a full house today. Speak to the caterers, please Rob,' Valerie says. 'Let's all retire to our private quarters for a while and cool off these high spirits.'

The private quarters this time are not quite so luxurious. The hotel décor has been replaced with items more at home in a backpacker's hostel, but there are no bars, so it doesn't feel like the prison it clearly is. The guys in black put me, Ani and Jasper in the same room this time. I figure that the place is definitely wired, and when I pull out the notebook and pencil I nicked from the nicer room, I almost laugh when I see Jasper do the same. Great messed up minds still think alike. We all troop into the little bathroom.

Ani is the first to write in my notebook. 'We may not have long,' she scribbles, 'if they are watching us.'

'Use the bathroom, and cover the mirror,' I write.

To be fair, it's not really a bathroom, it's more of a toilet with a washbasin. It's completely cramped, but we all just about manage to fit in, and Ani tosses her jacket over the small mirror over the sink.

'Where is it?' I write.

'In the Old Shed,' she writes back. 'When we woke up and you'd gone, I went out and hid it in one of the huge pots at the back.'

'That's not safe!!!!!' I write, overdoing the exclamation marks to get my emotion across. 'I thought you put it somewhere safe!'

'Assuming they find out about its existence at all, why would they look in the shed?'

Ani writes. 'First place they'll look is somewhere safe.'

'That book is dangerous now,' Jasper finally writes, after watching our conversation. 'That might be the only copy that's left.'

I nod. Ani writes, 'I didn't read anywhere near all of it, but I never saw mention of the Witan.'

'They all still think that the keys are important,' I scribble. 'That you need a key to ride the Weys.'

'So the true info isn't in the Witan's book?' Jasper writes.

I shake my head no. 'I bet the real info about the Weyleighers isn't in there either. I need to -' but I don't get a chance to write what I need to let them know because there is a loud bang, and we all realise at once that someone or ones have come into the main room. Jasper reaches across and locks the door.

'Why are you all in the toilet together?' an unfamiliar voice calls.

As one we start tearing the messages from the notebooks. Ani runs the tap and we drop the small balls of paper into the toilet bowl. Luckily, being 21st-century kids we don't waste paper, and we haven't used too much. I throw a bit of loo paper on top and flush, crossing my fingers for them all to see.

'What are you doing in there?' the voice asks again.

I look down into the empty pan.

Jasper unlocks the door, walks out and puts his hands on his hips in his very best indignant pose. 'What do you think we were doing in there? And what gives you the right to storm in here without knocking? One of us could've been undressed ...'

The guy in black pushes him out of the way and comes into the toilet room. Ani finishes washing her hands and turns off the tap. He looks down into the clean pan.

'I did knock,' he growls. 'Three times. And the Witan give me my rights, in case you hadn't noticed.' He turns and looks at me. 'Why are you all in here at the same time?'

'Haven't you ever been to a club?' I ask enigmatically and push past him back into the sparse room.

'You put your jacket over the mirror,' he says, scowling.

'I hate seeing my reflection when I'm not looking my best,' Jasper replies sweetly.

After a few more minutes of ineffectual grunting and searching, the man comes out of the toilet room.

'So why did the Witan give you the right to come storming in here like Black Ops?' Jasper asks.

'You didn't answer the door,' the guy in black says.

'We might've been asleep,' Ani replies.

The guy in black gives her a pitiful look. 'You look more intelligent than that answer suggests,' he says, not unkindly.

'So they are watching us,' I say.

'Where have you been?' he says, almost laughing. 'If you're of interest to the Witan, they'll be watching every step you take.' With that, he leaves the room and shuts and locks it firmly behind him.

'You were about to tell us something,' Ani says.

'Not a chance now,' I say.

'Back to the toilet?' Jasper asks.

'Not a chance now,' I repeat.

We are all standing looking at each other like noobs at a house party when I hear voices from outside the room. The door is too thick to make out the words, but it sounds like the guy in black is being hung out to dry by someone. We hear the key in the lock, and the door swings open to reveal Rob, looking hot and cross.

'I didn't get an authorisation -' the guy in black starts to say.

'That's because I have the authorisation,' Rob snaps before he can finish. 'I, in case you hadn't noticed, am a member of the Witan family that you serve. My mother is now unhappy with these three being in the same room. She asked me to move them to more appropriate accommodations.'

'Jeeez, I can see why Brian hates him,' Jasper whispers.

'Don't make things worse,' I mutter, ignoring the look of shock he gives me.

'Out. All of you. Now,' Rob barks.

'Where are we going now?' Ani asks.

'Somewhere we can keep a better eye on you,' Rob replies.

'What if we don't want to go with you?' she says.

I nudge against her so hard, I figure the guy in black must have seen it. 'What's the point in arguing?' I say slowly, trying to make each word have a meaning it doesn't usually carry. 'We should just go with him.'

She looks at me, and I can tell she's not happy, but she's intelligent enough to know I'm trying to convey some information to her that I can't come out and say.

'If anyone lays a finger on me I'm suing, and I don't give a flying feck what year it is,' Jasper says loudly, but he moves out through the door and Ani and me follow, Rob at the back.

This floor of the hotel is a maze; I've got no idea where we are when we finally arrive back at the end of a corridor, facing a lift that looks a lot like the one we arrived in when Valerie first found us.

The lights above are low. There are no guys in black around, but there are Kim and Brian instead.

'Where is Lizzy?' I ask quietly.

'I can't get to her,' Rob says. 'I've done all I can.'

'And what exactly,' says Ani, 'is that?'

Chapter Twenty-Six – Lean On Me - (Club Nouveau, 1987)

~

'Stop asking me questions about a life you never knew you had. I told you, it was more than another timeline – it already feels like another lifetime,' I add, quieter now. 'You aren't the same boy, and after all I've been through lately, I'm probably not the same girl either.'

'Then why was it that as soon as you walked into the room last night, I felt as if I had been smacked in the mouth? That I had known you forevermore?' he asks as quietly. He reaches out, and I pull away.

That word. Echoing down through the decades, last spoken by an older man in desperation as he gave me another means of escape across the Weys, should I ever need one.

'Don't touch me with your ring hand.'

'Whyever not?' He looks confused, with good reason.

'Just trust me, okay?'

He takes my hand with the other, gently. 'Would it be all right if I touched you with this one instead?"

'Rob! Come back in here now, please,' Valerie's shrill voice cuts through the tension that's building between her son and me. 'Lizzy's family are here.'

I look down at the ringless hand holding mine and based on that one word, I make a decision that could make or break everything.

'Are we being watched here?' I ask quietly.

He shakes his head no. 'This part of the hotel is our home.'

I pull away from him, and I reach down towards my foot, unlacing and pulling off the Converse boot, and carefully peeling the hidden secrets from inside my sock.

'Why the hell have you got a bloody bandage in your sock?' he asks. When his face screws up, he's still hot AF.

'Forget about that,' I say. 'Don't touch me. Just look at this.'

As I take out the ring that I was given in the future, he lets out a massive gasp. 'And how the hell do you have a Witan ring?'

'Because you gave it to me. In a future that probably doesn't exist now any more than the one I came from. Be careful not to touch it with your own,' I say, holding it out for him to look more closely. 'You were the same age as Valerie is now when you gave this to me. Take off your own ring.' Seemingly bewildered, he does so. 'Look inside the band. Is there anything written there?'

'I know without looking. An inscription,' he says. 'To Rob, Love Always, Mum.' She gave it to me on my 18th back in November.'

'Look inside this one,' I say. 'Tell me what you can read. I couldn't make it out in the bathroom; the strip lights were too dim.' He peers at the version of the ring that I'm holding, and as he registers what's written there, his whole face fills with emotion, eyes bright and brimming as he looks back at me. 'Tell me what it says?'

'It says, 'To Rob, Love Always, Mum.''

I nod. 'It's the same ring. That's what I thought. We mustn't touch them at the same time. They'll create a physical paradox like the one that knocked Glenda out.'

'That's not all that's written here.' He puts his own ring back on, sweeps a hand roughly over his face, and looks into my eyes. 'It also says, 'Remember Maisie. Forevermore.'' Reaching out a slow, uncertain hand, he touches my face, and we have frozen again, together in time. 'If I gave this to you, then you must've been someone very special to me once.'

I refuse to let myself react the way I want to, but I allow myself a shrug. 'When do you first remember knowing about the Weys?'

'I've always known about them,' he says, a finger twirling a piece of my hair. 'I'm a bloke in a Witan family. She may be my mother, but the Witan come first. They always have. It's all about power and control. Everyone thinks I lead a charmed life,' he says bitterly,' but I might as well not exist. I'm not important enough to protect the Weys, but I'm important enough to keep their secrets, and if I don't she'll throw me in the Bergh, don't doubt that.'

The Bergh. I remember that word, the last time I was somewhere he touched my face.

'I have to get you away from here,' he says, after some time. 'We need to get to the Weydoor.'

'I guess that explains why you're on our side all of a sudden,' Brian mutters after we briefly explain.

Rob stares at him, and unexpectedly holds out his hand. 'I haven't always done right by you,' he says, 'but Maisie had a little time to explain what's going on. I'm sorry. I only shot my mouth off to protect myself. I want to start to put it right tonight if I can.'

Brian looks down at the outstretched hand of apology, and just as I think he's going to refuse, he takes it and shakes it hard. It seems to have an effect on everyone. 'To be fair,' he says, 'I'm only just getting up to speed with all this.'

'Get in the lift,' Rob says. 'We need to get out of here fast.'

'I'm not leaving without the others,' I say firmly.

Rob sighs in frustration. 'I don't know how long we have before the Guard checks with Mum or Scott that they sent for you!'

'I'm still not leaving without the others,' I repeat.

'Why not?' Rob asks, beginning to lose patience.

'Because I owe Lizzy. I promised her a few timelines back that I would help look after her family,' I say. 'I'm not going back on my word.'

'What can you do? I can't even ride the Weys safely and I'm Witan.' He pulls a face. 'Because I'm a bloke, I don't have any authority to say what should be done with them. I don't mean to be cruel, Maisie, but you're just a bystander.'

Jasper and Ani look at me then, and I realise the time has come to really test his loyalty.

I reach into my top, and I pull out my key.

'Well, I think it's fair to say I wasn't expecting that,' Brian says into the silence. Kim has the common sense to stay quiet since she knows having a key doesn't make me Weyfare, and Jasper and Ani have enough common sense to stay quiet because they know I am Weyfare regardless of the key.

After another lifetime, Rob says, 'So you're Weyfare.' We stare at each other for another breathless moment. Do I trust him yet? Can I risk everyone's safety because he has the face and body of the boy whose soul connected with mine?

It's still too big a risk. 'It's a long story. It's not mine. It was lent to me,' I say, unravelling a few layers of timeline in my lie.

He stares at me for a while, and then he seems to pull himself together. 'They are in the Vaults.'

'Vaults?'

'The passageways that link the oldest part of this building to Trinity.' He turns on the spot and leads us away from the lift. 'This won't be easy.'

'The hospital was linked underground to the church?' Ani asks.

'Everything's linked,' I tell her. 'Rob's granddad was the last vicar of Trinity before it was desanctified.'

'Grandma wasn't allowed to be a vicar, so Granddad was the figurehead. The family only knew vaguely about their ancestry; it wasn't until Mum met Scott that the Witan really came back into existence.' Rob is leading us down increasingly dark corridors, the clean painted walls with their smart colour prints are giving way to pale blocks of stone, and my spider-sense is telling me we're moving back towards the older part of the building and the original hospital. 'Scott told Mum about the Wey in the Old Library at Drake's School for Girls, and about Glenda being Weyfare, and the two of them started to monitor the Weys properly again with Glenda's family.' We start to descend some steps, and instead of being covered in carpet, they are bare stone. 'I don't know why he said all that about Lizzy stabbing him. He's never said anything like that before.'

'And what did Glenda's mother have to say about that?' I ask, thinking that my great-grandmother would surely have known the contents of the truth.

'I don't remember Glenda's parents at all. I was pretty small.'

All the same, I have a bad feeling about this.

'So what exactly is the Moot?' Ani asks.

'A council of Witan assigned to monitor the Weyferere in the local area.'

'There are more families?' I ask. This was not something I'd considered either. Glenda had made it sound like our bloodline was the only one still active – but that had been before Scott spilt the tea. Just how much damage had we done, leaving him in 1971?

At the foot of the steps, he stops. 'All over. I can't say any more for now. This is the last safe place I can speak. The guards will have walkie-talkies, but there are no video cameras or audio down here yet. I am going to try to convince the Guard that Mum has given you permission to say goodbye to the Brookes family.'

'And once we're in the Vaults, then what?' Jasper asks.

Rob shakes his head. 'That's it. That's all I can do. I can give Maisie the chance to say goodbye and explain. Only Mum has the keys that open the actual cells in the Vaults.'

'That's not cool,' Kim says. 'We can't leave them behind! What will your Mum do to them?'

'Her mouth is bigger than her bite,' Rob says thinly, 'but she likes power. If Glenda and Lizzy tell the truth and do enough cow tailing, then she may ask the Moot to give them a reprieve.' He nods at the key that I haven't yet hidden back until my top. 'Best to hide that. Stay here, and I'll come back for you once the coast is clear.' He strides off and vanishes around a corner before any of us can ask him another question.

'Maisie. Do you trust him?' Jasper asks. 'I mean, really trust him? He isn't Rob. Rob is gone. You know this.'

'I know that,' I say, 'but just like Ani isn't Ani, every now and then I see a glimpse of her. She's almost there.' I smile at her, and she smiles a little back. I feel the same about Rob. And if we don't give him a chance to prove we can trust him, then we might as well go back to our rooms, curl up in a ball and surrender.'

'I've been almost there my whole life,' Brian says. 'Nothing changes.'

'I don't think you should have so much faith in me,' Ani says quietly.

'We've got over the fact that you aren't the Ani we knew,' Jasper says, 'but we're getting to quite like the new you.'

'I think this is all my fault,' Ani replies.

'How can this possibly all be your fault?' Kim asks.

Before Ani can answer, I say, 'What's the point in laying blame here? We are at this point in time, and we have to get on with it. The most important thing to consider now is how we are going to get Lizzy and her family out of the cells if Val is the only one with a key.' My family.

There is a longer silence between us than I'd like.

'There's a chance that Rob is right,' Jasper says, 'and all we can hope for right now is a chance to tell them goodbye, and that we will do our best to sort things out.'

'How do we do that?' I ask, but before any of us can speak, Rob is walking back towards us.

'We have five minutes,' he says.

Along two corridors and at the end, there is a large wooden door not dissimilar to the entrance to the Old Library. The Guard that Rob asked to stand aside is sitting at a low table, smoking a cigarette. The large wooden door is open.

We walk through it, and instantly it feels like we've walked back in Time because the lights on the walls aren't electric, they are gas lamps like in Victorian times, and the ground feels muddy and smells of earth and rotten plants. Rob closes the wooden door behind us, and moves to the front of our group; we follow him quickly as the floor falls away and we seem to be walking down deeper under the ground. Eventually, the ground levels out, and the gas lamps flicker as we all walk past them, door after wooden door appearing on the left, each with a small barred window looking out from darkness. I can't believe they are being kept down here. It's barbaric.

'Remember we don't have long,' Rob says. 'I'm so sorry I can't do more.'

He stops in front of a door that looks like its been dug out of the rock, but to touch it feels like metal and there is a keyhole lit by the flickering gas lamps behind us.

'Lizzy?' I call out.

She is at the bars in seconds. 'Maisie! Get us out of here!'

'Well, duh,' Jasper says.

'Are you hurt?' Kim calls in.

'No. They took our keys, but they didn't knock us about.'

I look down at the keyhole. I have no reason to think this will work, but I have every reason to try. These Vaults have been here a very long time, and so have the Weyfare – far longer than these fake Witan. I take my key out of my top, and keeping it on its chain, I lean forward and push it into the lock. I turn it once, twice, and there is a satisfying thud. The next thing we know, the cell door is open, Lizzy is throwing her arms around me and Glenda is being helped to her feet by Paul and Henry. Rob is staring at the lock in utter bewilderment.

'These are Weyfarere cells?' he says incredulously.

Lizzy catches sight of Rob as he speaks. 'What's he doing here?'

'Long story, no time.' I say.

'Turns out another new timeline hasn't stopped him having the hots for Maisie,' Jasper says.

'No, it turns out that he's just not as much of a tard as everyone thought he was,' I say, my cheeks burning under the protection of the poor lighting. Rob doesn't reply.

'Where do we end up if we go that way?' Ani points in the opposite direction to the one we came from.

'It comes out somewhere on the Trinity site, I think.' Rob walks across to where Glenda is standing. 'It's our way out. I'm sorry about what's happened, Mrs Brookes.'

Glenda looks far from okay, but her voice is strong. 'Show us you're sorry by getting us out of here.'

'Won't they come down here once they realise we're missing?' Kim asks.

'They won't expect anything to be wrong down here,' Rob replies. 'They don't expect anyone to have a key.'

'Come on, let's get going,' I say quickly, seeing Glenda's face pull into a frown of confusion.

The Vaults get narrower and narrower the further we travel away from the cells and the Guard. In the end, even the oil lamps aren't lit, and all we can do is feel along the cold stone walls to guide us, as there is no light at all. The smokers fire up their lighters every now and again, just to make sure we aren't heading straight for a bottomless pit, but they can't keep the flame up for long or it becomes too hot to hold. When the top of Rob's head touches the ceiling, he warns us all that we might need to bend down, and one by one we are reduced to staggering along sideways, knees bent like Sumo wrestlers, hoping that the Vaults aren't blocked and that we've travelled further than we think we have. The Tunnel between the Old Library and Travellers' Rest is only the distance of the Park that separates the two buildings. Right now, we are somewhere in the bowels of Stoneford.

We've probably been moving for half an hour when we all have to drop to our hands and knees, and I'm becoming increasingly worried about what we're going to find at the end. At least the dirt floor isn't wet.

Five minutes after we start crawling, Paul, who is at the rear of our freaky little blind caterpillar, says, 'Stop. I can hear something behind us.'

Rob at the front of us stops, and we all barge into each other's rear ends. 'It could be the noise from above ground if we're under a road or something?' he whispers. It sounds amplified in the dark.

'No, it's voices,' Glenda says. 'Quiet.'

We all listen, and sure enough, I can make out footsteps crunching the dry dirt floor and muttered voices.

'I think they're still some distance back,' Paul says.

'So they've discovered we're gone,' Ani says.

'They're coming after us!' Lizzy hisses. 'You said they wouldn't think there was a problem!' she adds, clearly at Rob, although they can't see each other.

'Well, not for a while, but I knew they'd look eventually,' Rob replies, barely loud enough for me to hear him. 'I just didn't think they'd come out this way. Keep your voices down and don't move. If we can hear them, they can hear us.'

We all stay still then in the dark, the moisture in my breath turning to vapour in the chill dank of the Vault. The voices and footfalls seem to be getting louder, and I'm about to prod Rob hard in the butt and tell him we need to be getting a wiggle on, when the voices seem to be ebbing away again, like liquid going down the drain. Eventually, all I can hear is the sound of our breathing.

'I think they've gone,' Henry whispers.

'They might be sneaking up on us,' Kim replies, fear turning her voice to ice.

'I can't hear any more footsteps,' Glenda says. 'I think they've turned back.'

'Why would they have done that?' Jasper asks.

'Perhaps they think the Vaults are blocked,' I say.

'That's what I'm hoping they think,' Rob says.

'And are the Vaults blocked up at Trinity?' Glenda asks. 'More to the point, what do we do if they are?

'I'm pretty sure I know where this Vault comes out,' Rob says, 'but I have to be honest with you, I have no idea if there have been any rockfalls or blockages before we get to the end. This was our only chance of escape. We wouldn't have had any chance of trying to get out through the Hotel.'

'I think it's more likely that they're going to be waiting for us at the other end,' Brian suggests.

Chapter Twenty-Seven –
Born To Run (Live) (Bruce
Springsteen, 1987)

Suddenly I'm not in so much of a hurry to get the end of the Vaults.

Lizzy has other ideas. 'We can't just stay here,' she says, 'we've come this far, so we may as well carry on until the bitter end and face whatever crisis is served up next.'

Time doesn't mean much when you can't see your watch even if it is working, but I reckon it must be at least another 20 minutes before Rob speaks for the first time in an age. 'There's light ahead,' he says, and I can hear the excitement in his voice.

'Light means there's no blockage up ahead, surely?' Jasper says.

'That's a good thing, isn't it?' Kim asks.

'Yes and no,' Brian replies. 'No blockage means we can get out, but it also means they can get in. Quack Quack oops.'

'Excuse me? What does that mean?' Ani says.

'It's the sound of a mistake being made on DLT's radio show,' Lizzy says, 'forget about that for now. Shut up and listen. Can you hear any voices, Rob?'

Everyone obediently remains silent. 'Nothing,' he says. 'Can't even hear any movement.'

'Do you know anything about these Vaults, Mum?' Paul

asks.

'Nothing,' Glenda replies, sounding bitter. 'I only know about the tunnel that connects the Old Library to our house. I've always known there's a link with Trinity and the old hospital though,' she adds after a short pause. 'Anyone who knows the sign of the Valknut would make the connection. I just didn't think it was physical. The Witan tell me nothing. I just have to watch out for bystanders and send them on their Wey.'

'So you just chuck these bystanders back through the Weydoor and hope for the best?' Brian remarks. 'Brutal.'

There is a muffled noise of indignation. 'That's not what I do at all!' Glenda splutters.

'This is not the time or the place for unhelpful accusations, Brian!' Henry exclaims.

'Sorry,' he replies gruffly. 'Shall we just push on, and see what happens?

With the light getting brighter, we realise that we can now stand hunched over again, and the walls are beginning to widen out. A little further on and I can stand; a few metres further still and everyone is upright again. I can make out the stone in the walls again and the unlit gas lamps.

'This is reminding me of the Crypt,' I say. 'Guys? The Crypt at Trinity where we saw Frank's band?'

'Frank Bennett's band?' Glenda asks in surprise.

'My uncle had a band?' Rob asks, stopping suddenly and letting me bounce uncomfortably into the back of him. 'Sorry. But no one ever told me Uncle Frank had a band.' He starts to shuffle forward again.

'He looked like Marc Bolan,' Lizzy says helpfully.

'Cool.'

'Maybe we should keep quiet now,' I say, 'the light is getting well bright down here.'

Actually, we walk carefully around only one more corner and then freeze in our tracks. There is a wooden door in front of Rob, and before anyone can give useful words of advice the latch has somehow opened into the back of what looks like a big storeroom, filled with all kinds of things: glass bottles of beer, crates of cans, juice boxes, burger and hot dog buns and plastic bottles of various coloured sauces. Along one side of the stone wall, there are large white chest freezers. One of the lids is open, and a guy about Paul's age is taking out a big cellophane packet of burgers.

I'm trying to make everyone behind me retreat backwards through the wooden door without using my voice, but before I have any success, the guy with the burgers turns around, spots us all in what must be the back of the store, drops the lid with a bang and the pack of frozen burgers on his foot.

'Ow!'

'No, no - shh,' Rob says, stepping into the room and allowing the rest of us to emerge.

'Bugger me!' the other guy says again, lifting up his injured foot and rubbing it, leaning against the closed freezer.

'Ed?' Paul says, having finally appeared from the Vault. 'Ed, it's me, Paul.'

'Brooky? Is that you? What's going on, my man? Where the fuck did you come from?' He peers at us. "Kimmy? What you doing back there?'

Kim giggles, blushes and waves.

'Long story. Ed, I need you to close it down, mate. We

don't want any company.'

As if cued in by an unknown force, there is suddenly a blast of voices coming from the other side of the main door to the storeroom. Ed nods once, looking pretty much the same as he did the day he let Jasper drive the shagmobile and the way he looked at Tracy's barbeque last night, except for sounding and smelling sober.

'Is it the Old Bill?' he whispers.

Paul shakes his head no. Come to think of it, I have no idea how much real power Valerie and her family wield in the real world. 'But they're trouble.'

'We need your help, Ed,' Kim says, her blonde curls all grubby from the Vaults, still bobbing sweetly.

Ed nods again just once, picks up the frozen burgers and launches himself through the main door. We can hear him locking it.

'Jesus H, man, you scared the living shit out of me,' Ed says loudly from behind the door. 'What you doing back here? This is for Trinity personnel only, mate.'

'What's behind the door?' a gruff voice asks.

'Bread rolls. Beer. Burgers. Staple diet for the waifs and strays that turn up here looking for some grub,' Ed replies. 'You hungry?'

'We need to go in there,' another voice says.

'Hey, no way, man. Contamination and foodstuff standards crap. When was the last time you washed your hands? Or your boots? You want to lose me my job?'

There is a thud, which sounds worrying like someone tall and slim is being rammed hard against the door. 'I don't give three fucks about your job,' Gruff One snarls.

'Well I do, and unless the boss says you can check in the storeroom, I ain't letting no one in.'

I'll give it to Ed; he may have a drink problem, but he's also got balls the size of coconuts.

There's another thud, and what sounds like a slither, and footsteps moving away from the door.

'If Mum only sent a couple of Guard, then she can't really believe that we escaped through the Vaults,' Rob mutters.

'So where are all the others?' Glenda asks.

The door unlocks, and Ed comes in and locks it behind him. 'Bugger me, Brooky, what the hell kind of mess have you got yourself into now? You involved with the Firm?'

'No time to explain. We need a ride. Is the van here or the Shagmobile?'

'He has a van?' Rob asks.

'He's in a band,' Paul explains. 'Divine Morrissey.'

'Is everyone in a band?' Rob asks, faintly.

'I got the van out back,' Ed says. 'I said I'd do the Cash and Carry run for the boss today as the regular bloke is off. Double time. Bank Holiday.' He rubs his hands together.

Paul nods in approval. 'I need the biggest favour ever, Ed.'

'You paying me double time for it?' Ed asks.

'You'll get your reward in Heaven.' Paul steps in front of us all and throws a friendly arm around Ed's shoulder. 'Can you run us back home in the van?'

'I'll give you a kiss if you help,' Kim says.

'I'm in,' Ed replies, flashing her a toothy smile. 'But you'll never get out of here without them eyeballing you. What's the script, mate? Who are they?'

'They're from St Peter's,' Glenda says.

'Bennett thugs?' Ed asks, his eyes widening. 'What you doing tangled up with the Bennetts? They're mean sons of bitches.'

'We're not that bad,' Rob says, stepping forward.

Ed does a double-take. 'You're Rob Bennett.' He steps away from us and pins himself to the door. 'Kimmy baby, what you doing getting yourself tangled up with a Bennett?'

'Not her. Us,' Paul says.

'Don't do this, mate. Don't go kidnapping no Bennetts.'

'No one's kidnapping me,' Rob says.

'We need to get home,' Glenda says. 'We need a lift, and we need a distraction.'

'I can provide the distraction,' Rob says. 'I can convince the Guard I came through the Vault, and that I didn't find anyone in it.'

'Then what?' Brian asks. Everyone looks at him as if they only just realised he was still here. 'Where are we going, with the Bennett family chasing us down like Miami Vice? You don't think that 'home' is the first place they'll look for us?'

'We have to go back,' Ani says. 'I left something there.'

The Truth. She hid it in a pot in the Shed.

'It's not safe, though. Brian's right,' Kim says.

'Well, we can't stay here.' Rob steps forward. 'I'm going to get the Guard out the front. There's a way out to the back car park from the side of the stage, isn't there?' Ed nods. 'Give me the keys to this room, and come with me,' he says authoritatively. I guess being a Bennett in this version of 1987 gives you some clout. 'Give them the keys to the van,' he adds.

Ed salutes like a soldier on duty, throwing the van keys

into Paul's waiting hands.

'Leave the door open a crack,' Rob says, and when you see me go out with the Guard towards the lych gate, come out and head for the back car park.'

He slips out of the door.

'Why is he even doing this?' Jasper asks. 'Okay, I get the inscription on the ring and the feeling of neglect, but is he really giving up a life of luxury and throwing his hand in with us?' He looks at me. 'Surely it's a trap? I'm sorry, Maisie, but I'm not convinced.'

'Well after all this, we'll know one way or another, won't we?' I say, peering out the tiny crack in the almost closed door.

'So do we get Ed to take us home or what?' Paul asks.

Everyone replies, but the response is 50-50.

'The Guard will be waiting for us,' Brian says. 'It's the first place I'd look.'

'And the second place they'll look is the Old Library,' Kim says, 'as they'll be expecting us to escape using the Weys.'

'I don't think so,' Glenda says. 'The Witan took our keys. Even if we were to break the codes again, they know we can't possibly ride the Weys safely without them.'

So she thinks.

'Look, we'll answer all the questions once we are somewhere safe, but right now we need to be watching for Rob's signal,' Lizzy says.

'And that'll be about now,' I say, watching as Rob, Ed and the two Guard walk slowly towards the doors at the front of Trinity. I can't see for sure, but I think we're in the room next to the one St John's Ambulance used at Lizzy's party. 'Give it another few seconds. Okay. They've left.'

'We're on,' Paul says.

It's hard to be inconspicuous when you are part of a group of ten people leaving a storeroom, but the sun high in the sky through the window suggests it's the middle of the day, Trinity is fairly busy, and no one seems to be taking much notice of us. There are lots of tables outside the canteen hatch, and there's still a big metal urn there, but they are cooking hamburger that smells really good. I wish I'd eaten lunch as my tummy grumbles, but there's no time for food regrets, we are making our way over to a door next to the stage, right at the front of the huge hall. Ed opens it, and another beautiful May day floods in.

Ed's van is a blue Ford Transit, and the back is completely stripped out, so it's big enough for the eight of us to squeeze in if we don't expect any leg or arm room.

Paul gets in up front and starts the motor.

'Wait,' I call. 'What about Rob?'

'He didn't say anything about waiting,' Paul says.

'He didn't say anything about leaving without him, either,' I snap back. 'And we can't just drive off with Ed's van.'

'Maisie, we need to get going,' Jasper says, trying to be soothing.

'Can we just give him another minute or two?' I ask. 'If it hadn't been for him, we wouldn't have got this far.'

'And if he runs around the corner in two minutes with the rest of the Guard? Then what do you propose?' Glenda snaps. 'You're just a bystander.'

I look at Jasper. He reads my mind, and shrugs: what choice do you have? Without *The Truth*, there is no evidence of the blood tokens, and it might be safer to keep that secret for now. The Witan and the Weyferere think that the keys are the safe way to ride, but I'm so much in sympathy with Rob right now; I'm getting sick of being treated like an underclass when I am currently the G.O.A.T.

I pull the key out from under my clothing.

Glenda gasps. 'Where did you... did you steal that?'

I shake my head. 'There's no time for this. I was lent it in the future by Lizzy. Stop with the treating me like I'm a piece of crap.'

'Lizzy lent you a key?' Glenda is starting to look green again.

'Did you have to show her that now?' Lizzy asks, rolling her eyes.

'This version talks down her nose at us,' I say. 'I wanted some equality.'

Lizzy chews on her lips and nods. ' I know,' she says. 'I don't like it. It wasn't like that before, was it?'

'I'm not talking down to you. I don't know what to make of you,' Glenda sighs. 'I've never met bystanders who know so much. I've never met a bystander with a token key.'

'Every day's a school day,' I say lightly.

'We need to leave now,' Paul says.

'Another minute,' I reply.

'No more minutes! Oh, bugger,' Paul finishes, and although I can't see what he can see through his window, I'm guessing my hunch has paid off. Moments later, the passenger door opens, and Rob squeezes in next to Paul on side, and Ed pushes him out of the way of the steering wheel.

'Leave. Now,' Rob says firmly, and Ed roars off like he's

driving a Grand Prix.

Rob turns back to us. 'So I didn't get a lot of info from the Guard, but reading between the lines, it sounds like Mum thinks you got out through the hotel somehow. and most of the Guard are trawling through town trying to spot you in the street. Mum wasn't expecting you to come through the Vaults because she thought the end door was locked. There's a local music festival on at the Railway Gardens, and it's generating more traffic on the road than your usual bank holiday.'

'Bunch of snobs,' Ed offers. 'We said we'd play, but they wanted a "better class of act on the bandstand," I quote you.'

'Trouble is, Mum has sent a team up to your place, Glenda,' Rob says. 'Apparently, they can't work out how you got out of the cells, but they reckon one of you must've managed to hide a token key from them. So another team has gone on to the Old Library, just in case.'

'Well, that's us scuppered,' Brian says.

'Where are we supposed to go then?' Lizzy asks, her voice sounded even shakier than the Transit's suspension.

'How badly do you need to get to Travellers' Rest?' Rob asks.

'It's quite possibly a matter of life and death,' Ani says.

'Maybe just a touch overdramatic there,' Lizzy says, 'but if we can't go home and we can't ride the Weys to somewhere else, where else can we go?'

'No, you don't understand,' Ani says loudly, 'we really do need to go to Travellers' Rest.'

Everyone starts on her then, and I don't like it; sure, she's a bit up herself and she's not my BFF, but actually, she's trying to help and no one's giving her a chance, and in this new world of us and them, I'm not happy about more divisions.

'Shut up!' I shout, and to my complete surprise, everyone does. 'Rob, what can you do at Lizzy's house to help us?'

'I'm not sure,' he says seriously. 'They didn't tell me how big the teams were. If they're small enough, maybe I can distract them like I did back there at Trinity.'

'It's not worth the risk,' Lizzy says.

'No, it really is worth the risk,' Ani says.

'Last time I looked, you weren't in charge,' Lizzy snaps at her.

'Last time I looked, you hadn't got a clue what to do either,' Ani snaps back.

'Bitch fight. Just what we need right now,' Jasper says calmly.

'Why are you so keen to go to my house?' Henry asks. 'We are currently on the run from the Witan! What was the point in the escape through the Vaults, if we're effectively going to hand ourselves back over to them later the same day?"

I watch as Ani leans forward, elbows on her knees and her hands over her face.

'Henry, Glenda,' I say. 'You don't trust us. We get that. You have no idea where we're from, or how we got here. I know you think we're just bystanders in all of this, but actually, we're far more important than that. Some of us have known you on other timelines. We are the architects of all this; we didn't know it at the time, but we made this mess, and if we have the faintest hope of ever learning how to sort things out and return everyone to the timeline they should be following:' I take a deep breath and place a reassuring arm on Ani's bowed shoul-

der, 'then the first thing you need to do
is listen to Ani.'

She looks up guiltily but gratefully at me then, the closest I've felt to her since she returned, and she nods. 'I only need
five minutes,' she says.

I look at Rob, and as our eyes meet, he nods too. 'I'll
do what I can,' he says quietly, just to me, 'but she'll have no
longer than that.'

'I'm still not leaving without the others,' I say, so only
he can hear.

'And I'm still coming with you,' he says firmly.

I take a deep, calming breath, but it doesn't work. 'That
has to be your decision in the end. If they catch us, they
won't put us in the Bergh now,' I say quietly. 'They'll throw us
through the Weydoor. You know I'm right. We're too dangerous.'

He nods. 'I'm still coming.' When I don't reply, he adds,
'Do you have a plan?'

'Nothing so elaborate as that.' I look at him as Ed speeds
the blue Transit van through the streets of Stoneford as if he's
driving a Tesla through the streets of Monte Carlo, ever closer
to what awaits us.

Chapter Twenty-Eight – Serious (Donna Allen, 1987)

The van pulls into the bottom of the long garden, slightly shielded by the caravan.

'Don't kill the engine,' Rob says, 'we might need to shift sharpish.'

'Can you see anyone?' I mutter.

'Hard to say,' Paul says. 'Nothing obvious.'

'You told us your mother had sent a team here just in case,' Henry says to Rob.

'That's what the Guard at Trinity told me,' he says.

'It's too quiet,' Jasper says. 'I've seen so many of those films where they think the street's deserted and then Bang!'

'This isn't a Western,' Lizzy says, 'but I agree. It feels like a trap.'

'Why don't I go up to the house with Dad?' Paul asks. 'The Witan said they weren't holding us – we chose to stay at the Hotel. They couldn't have found us in the Vaults without raising suspicion, but surely there's nothing wrong with finding us two in our home?'

'It's nearly three,' Ed says, tapping a plastic watch that can't be a fitness tracker. 'Look, man, I'm not being funny but I got to get my collection done, and the cash and carry shuts early on bank holidays.'

'What do you need from the house, Ani?' Lizzy asks.

'It's not in the house. It's in the Old Shed,' Ani replies.

'We're risking our freedom for a spade?' Brian asks. She scowls at him, and he nudges her playfully.

'What do you need from the house, Mum?' Paul asks.

'It depends where we're going next and for how long,' Glenda leans forward and rubs her hands over her face. 'Clothing and money for a start.'

'Right. We can't sit here doing nothing because if there are Guard up there watching us, they're going to think something is fishy,' Rob says. 'I'll go up to the house with Paul and Henry. They can get whatever they need, while I go to the Old Shed. What is it that's so important, Ani?'

The anxiety bubbles over me like a Mentos sweet in cola. 'I have to get it,' she says, and I realise that, like me, she has probably felt like this all along.

Rob frowns. 'I can't fetch it for you?'

'I'd prefer to get it myself,' she says, and adds quickly, 'it's from the future. I'm not sure you should touch it, in case it causes problems like before with Glenda and the keys.' Rob looks sceptical.

'And your rings, remember?' I say, hoping that the thought of the few moments we shared in the Quad at the Hotel is enough to put him off the scent of a very shaky story. Why don't we want him to get *The Truth* from the Old Shed? Does something inside me not trust him? Sure, he's saying the right things, and he helped us escape from the Hotel, and he helped us escape from Trinity as well – but he's Witan. I don't know how long that's going to matter. A lot longer than a day or two, I'm guessing. Is it wrong that I need more evidence than the ring?

'Okay,' he shrugs. 'If the house is clear, I'll signal down

to the van, and you can come up and find whatever it is.'

He slips out of the van with Paul, and Henry places a firm kiss on Glenda's head before opening the back and jumping quietly out.

'What the hell fuck have you lot got yourselves into?' Ed remarks, and he lights a cigarette. 'I haven't understood a bloody word for the last five minutes, and I'm sober today!' He too slips out of the door with a huff of impatience.

I lean forward and peer out of the passenger window as they walk casually up the garden path.

'So are we destined for a road trip to the cash and carry with Ed, or can we get out as well?' Jasper asks.

'Where exactly are we going though?' Kim asks. 'Even if there's no one in the house right now, we can't stay there, can we?'

'We're on the run from the Witan,' Brian says. 'Is there anywhere we can go that's safe?'

I sneak a glance at Lizzy and nod, and we look at Glenda.

'Mum, we're going to have to ride the Weys,' she says.

'Really?' Brian's voice comes out in a squeak.

'Absolutely not,' Glenda exclaims. 'It's got you in enough trouble.'

'Which I can't undo,' Lizzy says, 'if we can't stay here. In this 1987, I mean. Not the way things stand.'

'What do you mean by that?' Glenda asks.

'This 1987 is different,' Lizzy says. 'The only way we can change it is to ride further back.'

'Elizabeth Brookes, you never ride the Weys intending to change time events!' Glenda shouts. 'Why don't you ever listen?' and I look away again through the window.

I can see the three men are now pretty much at the top of the garden next to the Old Shed.

'Don't go until they give the signal, Ani,' I say.

Afterwards, I realised that if I'd stayed looking out of the window for a few seconds more instead of turning to look at everyone as they tried to get their heads around what was happening, I would've seen Paul frantically making signs to abort, run, leave, escape or any combination of the three, shortly before being grabbed from behind by two Guard.

But I didn't.

The rear doors of the van swung open with a bang, and 30 of Valerie's Guard piled into the back. Okay, it wasn't 30, but it felt like 30 as they jumped all over us, stamping on feet and hands, man-handling us out of the van and onto the tarmac next to the caravan. Some people are screaming, there are thuds of feet meeting limbs and fists meeting faces but we don't stand a chance.

'How did they know where we were?' Jasper hisses at me as they lead us up towards the house. He gets a smack on the back of his head for the comment, hard enough that he doesn't ask anything else, but it worries me. Surely I can't have been that naïve?

The faithful old clock on the wall detonates another minute into the cold atmosphere of the kitchen as we are led inside, but no one is sitting at the pine table. We are walked into the hallway, and then up two flights of stairs, past Lizzy's room and Paul's room at the end of the first-floor landing, my heart sinking lower and lower in my chest until we arrive at the door to Glenda and Henry's bedroom.

It's a big master room, and it's just as well because there are bloody loads of us here. Paul and Henry are sitting on the bed. Valerie is standing between them. As we are all pushed into her presence, she barks at the Guard holding Ed.

'Who is that?'

'I've got nothing to do with this, lady, I just drove them here,' Ed splutters. 'I was doing Brooky there a favour, but he won't get any fucking more!'

'Sorry to drag you into this, man,' Paul says, without looking up.

'I've got no business with the Bennetts,' Ed squeals. 'I'm just a bass player.'

'Let the idiot go,' Valerie says, and the moment the Guard follows orders, Ed is out the door so fast, we can hear him almost tumbling down the two flights of stairs to get away.

'Rather stupid of you, coming to the first place we'd look?' Valerie says, crossing her arms in front of her. 'The Moot won't look kindly on such behaviour as this. You were simply being questioned earlier. I wonder to myself, why is it that you would see the need for escape if you believed you had committed no crime against our code?'

'Let's just say we fancied our chances better outside the cells,' Lizzy says.

'I'd say you were prepared to risk a great deal to get back here, Valerie replies. 'Fortunately, Scott has a very good memory.'

'So good that when it really matters, the two of you choose to rewrite History.'

'Isn't that what you and your cronies are doing?' Valerie smiles thinly.

'How is all this relevant to anything?' Jasper asks.

'Well, Scott was pretty sure that on the timeline he left, my son was friends with you all.' She looks at us all. I'm trying desperately to keep my face from showing my fear, but I never played Poker. 'I told Rob to help you escape. To tell you it was for old time's sake. He always enjoyed charades when he was smaller. I knew you'd believe him and lead him to anything important. And you brought him here.'

Something doesn't sit well here, but I stare so hard at my filthy Converse, that tears come to my eyes.

'He betrayed us?' Kim asks, echoing my hurt, screaming from every word.

'You don't think he's done this sort of thing before? Poor, green girl.' Valerie gave her a smug look. 'So, Glenda. What brings you to your house, when the most sensible thing would have been to get your son's gormless friend to drive you miles from here?'

Glenda just shakes her head, staring at Henry, who is twisting the silver bracelet round and round, not taking his eyes from her.

'Perhaps I'll tell you why then,' Valerie says and without warning, she flings open the wardrobe doors. 'Pull out the safe,' she tells the Guard nearest to it.

Glenda lets out a squawk of emotion then, and it seems to set us all off: Kim, Brian and Ani make a run for the door; me, Lizzy and Jasper make a grab for the dressing table, trying to pull it over and Paul and Henry dive onto the boots of the Guard as he tries to pull the safe out from underneath the boot boxes and clothing. It doesn't take long for them all to restore order, but Valerie is pinker in the light of the fading afternoon, and she's seriously pissed off.

'Get that bloody safe out now,' she shouts at the Guard who is still head first inside the wardrobe.

'You were my best friend!' Glenda cries, and my heart breaks for her. 'How did you end up such a bitch?'

'I'm just doing my job, like all of us,' Valerie says, running fingers through her hair to smooth it back down.

'You need a key to open that safe,' Henry says through gritted teeth; the Guard is holding his arms back tightly, 'and you stole my wife's and my daughter's.'

Valerie reaches into the pocket of the dark blue hotel uniform she's still wearing, and she pulls out an ornate key. I can't see if it's Lizzy's or Glenda's, but I'm guessing it's Lizzy's – she's too clever to make that mistake. 'Borrowed, Harry. And it's a piece of luck I brought them with me then,' she says smoothly. 'And I'll bet good money that the code is a birthday. One of your children, in fact. Your most important child, let's say.'

I can feel Paul's anger from where I stand, anchored to the spot by the Guard holding me, while the one on the floor keys in 2-3-0-5-6-9 and uses the key passed to him by Valerie to open the door and pull out the contents: a purple bound book and a silver key.

'So here's the other key,' Valerie takes it and holds it up. 'Your other key, Glen? You'll notice I gave yours to my Guard so that I didn't suffer the same fate as you by touching them both.' She looks at it closely. 'Fascinating. A physical paradox, here in front of me. Most importantly, proof of unauthorised riding of the Weys.

'So I get why you would want to come back here and rescue the only other key you have access to, but surely you didn't come back here for a diary?' She opens the pages of *The Truth*, safe here for so long away from eyes that shouldn't see, and her eyes widen as she flicks across the pages, so wide that I think she's about to have some kind of seizure. 'What is this?'

'I don't know,' Glenda says, honestly. 'I've never seen it before.'

'You don't know what it is, but you keep it in your safe?' Valerie screeches. I glance at Jasper, and he nods in agreement: she's losing it. 'Get me a bin.'

None of the Guard seems to understand what's being asked of them, and anyway, they are all hanging onto us in case we try anything else.

'Get me a bin!' she yells, and Kim's Guard runs out of the room, and comes back a few moments later with a metal bin from the study.

Valerie takes a lighter from her jacket pocket, opens the delicate and fragile pages of *The Truth*, holds the flame to them, and to all our horrors, they catch fire, one by one, little orange curls turning the ancient pages to brown and then blackening and, as she drops the priceless true history of Wayland and his brothers into the bin, the flames blaze away, turning the precious writing to ashes.

Her face red like a demon in the reflection of the flames; Valerie looks at us in triumph. She puts the key from the safe around her own neck, takes a thick woollen scarf from the open wardrobe and holds her hand out for the other key that the Guard removes from the lock of the safe.

'Enough of this nonsense now. I think it's about time we put all this business to rest once and for all, don't you?' she asks.

I'm certain that no one in the room thinks she expects a reply.

There's no opportunity for Ani to grab the only other copy of *The Truth* from whichever pot she hid it in. There are Guard in front of us, and Guard behind us, forcing us down the slippery stone steps into the belly of the ground and the Tunnel to the Old Library. There is no room to create a distraction or change direction. We can do nothing about *The Truth* in the Old Shed, and we can only hope it's in such an obscure place that it won't be found since no one knows it exists. We know what is going to happen to us, however, and we (at least Jasper, Ani, Lizzy and me) know why.

What we don't know is the details. I have no idea what we're going to be facing when we get to the Old Library. I don't know how it's all going to work out. In fact, everything could be a total mess, and that's not even considering my own personal emotional trauma, but I have too much to do to consider my options, while we march along the Tunnel in silence. In the dark, the Guard can hear everything we say, but they can't see what we do.

Eventually, the Guard at the front opens the door into the Old Library, and I have the small satisfaction of knowing that in this part of the next few minutes, I was right.

Scott and Rob are standing in front of the Weydoor.

Chapter Twenty-Nine – 87 And Cry (David Bowie, 1987)

Having dutifully led us out into the room, the Guard stand behind us, their arms folded.

'There's no reason for you to stay,' Scott says. 'Lock the outer door, and I will resolve the difficulties.'

'Miss Bennett said -' one begins, but Scott lifts a hand lazily as if he'd been raised to do it.

'Miss Bennett is my partner. You do not question my judgement. I am here under her direction. Leave, or you can answer to her yourselves.'

I can see they aren't happy, but they do leave, having locked the door that leads out to the school, they disappear back into the Tunnels, and finally, we are alone.

'You freaking liar,' I say.

'You son of a bitch,' Lizzy says.

'You betrayed us,' Ani says.

'I love a reunion,' Brian says lightly. 'Anyone got a lighter?'

'You don't smoke; it's a disgusting habit,' I say, staring at Rob. He doesn't meet my eyes.

'I didn't time travel either, but I've recently decided to take that up as well,' Brian says. Henry throws him a packet like a fast bowler, and he catches it like he's playing in the World Series.

'So come on then, Scott,' Ani says, 'who was it who

stabbed you and threw you through this Weydoor like a piece of old garbage?'

'Yesterday's news,' he says smoothly.

'But it wasn't me,' Lizzy says, 'and most of the people here know it.'

'And now you're going to do the same to us,' Jasper says.

Scott shakes his head. 'I'm not the mercenary you think I am. I don't need to hurt you. I just need to throw you through the Weydoor,' and without any more warning, he grabs hold of Henry, who is already holding hands with Glenda, who is already holding hands with Paul, and he pushes his hand through the Weydoor, and there's white heat, purple light, black – and they are gone.

Scott looks back at us, and I shout loudly at him. 'Where have you sent them?'

'Who knows?' he says. 'Where will you go when it's your turn?'

Brian steps forward. 'Maybe we'll just take our chances,' he says, and before Scott and Rob can react, he has taken hold of Kim and Lizzy and he jumps through the Weydoor, and there's white heat, purple light, black – and they are gone.

I look back into Scott's face and I can see frustration there. 'What's the matter?' I ask calmly. 'Is it not such fun when they aren't forced to ride?'

'You think you know so much,' he sneers, those beautiful blue eyes flashing who knows what dark motives.

'I know so little,' I say. 'But you know so much. Here you are, banging a Witan queen in the lap of luxury, living a life that wasn't supposed to be yours. In fact, you made everything different, didn't you Scott?'

'You fucking left me there to die!' he shouts at us.

'We took you to hospital, you asscloth,' Ani says. 'I sat with you as you were slowly bleeding out. I tried to give you reassurance. I tried to give you a sense of what happened, in case you died. I wasn't even sure you could hear me. Oh, you heard me all right. You heard every tiny secret I told you about them, and you spilled the lot. You're such an angel, aren't you?'

He stares at her then; it's an unnerving look that I can't understand. 'It doesn't matter,' he says quietly, 'and it can never matter again.'

'I would have gone back for you!' Ani yells unexpectedly.

He shakes his head. 'You need to go. I don't care where you go, or how long you stay as long as you stay off this timeline. You want my advice? I fell on my feet. You don't belong here. You aren't safe here. Leave of your own accord if you will, but leave.'

He looks at Rob. We all do. 'Which one of them were you in love with?' Scott asks. 'I remember you were with one of them, but it's too long ago to be clear.'

I look at Rob's face. It is chiselled like stone. It is impossible to read. It makes every part of my being ache. 'As you said, it was another timeline. What does it matter? You loved Lizzy once,' I say defiantly.

He laughs then, and my insides crumple for her. 'Love? It was absolutely never that. Do yourselves a favour and leave. Ride the Weys until your insides shrivel to dust, but don't come home. Your time here is done.'

I step forward and slap him hard on the face, and he laughs at me, but it is time we leave before he can control our ride. He reaches forward to push me, and I grab hold of Jasper first, hoping that he gets a hand onto Ani, hoping that the plans we made back in the caravan work out.

With my other hand, I simply reach out and wait to see what happens, my heart in my mouth, and just before I fall against the bookshelves, my heart leaps to life again as I can feel fingers wrapping around mine against a shout of horror, and there's white heat, purple light, black – nothing.

'What the hell fuck have you lot got yourselves into?' Ed remarks, and he lights a cigarette. 'I haven't understood a bloody word for the last five minutes, and I'm sober today!' He too slips out of the driver's door with a huff of impatience and stares out over the orchards.

I lean forward and peer out of the passenger window as they walk casually up the garden path. 'So are we destined for a road trip to the cash and carry with Ed, or can we get out as well?' Jasper asks.

'Where exactly are we going though?' Kim asks. 'Even if there's no one in the house right now, we can't stay there, can we?'

'We're on the run from the Witan,' Brian says. 'Is there anywhere we can go that's safe?'

I sneak a glance at Lizzy and nod, and we look at Glenda.

'Mum, we're going to have to ride the Weys,' she says.

'Really?' Brian's voice comes out in a squeak.

'Absolutely not,' Glenda exclaims. 'It's got you in enough trouble.'

'Which I can't undo,' Lizzy says, 'if we can't stay here. In this 1987, I mean. Not the way things stand.'

'What do you mean by that?' Glenda asks.

'This 1987 is different,' Lizzy says. 'The only way we can change it is to ride further back.'

'Elizabeth Brookes, you never ride the Weys intending to change time events!' Glenda shouts. 'Why don't you ever listen?' and I look away again through the window. I can see the three men are now pretty much at the top of the garden next to the Old Shed.

'Don't go until they give the signal, Ani,' I say.

'It was never our intention to change things,' Lizzy says, but I can hear the hesitation in her voice. Of course, it has been our intention for a while to change events. Ever since I stepped foot in 1987 the first time, I've been changing events, but we went back to 1971 with the actual sole purpose of changing them. 'We went back to hide *The Truth*,' she admits.

'What is this Truth you all keep hammering on about?' Glenda asks.

'It's the history of your ancestry,' Ani says.

'It's the reason we came here the first time,' Jasper says.

'I told you, the history of our ancestry is called *The Book of the Witan*,' Glenda says, sighing as she runs her fingers through her hair over and over.

'It's a fake,' Brian says.

Something occurs to me, and I don't have to speak in riddles this time.

'So there are two versions of *The Truth*?' I ask Ani.

She nods. 'The one Lizzy hid in the safe in 1971, and the one I took from the study in 2019, hidden in the pots in the Old Shed.'

'2019, for God's sake,' Glenda breathes the word out like a sigh.

'There's definitely a book in the safe,' I say, 'Also there's the other key.'

'Other key?' Glenda repeats again.

Jasper pulls fingers through hair that has definitely seen better product days. I look away from the garden then to see Kim and Brian looking at me, totally confused.

'We need to get hold of *The Truth* and the key,' I say. 'The books especially. They are far more important now, far more now than they ever were.' I look at Glenda. 'The key is Glenda's, from the other future timeline. *The Truth* is the original history of Wayland's descendancy. We've never really talked about it -' I glance at Lizzy, Jasper and Ani and they all nod – 'but we think the *Book of the Witan* is probably a document which only dates back to 1971.'

'That's ridiculous,' Glenda splutters. 'That book has existed for generations.'

'You need to trust them, Mum. If they say we need to get away from here, we need to get away,' Lizzy says. 'Ride the Weys back to the time when we can maybe put this right.'

'So what are you suggesting? That we all high tail it back to 1971? Why is 1971 so important?' Glenda asks.

'Not least because it's where the Weyleigher threw Scott Kelly after she stabbed him,' I say. The silence that follows is suffocating.

'Of course, they don't know the real smackeroonie here,' says Jasper.

'But that's not for now,' I say firmly. 'We can't get into the house, so we can't get that version of *The Truth* now, but we can if we go back to when Lizzy put it in the safe.'

'Will you stop talking in riddles and explain to the rest of us in words of one syllable?' Brian asks.

'I believe they're going to throw us through the Weydoor, with no way of knowing we're going to end up,' I tell him.

His eyes grow very round, and he nods slowly. 'We are a danger to them.'

'So we need to get hold of grounding tokens for 1971 then. The more the merrier,' Lizzy says. 'Pressies that you were given on your 21st birthday, Mum? Or near as damnit.'

'My God, you're serious, aren't you?' Glenda says, her frustration turning to disbelief.

'It's the best chance we have. Go back into the past to the point it all changed. and sort out the mess we made,' I say.

'We might just make it worse,' Ani mutters. 'We've changed too much already. We can't go on and we can't go back. What's the point?'

'There has to be a point,' I say loudly, suddenly cross that she's being so defeatist. I need them to be strong right now or I'm likely to crumble. 'Everyone has to believe there's a point, or they'd never get out of bed in the mornings. Whatever life is like, you have to make the best of it, even if it isn't the life you were expecting. Or the one you had yesterday.'

'Confucius she speaks wisely,' Brian says, putting his hand on Ani's. I notice she doesn't pull it away.

Glenda rubs her hands over her face as if to wake herself. 'Okay,' she says eventually, 'I don't really understand what's happening, and I don't believe for one minute that riding the Weys is going to improve our situation in the long term, but I'm too exhausted to come up with a better plan, and if we don't stay away for too long -' Her voice trails off.

'Apart from your key, have you still got anything precious in the house that was given to you on that birthday?' Lizzy asks. 'Not at the same time though?'

'There's a little cocktail watch that I think is in a velvet bag in one of my dressing table drawers,' Glenda says slowly as if thinking out loud, ' and there's a gold Dunhill lighter up there that your dad still sometimes uses. I got those in the evening. Mother gave me my key earlier on in the day.'

'I'm sorted,' Jasper says, patting the bottom of his leg.

'We can't use that,' I say, avoiding Lizzy's frown, 'We'll bump straight into the Other Us as we come through the Weydoor.'

He sighs. 'Glad I kept it all this time then.'

'Anything else, Glenda?'

She pulls a face. 'Only my signet ring.' She holds up her right hand, showing us a band of gold on her ring finger.

'That'll do. There is one other thing,' I say. 'Me, Jasper, Ani and Lizzy – we've all ridden out and back before, and, well it changes things.'

'This is what I've been trying to tell you for the last five minutes!' Glenda throws her hands up in the air all gospel.

'So are you all prepared to come back to a different 1987 then?' Jasper says abruptly.

'You might lose some friends. Or worse,' I say, not allowing myself to look at Lizzy.

'People might be extinguished,' Ani says.

No one says anything for a few moments.

'My parents told me not to come back home when I walked out,' Kim says, 'and I don't think for one minute that they will have changed their minds. I'd miss Tracy and the gang if they forget about us but,' she looks shyly at Lizzy, 'the people I care about most are here with me.'

'I could be the next Einstein, and my parents would still be more interested in what my sister had for breakfast,' Brian says. 'Count me in.'

'This is madness,' Glenda says,' total and utter madness! I don't know why I'm even considering going along with such a foolish, hare-brained idea like this! Me and Lizzy have no keys, and yours,' she nods disdainfully at me, 'is from God only knows when! We have no way of getting back here! We don't even know that the Witan are going to punish us! They'll probably just cancel my leave and monitor your training a bit more closely, and as long as we get rid of you bystanders, that'll be an end to it. Do we really need to jeopardise our safety in this way?'

I can see she really believes this, but then, she doesn't know what we know, and right now, she's safer for it. Now is not the time to fight this particular battle.

'So what do you want us to do, Mum?' Lizzy asks impatiently. 'Go back up to the house so you can make us all a nice cup of tea while we're waiting for the Witan Guard to chuck us into the Weys?'

'Save your teenage attitude, Lizzy, and start acting like the grown woman you're becoming,' Glenda snaps. 'I need to go somewhere where I can at least get some proper thinking time, instead of this rushing headlong into panicked decision making.'

'But where can we go?' Kim asks, and the van starts shaking violently.

If I'd stayed looking out of the window for a few seconds more instead of turning to look at everyone as they tried to get their heads around what was happening, I would've seen Paul reappearing fast at the top of the steps, skidding to a stop and frantically making signs to abort, run, leave, escape or any combination of the three, shortly before being grabbed from behind by two Guard.

But I didn't.

Chapter Thirty – Dancing With A Stranger (Sam Smith And Normani, 2019)

I manage to land quite gracefully and even Jasper and Ani stumble into the room and stay upright, but Rob flops onto the floor beside us in an unconscious tangle of limbs and dust. We prop him up against one of the bookcases that isn't a Wey-door, and I pat his cheeks gently to try and bring him round. I'm not worried; we all passed out the first few times we Rode.

'You were right then,' Ani says grimly, wiping a few specks of dust from her jacket. 'They did intend to throw us into the Weys.'

I nod. 'We know too much about a world where Val isn't Queen Bitch. Whatever plan she hatched with Scott Kelly, we threaten it big time. Did you see her face when she looked at *The Truth*? She went the colour of last week's porridge oats.'

'So did our plan work out?' Jasper asks.

I shrug and carry on patting. 'We won't know until the next Ride out.'

'He came through then,' Jasper says, crouching down and shaking one of Rob's legs ineffectually. 'You were right about him too. That must be a relief for you.'

'You know it only makes a whole lot of other things more difficult,' I tell him, and we all jump back then as Rob's eyes snap open and he struggles to get to his feet. 'Hey! Hey, Rob – it's all right. You're all right.'

Rob stares out at us all. I watch as the last few minutes sink into his brain and then shine out through his eyes until the recall turns to accusation. 'Why didn't you warn me you were going to do that?' he says. 'Why didn't you grab me? I very nearly didn't get hold of you!'

'I had to be sure that you really wanted to come with us,' I tell him simply.

The accusation fades a little. 'You,' he says more quietly. 'I wanted to come with you.'

'Squatting right here,' Jasper says. 'Don't mind us.'

'So Valerie thought you were leading us to her,' Ani asks.

Rob nods, and brushes the dust from his trousers. 'It was the only way I could guarantee getting you to the Weydoor.' He pauses, looking around. 'Did I do it?' I nod at him yes, with a smile. 'I can't believe I actually Rode a Wey!" he exclaims then, sounding more like an excited toddler than the son of a Witan leader. 'Where is everyone else?'

'1971, we hope,' I say. 'I managed to get the watch that I found on Glenda's dressing table passed back to her as we came through the Tunnel. Hopefully the plans we made back in the caravan worked.'

'I bloody nearly dropped that watch as well,' Jasper says.

'And I'm guessing that Brian hasn't taken up smoking,' Rob asks.

I shake my head no. 'The lighter in the packet that Henry threw at him was a token for 1971 as well. We hope.'

'So this is 1971,' he says, looking around.

'No. This is 2019,' Ani says.

'You didn't have a token for 1971?' he says, the pitch of his voice slightly raised.

'Wouldn't have made a lot of difference, would it, Maisie?' Jasper pats me on the shoulder. 'We'll leave you be for a bit. Be up the front if you need us.'

'Don't be too long. We have no idea what's going on here any more,' Ani says, walking after him as he goes back towards the main door into the Old Library.

Rob stares at them, and then back at me. I can barely see his face in the shadows cast by the moonlight shining through the high windows.

'I had to jump back here first. Jasper and Ani came with me. They didn't have to,' I say. I've got no idea right now how this conversation is going to pan out, even though I've been rehearsing it in my head for the last hour or so. Maybe longer.

The mist clears, and he nods confidently. 'Oh, I get it. The key you're wearing. It's a token for 2019.'

I hesitate and look at the floor. A little voice in my head says, He chose to follow you. He could have stayed. Another little voice says, It's too early to trust him. You've known him even less time than you knew him before. I shake my head. Last time I was standing here in 2019, I was holding hands with the Rob I let down because I didn't trust him enough with my secrets – and he never stopped believing in me. Whatever the consequences, whatever the cost, I'm not making that mistake twice.

'It wasn't lent to me. It was given to me,' I say. 'I'm Weyfare.'

It must be about three in the morning here. Saturday

morning, May 25th. I can hear nothing except the low mumbling of the two voices at the front of the library.

'I should've guessed,' he says, after a few moments. "Of course you are.' Like little pieces of electricity, his fingers gently twine themselves around mine in the dark. 'Did I always know that you were?'

'No,' I say, swallowing hard, 'no, you didn't. Actually, I never told anyone. I never told you.'

He frowns. 'Why not?'

'I thought I couldn't trust you. I thought that if I told you, you'd work out the rest of my secret.'

'And now?'

I take a step closer to him, still not looking up. 'Lizzy, Glenda, Brian, Kim – they don't know I'm Weyfare. But Ani and Jasper worked it out, and I've decided to take the chance that I can trust you. Don't you dare let me down.'

His fingers take my other hand. 'Thank you.'

We stand there silently in the shadows cast by the moonlight for some time, not speaking, not touching apart from our joined hands. It feels different this time; when we first met, we were all over each other in a matter of hours. This feels slow and careful. I guess I know a lot more now, about how to be with him in the past like this, about how the slightest touch can make such a difference to a life. Somehow, it feels as if it means more like this.

'I have to warn you that if we go back to 1987, things might have changed,' I say. 'With your family, your situation -'

'I don't care about any of that,' he says shortly. 'I knew what I was doing when I took hold of you all back there.'

'What about Yvonne?'

He looks down, at where his hands are linked with mine. 'We're not together,' he says. 'She turns up for nookie when she's home from Uni, that's all. She's seeing at least three other fellas.'

'Nookie?' I ask.

'You know what nookie is, don't you?'

Suddenly it's obvious to me what nookie is, and then we're giggling away like five-year-olds over a poo joke.

'You haven't asked me about the rest of my secret,' I say eventually.

'I didn't want to push you,' he says. 'I thought you would tell me in your own time.'

'In my own time?' I laugh suddenly. My own time? Is there such a thing any more? 'Rob, I'm Weyfare. I've already lost count of how many times I've ridden on the Weys and every time I come back here, it isn't my own Time. I have messed up royally.' My eyes fill up with tears, and I'm grateful for the darkness.

'I don't understand,' he says.

'Why should you understand?' I say. 'I didn't understand a thing the first time I rode the Weys – I didn't know what I was. Who I was.'

'Maisie, you're not making any sense,' he says, 'but I'm not going to force it out of you –'

'No. No, you're not.' I pull my frayed emotions together with a big breath and dive into the unknown. 'You didn't force it out of me before. When I knew you before, in 1987. I chose not to tell you my secrets because I was too scared of making a commitment to someone from the past, of changing lives, and you respected that, and you stepped away and I lost you.

But things happened even though I didn't tell you my secrets, Rob. Now I know lives change every time I Ride, or Lizzy or Glenda Ride, and right now there is no way of knowing how to put those lives back the way they were, or even if it's possible. And you still made a commitment to me even though I didn't trust you, and you engraved it on a ring that you gave to me 32 years later. So, you see, I have decided to trust you now because somehow we are committed, whatever I do. I came back to your 1987 to tell you my secrets, and then nothing was the same, and I was worrying that you were gone forever, and when I found you at the Hotel, you were safe but you were Witan, and yet tonight, you still chose to Ride with me. Why did you do that?' I ask finally, hoping to hear the words I need to hear.

'You walked into the room and I felt like I had known you my whole life, even though I'd never seen you before.' In the darkness, I can feel his fingertips release one of my hands, and brush against the side of my face. 'It was as if my future had walked in with you.'

'I wanted you to choose this. I didn't want to take you away from your life,' I tell him, ' but coming with me means your life will likely never be the same. Now at least, if you are here with me, if we are going to change our futures, we change them together.' I take another deep lungful of air; I can't remember breathing during all my speeches, and before I can say anything else, his lips are gently against mine. I feel his fingers pushing through my hair, and I wrap my arms around him and pull him closer.

The Old Library is writhing on its ancient foundations, and I can hear angels. No, I can hear Jasper and Ani; they're no longer at the front of the room.

'Rob, please put her down bro; you don't know where she's been,' Jasper says.

I can feel Rob's lips curve into a smile, as he draws away. 'Actually, I'm beginning to find out.'

'Look, we can hear somebody outside,' Jasper hisses. 'It's time to leave.'

Rob pulls his body away from me but still holds me close. 'Leave?'

'We have to go join the others,' Ani says.

'I haven't finished telling him everything yet,' I say frustratedly, my cheek against his warm chest. I prefer the black rocker T-shirt, but I'll live with the polo.

'Were you eating each other's faces the entire time you were back here?' Ani says snarkily. 'I credited you with a bit more sense, Maisie. Still, you've waited across three decades and back again to be straight with him, what difference are another 40 years going to make to you both?'

We all look back suddenly at the sound of a key turning over in a lock. 'She's right. We need to go now," I say, pulling Rob back towards the glowing Weydoor. "Jasper?"

'40 years?' Rob asks.

Jasper waves at us, a gold signet ring reflecting the light from the Weydoor on his pinky finger. 'Have you any idea how painful it is, keeping a pen in your sock?' he moans. 'And all that time I needn't have bothered. This is not even my size.'

He reaches forward with the hand holding the ring, and he takes my hand with the other. I hold on to Rob with my other hand, the other ring buried safely in my sock. 'Trust me?' I ask, and he nods and takes hold of me as if he never intends to let me go. 'Hold on to Ani," I tell him. 'Don't you let her go.'

'I won't let go,' he says.

Jasper's arm just seems to slip through the bookcase as if it is a kind of projection, and the next thing I know we're falling against the bookshelves, and there's white heat, purple light, black – nothing.

ABOUT THE AUTHOR

S. J. Blackwell

I'm a British author with a passion for writing middle grade and New Adult fiction, sprinkled with the fantastic or paranormal. My favourite thing is writing in the magical den at the bottom of my garden with the squirrels and the fairies, but sometimes you can find me adventuring in my vintage camper van or playing with my two very soppy greyhounds.

I hope you enjoyed No Wey of Knowing. If you did, please leave me a review on Amazon!

Watch out for the third book in the Weys series, Long Wey Round, due to be published Autumn 2020!

BOOKS IN THIS SERIES

The Weys

Wey Back When

Meet Maisie Wharton. She's been invited to a party, but it's in 1987, and it's her mother's 18th birthday ...

As if coping with a teenage mum, big hair, vinyl records and power ballads isn't enough for her, Maisie's also trying not to fall in love.

Then her grandmother reveals a family secret that alters everything - not just for Maisie, but for the mother who has no idea her daughter has turned up from the future, and also for the boy who has fallen for the girl who changed everything when she travelled Wey Back When in time.

No Wey Of Knowing

Maisie's already discovered that 1987 is all not all big hair, vinyl records and power ballads. Her love life's beyond complicated, and she's already lost one best friend. Now she's got a big secret and she needs to protect it, but she's also on a mission to mend her family's future.

When one old friend unexpectedly turns up through the Weydoor, it's clear that this mission is going to be far from straightforward, but when another old friend needs urgent help, Maisie and her friends put in motion a chain of events, and everything's going to change. Will it be for the better, or a whole lot worse?

Long Wey Round

Expected Autumn 2020

Printed in Great Britain
by Amazon

60188502R00225